"Heads up!" Sery sang out from the console. "A cloud of missiles rising—I make out fourteen with more still launching. Target appears to be *Zuiho*."

Captain Jankowskie slammed the panel to sound action stations and opened a channel to *Zuiho*. "Jankowskie here. You're being fired at. It looks as though they plan on swamping your defenses, and the missiles probably have nuclear warheads. Put some distance between your ship and those warheads."

"Maybe we still have time to launch corvette *Chokei*," the ship's executive officer said hesitantly.

Jankowskie shook his head impatiently. "They were waiting to catch us like this, and we haven't got ten minutes. We'll have to dance with who we have."

"Twenty-seven missiles now fired," Sery noted. No one else had much to say.

By Robert Frezza
Published by Ballantine Books:

A SMALL COLONIAL WAR
McLENDON'S SYNDROME
FIRE IN A FARAWAY PLACE
CAIN'S LAND

CAIN'S LAND

Robert Frezza

A Del Rey® Book
BALLANTINE BOOKS • NEW YORK

A Del Rey® Book
Published by Ballantine Books

Copyright © 1995 by Robert Frezza

All rights reserved under International and Pan-American Copyright Conventions. Published in the United States by Ballantine Books, a division of Random House, Inc., New York, and simultaneously in Canada by Random House of Canada Limited, Toronto.

Library of Congress Catalog Card Number: 95-92521

ISBN 0-345-39025-3

Manufactured in the United States of America

First Edition: January 1996

10 9 8 7 6 5 4 3 2 1

To Steve, Dan, Ellie, Teresa, and Angela, who helped. To Margie, who cheerfully endured while Steve helped. And to Suzie, who thinks I need to get a real job. Thanks for trying to keep me sane.

PRINCIPAL CHARACTERS_____

Former Personnel, 1st Battalion, 35th Infantry (Rifle)
Lieutenant-Colonel (retired) Anton Vereshchagin ("The Variag"), former battalion and task-group commander
Lieutenant-Colonel (retired) Matti Harjalo, former battalion commander
Major (retired) Piotr Kolomeitsev ("The Iceman"), former A Company commander
Major (reserve) Meri Reinikka, former Engineer Company commander
Major (retired) Saki Bukhanov, former battalion intendance officer
Captain (retired) Gennadi Karaev, former C Company executive officer
Platoon Sergeant (retired) Roy "Filthy DeKe", "The Deacon" de Kantzow, No. 9 rifle platoon
Recruit Private (retired) Woldemar Prigal, formerly assigned to 1st section, No. 15 light attack platoon

Active Personnel, 1/35th Infantry
Lieutenant-Colonel Hans Coldewe, battalion commander
Major Daniel "Danny" Meagher, executive officer
Lieutenant Resit Aksu ("The Smiling Buddha"), intelligence officer
Captain Detlef Jankowskie, commanding frigate *General Hendrik Pienaar*
Chief Gunner Nicolas Sery, frigate *General Hendrik Pienaar*
Senior Communications Sergeant Esko Poikolainnen
Major Tikhon Degtyarov, A Company commander
Major Jan Snyman, C Company commander
Natasha Solchava-Snyman, battalion surgeon
Company Sergeant Isaac Wanjau, C Company
Flight Sergeant Ivan "Coconut" Kokovtsov, aviation company

Section Sergeant Mikhail Remmar, 1st section, No. 15 light attack platoon

Superior Private Valeska Remmar, 1st section, No. 15 light attack platoon

No. 17 Reconnaissance Platoon, 1/35th Infantry
Section Sergeant Thys Meiring, 1st section
Section Sergeant Markus Alariesto, 2nd section
Section Sergeant Vsevolod Zerebtsov, 3rd section
Assistant Section Sergeant Kalle Kekkonen, 1st section
Superior Private Denys Gordimer, 1st section
Superior Private Blaar Schuur, 1st section

No. 9 Rifle Platoon, 1/35th Infantry
Lieutenant Mika Hiltunen, platoon leader
Platoon Sergeant Kaarlo Kivela
Section Sergeant Dmitri "Bory" Uborevich, 1st section
Section Sergeant Fedya "Mother Elena" Yelenov, 2nd section
Superior Private Gerrit Myburgh, 3rd section
Corporal Kobus Nicodemus, assigned special duties
Superior Private Brit Smits, assigned special duties

Suid-Afrikans
Dr. Simon Beetje, professor of Suid-Afrikan ecology, University of Suid-Afrika
Dr. Maria Beetje, professor of Suid-Afrikan ecology, University of Suid-Afrika
Betje Beyers, widow of Republic of Suid-Afrika president Albert Beyers
Father Nicola Bosenac, Franciscan priest
Klaes De la Rey, *Suiwerheidwagte* (Silvershirt) leader
Dr. Connie Marais, associate professor of modern languages, University of Suid-Afrika
Eva Moore, hospital director and former Imperial lieutenant-colonel
Hendricka "Rikki" Sanmartin, student
Andries Steen, president of the Republic of Suid-Afrika and Reformed Nationalist party leader
Prinsloo Adriaan Smith, burgemeester of Johannesburg and Union party leader
Hannes Van der Merwe, *Suiwerheidwagte* (Silvershirt) adjutant
Liyu Ssu, political analyst and former Imperial censor

Imperials

Major Mitsuru Aichi, No. 305 Independent Infantry Company
  commander

Ship Captain Yotaro Kobayashi, commanding Imperial frigate
  Aoba

Dr. Tomomi Motofugi, professor of linguistics, University of
  Go-Nihon

Akira Mutaro, sector commissioner

Commander Jochi Nitobe, commanding Imperial corvette *Jintsu*

Dr. Kantaro Ozawa, assistant professor of biology, University of
  Go-Nihon

Dr. Inagi Seki, deputy sector commissioner

Dr. Ferenc Szuba, professor of physics, University of Go-Nihon

Dr. Pia Szuba, professor of sociology, University of Go-Nihon

Blues

Ekpalawehud

Meniolagomeka

Spoagusa

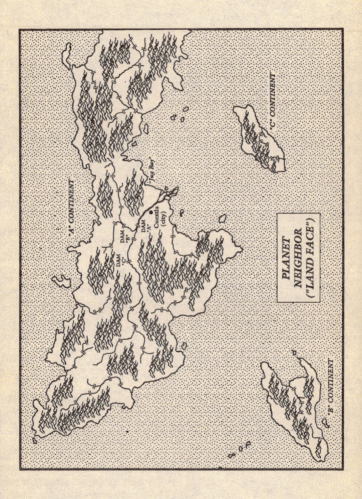

PLANET NEIGHBOR
("LAND FACE")

"A" CONTINENT

"C" CONTINENT

"B" CONTINENT

DAM "C"

DAM "B"

DAM "A"

Cucurdia (city)

Tug Bay

PROLOGUE

Go-Nihon system, Inbound

AS THE PROBE ENTERED THE GO-NIHON SYSTEM, IT DECELER-
ated in accordance with its programming, and prepared to assume orbit around the third potentially Earth-like planet it had come across in its travels. Imperial frigate *Aoba* broadcast a coded signal to shut the probe down, and set a course to intercept it.

Dwarfed in *Aoba*'s cavernous shuttle bay, petty officers Ryohei Noma and Kazuo Hosoya waited in space suits. "It appears strange," Hosoya commented indignantly in the somewhat stilted classical English the Imperial Navy still favored, "almost wasteful that this probe was not programmed to ignore worlds that have already been colonized. It is fortunate that our ship will reduce by a year the amount of time it will take the probe's data to reach Earth, but the matter should have been thought of."

Grateful for the diversion from the ship's otherwise monotonous colonial routine, a dozen more of *Aoba*'s crewmen watched and waited above the bay to assist Hosoya and Noma.

Noma checked his helmet one final time and gave his younger colleague an amused and pitying look. "If Go-Nihon had been discovered at the time the probe was launched, it is possible that its programmers might have anticipated this."

"How long has this probe been traveling?" Hosoya asked in a moderately embarrassed voice.

"Forty-two years have elapsed for the probe since it was launched. As our computer could have told you."

The crewmen above them began opening the shuttle bay's clamshell doors. "What will happen to the probe after we recover it?" Hosoya asked.

"I am certain that it will be given to a museum somewhere," Noma said, with greater accuracy than he realized.

1

As they jetted out to the probe on a "pig"—essentially a manned torpedo—trailing a cable, Hosoya continued a long-running discussion. "I am of the view that you should at least consider the possibility of settling on Go-Nihon."

In the pig's rear seat, Noma wrinkled his nose. "And become a dirt dweller?"

"With time dilation, hardly anyone on Earth will want to know us if we go back, and for persons like ourselves, there are plenty of opportunities here as well as on the other *zaibatsu* worlds. Don't forget, an immigrant ship is arriving in two months' time with Amida knows how many young ladies eager to meet a pair of clean-cut sailors, so you should not make up your mind so firmly. Another colonial tour on a Navy ship would drive both of us mad!" Hosoya argued.

Colonial tours were peaceful affairs. The only potential trouble spot in *Aoba*'s sector was the planet Suid-Afrika with its single frigate. "We are almost there," Noma said firmly.

As they slowed beside the motionless probe, Hosoya extended a gloved hand, pointing to a scarring along the side of the probe's fusion bottle. "Look, a meteor strike. It was fortunate she survived."

"Not a meteor. Possibly a flock of micrometeoroids. Pull us up alongside."

After they finished hooking the cable to the probe's nose, Noma drifted back to examine the damage.

"What does it look like?" Hosoya asked.

Noma pulled a pair of needle-nosed pliers from his equipment belt. Deftly feeling under the probe's metal skin, he extracted a thumb-sized object and focused his light on it for his companion.

"What is it?" Hosoya asked.

"It is an octahedron made of very hard metal, possibly tungsten steel."

"The Suid-Afrikans must have fired a satellite-killer at it! But why would they do that?"

"The Suid-Afrikans' frigate has never come within light years of this probe," Noma said flatly.

"But if the Suid-Afrikans didn't shoot at it, who could have?" Hosoya protested.

Noma ignored him. Carefully tucking the octahedron in his belt, he keyed his radio to *Aoba*'s operating frequency. "Noma here. Please advise Captain Kobayashi that it would be exceedingly desirable for him to come to the shuttle bay."

FAITH ————————————————

"Oh, we're having a war, and we want you to come!"
  So the pig began to whistle and to pound on a drum.
"We'll give you a gun, and we'll give you a hat!"
  And the pig began to whistle when they told the piggies that.
    —Excerpt from "The Whistling Pig," anonymous

Suid-Afrika, Landing Day plus 1167 weeks
Monday (1167)

WARMED BY SUID-AFRIKA'S SUN, LIEUTENANT-COLONEL HANS
Coldewe walked briskly down the Krugerstraat. A few of Johannesburg's younger boys followed him at a discreet distance. Of medium height and slender, Coldewe was commanding officer of Suid-Afrika's only permanent military unit, the 1/35th Rifle Battalion, and as such, the planet's ranking military officer.

As he walked, he whistled, as he often did, with an unlit pipe clenched upside down between his teeth. The soldiers of the 1/35th were fond of pointing out that it had taken Coldewe quite a few years to perfect his technique. The song varied, depending on his mood. His current favorite was "The House Carpenter," a grim old ballad of the sort that Coldewe whistled to cheer people up.

As he reached the door he was looking for, a corporal named Gu opened it and admitted him.

"Where's Anton?" Coldewe asked pleasantly.

"In the study waiting for the Imp commissioner to appear," Gu responded, moving his body a fraction so that Coldewe could enter. Gu's scowl deepened. A stocky Manchurian, he had served as an Imperial soldier before Suid-Afrika won its independence. Like many of Suid-Afrika's inhabitants, he disliked Imperial officials intensely.

3

Coldewe patted him lightly on the arm. "Apart from the fact that we half wrecked the city of Tokyo, what could His Imperial Majesty's commissioner possibly have against us?" He followed Gu into the study where Anton Vereshchagin was waiting.

Even with nearly twenty years of time dilation factored in, the years had treated Vereshchagin kindly. Although his graying hair was streaked with white, his body and unlined face belonged to a much younger man. He set down the book he was reading. "Hello, Hans."

The younger man smiled. "Hello, Anton." He walked over to the samovar and poured himself a cup of tea. "Do we have any idea why His Imperial Majesty's representative has acknowledged your existence?"

"None whatever. I, of course, reported Commissioner Mutaro's request to President Steen's government."

"Steen and his cronies must be collectively excreting bricks."

"I must admit that Mutaro-*san* has an exquisite sense of timing." Vereshchagin handed Coldewe a copy of *Die Afrikaner* and pointed to an article written about Steen's latest speech. "Steen announced economies in government spending, which means he wishes to further pare your budget."

Coldewe nodded. "Yes, he's serious about clipping our wings, and he thinks he has the votes. What I would really like is to have Albert Beyers back to life for forty-five minutes." Beyers, Suid-Afrika's first president, had died in the middle of his third term of office partly of a broken heart. "It would be almost as much fun as watching Christ in the temple with the money changers."

Gu reappeared, escorting a frail-looking Japanese man. "Commissioner Akira Mutaro," he said with obvious distaste before departing.

Coldewe and Vereshchagin exchanged bows with Mutaro. "I am Colonel Anton Vereshchagin, retired, and this is Lieutenant-Colonel Hans Coldewe. Please, make yourself welcome." Vereshchagin drew his guest a cup of tea.

Mutaro seated himself in a large armchair, his deceptively soft eyes twinkling with amusement. "Now, it is possible that you are asking yourselves why I have come here insisting on meeting former Colonel Anton Vereshchagin, after my government acquiesced for nine years in the polite fiction that Anton Vereshchagin died in his attack on Tokyo."

"I do find your government's sudden interest unsettling," Vereshchagin admitted.

"Let me see," Mutaro said in accent-free English. "As an Imperial officer, you fought in six campaigns on colonial planets, rising to the rank of lieutenant-colonel. You took command of the task force sent here after all officers senior to you were killed, and suppressed a revolt by this planet's Afrikaner inhabitants. When a second Imperial task force arrived here under orders to uproot potential opposition and return the planet to the control of the United Steel–Standard corporation, you led a second Afrikaner rebellion and annihilated the task group."

Vereshchagin inclined his head, acknowledging this.

"You then took a captured frigate back to Earth and attacked the warships based at Yamato Space Station and selected targets in the city of Tokyo. You destroyed the headquarters of United Steel–Standard, assassinated several leading politicians, and gassed the ministries that advocated exploiting the federated nations and colonial planets. Eleven hundred company employees and nearly two thousand civil servants were killed. Very tragic."

"Very tragic, indeed," Vereshchagin agreed.

"The reaction to your attack and the resulting financial dislocation, which I understand you also had a hand in, resulted in profound changes in the Imperial system, as well as eventual recognition of Suid-Afrika's independence." Mutaro turned his head toward Coldewe. "Colonel Coldewe, I recall seeing you on television as spokesman for the landing force."

"We were broadcasting from the New Akasaki Prince Hotel. We left the rooms a mess, so I don't think the hotel's going to welcome me back any time soon," Coldewe quipped.

Mutaro cocked his head as he sipped his tea. "Your secretary quite clearly disapproves of Japanese, Vereshchagin-*san*."

Vereshchagin smiled. "Corporal Gu came here with the second task group. He was somewhat disillusioned by his experiences as an Imperial soldier and, I expect, somewhat apprehensive about returning to Earth after surrendering. He declined repatriation and requested permission to enlist in our battalion."

Coldewe grinned. "The Manchurians weren't too popular here, so we turned him down. We finally accepted about a dozen of them after they went on a hunger strike."

"It is curious that you should choose a Manchurian corporal to become your secretary," Mutaro said, by indirection moving toward the question he really wanted answered.

"Gu has earned himself a degree in communications from the university here," Vereshchagin said, enjoying the fencing.

"He's a wizard with a camera," Coldewe interjected. "Anton is our War Academy, and I've been making Gu tape lectures. As I'm sure you're aware, Suid-Afrika's standing military forces aren't very large, so we have to make good use of our talent."

"Suid-Afrika's military forces are very small," Mutaro agreed politely. "I believe that the active force is restricted by law to forty-five commissioned officers and 750 men. You currently have, I am told by my experts, one warship—the frigate *General Hendrik Pienaar*, formerly an Imperial ship—and the 1st Battalion, 35th Rifles, consisting of three infantry companies, a light attack company, an aviation company, a combat engineer company, and a reconnaissance company. Yet some persons in your planet's Assembly have recommended abolishing your active military forces as a useless drain on Suid-Afrika's treasury. Politics here seems to be taken quite personally. What was it that Heer Pirow called Colonel Coldewe in his speech last week?"

"A *vreemde fortuin-soeker*, a foreign fortune-seeker," Coldewe replied curtly.

"If my sources are correct, President Steen intends to further reduce the number of active soldiers."

Coldewe and Vereshchagin exchanged glances. "Your sources are to be commended," Vereshchagin said dryly. "And since the Imperial Government, which you have the honor to represent, is Suid-Afrika's only potential enemy, I am not certain President Steen would be pleased to know that you are in possession of this information."

"I would suspect that you are correct to say this," Mutaro said blandly. "Indeed, my sources tell me that President Steen views Suid-Afrika's military forces as a source of political patronage, and is motivated to reduce military spending partly out of pique at Colonel Coldewe's disinclination to steer contracts to his supporters. Colonel Coldewe's soldiers are also quite zealous in acting as game wardens. I understand that the planet's hunting lobby has promised Steen considerable financial support in his endeavors."

Coldewe began choking.

Mutaro winked solemnly. "I assure you from my inmost feelings of my belief that Imperial Japan is committed to a peaceful course of existence with Suid-Afrika. Nevertheless—"

"Nevertheless, it would be a sin to lead the Imperial Government into temptation by reducing our forces too drastically," Vereshchagin concluded for him. "Colonel Coldewe and I will, of course, report the substance of this conversation to President

Steen's government. I hope you will not mind if I quote you on this word for word."

"Naturally I would not be offended in any way." Mutaro set his teacup down and leaned back in his chair. He looked at Vereshchagin. "Periodically, Japanese patriotic organizations demand punitive action against this planet to wipe the stain from the nation's honor, and such organizations have suggested that peace terms with Suid-Afrika should include rooting up your corpse and returning it to Japan, presumably for the nation to vent its outrage upon."

"Do you concur in these opinions?" Vereshchagin asked quietly.

Mutaro studied Vereshchagin's face for a moment or two. "I recollect," he said softly, "being inordinately impressed by the restraint your forces demonstrated. It was well within your power to destroy Tokyo. Your attack was clearly intended to achieve a particular political result with minimal casualties." The humor left his eyes. "I do not lightly intrude upon your solitude, but I must ask you to trust me. Please tell me, if it had been necessary to achieve your goal, would you have destroyed the city?"

"Truthfully, I do not know," Vereshchagin admitted. "I do not think so."

"Why?" Mutaro demanded.

Vereshchagin pondered the answer for a moment. "Because any good I would have achieved would not have been commensurate."

Mutaro persisted. "But, hypothetically, what if the good to mankind outweighed the destruction of the city and tens of millions of inhabitants?"

Vereshchagin looked at him. "Hypothetically, yes. I would have done so."

His small figure almost lost in the cushions of the armchair, Mutaro nodded slowly. "Vereshchagin-*san*, you were a brilliant military officer. I have been told, however, that genius in a military officer is superfluous, even dangerous, and that reliance should instead be placed upon average officers who subordinate themselves to a collective will and intelligence."

Coldewe coughed politely. "Anton won't speak for himself, so I will. That particular nonsense is an outgrowth of the old Prussian General Staff System and reflects the notion that a hundred average men who react the same way will achieve better results than a hundred brilliant men who don't. It has some validity when you have corps and armies and the sum of a thousand tiny combats, but colonial wars are little wars. Out here, brilliance wins. I might add that the Prussian General Staff never selected average men."

"Tell me, Vereshchagin-*san*," Mutaro said languidly, "are you still a soldier?"

"I have been retired from soldiering for a number of years. I am retired from all pursuits now." Vereshchagin studied Mutaro's face for what it might reveal.

Mutaro sucked in his breath. "So! Tell me, do you believe that there is other intelligent life in the universe?" Mutaro rested his elbows on the arms of the chair and rested the palms of his hands against each other, steepling his fingers. "Four months ago, a probe we dispatched almost half a century ago was intercepted near the planet Go-Nihon. The matter was brought to my attention. My experts assure me that one of the planets the probe surveyed is indeed inhabited by intelligent creatures."

Mutaro paused. "This news was immediately dispatched to Earth, but it is an eight-month voyage from Go-Nihon to Earth, and with the effects of time dilation, several more years will elapse before Earth can respond. I find this unacceptable. As Imperial commissioner for this sector, I have determined, therefore, to take action using resources available in this sector."

"How advanced are these folks?" Coldewe asked sharply.

"The probe was only intended to survey planets for possible habitation, so the data it could provide is unfortunately quite limited. Nevertheless, my experts assure me that there is unmistakable evidence of extensive telecommunications and electromagnetic power networks, so I would assume that they are quite advanced, although not nearly as advanced as humanity."

"Have they developed spaceflight, and are they aware of our existence?" Vereshchagin asked.

"Such evidence as the probe was able to provide suggests that they do not possess spaceflight," Mutaro replied. "However, the probe was damaged by an explosion, so it would appear that they are somewhat aware of our existence." He waited for Coldewe and Vereshchagin to digest this information.

Vereshchagin looked at Coldewe. "If they do not possess spaceflight, they will."

"Perhaps twenty standard years have elapsed since the probe made contact. I believe that it is imperative for us to contact this intelligent, alien species. The potential for mankind to benefit from this contact is enormous. The potential danger to mankind is also enormous."

Mutaro folded his hands. "I am told that the planet itself is habitable. Although the average surface temperature of the planet is quite warm, averaging 32° centigrade in many places, the atmosphere is dense and entirely suitable, with an oxygen content similar to that of Earth. I am told that this is normal for a planet with an ocean."

Vereshchagin nodded. "On Earth-like worlds, evolving plant life breaks down carbon dioxide, freeing oxygen in quantity until a balance is reached between plants and the animals that feed on them. Raul Sanmartin, who was one of my officers, once told me that after a few thousand millennia, the oxygen content on such worlds stabilizes between 19 and 23 percent."

"Indeed," Mutaro said politely, having heard of Raul Sanmartin in a different context.

"Why are you bringing this to our attention?" Coldewe asked bluntly.

Mutaro shifted his weight. "Coldewe-*san*, I intend to send an expedition to contact these aliens. I require a special individual to lead such an expedition. Although soldiers are skilled in the management of violence, the person I require must be something more than a soldier."

For a period of time, Vereshchagin said nothing. Then he said, "Why would you consider me?"

"Vereshchagin-*san*," Mutaro replied, choosing simple words, "I feel the weight of history pressing upon me. I do not believe I exaggerate when I say that this expedition may have extremely serious consequences. The man I select must attempt with all his heart to establish peaceful relations, but he must also judiciously weigh the risk this alien people presents to mankind. I have studied your career with some care, both your service record and the additional information Imperial Intelligence has been able to gather on you—as you may guess, you have been an object of some interest. You have demonstrated that you can be a ruthless man in the cause of peace. My mind tells me that you are the man best suited. After speaking with you, my heart agrees. Do you disagree?"

Whatever remained of Vereshchagin's smile faded. "As much as I would like to deny the charge, I cannot."

"I'm not sure I understand," Coldewe said slowly.

The expression on Mutaro's face hardened. "I believe that you do understand, Coldewe-*san*. If these aliens are not hostile or dangerous to Earth and its colonies, it would be a crime to deal with them in a hostile manner. The damage to the probe suggests, however, that they may be hostile. If a grave threat exists to mankind, it must be neutralized. Yet could you assess the threat presented by a completely alien civilization and neutralize this threat with the limited forces available for me to send?"

"God in heaven, I don't know," Coldewe admitted.

Mutaro chuckled, a dry, rasping sound. "Any honest man would say the same."

Vereshchagin reclaimed his old pipe from Coldewe's hand and tapped it absently on his thigh. "After what I have done to Tokyo, you will be severely censured for sending me."

Mutaro laughed. "When it becomes known that I have selected a notorious and—forgive me—bloodthirsty rebel, long assumed to be dead, to lead this mission as an emissary of the Imperial Government, there will be considerable criticism, but it will be far too late to matter."

"They're going to fry you," Coldewe said.

"Only figuratively, I hope, but I am no longer a young man. I may not live to answer my critics. But please also understand that if you find it necessary to take military action, there will be a fire storm of protest on Earth, regardless of the necessity."

Vereshchagin smiled, tightly.

"The man I send must not waver in the face of such disapproval. I doubt very much whether I could find another man sufficiently capable of ignoring such distractions."

"More to the point," Coldewe commented, "if it became expedient, the Imperial Government could disavow Anton in a heartbeat."

"Of a certainty, they would do so. But that would scarcely matter, would it?" Mutaro's eyes danced. "Indeed, if military action became necessary, what better way to assuage the collective guilt of humanity than to blame the attack on a dead Imperial Commissioner and the traitorous Colonel Anton Vereshchagin?"

Again, the humor left Mutaro's face. "Vereshchagin-*san*, I ask you to set aside your saffron robe and undertake this mission for the good of humanity. I believe you possess the wisdom to work wholeheartedly toward an understanding with these aliens, as well as the steadfastness of purpose to do whatever is necessary if an understanding is not possible."

"What forces do you have available, and what authority will you give me?" Vereshchagin asked.

"I have a frigate with two corvettes, two supply ships, and an assault transport arriving within thirty days. They are outfitting now. The best interdisciplinary scientific team that my deputy can assemble will arrive with the ships. I regret that I can only provide you with one infantry company of Imperial troops. I will delegate complete authority to you, and all expedition personnel will be instructed to obey your orders without question. For the record, I will dictate detailed instructions as to how you will conduct the expedition. I fully expect you to disregard these instructions as soon as you leave orbit."

"One frigate with an ordinary weapons load and a couple of corvettes isn't much to take on a whole planet," Coldewe observed.

"The frigate will carry forty nuclear missiles in place of a third corvette, and I will provide a skilled team of biological and chemical warfare experts."

Vereshchagin raised one eyebrow. "I assume that the missiles and these experts were intended for deployment against Suid-Afrika under the correct circumstances."

"Indeed." Mutaro chuckled again, a thin, rasping sound. "You are quite dangerous. I wonder if I should tell President Steen this?"

"That does bring up a problem," Vereshchagin said. "I will need to draw personnel from Suid-Afrika's military forces."

Mutaro nodded slowly. "I had not anticipated this."

"Some anti-Imperial Assemblymen will see this as a plot to strip Suid-Afrika of its defenses," Vereshchagin surmised, "while President Steen's fiscally prudent allies may view the 'alien threat' as a myth concocted to avoid military budget cuts. I suspect that even the sober and responsible politicians here are going to have some difficulty accepting the notion that Suid-Afrika should provide volunteers for an expedition."

"I trust that we will find a way around this dilemma," Mutaro said.

Coldewe shrugged. "We have thirty days until your ships arrive."

When Mutaro left, Coldewe looked at Vereshchagin. "Saffron robe?"

"Metaphoric," Vereshchagin said absently. "Are you interested in coming along? You do not have to, you know."

"Dear me, what would keep me here? There is the crazy lady who keeps hitting me with a plastic scythe in public places, the insect watchers who congregate next to the flagpole while I'm trying to eat my breakfast, my ex-girlfriends, and, of course,

Professor Dr. Anneke Brink who still calls me up when she's feeling maudlin about Cousin Raul and nips too hard at the brandy. You know full well I wouldn't miss this for the fairy gold in the mountains. Besides, if I go, Danny Meagher will take command of the battalion, and won't Andries Steen love that!"

Meagher, a caustic Irishman once employed as a mercenary by United Steel–Standard, had joined the battalion as a private and risen through the ranks.

"Who do you want?" Vereshchagin asked suddenly.

"God alone knows what we'll need, and I'd rather not have to depend on that rifle company Mutaro is bringing. I want Jan Snyman and two rifle platoons, a recon platoon, half of No. 15 light attack platoon, and a section of engineers. We'll have to take a look at the probe data, but I see no reason why we can't take aircraft. That and a few puppies should be enough."

Vereshchagin hid a smile. One of Coldewe's innovations was the pint-sized scout dogs added to No. 18 recon platoon, which Coldewe considered to be cheaper, more effective, and a lot more fun than portable sensor units.

"We'll also want to look around the university to find some more would-be scientific experts to bring along. The scientists Mutaro scraped up probably think they are hotter than plasma, but nobody knows an awful lot about how to approach this sort of thing." Coldewe remembered a world called Ashcroft and paused. "It's warm here, but it'll be hotter than hell there. We'll need to modify our gear."

Vereshchagin nodded.

"I assume that you'll want Detlef Jankowskie to command the frigate, and that you plan on dragging Piotr out of retirement."

"Yes," Vereshchagin said. Major Piotr Kolomeitsev, "The Iceman," was formerly the commander of Vereshchagin's A Company. As a tactician, The Iceman had no living peer. He had buried a wife once, and a lot of men since. Vereshchagin could count on him to provide advice that was untainted by anything save the coldest of logic.

"What are we going to say to Matti?" Coldewe asked in a troubled voice.

Matti Harjalo, once Vereshchagin's executive officer and Coldewe's predecessor as commander of the 1/35th Rifle Battalion, had been forced into retirement when Andries Steen took office and had largely become a recluse. Harjalo had been left behind from the Tokyo raid to organize Suid-Afrika's defenses.

For Anton Vereshchagin, part of the price paid for the raid was the friendship he had once had with Matti Harjalo.

"You talk with Jan. I will deal with Matti," Vereshchagin said.

Tuesday (1167)

LYING IN WHAT WAS BECOMING A CONSIDERABLE PUDDLE, MAjor Jan Snyman felt the familiar hum as a radio signal crept up his back and under his cap before registering through the bone-induction plates over his temples.

"Coldewe here. Hello, Jan."

Snyman silently cursed the rain and all communications with headquarters. "Hello yourself, Hans. If you are calling about poachers, can it wait? Heaven knows they should have better sense than to be out in the forest tonight."

"No, it isn't poachers, but I'm pulling you out anyway."

"Colonel Hans, sir," Snyman protested, "we finally have those street sweepers from No. 2 platoon nibbling at the cheese. We owe them an ambush, and having sat in the same patch of mud for two days, the boys will probably wish to shoot both of us if I pull them out now."

He heard Coldewe laugh. As the reserve companies had ruefully learned, the 1/35th took company maneuvers very seriously. Failure carried a price—losers bought the winners beer.

"Can you wrap things up in another hour or two?" Coldewe asked.

"Possibly," Snyman conceded.

"You have until midnight, and then I'm calling off the exercise. March everyone to Landing Zone Beppu Beppu, and I'll send aircraft to pick you up."

"Any particular reason?" Snyman asked.

"Think of it as another Tokyo mission, across the sea of stars. I want you to quietly find me two platoons of volunteer infantrymen and a recon platoon. No married men unless we can contrive to take their wives along. Get as many of the old laggs as you can. Tell them that they can talk it up among themselves, but if it leaks outside the battalion, like Salome I'm going to want somebody's head."

"Yes, sir," Snyman said, stunned.

"And while you're at it, speak with your charming wife." Snyman's wife, Natasha Solchava, was the battalion surgeon.

"Ask her if the two of you have plans for the next few years. I will explain in detail when you get in. Coldewe out."

Snyman glanced over at one of his troopers—a stocky Afrikaner named Meier, whose nickname was "Snack Bar"—lying in another puddle a few meters away. "This is shaping up as one of those evenings," he commented.

Major Tikhon Degtyarov's A Company called itself "The Night Shift," and his No. 2 platoon called itself "The Devil's Own," only partly in jest. As Degtyarov himself said, they would have rescued Christ from the cross to pocket the nails.

They somehow sniffed out C Company's careful ambush, escaping with fewer than a dozen casualties. It was, as Jan Snyman observed sourly to his wife a few hours later, one of those evenings.

Wednesday (1167)

AT DAWN, ANTON VERESHCHAGIN DROVE HIMSELF TO THE BATtalion's casern on the outskirts of Pretoria and paused for a few moments in the battalion cemetery.

A small crypt held the ashes of Paul Henke. After suffering a small stroke, Henke had quietly retired as D Company commander and ended his life with a chemical grenade. As always, Vereshchagin paused to say a prayer for The Hangman's troubled soul.

As he stopped beside the cenotaph to Raul Sanmartin, Yuri Malinov, and the others who had died on the Tokyo raid, he saw a young woman approaching. "Rikki, what are you doing here?"

Hendricka Sanmartin came up to stand beside him. "Tant Betje sent me to ask what you are up to. Hans said you were coming to Pretoria this morning, and I thought I would find you here."

"I am becoming too predictable." Vereshchagin asked innocently, "What makes Betje believe that I am up to anything?"

"Uncle Anton!" Hendricka squeezed his hand. "She can smell when you are up to something, and I am sure I can, too."

Blond with a heart-shaped face, Hendricka bore a strong resemblance to her mother, Hanna Bruwer, who had served as the first speaker of Suid-Afrika's Assembly. In temperament, charitable people said she favored her father, Raul Sanmartin. Les charitable people said she favored her great-grandfather, Hendrik Pienaar, who had scant use for fools in his lifetime. With her mother executed by Imperial soldiers during the second rebellion and her father dead in the attack on Tokyo, Albert and Betje Beyers were the only parents Rikki Sanmartin had known for most of her life.

"I have not spoken with Betje. How is she?" Vereshchagin said aloud.

"As well as ever. I keep trying to coax her into doing things and meeting new people, but she always says no. Our fractious and stiff-necked people killed Oom Albert as surely as a bullet, and I doubt whether she will ever completely forgive them. Friedrick and Bret visited her last Thursday to talk her into moving in with Bret and his wife, but she called my foster brothers a pair of amiable louts and threw them out."

Vereshchagin knew both of Betje Beyers's sons, well-meaning, middle-aged engineers. To their credit, they never begrudged Rikki the place she had usurped in their mother's affections. Still, Vereshchagin sympathized with Vroew Beyers. "Before I explain my plans, what are yours?" he asked, his eyes half-shut.

She reached out to touch the cenotaph. "I can sit for the last part of my degree anytime I choose. Simon Beetje wants to give me a faculty position in his department."

With Albert Beyers's connivance, twenty years earlier Raul Sanmartin had established the university's Department of Suid-Afrikan Ecology, and Simon Beetje and his wife Maria were two of his first students. Rikki Sanmartin, who had a houseful of pets to take care of by the time she was five, had inherited his passion.

"When did Simon say this?" Vereshchagin asked.

"A week ago." She studied his face. "Other than you, Simon and Maria are about the only ones who have noticed that little Hendricka is all grown up. I told him that I would have to think about it and consult with my crafty old Uncle Anton."

"Me?" Vereshchagin protested.

"Yes, you." She tilted her head sideways to observe him better. "For as long as I have been alive, not very much has happened on this planet that you have not had a hand in, and for the last few years I have felt you watching and waiting."

"So what do you think of Simon's offer?" Vereshchagin asked in a neutral tone of voice.

"I wish the timing were better. This is the first election that I am old enough to stand for. Steen's Reformed Nationals can be set to take a tumble, so this is a chance to make my mark. If I wait, it might be years before another opportunity comes. 'Green fruit will make your stomach ill, but you must pick it when it ripens'—isn't that what Oom Albert used to say?" She searched Vereshchagin's eyes. "Friedrick and Bret have never had any interest in politics, which makes me the heir apparent."

"Who has been after you to stand?" Vereshchagin asked, understanding her.

"Adriaan Smith. Dear old Adriaan, of course—he is tired of being burgemeester and is hoping I will be ready to take the job from him in five or six years. I remember sitting on his knee listening to him tell droll stories about the other sharks in Suid-Afrika's political pond. He was really very sweet about it. He thinks that if he can set me up in a safe Jo'burg assembly seat, he will pay the debt he owes my mother."

"And what do you think?"

She sat down among the short ferns carpeting the cemetery. "I think that this is the year you should run for president. If anyone can sink Steen, you can—people love war heros. I will ride to victory on your coattails. I think that you have thought about it, and I think that Heer Mutaro dropped by to tell you that His Imperial Majesty will not object."

Vereshchagin smiled. Little Rikki was a curious mixture of wistful idealism and hardened cynicism. "An excellent surmise, but not a correct one. Tell me, do you think enough of politics to wish public office upon me?"

"It is a filthy business," she said with callous candor, "but it is filthier when good people avoid it."

"And would the people here elect me?"

"Dear old Uncle Anton." She clicked her teeth disapprovingly. "You were the first one to call me a precocious brat and mean it. I could count votes before I had my teeth straightened." She tossed her hair. "Adriaan will get the Union party's endorsement for lack of anyone better, but he doesn't want to be president. He would rather be gelded, I think. So he expects to run and lose. It is a shame—he is a good man. If you announced as a candidate, he would be the first to cheer."

"And who told you this, young lady?"

"My little voice, but anyone else who pays attention could tell you the same," she said indifferently. "You will pick up at least half the Afrikaners even if Steen runs well, which he won't, and the cowboys and the sects would vote for you to a man."

While 66 percent of Suid-Afrika's population was of Afrikaner descent, both the cowboys, a mixed population from the continent's largely agrarian south, and the descendants of the five sects who were the planet's original colonists were guaranteed representation in the Assembly.

During the years of anarchy that preceded Vereshchagin's arrival, an Afrikaner *kommando* had burned the inhabitants of one sect village alive; and during the first Afrikaner rebellion, extremists had detonated a nuclear device in the cowboy town of Reading. Both the cultists and the cowboys were understandably sensitive about the incidents, and whatever slight support that President Steen had enjoyed among them evaporated the morning after his finance minister was quoted as saying that the solution to Suid-Afrika's problems was "a bomb and some gasoline." While the minister in question found himself unemployed even before he was sober, the damage to Steen was considerable.

Vereshchagin did not venture to disagree. "Your little voice?" he queried, sitting next to her.

"Oom Albert. I sometimes hear his voice in my head. The things he would say to me." She grinned. "Last week, when Fanie Slabbert came by to see if I had designs on his seat, I could hear Oom Albert, clear as a bell, saying, 'Smack his nose, and he will lick your feet.' "

"Sound advice. What about you? Are you certain that you wish to go into politics? Why not the university?"

"You taught me about duty," she said, her inner self speaking. "You know the way of things. I can be a researcher and catalog all of Suid-Afrika's plants and animals before they disappear, or I can put myself in a position to do something to prevent it."

"Tell me, in the university, which are the best minds? Simon has already given me his choices."

"Simon probably left out himself."

Vereshchagin nodded.

"Which departments then?" she asked.

"Linguistics, communications, anthropology, xenobiology, for a start."

"That is an odd assortment. I still want to know what the Imperial commissioner wanted with you. Let me see if I can puzzle it out from the clues you've given me." A sudden thought struck her, and she held her hand to her mouth.

"Yes," Vereshchagin said, "an intelligent, alien species on our doorstep. Mutaro-*san* has asked me to lead the expedition. Simon has not guessed yet. You may tell him that I need a xenobiologist."

"That should have been my father," Rikki said, reaching out to touch the cenotaph, one tear coursing down her cheek.

Vereshchagin waited to see if she would say more.

"I used to dream that he really wasn't dead, that somehow he survived and they put him in prison, and that when I grew up, I would go to Earth and rescue him. I used to act it out with my dolls. Isn't that silly? Tant Betje never knew."

Vereshchagin smiled very slightly. "Tant Betje gave me regular reports, and from what she told me, your plan was better than some I have seen from my junior officers."

"I always meant to ask you, Uncle Anton, whether he really had to die."

Vereshchagin hesitated. " 'Had to' is a very difficult standard to apply. In truth, to this day I do not know if he had to die, and I doubt whether he knew either. But I know that he was unwilling to accept the risk of failing, and neither was I."

"He was the last man to die in our war for independence. At times, I hated him for it, you know. Mother only had time to write me one letter before they killed her, but he had time to plan. He left me thirty letters altogether—one for each of my birthdays and a few more besides. The one I remember best is the one he left for my seventeenth birthday to try to make me understand why Mother died." She looked at him. "I don't have her kind of faith. Or her kind of courage."

"I have been a soldier for a long time, Rikki, and I know that you will not know whether you have the faith or the courage until you are asked to show it. But I would be very surprised if you do not."

"Who are you taking with you?" she asked in a subdued voice.

"I will need a team of scientists, and Hans is assembling a company-sized strike force for me. There will be Imperial scientists and soldiers as well."

"Why would you take soldiers along? Seriously, Uncle Anton, if these aliens are unfriendly, what can one company of soldiers do?"

Vereshchagin smiled. "We took less than a company to Tokyo and accomplished a great deal." He touched the ferns around him. "Mostly, we will have them for reconnaissance, which is field research by another name. Orbital sensors are effective at gathering certain types of information, but even if the natives are extraordinarily friendly, we will need men on the ground observing and collecting specimens to tell us more about the planet and its inhabitants. Certainly, some of it will not be terribly different from the wildlife research we do for Simon and Maria. Moreover, if these aliens are unfriendly, although I can do a great deal with warships and precision-guided munitions, they are no substitute for poor, bloody infantrymen; and I know that the men Hans will select will accomplish whatever I require of them." He looked up. "So, Rikki, are you the promising young xenobiologist or the budding politician?"

"You are asking whether I want to go with you. And my answer is yes." She tried not to allow her voice to falter.

"What I am really asking is whether you are willing to stay behind if I need you to do so. I am very much afraid I might."

He left her lost in thought beside the cenotaph and walked inside Coldewe's headquarters bunker to meet with Coldewe's "brain trust"—Danny Meagher, his executive officer; Battalion Sergeant Aleksei Beregov; and the officers commanding his four maneuver companies: Tikhon Degtyarov, Per Kiritinitis, Jan Snyman, and Sergei Okladnikov. Saki Bukhanov, Vereshchagin's former intendance officer, was also seated, wearing mufti and looking ill at ease. A ninth officer, Detlef Jankowskie, still orbiting overhead in his ship, was present via a telecommunications relay.

"We were almost ready to send out a search party to look for you," Coldewe joked.

"Rikki accosted me on my way in." Vereshchagin took a seat.

"I've brought everyone up to the mark, and we've looked at the materials Mutaro-*san* provided." Coldewe glanced at his officers. "Jan, do you want to tell us what they mean?"

Snyman rose and turned on the room's large electronic map. "This is a space shot of the planet the Imps have named 'Neighbor.' It is a shade closer to its primary, and a hair smaller than Earth. The planet has a rotation of about nineteen hours, a modest axial tilt, and two small satellites—orbiting cover and concealment, as Detlef would say—with a combined mass about a quarter of Luna's."

He superimposed a closer shot. "As you can see, there are three major landmasses: one equatorial supercontinent and two island continents, one about the size of Australia and another slightly larger than Greenland. Mutaro's climatologist says that all three continents exhibit severe seasonal patterns of rainfall distribution, which means, in English, that they alternate between monsoon season and drought season. In general, winds are fierce, particularly in storm bands north and south of the equator, and tides are minimal. There is very little snow except at higher elevations."

"Polar ice?" Okladnikov asked.

Snyman focused in on the top third of the planet. "No ice caps. The continents are superhot—equivalent to Earth's Eocene—in the equatorial band." He switched the map image to a shot of the main landmass. "The mountain chains are not much to look at. Based on this and some other data, the geologists think that Neighbor has significantly less vulcanism and crustal plate movement than either Earth or Suid-Afrika. While marine life appears abundant and sophisticated, the vegetation on land isn't especially impressive. Significant portions of all three continents are desert—hot as blazes during the day and chilly at night."

"We remember Ashcroft—we were young once," Coldewe commented. Ashcroft had been a hellish, barren world with only scraps of an atmosphere. "We can think of it as *déjà vu* all over again."

"The planet shows obvious signs of cultivation and urbanization," Snyman continued, focusing on a medium-sized city. "Interestingly, it doesn't appear to have anything resembling grasses, which provide most of humanity's staple food plants."

Danny Meagher rubbed his eyes impatiently, "Jan, is this the best resolution the probe can give us?"

Snyman turned off his magic map. "For some reason, the people who designed the probe never considered the possibility that it might come across an inhabited world. We have all kinds of things—atmospheric content, weather patterns, spectral analysis of vegetation. But if we want any useful military data, we will have to look for it ourselves."

Coldewe turned to Saki Bukhanov, who had red-rimmed eyes from studying shipping manifests and who was arguably the most important person in the room. "How do the logistics look?"

Saki patted his belly—the way his wife, Petronella, fed him, his old uniform didn't fit, but five years as a banker had done little to dull his mind. "The Imperials have severely underestimated requirements, and bringing an additional company will make matters worse. They are only shipping thirty days ammunition at a limited conflict expenditure rate, which might last all of a week if you had to use it, and they omitted a lot of ancillary equipment—I don't know where they expected to find a machine shop. But the food situation concerns me most. I doubt whether there will be any food on this planet that men can eat, and hydroponic gardening to recycle nutrients is well and good, but in practice, the wastage rate is far higher than is assumed here."

"Can we do the mission with the shipping space available?" Coldewe asked.

"How long do you plan on staying in orbit?" Bukhanov asked.

"Plan on at least two years," Vereshchagin said.

Bukhanov consulted the little laptop computer that rarely left his side. "We'd have to freeze-dry everything and Heer Mutaro would have to guarantee two supply ships a year," he conceded reluctantly. "I will get with Vulko Redzup and put something together. We will still have to dip deep into our stocks to get the expedition outfitted initially."

"Give me the figures," Vereshchagin told him.

WHEN SIMON BEETJE TOOK THE CALL, HE LISTENED FOR SEVeral minutes. Stunned, he hung up the phone. His wife, Maria, looked at him.

He slumped down in his chair. "That was Rikki." Unlike most Afrikaners, the Beetjes spoke English at home.

"Well, is she going to accept or not? If she is, we will have to ask for a supplement to the budget by Tuesday at the latest," his wife replied, ever practical, as she busied herself cleaning up from dinner.

"We didn't discuss that." Tall, extraordinarily thin, and perpetually youthful, Simon Beetje fit no one's image of a department head, while Maria was short and rounded. Their students called them "stick and stone."

"Well, what did you discuss?" She gave the countertop a final flick with a cloth.

"The Imperials have discovered an intelligent alien species not very far from here. They have asked Anton Vereshchagin to lead an expedition to contact them."

"That's silly." For a moment, she seemed surprised. "Rikki must be imagining things. The Imps would never trust Anton Vereshchagin with anything."

"What if it is true? It would be the opportunity of a lifetime!" He looked away. "It must be true. Anton asked me yesterday who the brightest faculty members were, but at the time, I didn't know what he was after. Rikki said he plans on leaving about six weeks from now. He wants to know if you and I are interested."

"You don't imagine that we could leave, do you?" She held up fingers to make her points. "The university would never give both of us a leave of absence at the same time. Who would look after the department? Surely not Karol or Mannie! And they couldn't take all of our classes. And what about our ongoing research—we cannot simply abandon it. And if we did go, what would there be for us to do? They will not allow xenobiologists to study these aliens—the linguists and the anthropologists will do that—and there is no reason in our going off to study another planet's ecology when there is so much still to be done here."

"Don't you see how important this could be?"

Maria pushed aside her hair impatiently, and her voice took on a sharp edge. "What I see if we go off like that is our department being abolished and our tenure taken away. We would lose everything we've worked for. And the idea that we could pick up our lives and flit off into space is simply ridiculous. With time dilation, how could we ever pick up again when we returned? Don't be silly. Think of the work we are doing here and the students we are preparing. Rikki is a young girl and can do flighty things if she likes, but we are established professors."

When he failed to respond, she said, "For dinner tomorrow, why don't you make something light, maybe a chicken dish." Her point made, she left the room, leaving Simon Beetje staring at the surface of the table.

Thursday (1167)

HENDRICKA SANMARTIN FOLLOWED SENIOR COMMUNICATIONS Sergeant Esko Poikolainnen into the small room that served Coldewe as office and living quarters. "Uncle Hans? Are you here?"

"Down here. With the rest of the mess." The room held two chairs, a field desk with a computer terminal, a hammock, and a fair amount of junk. Coldewe was seated cross-legged in a corner.

Rikki moved a rumpled battledress uniform from one of the chairs and sat down. "Could you be more specific?"

"The maid doesn't come until Wednesday."

"Of what year?" Rikki inquired innocently.

Poikolainnen smiled and left.

She pointed into the closet. "What is that?"

Coldewe reached for the object in question, a wide-brimmed black hat, handling it reverently. "This is my cowboy hat. The mayor of Upper Marlboro gave me it last year."

"Do you still read those Karl May western books?" Sanmartin thought better of the question. "I thought only outlaws wore black hats."

Coldewe yawned. "It seemed more appropriate somehow."

Sanmartin folded her arms. "Uncle Hans, have you been up all night?"

"I'm sure I got a nap in somewhere. Ask Esko." Coldewe waved his hand impatiently. "I need your help. You're the only xenobiologist in on the secret."

"When does the news become public?"

"Tomorrow, probably. Anton and I turn in our reports to Steen today. The Nat leaders will meet tomorrow, and in case they decide not to say anything, Anton has asked a few old friends of the press to join him for breakfast on Saturday."

"Simon knows already. Uncle Anton asked me to tell him."

"You're family. You're prettier than he is, anyway." Coldewe shrugged and sat down in the other chair. "After I went through munitions requirements with Saki Bukhanov, I started having second thoughts. What works for killing people might not work on Neighbor." He added in a strained voice, " 'Even more than other subjects, affairs of war are subject to continual change.' "

Rikki rubbed her temples, "Who are you quoting now, Helmuth von Moltke or Karl May?"

"*Don Quixote*. I find myself assuming that people on Neighbor are a lot like us, but what if they have chitinous armor—"

"Like giant beetles?"

"Or whatever. Is it safe to assume that they're carbon-based blobs of protoplasm? Why not silicon beings, or energy beings?" Coldewe sighed. "Can I use 5mm caseless, or do I have to figure out how to build ray guns?"

"How much do you know about amino acids, Uncle Hans?"

"Not one thing," Coldewe said cheerfully.

"One of these days, people are going to take you seriously when you make jokes like that," Sanmartin warned him darkly.

"I was educated as befits a gentleman, which is to say I learned literature and tactics and several foreign languages."

"I have heard you try to speak some of them." Rikki pondered. "Let me think how simple I can make this."

"Very simple, I hope."

"I will try. First, the living organisms on *every* planet human beings have visited are aggregates of amino acids. This seems to be the basic autocatalytic process in the universe."

"But—" Coldewe began.

"I am coming to that part. Life on different planets arises from different groupings of the base amino acids. Simon made me do a paper once in which I compared the enzymatic conversion of dUMP to dTMP in Suid-Afrikan organisms with the same process in Terran organisms. This is a very basic process, and the sequence of the amino acids that assist in binding the pyrimidine remain remarkably stable over time."

"Whatever," Coldewe agreed, nodding.

"In Earth's common *E. coli* bacterium, the last twelve amino acids in this sequence are arginine, serine, cysteine, aspartate, valine, phenylalanine, leucine, glycine, leucine, proline, phenylalanine, and asparagine. In a human being, the amino acids in these positions are arginine, serine, glycine, aspartate, methionine, glycine, leucine, glycine, valine, proline, phenylalanine, and asparagine, which clearly shows that the two organisms— the bacterium and the human being—share a common ancestry, however remote. In Suid-Afrikan organisms, while the process is essentially identical, the sequencing of amino acids is completely different."

"I'm glad this is the simple part."

"Neighbor is an Earth-type world, which is to say that the average temperature of its landmasses and seas is comfortably situated between the melting and boiling points for water. As the probe data shows, the planet now has a remarkably Earth-like atmosphere. This did *not* come about by chance. Oxygen is extremely reactive, and free oxygen does not occur naturally in such quantities. Neighbor's high oxygen and low carbon dioxide levels obviously result from aerobic processes, which is strong evidence that evolution on Neighbor followed the same general path as evolution on Earth, or Suid-Afrika, or a dozen other worlds. On such worlds, the prebiotic atmosphere is mainly carbon dioxide, carbon monoxide, and nitrogen, with significant amounts of hydrogen, methane, and ammonia vented from rocks. Through a simple series of chemical reactions, these compounds are transformed into hydrogen cyanide and formaldehyde, which in turn react with water and ammonia to form amino acids. Eventually, these amino acids string themselves into self-replicating polymers that become life, as we know it. This is to say that in my professional opinion if the organisms you encounter on Neighbor are grossly dissimilar from Terran or Suid-Afrikan organisms, I will eat your precious hat there."

"No bulletproof silicon beings?"

"A number of scientists have postulated the existence of silicon-based life, but no one has worked out an appropriate mechanism, and the atmosphere that would evolve on such a world would probably not be significantly Earth-like. There are no guarantees in the universe, but you were not the only one to stay up late, and everything I have seen from the probe data suggests that the Neighbors are not too terribly different from us."

"Those poor, benighted beings," Coldewe said in a tone of wonderment that broke Rikki Sanmartin up completely. "So, Madame Scientist, what are these people like?"

"They are almost certainly bipedal, between a meter and two and a half meters in height. If you smoked, I would bet you a cigar that they average out at a little over two meters. And they reproduce sexually, which would be a helpful thing for you to know."

"How do you know all that?"

She shrugged. "Four limbs is obvious. Life from the seas colonizes the land, and no one has come up with a reason why a fish that does this would develop more than two limb girdles. Bipedal is equally obvious. Civilization implies grasping hands as well as intelligence. At some point, there is no reproductive advantage to developing intelligence without hands to manipulate the environment."

"And the size?"

"The gravity on Neighbor is 94.32 percent of Earth's, which dictates to a large degree the maximum size of plants and animals. Intelligence is not necessarily an optimal adaption for all creatures." She smiled impishly. "Anything smaller than a meter is very likely to be too far down in the food chain to concentrate on becoming smarter, while anything larger than two and a half meters tall probably doesn't need to."

Coldewe threw up his hands. "I used to have conversations like this with your mother. All right, why do they reproduce sexually?"

"The sexual selection process is a powerful force in nature. Organisms that reproduce sexually preserve greater genetic variation and are able to evolve much more quickly than asexual organisms. An asexual organism either stabilizes to fill a particular environmental niche, or quickly becomes extinct."

There was a knock at the door. Coldewe called out, "Come in."

Esko Poikolainnen stuck his head inside and said apologetically, "Saki Bukhanov is on the line. He is agitated."

"May I take the call?" Coldewe swiveled around in his chair and chose the appropriate menu selection on his computer. Bukhanov's round, homely face appeared. "Hello, Saki."

Bukhanov was wearing a gray suit and a white shirt and tie. "Hello, Hans. Who is that behind you?"

"That's Rikki Sanmartin."

Bukhanov nodded. "You've grown since I saw you last. Tell Hans to mind his manners."

Coldewe interrupted, "What's the problem, Saki?"

"Sir, I am feuding with that intendance officer of yours." Bukhanov wore a pained expression. "I want four engineering vehicles, and he says he won't release them—he'll lay down in front of the wheels first. The Imps only loaded four, and that isn't nearly enough. We are going to have to plan on a succession of supply ships, and I do not want to even think about moving that kind of tonnage by hand."

Lightweight and powerful, the little engineering vehicles were excellent as forklifts and light bulldozers. With electromagnetic strips mounted in the tires, they were as adept at moving cargo in orbit as they were at digging bunkers dirtside, and for that reason, they were worth their weight in precious metal.

"I'll talk to Christiaan. He's young enough to be miffed that I didn't include him in on the planning. Is there anything else I can do?"

"Yes, sir, there is." Bukhanov adopted an even more pained expression. "Before the news breaks, call my wife and make sure she understands that I am not going with you. Otherwise, I will find my clothing in a pile in the street, and it's a nuisance getting it dry-cleaned."

"Right. Coldewe out." Coldewe blanked the screen.

"His wife wouldn't really do that, would she?" Rikki inquired.

"You haven't met the gay divorcée, have you? Petronella latched on to Saki after we got back from Tokyo. Until he became a banker, he used to keep extra clothes in the armsroom in case we ran late." Coldewe looked away. "I'd love to have him along, but he almost didn't get back from Tokyo, and I think he's seen enough."

"I notice he called you 'sir.' "

"My officers usually do that when they're telling me my head needs soaking. I find it difficult to give myself airs—too many people remember me as a lieutenant with a questionable sense of humor."

The corner of Rikki's mouth turned down. "Your sense of humor hasn't gotten any better, Uncle Hans. Can't you be serious about anything?"

"You know, Rikki-tikki-tavi, I was serious once." Coldewe's eyes took on a faraway look. "At your age, I was serious about everything. And one day among the pebbles in a very dry wadi, I stopped. Being serious, that is."

"That was Ashcroft, wasn't it?"

Coldewe coughed, remembering the desert. "Who told you about Ashcroft?"

"Uncle Matti, of course. He is really the only one of you who will say anything about what my father did as a soldier. Ashcroft left its marks on my father."

"On all of us."

Esko Poikolainnen rapped on the door. "Colonel, it's time."

"Right." Coldewe looked at the time display on his wrist mount. "I'm due in court."

"What did they catch you at?"

"I'm being called as a character witness for a former D Company soldier named Prigal. He's up before the landrost for dangerous driving." Coldewe coughed. "He's a trifle hard up for character witnesses."

"Not *the* Prigal?" Rikki exclaimed. "You mean, there really is a Prigal?"

"You know him?"

"You used to tell me Prigal stories. When I was a girl." She glared at him accusingly. "You should be ashamed of the stories you made up about him."

"Prigal, the world's oldest recruit private—this world or any other." Coldewe began coughing. He started to say something and then began coughing again. "As God is my witness," he finally managed to say, "every word was truth. Misfortune is Prigal's ruling star and his mishaps the stuff of legend."

"Even Prigal's Island?"

Tears of mirth trickled down Coldewe's cheeks. "God is my witness." He waved a finger weakly. "Prigal, through skillful manipulation of the air pressure in his tires and a 45-degree compass error—I never got the details straight, but I understand it had something to do with the magnet he used to hang a pinup—managed to bury his armored car in the heart of the largest swamp on the continent. A Cadillac will float, so don't ask me how. We had to drop forty-three tons of stone before we could fly in a crane big enough to haul him out."

"Oh, my."

"Meri Reinikka, our engineer company commander, got stuck with the salvage job, and we had to take his rifle away, he was so mad. He actually fired a couple of shots in Prigal's direction, but he usually hits what he aims at, so nobody took him seriously. Prigal's Island has the dubious distinction of being the only named terrain feature in a five-thousand-hectare area."

"Oh, dear."

"Prigal now drives a taxi as if it were an armored car. Wish me luck as I perjure myself," Coldewe said. "If I told the court a fraction of the truth, he'd never get his license back."

Friday (1167)

"THE NEXT ITEM ON THE AGENDA," PRESIDENT ANDRIES STEEN said primly in Afrikaans, glancing up and down the table, "concerns Colonel Vereshchagin's meeting with Imperial commissioner Mutaro." The absence of non-Afrikaners obviated the need to use English.

Having purged "softs" from the Reformed Nationalist party's leadership council, Steen and his middle-aged "hard" supporters kept tight control.

Near the foot of the table, District Leader Jooste van Drooste ventured incautiously, "Vereshchagin is no friend of ours. If the old man wants to go, we will never have a better chance to get rid of him."

Wiser heads waited to take their cue from Steen.

Andries Steen was a sleek man with piercing eyes, his face framed by an imposing gray Vandyke beard and a dark mustache that ran like a streak to either side of his jawline and gave him a strikingly effective television presence.

Steen waited half a moment before turning on van Drooste. "The Imperials are our enemy. One does not compromise with enemies." In his path to power, Steen, notoriously humorless, had repeated that maxim more than once. Although never a soldier, Steen fully understood that an enemy who is given a line of retreat lives to fight again.

Again he paused, to give weight to his remarks. "It is clear that the Imperials have bribed Vereshchagin to betray us. He betrayed the Imperials once, and once a traitor, always a traitor. Any compromise would cause our people needless confusion at this juncture in history. This proposed expedition is nothing more than an attempt to weaken Suid-Afrika."

During the second, ultimately successful rebellion, Imperial intelligence had coerced a large number of Suid-Afrikans into providing information. A former trial lawyer, Steen had achieved political eminence by crafting Suid-Afrika's lustrance law, which debarred such individuals from participating in politics.

With an election pending, it was abundantly clear to most of the party leaders present that having played the anti-Imperial card to propel himself into power, Andries Steen proposed seeing if it would capture another trick. No one present had the audacity to ask Steen how much of what he had said he believed.

Discussion stopped at the faint sound of children's voices singing, " 'Oh, we're having a war, and we want you to come!' So the pig began to whistle and to pound on a drum."

Steen made an effort to control his face.

Until Steen took office, "The Whistling Pig" had served as Suid-Afrika's national anthem, and it still served the 1/35th Rifle Battalion as its official drinking song.

He spoke to one of his bodyguards. "Seivert, go out in the plaza and make them stop."

Some part of Steen's mind knew that he was trying to hold back the tide with a very small bucket, but it is a prerogative of kings and princes to try.

That afternoon, when his speech aired, bitterly attacking the Imperial Government and cautioning Suid-Afrikans to guard their independence, in the security of his quarters, Hans Coldewe bounced a paperweight off the television screen.

Used to Coldewe's eccentric mannerisms around televisions, Esko Poikolainnen, Coldewe's communications sergeant and constant shadow, touched a button and turned the set off. "Sir, he hasn't turned down the expedition, yet."

"No, but I know the difference between a hawk and a hand saw." Coldewe looked around for something else to throw. "Depend on it, Esko, Andries Steen just declared war."

Poikolainnen smiled thinly. "War is what we're good at."

Saturday (1167)

"HEER MUTARO?" SEEMINGLY OBLIVIOUS TO MUTARO'S AP-
proach, Vereshchagin continued to observe the small amphtiles
playing around his feet. "I trust your trip was uneventful." Camouflaged by the battledress he was wearing, Vereshchagin's outline seemed to blur into the backdrop of the forest's edge.

Mutaro glanced back at his escort, Roy "Filthy DeKe" de
Kantzow, with a degree of amusement. "It was quite interesting."

"Frosting straight," the tall former soldier affirmed.

Although Vereshchagin discouraged his soldiers from using
profanity, Filthy DeKe had always been a glorious exception.
When The Deacon left active service to marry a sweet thing half
his age, several colleagues reported that de Kantzow had visibly
purpled under the strain of keeping a civil tongue during the ceremony.

De Kantzow walked away, and Mutaro sat down gingerly on
a small camp chair that Vereshchagin had provided.

"I rather like the forest," Vereshchagin said. "I find it tran-
quil."

Mutaro gazed up at the tall trees. "I understand that Heer
Steen has rejected the idea of assisting the expedition."

"The matter had become entangled in party politics."

Mutaro sighed deeply. "Vereshchagin-*san*, perhaps Steen does
not comprehend what is at issue. Perhaps someone could explain
matters to him."

Vereshchagin shook his head. "Heer Steen does not and perhaps cannot view Neighbor as a threat to Suid-Afrika. And he
believes that he is playing for the highest stakes of all—the
verafrikansing of Suid-Afrika. What he desires are changes in
Suid-Afrika's constitutional structure that would allow him to
disenfranchise non-Afrikaners and suppress opponents. Have
you been briefed on Suid-Afrika's political situation?"

Mutaro smiled. "Inadequately, it seems."

Vereshchagin paused to consider his words. "Over the past
three years, the Reformed Nationalist party has been radicalized
by the fear that the younger generation is losing sight of its Afrikaner heritage."

"They are losing their intolerance for other peoples, which is
perhaps not such an unfortunate thing," Mutaro rejoined.

Vereshchagin bowed his head, acknowledging the truth of the
statement. "The Afrikaners, descendants of refugees, have my-

thologized the gradual descent of Earth's Republic of South Africa into multisided civil war, and to a lesser extent they have also mythologized the brutal economic oppression they suffered under the dominion of United Steel–Standard. Ironically, the same 'intolerance, petty intellectual thuggery, and political dissembling' that wrecked nearly every political movement in the old Republic of South Africa has resurrected itself here. Steen skillfully played upon the resentments of many older Afrikaners to oust Christos Claassen as head of the Reformed Nationalist party, and he and his supporters now view the next few years as their only opportunity to radically alter Suid-Afrika's direction. Unfortunately, our contact with Neighbor could not have come at a more awkward moment."

Mutaro stroked his chin. "I am of the view that an effort could be made to persuade Heer Steen to reconsider the ill-advised path he has chosen."

Vereshchagin laughed softly. "To use one of Hans's metaphors, Steen is as white as the snow that Suid-Afrika doesn't have. He is a church elder with one wife and no mistresses, and as far as I know, he even pays his taxes honestly."

"A dangerous man has no vices."

"His vice is lust for power."

"And here, as in many places, lust for power is only an offense if one is detected." Mutaro pondered this. "Has President Steen placed you under surveillance?"

"It began yesterday. Several Silvershirts—members of the *Suiwerheidwagte*, the 'Purity Watch,' an ostensibly separate paramilitary organization that Steen formed a year ago—rented a house across the street from me to observe my movements."

"Heavens, how did you slip away?"

Vereshchagin smiled again. "At election time when passions are inflamed, Hans has a soldier on guard outside my door. One soldier in battledress and a face shield looks very much like any other, and my uniform still fits, so I simply exchanged places with the young man Hans sent, guarded my door for a few hours, and left in the vehicle that came to pick him up."

Mutaro laughed very gently. "What move is next in our game?"

"For my people to leave, Steen must lose the election."

Mutaro sighed, and his lined face, usually animated, suddenly appeared aged and haggard. "I had not anticipated this. It would be most embarrassing if you did not go. My deputy, Dr. Seki, a distinguished scientist, is available to lead the expedition, but I confess that I do not have great confidence in him. Yet President Steen dislikes and perhaps fears you. I cannot understand why he is not agreeable to having you go."

Vereshchagin tried to smile. "Unfortunately, the price he would demand for granting permission is one I cannot pay."

Mutaro folded his hands. "Perhaps it is a price I can afford," he suggested.

Vereshchagin shook his head emphatically. "The Uniates distrust your government, but the Nationalists view it as the very finger of Satan. Steen plays upon these fears. Economic concessions from your government would not tempt him. If anything he would restrict trade even more. What he desires is power."

Mutaro sighed. "It appears that Heer Smith will be the Union party presidential candidate. I am not sanguine about his chances."

Vereshchagin nodded. "I have an alternative candidate in mind."

"Indeed. Yet, Vereshchagin-*san*, permit me to suggest that it would be highly unfortunate for such a delicate matter as humanity's first contact with an alien civilization to hinge upon the vagaries of what is, after all, one more colonial world. Even if Steen were to deny Imperial ships permission to enter orbit, perhaps if you and personnel you deem essential were to quietly slip off planet, deficiencies in the expedition's equipment could be made at a later point in time."

Vereshchagin shook his head regretfully. "I cannot. If I were to do so, Steen would declare a state of emergency and initiate proceedings against anyone suspected of being involved. With proper management of the crisis, he could even impose a single-party dictatorship on this planet. I cannot allow this. I owe too much to persons who are dead."

Mutaro, who had already compromised himself far too much to draw back, said sadly, "I respect your reverence for the dead, Vereshchagin-*san*, but you must not forget the duty you owe to the living. I fear that I am tiring. Perhaps Heer de Kantzow could take me back now."

He rose and left, leaving Vereshchagin lost in thought.

Sunday (1168)

HANNES VAN DER MERWE HANDED THE DUTY ROSTER TO KLAES De la Rey, dazzling to the eye in his silver uniform. De la Rey glanced at it. "Oscar is going to moan about having to watch Vereshchagin's house on a Saturday. He is having trouble again with his wife."

"Change it if you like, but whoever gets stuck with a Saturday is going to moan about it."

De la Rey's adjutant, Van der Merwe, was one of the few *Suiwerheidwagte* members with military experience, and De la Rey attached great weight to his opinion on technical matters. "All right." He initialed off. "I will speak to Oscar. Being head of this organization is less fun than I thought it would be."

Van der Merwe, a pleasant man nearing his fortieth birthday, took it back. "You can have my job instead."

"Then there would not be anyone to do mine," De la Rey said frankly. "Are those signs ready?"

"I have one here to show you." Van der Merwe held it up.

The Movement claims and expects total allegiance without reservation. The Movement's strength lies in its discipline and political convictions, which bond the organization into one force. Volunteers must realize and understand the danger involved in drinking alcohol. A large body of information can be gathered by enemy forces from volunteers who drink. Volunteers are warned that drink-induced loose talk is the GREATEST POTENTIAL DANGER facing the organization, and in a military organization is SUICIDE!

"Yes, this is exactly what I want. Too many people think that the purpose of our Movement is to drink and shoot guns. Have every cell put two of them up." De la Rey looked at Van der Merwe. "What is wrong? You look as though you don't approve."

"You want me to speak candidly?"

"Yes, yes. Go ahead. I don't see anyone else here."

"I am not sure that the signs will do a lot of good."

"What do you suggest?" De la Rey trimmed a ragged fingernail. "We need to do something."

"I don't know, Klaes. Let me think about it for a few days."

"All right, I will wait to run it by the party heads." De la Rey cocked his head. "Is that the telephone in my office?"

He walked the length of the hall, shut the door behind him,

and switched on the phone. President Steen's image filled the screen. De la Rey saluted stiffly. "Yes, Heer President."

"I need you to watch Coldewe's officers, Klaes." Steen looked at him sternly. "Can you do it?"

"I will need to increase the stipend. We are stretched thin watching the Uniate leaders and Vereshchagin, and we are having trouble finding new volunteers," De la Rey admitted.

"The money you need will be forthcoming."

De la Rey saluted again. "Yes, Heer President."

Monday (1168)

SIMON BEETJE HEARD THE TELEPHONE RING IN HIS OFFICE. HE let it ring a few times with mounting apprehension. Finally, he picked it up. *"Hallo?"*

"Hello, Simon. This is Hans."

"Oh, hello, Hans, how are you doing?"

"I'm fine. When are you going to get your phone hooked up to your computer?"

"Hans, this is a university."

"Yes, I know—you people like being back in the Dark Ages, and if an extra twenty rand for fripperies ever showed up on one of your budget submissions, there would be the devil to pay."

"Ah, what may I do for you, Hans?"

"Remember the list of names Anton asked you for?"

"Yes, scientists for the expedition."

"Make sure the pedants on your list speak good English."

"Hans, English has been the universal language of scientific inquiry for more than two hundred years," Beetje said with wounded dignity.

"A lot of people who can puzzle through technical articles can't necessarily speak it. When you have the list, don't give it to Anton. His phone is being tapped. Give it to me instead."

"His phone is being tapped?" Simon felt his chest beginning to constrict. "Hans, what is going on?" He heard Coldewe chuckle.

"Politics, as usual. Steen is about to portray the expedition as an Imperial plot, so any preparations we make have to be made quietly. Things are getting interesting."

"Hans, I—"

"I might mention that there's a rally starting up in about an hour beside the founder's statue," Coldewe continued. "It seems that word got out that one of the university's newly appointed trustees is pressuring the library to cut back on off-planet purchases—the word *censorship* comes to mind—and your students and a few of their teachers are more than a little riled."

"Couldn't you have left the university aside?" Beetje asked, surprising himself with his own bitterness.

Coldewe laughed aloud. "We haven't even started playing rough yet. In case you haven't been paying attention, in places like Boksburg, the Silvershirts are holding their rallies in front of businesses that don't ante up contributions. Some places call that extortion. This isn't shaping up as just another election."

"Ah, Hans. I need to think. About things."

"Simon," Coldewe said quietly, "when I was a lieutenant and you were a weedy young thing, I remember Raul talked you out of enlisting in one of the reserve platoons because he figured you'd do Suid-Afrika more good as a professor than as a rifleman. I hope he didn't screw up. Give me the list. Or don't, but don't expect me to understand. In wartime, people look down on neutrals."

Beetje heard the phone click on the other end.

Tuesday (1168)

VERESHCHAGIN SETTLED INTO AN OVERSTUFFED CHAIR. "THANK you for meeting with me, Adriaan. I greatly appreciate it."

"You should." Prinsloo Adriaan Smith, Lord Mayor of Johannesburg and de facto Union party head, puffed placidly on his pipe, his unruly hair standing straight up in patches. "I have already had two of my colleagues ask me not to. You have become 'controversial.' Idiots! Are you under Silvershirt surveillance?"

"Yes, of course."

"Steen is too shrewd to raise a question in the Assembly about my meeting with you because then he would have to explain how he knew." Smith puffed away. "Thirty-five days until elections—Commissioner Mutaro's timing is terrible. Well, what would you like to have from me, a promise to back the expedition if we win? You have that, for what it is worth, which is little."

"Who will your presidential candidate be, Adriaan?"

"Me, I suppose." The former journalist turned politician shrugged. "A party caucus Thursday night will formalize it. We

had to run McClausland last time around or risk having the cowboys bolt the party, which makes it my turn, but the truth is, it
has been too many years in coming. I am an old man, and my
party is fast becoming an old man's party. The man we should
be running is Denoon."

"Who is dead," Vereshchagin pointed out.

"Yes, and you always thought there was something suspicious
about the accident."

"They covered their tracks well."

"None of the other youngsters is nearly as promising." Smith
absently tried to brush down a stray lock of hair. "We need Albert back, God help us. Albert as a dead hero is considerably
less valuable than Albert alive."

"This election frightens me, Adriaan."

"Perhaps it should frighten all of us," Smith said indifferently.

Vereshchagin scrutinized Prinsloo Smith's face for its usual
enthusiasm and found it lacking. "What do the polls say?" he
asked quietly.

"Steen looks and acts like a president, and with the economy
doing well, many people will vote for him for no better reason.
Former Senior Censor Ssu tells me that my candidacy has serious problems, and that any controversy is likely to make it
worse. So yes, I will run. Can I win?" Smith shrugged. "We
can't run a cowboy, and there isn't an Afrikaner in the party
worthy of the effort. Would you like to run? We could not do
worse."

"I have another solution. Run Rikki Sanmartin for president."

Smith's pipe went out. "Dear God, what a gamble!" he said
in a hoarse voice.

Vereshchagin waited.

"What was that toast you quoted me once?" Prinsloo Adriaan
Smith, the Lord Mayor of Johannesburg, asked in a sad voice.

"Montrose's toast. 'He either fears his fate too much/Or his
desserts are small/Who fears to put it to the touch/To win or lose
it all.' "

"Yes, that was it," Smith said in a soft, sad, satisfied voice.
"It would pay all of our debts, wouldn't it? What does Rikki
think about this?"

"I hoped that you would ask her," Vereshchagin confessed.

"I should, shouldn't I? No, stay there." Smith reached for the
phone. "She will know whose idea this was, and she might as
well get both of us at once." He chuckled. "Seeing how much

Steen has already paid for commercials attacking me, he will be annoyed!"

He waited for the phone to ring. "*Hallo*, Betje. Yes, I'm doing fine. Put Rikki on, I want her to run for president. . . . *Hallo*, Rikki? Congratulations. You are running for president. Put on something dowdy so that I can take you around to talk to the party leaders who will be dragooned into voting for you. Think of it as studying a different class of invertebrate." He paused to listen. He looked up at Vereshchagin. "She wants to talk to you."

SIX LONG HOURS LATER, HENDRICKA SANMARTIN SHUT THE door behind her, flung her handbag at the wall, and plopped herself down in a chair.

Her foster mother, Betje Beyers, looked at her sympathetically. "It went well?"

"McClausland was the worst!" Rikki announced. "He offered me a candy bar."

"I hope that you did not hurt your hand when you hit him," Beyers said in her strongly accented English.

"I was polite. Adriaan was standing on my foot at the time. Am I too young?"

Betje Beyers laughed, very softly. "Not at all. You have not been young for a very long time. Remember when you were five and you told me that you were too old to play with dolls? Of course, it surprised us when you burned them in the yard, and you frightened the neighbors. Have you started thinking about your campaign yet?"

"I will need a campaign manager."

Betje Beyers laughed. "Not me! I am going to be your treasurer." She looked at her foster daughter shrewdly and picked up the phone. "*Hallo*, Matti? This is Betje Beyers. You are taking my daughter to dinner tonight."

"Dinner theater," Rikki said promptly.

"Dinner theater," Betje corrected herself, "so be here at 6:30." She looked up at the clock. "That will give you two hours to find out what is up."

THE THEATER WAS BEGINNING TO FILL WHEN SANMARTIN AND Harjalo arrived. Harjalo, Anton Vereshchagin's executive officer and successor as battalion commander, was a gray-eyed Finn with a wiry frame and a moon face. He told the woman at the box office, "Colonel Harjalo and guest."

The woman giggled and passed the tickets across. "I recognized the dent in your nose from seeing you on the news. You have table eleven. Please enjoy our show."

Harjalo walked Rikki to their table. "I'm glad she didn't say she read about me in school."

Rikki nudged him with her elbow. "How did you break your nose? Hand-to-hand combat?"

"In a manner of speaking. It was during a football match. What's the show?"

"I think it is *Cry of the Phalarope*. Does it matter?"

Harjalo pondered this. "I suppose not."

"Thank you for taking me on such short notice," she said demurely.

Harjalo held her chair for her. "In twenty-three years of service I learned to duck when people shoot, and not to argue with Vroew Beyers. These are good seats. Did you tell them you were Albert's daughter?"

Rikki patted him on the arm. "I told them you were a little deaf. They were very understanding."

Harjalo was still sputtering as she led him over to the dwindling line at the buffet table.

The buffet was *braaivleis* style, which meant that the meat was roasted. "Pretty awful food," Harjalo said as he finished what he had taken.

"I squeezed in a course on theater, and I was told that bad food was traditional." She held her wineglass up to the light and stared at it.

"So. What is the business we need to discuss? Politics?"

She nodded. "Politics."

"I talked to Ssu, who is still the only political analyst on this planet worth the price of damnation, and he thinks your Uniates are going to get massacred."

She gazed into her glass with no expression on her face. "Steen and his Nationals rode the lustrance law to power. And they are still riding it. Nobody wants to admit this, but it is true."

"I always had trouble understanding the lustrance law. Admiral Horii's intelligence people coerced lots of people into providing information, but only a handful were real traitors. Most of the information Horii got was worthless."

"People still resent it," Rikki said tonelessly. "They saved the lives of their loved ones. Other people died as a result."

"Like your mother."

"Like my mother. Albert fought the lustrance law tooth and

nail and lost. He believed that stripping citizenship rights from persons who were coerced into collaborating—in the name of purity—would open wounds in our people that would take generations to heal, and he was right. Every election, the Nationals wave a bloody shirt and chant, 'No Softness on Traitors,' and people who feel strongly, people who lost relatives, vote for them as a result. But what is humorous is that people proscribed under the law give money to the Nationalist party and urge their families to vote the Nationalist ticket. The Union party preaches forgiveness for them, and they elect the other party."

"We humans are funny creatures, aren't we? Maybe some of them don't feel they deserve to be forgiven," Harjalo suggested gently.

Rikki spun her glass and caught it. "It is not their right."

Harjalo probed. "Are you bitter because it was your mother who died?"

"Yes, I am bitter." Rikki set her glass down with a thump and toyed with it. "It is my mother's blood on the shirt they wave, and she would have thought it an obscenity. But in a foul way, it makes me the best candidate. The Nationals can chant 'No Softness on Traitors' in a corner, but they don't dare challenge me openly. Not on that issue."

Harjalo stared at her. "Are you running for office this time around?"

"Yes. For president. And I need you to be my campaign manager."

"Little tin gods. And after your people put Albert through hell." Harjalo thought for a minute. "Is Anton behind this?"

"Of course." She giggled. "I just remembered that phalaropes are polyandrous birds—each female henpecks several dowdy little males into sitting on her nests and brooding her eggs."

Harjalo rubbed his bald spot reflexively. "Anton was probably planning this back when I had hair, but Anton is used to juggling planets, and I'm not so sure anymore. Sometimes I think that the planets deserve what they get, and that I ought to worry more about the people Anton uses."

Rikki stared through him. "I will not lie to you. It frightens me. I watched them eat away at Oom Albert. But this is my planet and my people, and they deserve better than they will get if I do not try to get myself elected."

"Speaking of nests and polyandrous birds, what about your personal life or lack of one?" Harjalo said grumpily. "When was the last time you went out on a date, young lady?"

"Oh, last year sometime, I suppose."

"That means the year before, most likely. It's a shame you're too old to spank." He shook his head. "You frighten them off, don't you?"

Rikki had the grace to blush, ever so slightly. "I suppose. Except for the ninnies, and the filth."

"Gods. If your mother ever came back, she'd bruise my shins for letting you grow up the way you did. What did Hans used to call you?"

"Rikki-tikki-tavi."

"So, Rikki-tikki-tavi, what is it you talk about when the young gentlemen come calling?"

"Animals and politics."

"Gods. You do scare them off. The good ones, anyway." Harjalo examined her face. "Who was he? The last one, I mean."

"An English professor." Her voice lost some of its assurance. "He sent flowers and poems."

"His wife didn't understand him, and he was in the process of getting a divorce, I suppose," Harjalo snapped.

Rikki used her knife to trace designs on the tablecloth. "I wasn't sure—I asked Aksu to look into it for me."

Matti nodded with approval. "Aksu is a damned good intell man. Shimazu trained him. And he found out that your young stud of a professor used the same line and the same poems on the last student he seduced."

Her eyes sparkled. "The last three." Her voice faltered. "I mentioned this to Simon."

"Who politely told the man that if your father's company ever found out, he'd need more health insurance," Harjalo said with a trace of satisfaction. He stopped abruptly. "I'm not going to change your mind, am I?"

"No. Not in the least."

Harjalo nodded sourly. "Let's move on to the next hard question then. Adriaan Smith must have agreed to this. Did you mention to him that you wanted me as your campaign manager?"

"No. Adriaan would probably be horrified."

"I shouldn't doubt. Do you remember Dominee Leibeck in Boksburg, or was that before your time?"

"Oh, yes. I remember."

Matti grinned, reminiscing. "The good dominee was partial to three-hour sermons of a distinctly political nature. He told me that I was going straight to hell, and I asked him if the devil needed a second in command. It looked good in the papers. You need my reputation like you need a lead weight strapped to your neck."

Sanmartin slammed her knife down on the tablecloth moodily. "The Devil doesn't need you as a second in command, I do. Ssu will handle the polling and political ends of things, and Tant Betje will raise funds, she has oceans of favors she can call in and no one is better at twisting arms. I already have campaign workers lined up—"

"The university?"

"Apart from the oceans of favors I can call in, I have a message that many students believe in. Adriaan will handle the Union party organization, but I need someone to help hold things together."

Harjalo frowned. "Far be it from me to teach you political taking tricks, but Rikki, darling, the electorate might not warm to a foreign ex-soldier helping run your campaign. Can't you find some well-connected Union party hack to do the job? Have you thought about the political fallout when I start running my mouth in public?"

"The Union party hacks haven't been winning very many elections." Rikki tossed her head impatiently. "I can't change my name, Uncle Matti, and I can't change who I am, so I might as well flaunt it. Any votes I lose because of you are votes I will lose anyway. As for political fallout from my stodgy, old Uncle Matti, dear me, I intend to shock more people than you ever could. My party colleagues haven't done very well being polite these last few years."

Harjalo scratched his chin. "I have been pretty stodgy, haven't I?" He shrugged. "How can I refuse tactfully?"

She laid her hand on his. "You can't. Deal?"

He nodded. "Deal."

"Now, hush! They are dimming the lights. The play is about to start."

During curtain calls, Harjalo noticed an older couple talking to each other at a corner table. Comparing his age to Rikki's, they were loudly discussing the nature of the relationship.

"Excuse me, this one's mine," Harjalo murmured. He stopped beside their table and smiled. "I couldn't help overhearing. I'm Matti Harjalo—you may have heard of me, I was a soldier when I had hair. This is my niece, Hendricka Sanmartin. You may have heard of her, too. She runs the family business, so I take orders from her." Harjalo paused. "And I couldn't be more proud."

The man began stammering an apology. Harjalo patted him on the shoulder reassuringly and reached into his pocket for one of the calling cards he carried out of habit. "Just act surprised when you read about her in the papers. Now, we truly have to run, but feel free to give me a call and chat sometime."

As they slipped through the press of the crowd, he whispered, "How did I do?"

Her eyes twinkled. "Middle class. Middle-grade executive of some kind. Slightly liberal. That is two votes anyway."

"How do you know all that?" Matti asked.

"That," his niece replied, tucking her arm firmly into his, "is why I am the candidate. Come take me home. It has been quite a day."

Saturday (1168)

HARJALO STEPPED ON TOP OF A BOX TO ADDRESS THE PEOPLE gathered in his backyard. It was an old ammunition box, which was a tradition of sorts, although only a few persons present realized this. "Good morning."

Although Harjalo spoke softly, something derived from a lifetime of command experience made people listen when he did speak. The mob quieted. "Although I've already met most of you, I'm Matti Harjalo, the campaign manager. By law, the campaign commences Monday, which gives us four weeks to get Rikki elected. She just spent four days locked in a cellar with a very shrewd and very nasty old man named Ssu trying to figure out what she stands for."

He held up a bulky wad of paper. "This is it. And since we don't have the chances of snow in Hades otherwise, we are going to spend the next four weeks campaigning on specific issues and programs, rather than the usual personalities, which should make a refreshing change for the electorate."

A young woman raised her hand, and Harjalo recognized her. "Mr. Harjalo, what if there are parts of it we do not agree with?"

"If there are parts of it you can't live with, we thank you for coming, and you leave." He looked over the crowd, among whom were nearly thirty reservists and former NCOs that Harjalo intended to use as assistant instructors. "We're purchasing a small amount of media time, but we don't and won't have a tremendous amount of money. The only way we're going to win is by organizing you to go out and talk to people."

He paused, and continued, "This farm is my home. Sleeping arrangements are a bit spartan. Think of the next two days as a cross between a religious retreat and military boot camp."

"Preparing us for combat?" a young man with a beard quipped.

"You get two hours of self-defense tonight and four more tomorrow," Harjalo said calmly. "I wish we had time to give you more. Any of you who want can come back next week for individual instruction. If you haven't already figured it out, the Silvershirts are going to try to rough you up, so we'll be sending you out in groups. We have two very long days plus four very long weeks ahead of us, so if any of you aren't really interested in doing this, please drop out now."

By midnight, they were calling him "Gideon."

Interlude

SUID-AFRIKA'S POPULATION, ALTHOUGH RAPIDLY GROWING, WAS still far smaller than the population of a medium-sized city on Earth, which made personal campaigning effective. In the cowboy country, the Purity Watch, the *Suiwerheidwagte*, was usually called the Sewer Watch, and the cowboy rancher magnates, who had even less love for Andries Steen than Steen realized, coughed up enough money to make Rikki Sanmartin's bid credible.

On a world like Suid-Afrika with only one professional sport, betting on elections runs a close second to betting on football results; and a canny and statistically significant fraction of the electorate had learned to lie to the professional pollsters to keep them from affecting the odds.

While Nationalist party pollsters continued to predict a Steen juggernaut, after the campaign's first week, Johannesburg bookies dropped the odds against Rikki to two-to-one, and Steen fired his pollsters and began to take the campaign seriously.

Meanwhile, Hans Coldewe's preparations for the expedition to Neighbor, never completely curtailed, began to assume a serious aspect.

Sunday (1170)

"BORY!" PLATOON SERGEANT KAARLO KIVELA YELLED ACROSS the ready room. "What platoon are you going to?"

Ostensibly, the motive for the reorganization of Coldewe's battalion was to add a recruit class. In point of fact, it was an open secret that the recon platoon, No. 9 rifle platoon, and No. 10 rifle platoon were being filled with the men who would be going to Neighbor.

Dmitri Uborevich, squat and barrel chested, was part Kalmyk and looked the part. He rubbed his chin. "Well, you know, I haven't decided. I mean, I've got a girlfriend now to think of."

Kivela snorted. "Since when? Last Tuesday?"

"Hey! I do so have a girlfriend!"

"Yeah, sure, you and the pope of Rome. If she's still seeing you next Tuesday, I'll take her out and buy her eyeglasses."

"That was unkind," Uborevich sniffed. "She likes me, I will have you know. And she doesn't use big words all the time, like the last one."

Kivela made a whistling noise through his teeth. "Whew! *That* young. You'd better go with us. I mean, they got laws against that sort of thing here."

"You! No, she's not *that* young. And she really does like me. Put it another way—she's grateful for everything I do."

Kivela whistled again, having attracted an appreciative audience. "Whew! *That ugly!* And with you looking the way you do? We've got to get you off world to protect this planet's gene pool."

A short chorus of laughter drowned Uborevich's muttered protests.

Sunday (1170)

ADRIAAN SMITH WAS WHIPPING UP THE CROWD IN JOHANNES-burg's Vryheidsplain from the back of a bakkie truck. Spotting Matti Harjalo near the back, Hans Coldewe elbowed his way over to join him.

"Hans!" Harjalo grasped his hand and shook it firmly. He shouted into Coldewe's ear, "You're just in time. Adriaan is about to wind up, and then Rikki is on."

"When she announced, I was probably the second most-surprised person on the planet. How did Anton talk Adriaan into this, anyway? Isn't she a little young?"

"Maybe." Harjalo was noncommittal. "But as Adriaan pointed out, the younger William Pitt, who was England's most successful prime minister, was twenty-four when he took the job."

Coldewe shook his hair out of his eyes. To his intense disgust, his hair that needed cutting was beginning to turn a violent salt-and-pepper. He spotted someone else in the crowd he recognized. "Excuse me, Matti."

He pushed his way over and returned just as Smith was finishing.

"Who was that?" Harjalo asked.

"I recognized him from the files. He does odd jobs for Steen. I told him if he caused any trouble, God would burn his house down and I'd make sure he was in it," Coldewe replied with a self-satisfied expression.

"Ssu says that it's going to be a very close election." Harjalo began clapping rhythmically with the crowd.

"Do not tax me, tax my children, is that what I hear you are telling me?" Sanmartin was saying in Afrikaans. "Suid-Afrika is becoming different. We will make it different, make it something our grandchildren will be proud of. Am I old enough and cunning enough to be your president? I tell you that the cunning comes natural, and by electing me, you will give me enough gray hairs to look the part in a year's time."

"What do you think?" Harjalo said with satisfaction. "That'll make the evening news."

"She's very good," Coldewe admitted.

"She knows these people. Suid-Afrika is beginning to change. She'd be unstoppable with a few more years behind her. Which, unfortunately, we don't have."

A heckler in the front of the crowd yelled out, "Heer President Andries Steen has ten years' experience. How many years have you?"

Harjalo held up his wrist mount so that Coldewe could see it. "We have a camera and a mike over the platform and an operator in back. We're tapping your database, which means that we have photos and voiceprints for 90 percent of the adult population, courtesy of the vehicle-registration records and those fictitious 'fire surveys' we used to do. Rikki has a flat monitor on the podium. His name is Bret Grobelaar." Harjalo shook his head. "Stupid of them to pick Grobelaar."

When Grobelaar repeated his catcall, Rikki acknowledged his presence. "Ah, Heer Grobelaar, how is the pharmacy business?"

She stepped away from the podium and walked to the edge of the platform so the crowd could see who she was addressing. "Napoleon Bonaparte once said that if experience were all that mattered, Prince Eugen's mules would be the greatest generals. I appreciate your coming to our rally. I shall have to come to one of yours to return the courtesy."

Grobelaar bravely bellowed, "The Bible says to respect your elders!"

Harjalo shook his head. "Stupid, stupid, stupid."

Rikki tilted her head. "Many a man who cannot direct you to the corner drugstore will get a respectful hearing after age has further impaired his mind." When the laughter ebbed, she added, "When you see your uncle, give him my regards."

"Bret's uncle liked little girls and bigotry, in that order, which a lot of people remember," Harjalo explained. "He suicided after he was indicted, around the time we declared war on Admiral Horii. The 'corner drugstore' remark sounds like one of your lines."

"It is," Coldewe said absently.

As Rikki ended her remarks and the crowd began cheering, a young girl came up to hand her a bouquet of roses. Spontaneously, she began peeling them off and tossing them to people.

"She's very good," Coldewe admitted.

Monday (1170)

"WHAT DO YOU THINK OF THE ELECTION?" SIMON ASKED HIS wife at dinner, in a neutral tone of voice.

"Rikki is a nice girl, of course, but the thought of her running for president is ludicrous. I do not know what possessed Adriaan Smith and the Union party to put her name forward. No, the election is already decided, and a good thing, too, because people who matter will be watching to see how we vote." His wife turned her head, unconcerned.

Simon picked at his food. "I meant to ask you, have you seen my tweed coat? I couldn't find it yesterday."

"Simon, that thing is ratty. It is a disgrace for you to wear it." Maria carefully scraped her plate clean, although conscious of her weight, she had taken very little. "I threw it out."

She got up and began stacking the dishwasher.

Simon put his fork down and began staring at the food in front of him, which had lost its savor. "Isn't it strange," he said after a moment, "how much in life depends on tiny coincidences?"

Maria stopped what she was doing and absently brushed aside a stray lock of hair. "And what is that supposed to mean?"

"The major events in everyone's life—your career, who you marry—just seem to happen." He considered the impulse that had led him to sign up for Raul Sanmartin's ecology course.

"Simon," his wife said sharply, "that makes no sense at all!"

Simon Beetje carefully pushed back his chair and began walking toward the door.

"Simon, where are you going?"

"Out." Beetje picked up his hat from the stand beside the door. His mouth twitched. "Rikki may need campaign workers."

"Simon! You're joking."

"No," he said carefully, "I'm not."

"Simon." Maria's mouth tightened.

The door shut quietly behind him.

Tuesday (1170)

THE LITTLE DOG GROWLED SOFTLY.

Concealed in the forest shadows by the battledress he was wearing, Assistant Section Sergeant Kalle Kekkonen stroked her head. "What is it, girl?" Then he touched his radio and spoke to his partner, Superior Private Denys Gordimer. "Recon point two-two. Kekkonen here. Gordo, stand fast for a second. Dolly thinks she's found something."

Kekkonen and Gordimer both froze, and listened.

Cloaked with epiphyte mosses, the tall spiketrees of Suid-Afrika's lowland forests were twilit at noon. Dripping water and eddying mists gave them a haunted look, and sounds traveled queerly, muffled by the hanging vegetation. A kilogram and a half of restrained energy, Dolly looked up expectantly.

Kekkonen touched his radio again. "Take it slow, bearing two-three-three, and let's see what we've found."

"Two-three-three, it is. Probably another big beastie for Simon Beetje. Watch you don't get your feet wet, grandpa. Catching cold is dangerous at your age."

Kekkonen grinned. Not counting time dilation and artificial hibernation in transit between worlds, Kalle K. was thirty-six years old, eight years older than Gordimer, and Gordimer rarely allowed him to forget it. Yet, while war is generally a young man's affair, older men held up better in the kind of patient war Coldewe's reconnaissance troopers fought. For recon troopers, the first enemy—often the only enemy—was the forest, or the desert.

Kekkonen found tracks a few moments later. He hunkered down, visually measured stride length, and stuck a finger into one of the boot prints to gauge its depth.

A moment later, Gordimer joined him. Kekkonen pointed to the boot marks, absently stroking Dolly's head.

"People?" Gordimer asked.

Kekkonen nodded. "Poachers. Two of them. The tall one is about two meters, massing maybe ninety kilos. The small one is about your size. City boys. They're maybe an hour ahead of us."

"City boys?" Gordimer questioned.

"New boots." Kekkonen stuck a thin whistle through the straw aperture in his face mask and blew a silent note. At his signal, Dolly bounded off through the trees, her battledress coat shielding her from sight and infrared detection.

Moving quietly and deliberately, they followed her uphill. As the moments passed, the choked spiketrees gradually thinned out and were replaced by the fern trees that were characteristic of Suid-Afrika's uplands. Through his radio, Kekkonen heard two short barks and paused, cursing softly, to take a reading on the transponder Dolly wore on her collar next to her radio. "Recon point two-two. Kekkonen here. Gordo?"

"Gordimer here."

"Okay. We're closer than I thought. They must have stopped for a break. I can't remember, have you done this before?"

"Amphtiles and stray hikers, yes. Poachers, no."

"Okay. We'll cut in ahead of them and set up an ambush. Kekkonen out. Recon point one. Break. Kekkonen here." He pushed his wrist mount to transmit his position. "We found some poachers. Get a platoon out here to back us. Kekkonen out."

With another, deeper sigh, he set out to catch up with his dog, deeply disquieted by the appearance of poachers this far from the roads along the forest reserve's southern boundary. As a generation of would-be poachers had learned, the recon platoons always had at least three or four teams in the field, night and day. With aircraft patrolling open areas and billabongs to restrict passage, the odds of getting caught were reasonably high—higher the deeper one penetrated into the reserve and the longer one stayed.

These poachers apparently didn't understand that, or didn't care.

In accordance with her training, Dolly was following the two men at a discreet distance. Using Dolly to figure their line of advance, Kekkonen lengthened his stride to overtake them.

"Recon point two-two. Break. Kekkonen here. Gordo, they're following the curve of the ridge line."

"So would anyone else with half a brain," Gordimer replied. The thick vegetation of Suid-Afrika's bottomlands was rough going for the uninitiated.

"I think we can cut across the floodplain and get ahead of them."

"Lead on. Gordimer out."

Nearly twenty minutes later, Kekkonen found himself a position with a relatively clear field of fire behind a toppled tree.

"Recon point two-two. Break. Kekkonen here. Gordo, take the patch of brush to my right. Backup is on its way. Remember, don't shoot unless they mean to shoot at us." Most poachers gave themselves up peacefully, but not all.

"I can hear them, grandpa. Sounds like two."

"I will initiate. Kekkonen out."

Kekkonen waited, tensed, until two men entered the clearing together. Then he whipped his rifle into position and yelled, "Halt! We have you covered! Drop your weapons, and lie down on the ground! Now! *Do it!*"

Both men wheeled and began running.

"Shit!" Kekkonen wheezed and burst from cover after them. Gordimer emerged from his position to join in the chase.

"You idiots!" Kekkonen yelled. "Stop!"

The smaller man tripped over a log and fell, sprawling.

"Stop!" Kekkonen yelled.

The other man halted and turned, swinging his rifle up. Without thinking, Gordimer and Kekkonen each put a two-tap burst into him. Hit by at least nine bullets, the man reeled and flopped onto his back.

"Oh, shit," Kekkonen said with feeling. He looked at the smaller man. "You! On your belly! Stretch out your hands. *Now!*"

The younger man immediately obeyed.

"Cover me while I get his weapon," Kekkonen told Gordimer. While Gordimer shifted position to give himself a clear field

of fire, Kekkonen went over and grasped the man's rifle, tossing
it out of reach. He spent a moment patting him down and then
used a plastic tie to secure the man's hands behind his back. He
then checked the corpse of the man he had shot. "Colonel Hans
is going to be pissed," he said to no one in particular.

He touched his radio. "Command point one. Break. Kekkonen
here. Colonel Hans? We got a dead poacher. . . . Oh, he's dead,
all right. Gordo and I both loaded him up. We will mark our firing positions and leave the body where it is until you get
here. . . . Yes, sir."

After Colonel Coldewe signed off, he looked at Gordimer and
sighed. "Colonel Hans is *pissed*."

After taking the call from Kekkonen, Coldewe handed the microphone back to Esko Poikolainnen and looked at his executive
officer, Major Danny Meagher. "Hell just broke jail."

The gaunt onetime mercenary, who had found himself
stranded on Suid-Afrika, stretched out in his chair and inter-
twined the fingers of his hands behind his head. "You're right
about that. While it's advantageous to periodically remind our
brethren of the poaching fraternity that stop means stop, I think
for President Steen, Christmas just came early." He unfolded
himself languidly. "One of us needs to see what those two
squirts have gotten us into, and given the mess this is likely to
become, that someone had best be me."

Coldewe thought for a moment and then nodded. "All right.
You go. I'll let Anton know."

As Meagher discovered when he arrived, both of the poachers
were Nationalist party members, and the survivor was a minister's son.

"We screwed up, didn't we?" Kekkonen inquired, as a couple
of Jan Snyman's troopers hustled the survivor away and began
methodically photographing the scene.

Meagher grinned and secured Kekkonen's weapon to hold for
the inevitable inquiry. "I wouldn't say that. You're alive, and he
isn't, which means that by the only completely objective standard, you two did just fine."

Kekkonen wrung his hands nervously. "Sir, look. Gordo and
I both know there's all kinds of stuff going on, and we both
want to go on the mission to Neighbor. If it'll help, we can both
plead guilty to something. If we did that, maybe you could
maybe talk the judge into kicking us off planet or something."

Meagher stared into space. "Thank you, Kekkonen. I shall die
complete."

"Sir?" Mystified, Kekkonen pulled off his face shield.

"Kalle, I consider myself deeply privileged to have heard such a hare-brained scheme from you direct. If you ever lie awake nights and wonder why you're a mere assistant section sergeant, think back to this moment." Meagher patted Kekkonen on the shoulder. "If you and Gordo are telling the truth on this one, we are going to get you off if we have to start a war to do it. Which, of course, we very well might have to do."

Wednesday (1170)

"UNCLE ANTON, WHAT ARE YOU DOING HERE?" HENDRICKA Sanmartin whispered as he took the seat next to hers.

"I have a friend or two in the Conservancy Front who pulled strings on my behalf."

"God sy dank," Sanmartin whispered fervently. "I thought I was here by myself."

"I had myself invited so that I could tell you about a serious incident yesterday. Two recon troopers killed a poacher. The surviving poacher is alleging murder, and they will undoubtedly be charged with that offense. Two minor Nationalist party figures spoke out at noon, demanding that Hans be suspended pending a full investigation."

"Uncle Matti already briefed me on all of the details. It is all right." She handed him a picture she was holding in her hand.

"A sea creature of some sort. Very pretty." Vereshchagin raised one eyebrow. "What is it?"

"It is a hibiscus fan star. I took the photo myself, the summer I spent studying marine life in Nobosuke Bay. I keep a few pictures with me these days to look at. It calms me."

As liveried waiters trundled out the meal, she stared down at the plate placed in front of her in utter horror. "Dear God," she murmured in a voice that only Vereshchagin was meant to hear. "Not vulcanized chicken twice in a day."

"You had a luncheon meeting?" Vereshchagin asked.

"With the businessmen of the Johannesburg chamber of commerce, or whatever they call it. Sandwiched around three speaking engagements. I spoke to them about your expedition."

"What did you say?"

"Oh, I lied shamelessly. In the same breath that I spoke of the money Suid-Afrika will make trading with Neighbor if we send Suid-Afrikans along, I direly predicted alien spacecraft raining destruction on Jo'burg if my crafty old Uncle Anton isn't there to keep the Imps in line. I was a big success, peddling fears and potential profits out of both sides of my mouth."

"And tonight?"

"Tonight, I shall speak blithely of environmental matters so that the concerned people who can afford to attend will fill my campaign coffers overflowing, so says the little cue card that Ssu laid on my dresser today. And I am so ... so ... very tired."

"Can you take a day off?"

"No. That is the difficulty with a short campaign. It is like being a boxer—the last one standing wins. If I want this badly enough, I will do it."

Vereshchagin looked at her, puzzled. "What is that in your hair?"

She reached up. "Where?"

Vereshchagin pointed.

"Oh, that is just part of a jelly doughnut. It is astonishing what parents will give their children to eat. The rest is on my jacket." She brushed the spot ineffectually. "Is it gone?"

Vereshchagin nodded.

She reached down and traced a mark on the back of his hand. "Your accolade. I told my staff that I was naming each of them knight commanders of the Holy Order of the Smeared Jelly Doughnut. I am thinking of asking my security detachment to frisk children for smearables."

"Are you sorry that I talked you into this?" Vereshchagin asked.

Rikki smiled. "This is my heritage. And it is only the start. If I win, I will spend years fooling people into thinking that I am older and wiser than anyone has a right to be, and I am tired already. Fortunately, my crafty Uncle Anton is the only one who suspects."

"Not even your staff?"

She laughed gently, causing a few heads to turn her way. "Especially not my loyal staff. They have to believe in me enough to fool everyone else." She shook her head. "What people want is another Joan of Arc—a Calvinist one, of course. And so, for sixteen more days, I play my part, as Steen plays his.

"This morning in Parys, six Silvershirts armed with sticks and truncheons went after three of my campaign workers, one of whom was a corporal in a reserve company. He tried to cripple as many of the six as he could. He came away with two broken ribs and a shattered jaw, and a student had her arm broken. And the Parys public prosecutor wants to prosecute him for defending himself." She spoke out of the side of her mouth as she made a pretense of eating. "In the end, it is the people who matter. I saw a few of them today, in between engagements."

Thursday (1170)

"HEER KEKKONEN, HEER GORDIMER?" THE OLD MAN TOOK A CI-gar from his pocket, looked at it longingly for a few seconds, and put it back. "My name is Abram van Zyl. Anton asked me to represent you. I was once the advocate for your battalion."

"Sir, *sir*." Kekkonen hopped to his feet. "But, sir—"

Van Zyl smiled indulgently. "Yes?"

"I thought you were dead."

"Well, maybe just a little. Are the two of you sure that you want me to represent you?"

Gordimer and Kekkonen looked at each other and nodded. "Yes, sir."

"Good." Van Zyl used his cane to help himself into a chair. "The preliminary inquiry into your case is set for this afternoon. The public prosecutor—a Steen appointee—has charged you with unpremeditated murder."

Hours later, as the court was called into session, van Zyl whispered to his clients, "Remember that this is just a preliminary inquiry in front of a magistrate. The magistrate presiding is Jan Oosthuisen. He is very fair." Van Zyl chuckled. "Jan was a student of mine, which never hurts."

Oosthuisen was a thin man with a pinched face, graying hair, and sharp, bright eyes. He said in Afrikaans, "The Republic versus Petrus van Blommenstein, Superior Private Denys Gordimer, and Assistant Section Sergeant Kalle Kekkonen. Heer van Blommenstein, are you to speak first?"

The blond poacher, now impeccably dressed, stood up. "Yes, Your Excellency."

"Have you consulted with an advocate, and do you wish to give evidence under oath?"

"Yes, Your Excellency."

As van Blommenstein proceeded to tell his tale, Gordimer felt the back of his neck turning red. He tugged at van Zyl's sleeve. "It wasn't like that at all. He was turned around with his rifle in his hand when we potted him."

Van Zyl patted his hand. "The public prosecutor had to have some evidence to charge you with a crime."

Oosthuisen adjusted the collar of his black robe. "Heer van Blommenstein, you are charged with violating the Wildlife Preservation Act. If I understand you, you are admitting guilt."

Van Blommenstein hesitated less than a second. "Yes, Your Excellency."

"Have you consulted about this with your advocate?"

The lawyer nodded, and van Blommenstein replied, "Yes, Your Excellency."

"Why would he admit that he was poaching?" Kekkonen whispered.

Van Zyl chuckled. "Mostly because he is guilty as sin. In determining a sentence, Oosthuisen will consider the fact that he admitted his crime at the first opportunity. Also, President Steen won't grant him a pardon until he has been convicted, and to hedge his wager, van Blommenstein might want to be convicted before the election."

Van Zyl stood. "Your Excellency, before this witness stands down, I have a few questions to certify to the court." He passed them forward. As he sat down, he explained to his clients, "At a preliminary inquiry, only the magistrate has the right to ask questions."

Oosthuisen frowned when he saw the questions, but asked them anyway. "Remember that you can decline to answer any question that may tend to implicate you in another crime, and that you are under oath. Are you or the deceased members of the *Suiwerheidwagte*?" When he saw van Blommenstein hesitate, he snapped, "Well?"

"Yes, both of us were, Your Excellency."

"Whose idea was it to go poaching?"

The public prosecutor stood up. "Your Excellency."

"Sit down," Oosthuisen told him. "Whose idea?"

"It was Vlause's, Your Excellency," van Blommenstein said hesitantly.

"Had he ever suggested anything like this before?"

"No, Your Excellency."

"Why did he suggest going now?"

Van Blommenstein caught his advocate's eye. "I would rather not answer that question, Your Excellency."

"Did Vlause Burger say what he planned to do with the hides of the animals you shot?"

Van Blommenstein's advocate rose. "Your Excellency, my client will have to decline to answer to this line of questioning."

"I see." Oosthuisen looked at van Blommenstein for a few moments and then dismissed him. "Heer van Zyl, are your two clients prepared to testify?"

"Yes, Your Excellency."

Kekkonen and Gordimer related their stories.

"Are there any other witnesses to be heard?" Oosthuisen inquired.

The public prosecutor stood. "No, Your Excellency. The photographs of the scene and the pathologist's report are appended."

"All right. With regard to the case against Gordimer and Kekkonen, I find that the only issue of fact is whether or not the deceased, Vlause Burger, tossed aside his rifle before he was shot as was related by witness Petrus van Blommenstein. Does anyone disagree?" Oosthuisen addressed van Blommenstein's advocate. "With regard to the case against van Blommenstein, do you plan on presenting any mitigating evidence?"

The lawyer stood. "No, Your Excellency. The public prosecutor's report provides sufficient information on the boy's family and his background."

"Is there any reason why I should not pass sentence on your client now?"

"No, Your Excellency."

"I thought not." Oosthuisen studied van Blommenstein. "Petrus van Blommenstein, I sentence you to six months confinement, loss of the rifle you carried, and a thousand-rand fine."

Van Blommenstein flushed, but said nothing. The public prosecutor bobbed to his feet. "Your Excellency, the Volk would request a thirty-day stay of confinement."

Oosthuisen glared at him sourly. "Denied. Put him in jail. The other two are remanded for trial. Court is closed."

"Jan is a fair man," van Zyl repeated, as soon as the judge left.

Gordimer looked at him. "I don't understand. What is going on?"

"They call it politics," van Zyl replied.

Friday (1170)

SIMON BEETJE HUNG UP THE PHONE AND MADE ANOTHER CHECK mark on his list. He poured himself another cup of coffee. After trying a sip, he pulled a bottle of brandy out of his desk drawer and used it to spike the coffee.

His student assistant knocked on the door timidly and stuck his head inside. Beetje looked up. "What are you still doing here, Wim? You should have gone hours ago."

"Your wife is here."

Maria Beetje pushed past him, and Wim wisely left them.

"Hello, Maria."

"I came to see if you have come to your senses."

Beetje made a pretense of considering this. "Probably not. Would you like some coffee? I have some brandy to flavor it."

"What are you doing here, Simon?!"

"Calling up people. Hans Coldewe was right. Most elections don't mean a great deal, but this one is different."

His wife burst into tears and began dabbing at her face. Simon stood up and tried to console her. She shook his arm off. "I mean it, Simon, if you don't stop this nonsense and come home, I am going to turn your things over to the clothing drive!"

"Hush! Hush. Please, don't shout." He nodded. "That will do, I think. I won't have much of a weight allowance, and it would be a nuisance to try to store them."

"You don't actually believe that you are going on this crack-brained expedition!"

He nodded again and looked at her directly for the first time. "I actually believe in something, which is a change."

"I don't understand you!" She swung her fist and dropped it. "Why are you throwing away your career, your life? You're in love with her—that's it, isn't it? You're in love with her, now!"

"Rikki? I should be, shouldn't I? She's young and pretty, and smart and dynamic, and she believes in something important—everything that you were once. But I'm not in love with Rikki, I'm not sure why. Probably it's because she is not in love with me. Look, Maria, I'm sorry. Please don't cry. You know how I hate it when you cry." He put his arm over her shoulder and stroked her hair timidly.

Pushing him away, she stormed out, slamming the door shut behind her.

Beetje sat down at his desk. Examining his coffee cup, he flipped its contents into the wastepaper can and refilled it with brandy. Then he took a long drink and began dialing the next number on his list.

Saturday (1170)

"MATTI SAID YOU WOULD BE BY, UNCLE HANS." RIKKI Sanmartin bent over to pat the little dog Coldewe had brought.

When her aide began making motions, she glanced at her watch. "I have precisely seven minutes. Is this one of your dogs?"

"Her name is Dolly. I'm taking care of her for a few days," Coldewe explained. "She's one of the witnesses in the case against Denys and Kalle. Say hello, Dolly."

Dolly barked enthusiastically.

"The case is giving both of us a terribly black eye, and it is set to go to trial only two days before the election." Rikki grimaced. "And, of course, I expect the prosecution to drag its case out until the day after the results are in."

"You are getting distressingly cynical in your old age," Coldewe observed. "Are things that bad?"

"They are not well. People from something calling itself the Women's Movement Against Militarism have begun attending my speeches to denounce the 'bloody-handed murderers' who fostered me. It has an impact, and I have to spend much of my effort on defense, which leaves me less time to attack Steen. Only a small number of people concern themselves seriously with politics, and to win, I must maintain my momentum. At best, the election would have been close. This might swing it back to Steen. And the violence is getting worse. Two more of our workers were forced from their vehicle and beaten this morning outside of Lydenburg."

"Are you frightened?"

Hendricka shook her head.

"I didn't think so. 'It is the hardest thing in the world to frighten a mongoose, because she is eaten up from nose to tail with curiosity. The motto of all the mongoose family is "Run and find out"; and Rikki-tikki was a true mongoose.' "

"You read me that story when I was three, Uncle Hans."

"Every child should be exposed to Kipling in her formative years. Although, come to think of it, Kipling wrote a few things about the Tweede Vryheidskrieg that probably wouldn't go over too well here."

She made an effort to smile. "So, then, is this the war fought single-handedly through the bathrooms of the big bungalow against Nag, the great black cobra?"

"And his cobra wife, and all the little baby cobras. For everyone knows that a mongoose's business in life is to fight and eat snakes."

Ignoring her aide, Sanmartin reached down to stroke the dog again. "With all of the modern military technology at your disposal, I can't think why you have dogs."

"Apart from the fact that modern military hardware costs real money, the recon troopers find the puppies useful in all kinds of situations. I'll show you." He pointed out the window. "See that girl there?"

"Yes."

Coldewe picked Dolly up, held her to the window, and pointed toward the girl. Then he pulled out a whistle, blew four short notes, and set her down. Dolly went out the door at a dead run, stopping at the girl's feet to fawn over her.

"Uncle Hans!" Sanmartin said in shrill disbelief. "You should all be ashamed of yourselves!"

Coldewe winked. "I suppose it does qualify as corruption of a minor." He said to the aide, "Could you be a dear and fetch Dolly back?"

The young woman shook her head in resignation and went to retrieve the dog.

"You have obviously forgotten what day it is," Coldewe volunteered, observing the aide's progress.

"What day is it?"

"Your twenty-first birthday. Happy birthday!"

"Thank you, Uncle Hans," Sanmartin responded, puzzled.

"And for your birthday present, I've arranged to have the charges against Kekkonen and Gordimer quietly interred."

Sanmartin's eyes went cold. "What have you been up to?"

"Last night, with a few hints and some excellent coaching from Resit Aksu, the Johannesburg screws went after our little friend, the surviving poacher, and he broke. This will never come out because we can't prove it and the other side will let the issue die, but the corpse went into the woods looking to get into a firefight. I expect the people who sent him in had a better idea of what probably would happen than he did."

"Dear God," Rikki Sanmartin said to herself.

Coldewe gave her a chaste birthday kiss. "Cheer up. Your birthday present cost like hell, but it was worth every cent."

She looked at him. "You mean?"

"Steen is not a fool. He's going to want to know how we knew, and he's going to assume that we have a source." Coldewe shrugged. "On the positive side, you've been keeping him rather busy lately, and he only has a finite amount of time to figure out who the source is before election day. Of course, I really hadn't planned on tipping my hand like this, and it took Ssu several hours and quantities of statistics to convince me. And I now calculate that your seven minutes is almost up."

"Thank you, Uncle Hans. Thank you very much." She made an effort to smile. "This has been the nicest birthday present I have had in a while." She raised her eyebrows and used her hand to trace a circle around her head. "But don't I get one of those little party hats?"

Coldewe coughed. "Er."

"Uncle Hans!" She looked up at him in shock. "You *didn't*!"

Coldewe stared out the window. "Frost and damn! There's the truck with the cake now. I told them not to come early." He turned to face her. "I hope you still like pink icing."

Sunday (1171)

EATING QUICKLY, ANDRIES STEEN CAREFULLY READ THE DAILY summary his staff had prepared. He laid it down. "Schreiner. Get in here."

Knowing Steen's habits, the party's chief strategist was no farther than the outer office.

Steen slammed down the summary. "Tertius, we are half way to election day, and this reads like dung."

"All of our projections envisioned the cowboy separatist parties running a presidential candidate to draw votes away from the Uniates," Schreiner replied calmly.

"We paid them enough!"

"You cannot trust a cowboy." Schreiner made a small joke of it, aware that he was the one man Andries Steen could not afford to fire. "They did not stay bought."

"We will deal with them properly when the time comes," Steen said grimly. He wadded the summary up and flung it away. "De la Rey made a fool of himself talking to the newspapers. He is an utter idiot!"

"Of course, he is. Fortunately, he is not an ambitious idiot," Schreiner agreed, well aware of the dangers in having someone in De la Rey's position who could think for himself. "But he has a leak somewhere in his organization. He assigned Geldenhuys and Van der Merwe to find it."

"Have them fired if they do not." Steen thought for a moment. "What can we do to Coldewe?"

Schreiner shrugged. "Abram van Zyl wrote the compact with Vereshchagin, and he did not leave any holes. Your predecessor signed it, he got the Assembly to ratify it, and he got its key provisions enshrined in the constitution. The constitutional court hates you. Short of paying Coldewe's men the value of the equipment they captured or brought along with them, I do not see a way to tamper with them. The *General Hendrik Pienaar* alone is worth a billion rand, give or take a few hundred million. Try explaining that to the voters. You can't trim his budget further and still campaign on the Imperial threat, and you can't appoint new officers—the last time we tried that, the poor man didn't last a week." Seeing the humor in the situation, he commented, "Most governments only dream of owning a frugal military."

Steen ignored him. "We do not have control of our destiny," he whispered.

"Forget Coldewe for now," Schreiner advised. "Deal with your enemies one at a time. If you don't do something about this election, we won't *have* a destiny."

Steen took a notepad and began writing notes to himself. "Get Telwyn in here. Tell him his last trick did not work, and he had better think of a better one—no, I will tell him myself. Six months of scheming, and he has not even found a way to make Coldewe's soldiers stop playing those awful bagpipes."

Monday (1171)

SCRIBBLING DESIGNS ON THE BACK OF A PAPER NAPKIN, KLAES De la Rey, a surprisingly modest man for the leader of a paramilitary organization, contented himself with the knowledge that he knew one thing that his squabbling district leaders in their silver berets did not—that each one of them hungered for his job. Although none of them obeyed De la Rey, none of them dared to disobey him too openly.

As for their interminable arguments over small parts of strategy, De la Rey, the direct descendant of several heros of the Second War of Independence, knew that it was all monkey talk to impress each other and Telwyn Zalm, President Steen's spy.

The Silvershirt movement was undergoing changes. Despite pressure from Zalm, De la Rey had permitted members of the organization to resign even as recruitment was stepped up. Those sickened by the violence were leaving. Others, who lusted for it, were being drawn in and outfitted.

As for the intimidation campaign, De la Rey could feel it tottering. Members were being arrested and charged, even in districts where the authorities were conscious of their racial identity, and many of the witnesses refused to be cowed. While the organization could easily afford to pay fines, even a few jail sentences might wreck it entirely. No one dared to voice the principal objection, which was the Nationalist party's cowardly refusal to allow itself to be publicly linked to the movement.

He calmly put his pen down and cleared his throat. "We are in agreement then? Volunteers on night patrols will wear hoods to conceal their identities. Are there objections?"

The cowboys still remembered an organization called the Klan, whose members wore hoods, but something had to be done and the party was in no position to contest cowboy districts in any case.

Nodding, De la Rey turned to the acting secretary, Hannes Van der Merwe, and asked him to read the next agenda item.

"Item: a telephone campaign to demonstrate to voters that Hendricka Sanmartin is racially and morally unfit to hold public office," Van der Merwe announced in a clear voice. "Proposed by Vereeniging district."

Observing the self-satisfied smile on Zalm's face, De la Rey had no doubt that the latter was a blatant untruth.

Rotund Anselm Wick spoke. "My people say that this should be party work. As it is, they complain that the movement is bleeding itself, running party errands." Eccentric and bloody-minded, Wick ran his Karoo district with more genuine democracy than most of the others would have dared.

No one contradicted him. Seeing which way the current was running, Telwyn Zalm looked around the room and tossed two packets of hundred-rand notes on the table. "It is only for a week, and the men will be paid for their efforts. The ones who can't stomach the patrols can do this instead. The party is doing its part, but every shoulder must be put to the wheel if Suid-Afrika is to achieve its destiny."

He left unstated the fact that most of those present could look forward to the inside of a jail if the Sanmartin girl won.

De la Rey idly wondered how much of the money the ordinary Silvershirt volunteers would see. "I see that there are no further objections. I move and second the proposal, which carries. Hannes, please read the next agenda item."

Tuesday (1171)

COLDEWE RAISED ONE EYELID WHEN ESKO POIKOLAINNEN ENtered and saw the troubled expression on his senior communication sergeant's face. "What's up, Esko?"

"Colonel Vereshchagin on the secure line, sir."

Coldewe got up, filled the sink with water, and threw his face into it. When he fumbled for a towel, Poikolainnen handed him one and keyed Coldewe's terminal.

Anton Vereshchagin's face appeared. "Good morning, Hans."

"Morning." Coldewe pushed his hair out of his eyes.

"Has Resit Aksu spoken to you about the whispering campaign?"

Coldewe's intelligence officer, Lieutenant Resit Aksu, was an urbane Turk from Antioch nicknamed "The Smiling Buddha." He was, as everyone who knew him more than casually agreed, good at his profession.

"No. How long have I been out?" Coldewe looked at the time display on his wrist mount. Poikolainnen pushed a mug of tea into his hand. "All I know so far is that the phone network lit up like a Christmas tree last night."

"Yes. It is a widespread, well-funded operation to convince vacillating voters that Rikki is an unchaste, wanton woman— quite untrue and quite effective."

Coldewe frowned. "Betje must want to kill someone."

"It was a predictable ploy. Such a rumor is believable by someone who does not know Rikki. Many people, particularly women, are uncomfortable with the thought of electing a young, unmarried woman to high office, and the rumors give this feeling an outlet. Steen has already flatly denied knowledge of the campaign, limiting himself to the cautious observation that where there is smoke, there is very often fire."

"Nobody with a gram of political sense is going to believe him, but a gram of political sense is not a prerequisite to vote."

"Politics and lies sometimes appear to be inseparable." Vereshchagin sipped his tea. "What kept you awake last night?"

"You'll see it in this morning's paper around page six. We had our first fatality last night, Reserve Corporal Nelson Bolaños, who had three children. Got his head cracked open with a steel pipe, and Eva Moore's people couldn't revive him. He used to be one of Orlov's kids. I put a hammock hook up for him," Coldewe said with cold certainty.

Whoever inherited the hook with the plaque with Bolaños's name on it would light a candle for him on December sixth, the Finnish national day, when Finns mourn their war dead.

Vereshchagin appeared disturbed. "The Silvershirts have orders to intimidate, not kill."

"I know what their orders are." Coldewe's voice rose shrilly as his temper for once began to get the better of him. "At least let's do something about the whispering."

"Resit has an idea for a response."

"I'll talk to Resit then and call you back," Coldewe said, partially mollified. "Coldewe out."

As Vereshchagin's face disappeared from the screen, Coldewe noticed Major Danny Meagher leaning against the door frame.

"Ah, Hans, a good night's sleep improves your otherwise negligible beauty." Meagher handed Coldewe a document. "A courier just dropped this off. It's an executive directive from the president's office abolishing military tribunals."

Coldewe skimmed the document, then read it through carefully. "Does this say what I think it says?"

"Probably."

Coldewe shook the offending document. "This obviously violates our compact. The constitutional court will kick this out in a heartbeat, so why bother sending it?"

"You had best talk to Ssu." The former mercenary took the directive from Coldewe's hands and smoothed it. "I expect it would play well with the crowd if we took it to court."

Coldewe flared his nostrils. "I was afraid you'd say that."

"That charming man Steen holds you and Anton responsible for the scare Juffrou Sanmartin is putting into him, and this is likely his way of saying he's going to get even," Meagher added.

Coldewe stared at a spot on the wall. "This is starting to get personal. And as I told Anton, the problem with going legitimate is that it seriously cramps our style."

Poikolainnen had reappeared during the exchange. "Sir, if we don't challenge it, we have to post it," he said unhappily.

Coldewe nodded. "Paste a copy inside every wastebasket."

Meagher grinned as Poikolainnen departed. "I don't suppose Steen will make an issue of it." He rubbed his chin. "Hans, it occurs to me that the battalion will need a new commander if your expedition ever does get off the ground."

"Yes. I suppose you want the job," Coldewe said, trying not to meet his executive officer's eyes.

"I would, but the man it should go to is Sergei Okladnikov." A smile creased Meagher's chunky face. "I'd rather tell you straight out that I'm the wrong man than have you wandering around thinking how to break the sad news to me."

"Why are you so sure I want Sergei?" Coldewe asked.

"Because you think the way I do, although not nearly as well. It's true Sergei loves that tin can of his—I've always thought that light-attack people have something wrong in the head somewhere—but he understands the lads with rifles and his heart and soul belong to the battalion. As much as I'd try to deny it, a part of me still remembers being on the other side shooting at your lot." Meagher punched Coldewe lightly on the shoulder to show there were no hard feelings. "You nearly killed me, you know."

"Thank you," Coldewe said softly.

"Don't mention it. Sergei will also get along with the civs here better than I ever could, although this week that may not be our top priority." Meagher glanced at his wrist mount. "I see the time I've allotted myself is up, and it's Aksu's turn. You're highly popular this morning."

Wednesday (1171)

HENDRICKA SANMARTIN PAUSED AT THE END OF HER PREPARED remarks. "Many of you members of the press have asked me to comment on the false and extremely offensive rumors being circulated about me. Although my learned opponent has denied organizing this campaign, I will not lie to you by saying I believe him."

"This should be worth half a column," Booyse Zwick, *Die Burger*'s morning editor, whispered to Seibert Wild, who was scribbling notes.

Sanmartin held up a large brown envelope. "This came to Matti Harjalo in the morning post. Some of you have already asked him about it. Uncle Matti tells me not to open it because it contains compromising photographs of six Nationalist party politicians and a note reading, 'People who live in glass houses should not sling mud.' " She paused. "I have been assured that Heer Steen is *not* one of them."

She tore the envelope and the pictures inside into small pieces. "I will not descend to their level." She left the stage.

"We both represent responsible news organizations," Zwick whispered. "We should stand upon our dignity."

Matti Harjalo adjusted the microphone. "That's all you get for today. I'm not taking questions either."

"Dignity," Wild agreed, grabbing for the pieces a half second ahead of Zwick.

Thursday (1171)

"NELLY ALWAYS LIKED THE BAGPIPES," BATTALION SERGEANT Aleksei Beregov said as Nelson Bolaños's funeral cortège passed, preceded by an honor guard from No. 9 platoon and the battalion pipers playing "Flowers of the Forest." "May God rest his soul."

"Does his widow have family here?" Vereshchagin asked unnecessarily.

"Yes, sir. She is an Afrikaner." A good battalion sergeant knew every conceivable thing, and Beregov was very good.

"Rikki should not cry," Vereshchagin said, remembering what Ssu had said. For the first day or two, outrage at an obviously politically motivated crime would move the indicators in Rikki's direction; then fear and the belief that Andries Steen was the person best suited to halt political violence would work to Steen's advantage.

"Colonel?" To Battalion Sergeant Aleksei Beregov, Anton Vereshchagin would always be a colonel.

"Yes?"

"The men have discussed the way of things, no officers present," Beregov said crisply. "Should you decide that Steen and his gang need turning out . . ." Beside him, Company Sergeant Isaac Wanjau nodded agreement. On a backward world, on the back side of nowhere, the endgame of a small-time election was being played out as if it meant life and death, as in a sense, it did.

"Have you discussed this with anyone?" Vereshchagin asked.

"No, sir."

"Please do not. Thank the men, on my behalf." He inclined

his head. "The record of military governments, however well intentioned, is abysmal."

He spoke to Piotr Kolomeitsev afterward. "Piotr, what is wrong? One casualty should not affect me like this. I feel as though we have lost our focus."

"We have," The Iceman said, including himself as a courtesy. "We care."

Friday (1171)

GRAAFF REINET WAS A QUIET TOWN, THE CENTER OF A CON-servative farming community in the rain shadow of the Drankensberg Mountains. The trees planted to line its streets had never grown very tall, and the cattle being driven to market sometimes nibbled its flowers.

A small house on Taalstraat served as Union party headquarters. At four minutes after nine, it exploded.

Sunday (1172)

WHETHER NEWS WAS GOOD OR BAD, ANDRIES STEEN NEVER AL-lowed his expression to change. Other men did, and Steen could see from the expression on Tertius Schreiner's face that the news was very bad indeed. "Well?"

Schreiner mopped his face nervously. As an economy measure, Steen kept the air-conditioning in the staatsamp turned off. Privately, Schreiner doubted whether the savings in electricity offset the loss of productivity. "Church and business boycotts against backsliders are having an effect in the smaller towns, and we have asked the dominees to make clear who they are neutral in favor of." He shook his head. "Still, with a week left, the race is too close to call. We purchased more television time. You have a lead."

"Made of sand, trickling through the hourglass," Steen said bitterly.

Schreiner spared a look of sympathy for Jooste van Drooste, who was gradually turning into a large pool of sweat in a corner of the room. Van Drooste had been demoted from his leadership position and reassigned to the president's entourage for the unforgivable crime of losing control of his district, which was likely to swing to the Uniates. "There is a time to attack and a time to compromise," Schreiner urged. "You may not have a lead come the day."

"Jooste?" Steen baited van Drooste, whose eclipse would presumably spur other Nationalist party members to greater efforts. "Do you also think I should tuck my tail between my legs and crawl?"

Van Drooste licked his lips and looked at Schreiner. "Perhaps there could be an accident."

Steen hurled his coffee mug against the wall, shattering it into pieces. The fragments cascaded onto the floor. "Jooste, were you always this much of a fool?"

Flinching, Schreiner explained in a low voice, "Jooste, God help us if Hendricka Sanmartin suffers an accident. Make no mistake of it—there would not be any hole deep enough for us to hide in." He returned his attention to Steen. "Andries, there is a time for stiff-necked pride and a time to be certain of the main thing. If we lose now, we may not have another opportunity."

"Our grandfathers came here to preserve the essence of the Volk. To make ourselves masters of our own destiny. People forget," Steen said with searing rancor. He touched the intercom on his desk. "Goetzee, are you there? Get in here."

When his personal assistant entered, Steen said, "Goetzee, get Vereshchagin to come here. Then help Jooste clear up that mess by the wall."

An hour later, Anton Vereshchagin found Steen seated at his desk, signing official correspondence. "Heer President."

"Sit down," Steen said. "Would you prefer English or Afrikaans?"

"English."

"English then." Steen studied him. "You are much shorter than I pictured you."

Vereshchagin inclined his head. "I will consider that a compliment, Heer President."

"Let us dispense with polite flattery. We are alone. Just we two, no witnesses." Steen used his handkerchief to mop a spot of moisture on his desk. "You are my enemy, and I am yours."

"Louis Snyman once said the same to me," Vereshchagin said, remembering Louis Snyman and Willem Strijdom and Suid-Afrika's other men of wrath. "In some ways, you remind me of him."

"Strijdom, Snyman, Steen—there is a continuity." Steen stood and began pacing the room in front of Vereshchagin. "Their mantle is mine."

"Strijdom was shot dead, and Snyman paralyzed. You might profit from their example."

Steen accepted the comment with an acrid satisfaction. "Old man, you were dead for years, why didn't you stay dead?"

"At one time, I thought that the Tokyo mission was the most important event in my lifetime. Our contact with Neighbor has the potential to be even more important."

Steen stared at him in surprise. He barked, "You don't believe that."

Vereshchagin said very quietly, "I do."

Steen continued pacing. "Perhaps you do. Enough then. Name your price."

"My price?"

"I erred," Steen admitted forthrightly. "I should have let you go to Neighbor. I admit this. I thought you safely buried. I should have checked your corpse to see if it was cold. You have shown that you can seriously inconvenience me. Now what are your terms? Call off the campaign you have raised against me and you have my word that your expedition will depart. I am sure you will find a way to gouge the treasury, but it will be worth it to see the back of you, and with luck you will not return."

With a sudden insight, Vereshchagin realized that Steen did not, perhaps could not, visualize Rikki Sanmartin as an opponent. "Heer President, the campaign is not mine to call off. In a sense, it is a campaign for Suid-Afrika's soul."

"Why did you come here then?"

"The campaign has gotten very dirty of late. I would like this to stop."

"As you have said," Steen remarked, turning away, "it is a campaign for Suid-Afrika's soul. I will not be defeated by a woman half my age." He touched his intercom. "Goetzee, show Heer Vereshchagin out."

Monday (1172)

AS HE WAITED, ADRIAAN SMITH FIDDLED WITH HIS PIPE. HE LAID it on the table. "Politics isn't the same without a smoke-filled room, but I can't keep it lit. Matti, have you done something to it?"

"Me?" Harjalo lied smoothly. "What did you tell McClausland to keep him away?"

"When McClausland ran three years ago, Ssu bet him that he would lose by ten thousand votes and he never paid up, so I told him that Ssu thinks he's a runny-nosed brat." Smith chuckled. "I sometimes enjoy telling the truth."

"Don't make a habit of it or they'll throw you out of the politician's guild," Harjalo said.

As he spoke, Ssu entered, precisely on time. Reed-thin, with a head almost too large for his body, the former senior censor was incredibly dignified. He turned his head from side to side. "Where is our presidential candidate?"

"Groggy with exhaustion," Harjalo told him. "Betje put her to bed."

Ssu bobbed his head abruptly, flexing the tendons in his neck. Then he sat to await questions.

Adriaan Smith set his pipe aside. "So, where do we stand?"

"The party will lose," Ssu said with icy precision. "We will fall three delegates short in the Assembly and Mistress Sanmartin will fail to gain the presidency."

"Are you sure? We have gained ground steadily, Rikki especially," Smith retorted.

"Despite high positive ratings, many voters who favor her will ultimately cast ballots for President Steen. If the election were held two weeks from now, the indications are that she would win. With the election one week away, she will lose. She will lose narrowly; nevertheless she will lose." He consulted his notes. "Over the last week, Union party candidates have been outspent by a margin of two to one. Mistress Sanmartin has been outspent by a margin of three to one."

"How is that?" Smith asked, surprised.

Ssu explained patiently, "There is a traditional bias toward funding incumbent candidates regardless of party affiliation, which currently favors the Reformed Nationalist candidates, and the Reformed Nationalists have prepared better. Over the last eight days, interests strongly opposed to the current environmental legislation have apparently struck a tacit deal."

"Why do you say we'll lose the Assembly?" Harjalo asked, dampening the anger he was feeling.

"In the Assembly, there are six seats in which the margin of victory will be no more than a few hundred votes." Ssu gave the two of them what could only be described as a pitying look. "The Nationalists currently control the Assembly, and any vote to resolve a disputed election will proceed along partisan lines. With an insignificant margin, it will be a relatively simple matter to disallow enough votes to ensure victory of the correct candidate."

"What can we do to change things?" Smith asked.

"What can be done has already been done," Ssu said primly.

Harjalo asked, "Does the other side know they're going to win?"

"They are very much unaware." A note of outrage crept into Ssu's voice. "Their methods are not scientific."

"God in heaven!" Prinsloo Adriaan Smith said, half to himself. "What do we tell Hendricka?"

"Nothing." Ssu shook his head firmly. "One does not say such things to candidates."

"If she asks, let me do the lying." Harjalo turned around and reached for a telephone. "I'll call Hans. He'll tell Anton. There is truly going to be the absolute Devil to pay."

Evening editorials, reacting to the increased violence, abandoned neutrality and called on the government to suppress the *Suiwerheidwagte*. Government spokesmen wrung their hands but downplayed the problem.

Tuesday (1172)

EVA MOORE, DIRECTOR OF PRETORIA'S LARGEST HOSPITAL AND A former Imperial lieutenant-colonel, grunted when her telephone lit up. She tapped a key and stared at her administrative assistant's image. "What is it, Kirsten?"

"You have a visitor. An important visitor."

Moore inhaled deeply. "Send him in."

She willed her body to relax. "Shut the door, Anton. Pull up a chair. It's been a few years."

"It has been a few years," Vereshchagin agreed, seating himself.

Moore propped her elbows up on her desk and looked at him thoughtfully. "For no particular reason, a few days ago, the feeling suddenly hit me that you'd drop by. I've been wondering what to say."

"How about, 'Hello'?"

She grinned. "Hello, Anton."

"How have you been?"

"Royally peeved of late. I'm coming up on mandatory retirement age, the hospital's board of directors is politely asking me what I want inscribed on my gold watch, and I am *pissed* that

I didn't have enough sense to shave a couple years off my age when I filled out that damnable application twenty years ago."

"I know, Eva."

"It occurs to me that if you get to jaunt off to that planet of yours, by the time you get back I'll be a little old lady. Probably with a damned cat. How does the election look?"

"Not promising."

"I figured as much when Natasha Solchava-Snyman called. I've been twisting arms for you."

"Thank you, Eva."

"Don't thank me. Thank Natasha. And thank Steen for being an ass. Want a cup of tea?"

"No, thank you."

"Good." She reached into a drawer and pulled out a bottle of local brandy and two glasses. "I hate diluting good liquor. So have a drink and tell me what you want." She tapped a key. "Kirsten, tell everybody not to bother me for a few hours."

Vereshchagin waited for her to finish. "Am I that transparent?"

"Anton, you are such a warm and caring person that occasionally even I forget how much of a snake you are." She filled a glass and handed it to him. "I was jealous as all hell when I heard Mutaro had tapped you. You remember Metal Molly?"

"Your adjutant?"

"Sweet and stupid. She lives in Komsburg, now. She called to tell me that she was going to name her third child after me, poor kid. That's immortality. I get a baby named after me. You get planets."

Vereshchagin shut his eyes. "I would rather have the baby."

"No, you don't. You just think you do." Moore sipped her brandy reflectively. "If you were half as self-effacing as you sometimes let on, I'd be scared silly."

"Cruel, but quite accurate, I am afraid."

"I've been keeping secrets for you for more years than I can remember, so tell the truth, who's going to win the election?"

"I am very much afraid that Steen will win," Vereshchagin said quietly. "So Ssu believes."

"Then you aren't here on a social visit, so tell me what you need."

"I need you to be ready to handle an influx of casualties."

"Gunshot, or something else?"

"Q-fever. QF^8 to be precise."

"Bio weapons?" Moore whistled. "And QF^8 is a killer." Biological weapons unleashed during the crack-up had decimated Earth's population. "Using that is likely to get you crucified. I doubt that folks here have forgotten the psittacosis[37] you used to finish off the first rebellion."

Vereshchagin looked mildly embarrassed. "I seem to have fallen into the practice of doing perfectly horrible things to prevent worse things from occurring."

Moore stroked her chin thoughtfully. "You know I can't make any kind of meaningful preparation without rumors leaking."

"I know. I am counting on it."

Moore stared at him. "I think I need more brandy. In fact, I think we both need more brandy."

At noon, Steen's finance minister released figures he had been sitting on for three weeks trumpeting a 3 percent upturn in the economy over the previous quarter. The best previous forecast had been 2 percent, and cynical observers, aware that someone would take a spill if the figures were later revised, noted that the minister failed to renew the lease on his Johannesburg residence.

Wednesday (1172)

"HANNES, YOU KNOW BETTER THAN TO COME IN HERE BEFORE I've had my coffee." Klaes De la Rey said mildly. The Silvershirt leader studied the two reports Van der Merwe silently placed in front of him. "What are these?"

"I pulled them from the stack of incoming material. The first one says that leave for soldiers in Coldewe's battalion was stopped early this week, Monday or Tuesday—our source wasn't sure. The second says that the Pretoria hospital is preparing to handle a serious epidemic."

"I suppose the first one has some meaning." De la Rey scratched the end of his nose. "I don't understand what the second one has to do with anything."

"Former Imperial lieutenant-colonel Eva Moore runs the hospital. Twenty years ago, she set up Vereshchagin's parrot-fever epidemic. I was a militiaman and after I was captured, I nearly ended up as one of the fifty men she sent out to infect everyone else." Van der Merwe shuddered, perhaps remembering his interrogation.

De la Rey clutched the two reports. "What are you telling me?"

Van de Merwe shrugged. "It is up to the president's advisers to say—they have better sources than we do—but if it were me, I'd say that Vereshchagin is plotting an uprising."

"We have to tell the president." De la Rey stood up. He reached over and held Van der Merwe by the shoulders. "Only we can stop them!"

ESKO POIKOLAINNEN INTERRUPTED HANS COLDEWE AS HE WAS discussing the machine tools the expedition would need with Major Jan Snyman. "Sir, do you have time to see Roy de Kantzow?"

"The Deacon?" Coldewe looked surprised. De Kantzow's broad shoulders filled the doorway. "Deacon. What brings you here?"

Filthy DeKe, a platoon sergeant for No. 9 platoon before his marriage, stood to attention, as awkward as ever in civilian clothes. "I frosting hear you're looking for some soldiers." The epithet "frosting," from Earth's crack-up years, dated him.

"We are full up, DeKe," Jan Snyman said quietly.

De Kantzow made no reply, waiting for Coldewe to speak.

"DeKe," Jan Snyman continued, "you must be pushing fifty standard years."

De Kantzow waited stoically, knowing that he and a man named Orlov and a dead man named Fripp had taught a boy named Snyman what there was to know about war.

"Don't you like being a civilian?" Coldewe asked.

De Kantzow merely shook his head.

"Are you in condition? That's a silly question. I'll have Natasha Solchava check you out, but you look to be in better shape than the day you retired," Coldewe said.

The Deacon nodded.

Coldewe studied the impassive face in front of him. "This isn't Tokyo, Deacon. I'm hoping there won't be any fighting, and if there is, we'll probably end up dead."

"Frost it, sir, I don't miss that part of it, no." De Kantzow searched for the right words. "It's being part of something."

"What about your wife?" Snyman asked.

"The silly bitch doesn't hold with swearing," de Kantzow said mildly, "and she cooks worse than old Frippie ever did."

Snyman, who knew de Kantzow's wife slightly, thought of her as three parts religion and half a part sense. They had no children. The truth was the Deacon had never adjusted to the civilian world, and probably never would.

Coldewe looked at Snyman helplessly. "What do you think, Jan?"

Snyman searched de Kantzow's eyes. "I already have my NCOs, DeKe."

De Kantzow nodded abruptly. "I used to be a cracking good private."

Coldewe threw up his hands in an outrageously theatrical gesture. "Start him walking."

The 1/35th Rifle Battalion discouraged profanity; The Deacon breathed it. By long-standing arrangement, Filthy DeKe walked punishment tours on the first day of every month to atone for his transgressions for the next thirty.

De Kantzow saluted. "Yes, sir!"

Snyman shook The Deacon's hand solemnly. "I give up. Welcome aboard. Of course, as Hans likes to say, you may be leaping from the frying pan into the fire."

"Be good practice for the place my wife says I'm going," the Deacon noted.

Thursday (1172)

CURSING THE SILVER-SHIRTED IDIOT WHO WAS SUPPOSED TO BE screening his calls, Hannes Van der Merwe flicked his terminal on at the fifth ring. "What is it, Joachim?"

There was a worried look on Van der Bergh's puffy face as it appeared on the screen. "Heer Adjutant, there is a voice-only call you must take."

Van der Merwe waved his finger impatiently. "You aren't grasping this, Joachim. You are screening my calls so that I don't have to take them, and I am screening the leader's calls so that he doesn't have to take them."

Van der Bergh nodded nervously, then his face disappeared.

Van der Merwe made an effort to pound the desk and stopped his hand in midair. *"Vervlaks!"* he said mildly. Then he froze as he recognized President Steen's voice.

"Adjutant Van der Merwe, is this call being recorded?"

"Yes, Heer President."

"Please cease recording."

Van der Merwe did so.

"We have reached a crisis point." Steen's voice hesitated. "Get De la Rey in here."

Van der Merwe did so. De la Rey saluted the blank screen. "Yes, my President."

"De la Rey, Anton Vereshchagin's men are planning to mount a coup." Bitterness tinged Steen's voice. "We cannot fight them."

"We must announce this to the people," De la Rey said, thinking aloud. "Arm them. My men will lead."

"No!" Steen's voice barked. "We have no proof. None! All of my advisers oppose this. Vereshchagin has undoubtedly made preparations, and the Uniate traitors hinder us. The people will hear them murmuring Satan's song, and they will not know who to believe. Listen! Months ago, we discussed several plans."

Van der Merwe could see sweat beginning to trickle down De la Rey's face.

"The Uniate leaders will meet in the National Assembly building on Saturday. I will ask for an emergency session at two o'clock, and it is their custom to meet together an hour beforehand. You must seize them there, and their documents. Then I will issue the call to arm the masses. Once you have the building and the traitors under lock and key, Vereshchagin will not dare attempt a coup. To clear the way, I have ordered Vereshchagin's C Company to leave Johannesburg." Steen's voice hardened. "We will then take steps to deal with all traitors. But the fate of Suid-Afrika rests in your hands!"

De la Rey stiffened with pride. "Yes, my President."

"A final warning—only persons you are sure of must know that you are preparing. Vereshchagin is watching, and Zalm tells me that there are traitors in your organization."

"I will tell no one more than he needs to know, my President."

"Good. May God guide your hands. Good-bye."

Ashen faced, Van der Merwe looked at De la Rey. "Klaes, this sounds insane!"

"All we have to do is hold the building for a few hours." The expression on De la Rey's face was exultant. "We will be a rallying point for the entire nation."

"Klaes, I fought against Vereshchagin's men years ago and nearly got myself killed. Holding the Assembly building for a few hours sounds like a good way to do that."

"We knew there would be risks when we joined. Are you with me to the death on this, Hannes? I need you."

Van der Merwe nodded.

De la Rey clasped his hand. "You are the truly loyal one, Hannes, the only one who never tried to undermine me."

Van der Merwe blushed.

De la Rey thought aloud, "We can't use men from the other districts, there is too much chance for our plan to leak. You told me yourself that Vereshchagin has spies in Boksburg and likely other districts as well. The men here are the only ones I trust. As soon as we are in control of the Assembly building, we will issue orders to the others to take to the streets."

"You make this sound very simple, Klaes."

"But we have rehearsed an operation like this, Hannes!"

"No, we have played at rehearsing an operation like this." Van der Merwe hauled off and kicked the wall. "I was a militia soldier once, and you know my other background," he said, alluding to his career as a terrorist who had, as De la Rey knew, just missed assassinating Imperial admiral Horii. "You cannot just throw together an operation like this as the president thinks. Damn! Damn, damn, damn!"

De la Rey put his arm around Van der Merwe's shoulder. "We two can do it. Our men are the best of any district. An order is an order, and the president ordered us himself. Cheer up, Hannes, the Volk rely upon us!"

"Damn!" Van der Merwe gave the wall a final kick. "I am trying to think. We will need all of our people. What about the two murderers we are hiding? The idiot who beat that man to death and the bomber?"

"Use them, but tell them nothing," De la Rey said indifferently.

"We also need some sort of diversion to keep the Johannesburg police occupied."

"I could order Pretoria district to hold a rally or a demonstration here."

"It might get them shot." Van der Merwe meditated. "We could have someone from Pretoria phone in a robbery—no, that's not good enough."

"What about a bomb threat?" De la Rey thought aloud.

"Why stop with one? Bomb threats! That will do the trick. I'll arrange it with Pretoria. Well, get all of the cell leaders in here, and then everybody else. Now!" Van der Merwe's face turned grim and foreboding. "We have two days. If we are going to do this, we can try to do it right. You had better have Boksburg or Pretoria send people to replace our men on the streets for the next two nights, but don't tell them why or everyone in the city will know."

De la Rey frowned. "Hannes, be reasonable. We can't expect our men to prepare day and night!"

"No, but they will need some time for getting themselves drunk, and tonight is as good a night as any. I plan on doing the same." Van der Merwe carefully unpinned one of the antidrinking signs he had posted. "Think of a good cover story to tell our men, maybe we can say we are planning to seize a polling station. That way, by midnight, every barmaid in town will know."

Friday (1172)

ANDRIES STEEN HAD NEVER FOUGHT A REALLY CLOSELY CON-tested election, and he was unpleasantly surprised when his seemingly limitless lines of credit miraculously disappeared, although Christos Claassen and Saki Bukhanov may have had something to do with it.

As the independent newspapers gleefully noted, funds were available at a price, payable upon delivery, and they referred to the emergency legislative session Steen called for Saturday afternoon as the *Skuldbekentenis*, which can either refer to an acknowledgment of debt or a confession of guilt.

Jan Snyman's C Company left Johannesburg and headed west for unscheduled maneuvers in the Vaal-Oranje Forest Reserve.

Saturday (1172)

"I KNOW THAT YOU DON'T WANT TO HEAR THIS, KLAES," Hannes Van der Merwe said in a low voice as he methodically packed packets of ammunition into his pockets, "but seven people called in sick—nervous flu. We are down to forty-nine people. I had to rearrange the *kommandos*."

De la Rey, resplendent in the decorations he had issued himself, looked around the room. "Where is Oscar? Don't tell me he is one of the seven!"

"No, I sent him out to find another vehicle. We are still one short." Van der Merwe shook his head and laughed a little. "No one wants to use his own car for this."

The Silvershirts around them sat and talked quietly. De la Rey had given the *Operasie Spuungslang*—Operation Spitting Cobra—strike force Friday evening off, and some of the pitifully young men who had taken him up on the offer had their heads between their legs.

Van der Merwe made room for De la Rey to sit, then said, "What did you tell your wife?"

"This is not something that a woman would understand. She still says that I should never have given up the pharmacy for politics."

"She has a point, you know." Van der Merwe waved his hand to encompass the room. "You could make a fortune selling hangover remedies. I left my girlfriend a note. She will see it tonight when she comes home from work."

"You should not have done that, Hannes," De la Rey chided him. "That is a major breach of security."

Van der Merwe blew away a speck of dust that had settled on his rifle. "Some things are more important than politics, Klaes."

"Well, done is done, as I always say. I don't want to fight with you." There were tears in De la Rey's eyes. "Of all of my subordinates, Hannes, no one could have done more to help me. You are the only truly loyal one."

Van der Merwe looked away, faintly embarrassed. "I saw in the papers that the president announced the special session. The papers say that the campaign has cost him half again what he expected and speculated that supporters who came through with large last-minute contributions want their thirty silver pieces in advance of the election."

"He scheduled the session, and Coldewe's soldiers left Johannesburg yesterday, so our way is clear. The president always comes through on his promises," De la Rey said confidently. "And that kind of talk from the newspapers is what we are fighting against. After the election, we will have a responsible press."

He was called away a moment later to take a call.

A young Silvershirt sidled up to Van der Merwe and swallowed hard. "Adjutant, it isn't true what they are saying, is it?"

"What are they saying?"

"That the party wants us to be killed so they will win the election?" He wouldn't meet Van der Merwe's eyes.

"Who said that?" Van der Merwe looked around the room which suddenly quieted. "No. It isn't true. And don't repeat your question to another soul."

"But—"

"Not one word. That is an order." Van der Merwe turned his head as the boy scuttled away. No one saw him smile.

De la Rey returned a moment later, his face serene. "That was Zalm. Voice only again. They must be very nervous up there. The president directed him to tell us that the plan is still on. Do you think Zalm knows?"

"I hope not." Van der Merwe watched his cell leaders, many of whom were hardly more than boys themselves, check weapons and equipment.

De la Rey handed Van der Merwe a copy of the proclamation he had drafted.

"This looks good, Klaes." Van der Merwe pocketed it.

"I wish we could have gotten another machine gun."

"I wish we could have gotten another machine gun and a mortar and a recoilless gun, and maybe a couple of tanks." Van der Merwe shrugged. "If wishes were fish, children would cast nets. I see a truck. That must be Oscar. I told Pretoria to make the bomb threats at 11:15. Let's get everyone loaded."

The strike force loaded into four trucks and three cars, which would travel separately to the Assembly building to avoid attracting suspicion. When the car carrying De la Rey and Van der Merwe reached Vaterlandplats, Van der Merwe stuck his head out the window. "I see Biks and Stoeffel waiting for us, but there must be half a dozen policemen in the plaza."

"There is no help for it," De la Rey said. "Everyone else should be around back waiting for us."

They slowed as they drove closer, and a Johannesburg policeman walked over and rapped on the driver's window.

"I am sorry. You can't come here, right now."

De la Rey froze. Van der Merwe reached down, grabbed his rifle, and leveled it at the bridge of the policeman's nose. "Yes, I can." The policeman was sensible enough not to argue. Van der Merwe turned to De la Rey. "I will take care of this, Klaes. Get everyone else inside."

Van der Merwe got out, using the policeman as a shield, and took his pistol. He motioned for the other policemen to leave the square as De la Rey and his storm detachment ran toward the Assembly building. As an afterthought, Van der Merwe handed the policeman a copy of De la Rey's proclamation.

Reaching the building, he found two Silvershirts guarding the door and a few more doing nothing. "What is going on? Where is everyone?"

De la Rey emerged from the inner chamber trailing a half-dozen men. "Hannes, the place is empty! Where are the Assemblymen?"

Before Van der Merwe could respond, one of the door guards murmured diffidently, "Sir, the policemen outside are shouting that there is a bomb in here."

There was a pregnant silence.

The door guard persisted, "Sir, what if there really is a bomb in here?"

"Small chance of that," Van der Merwe finally said. "I think we can say Pretoria district did its job. Klaes, is it too late to go back outside and pretend we made a mistake?"

"We must hold this building. The president is counting on us," De la Rey reminded him. "Also, we have already handed out our proclamation." He looked out the door anxiously. "Where is Oscar with the other truck?"

"I don't know. He may have lost his way. I hope he didn't lose his nerve when he saw the police."

"The truck didn't seem to be in very good shape. It could have broken down," Biks van Nagel volunteered.

"That would match the rest of our luck," Van der Merwe commented. "Either way, Oscar has the extra ammunition and the food. There's a Chinese carryout across the street, but I doubt the police will let us order. Are there vending machines in the basement?"

De la Rey slumped against the wall. "What will I tell the president?"

"I'd better call his office before the police turn off the telephone lines." Van der Merwe put the best face on things. "Maybe if we can find some of the documents he was talking about, things will turn out all right."

De la Rey gestured. "The rest of you, go look for Union party papers." He amended, "Not all of you. Jordaan and Cloete, you two watch the door. Keep watching the police. Keep me informed if anything occurs."

TELWYN ZALM TOOK VAN DER MERWE'S CALL. ZALM IMMEDI-ately pulled Steen out of a meeting. Steen's reaction was one of stunned incredulity. "How could those idiots—" His voice trailed away.

"They are holed up in the National Assembly building by themselves. Apparently some other dolt in the organization phoned in a bomb threat a few moments before they arrived,"

Zalm explained. "I made Van der Merwe read me De la Rey's proclamation over the telephone."

"What a monumental blunder!" Steen thought furiously. "Where is Schreiner?"

"You sent him off to keep Bloemfontein East from backsliding. It will be hours before he returns."

"When this is over, remind me to cut out De la Rey's manhood with a dull knife," Steen commented.

"Not even his wife would notice," Zalm rejoined, ever practical. "What do we do? De la Rey is telling the world that you ordered this to forestall a coup by Vereshchagin. Our best option is to simply throw him over and tell everyone that he is lying."

"The election is on *Monday*," Steen hissed. He thought for the space of five minutes. Finally, he said, "We are committed. There is no turning back now. How long will it take to assemble the press here?"

"An hour or two."

"Bring them here in an hour. Vereshchagin planned a coup. De la Rey acted to forestall him. That is all there is to it. Now, get out of here. I must think what I will say."

"THESE ARE AWFUL." VAN DER MERWE SPEARED ANOTHER COCK-tail sausage with the point of his knife and ate it. "If our legislators have to eat them, they are worth every cent of their pay."

De la Rey fumed. "Nothing! Not one shred of evidence toward a plot. What do we do now?"

"We have been here nearly two hours. If we don't leave, we have to start thinking about setting up a defense," Van der Merwe urged.

"We would stay in any case. It is a matter of honor," De la Rey said stubbornly. "The president is counting upon us."

A light machine gun sprayed fire over the heads of the two men guarding the door. They dropped to the floor as bits of plaster pelted them.

The older of the two, Deon Cloete, lifted his head cautiously. "Sir, there is a man waving a handkerchief who wants to talk to us."

Van der Merwe punched the intercom savagely. "Listen, everybody hold your fire."

Crouching, Van der Merwe and De la Rey went to the door. Seeing Roelf Jordaan aiming his rifle, Van der Merwe kicked it aside. "Stop that." He shouted out the door, "You! That is close enough. What do you want?"

A tall officer with broad shoulders tucked his handkerchief in a side pocket. "I am Major Tikhon Degtyarov, A Company, 1/35th Rifle Battalion. I presume that I have the honor of addressing Klaes De la Rey." Degtyarov chuckled. "Someone handed me a copy of your proclamation." By some trick, his words were broadcast over the building's intercom.

"Klaes, we are in deep trouble," Van der Merwe said very quietly. "That is The Iceman's company out there. Degtyarov is The Iceman's handpicked successor."

De la Rey looked stunned.

Degtyarov continued in a conversational tone, "The local police gave me a call about two hours ago and said something about a bomb. You have not blown up, so I presume there is nothing to it."

"This business of calling in bomb threats is sounding less and less like a good idea," Van der Merwe muttered.

Degtyarov adjusted the microphone around his neck. "Until a few moments ago, you had one of my engineers crawling around in the ventilation system. You needn't look—he's gone—but you really should have put someone on the roof to keep us from landing there."

"What do you want?" De la Rey asked.

"The usual. The Johannesburg police have informed me that you have broken any number of municipal ordinances relating to breaking and entering, unlawful possession of firearms, high treason, and willful destruction of vending machines. Colonel Coldewe and I flipped a coin to see which one of us would attend to the bomb and he lost, but to repeat one of his favorite aphorisms, 'We have you surrounded. Come out with your hands up.'"

"Never!" De la Rey shouted back, looking around for support. "Come in and get us!"

"Sir," the older of the two door guards murmured, "you really oughtn't to make him mad."

"Heer De la Rey," Degtyarov said patiently, "when we had to blast Admiral Horii's troops out of the spaceport, we lost good men, and we are not going to go through that again. Moushegian, now, if you please. The gas only."

Above De la Rey's head, the sprinkler system began discharging a cloud of acrid white gas.

Degtyarov continued, "As you may have noticed, we have control of your building's systems. What you are smelling right now is tear gas with a convulsant agent."

"We have gas masks!" De la Rey shouted. Choking, he put his mask to his face, as his stomach began turning flip-flops.

"In a few moments, anyone in there who caught a lungful of gas will begin vomiting, which will make it exceedingly difficult for you to keep your masks on. It may have occurred to you that we could have introduced something lethal, and you are probably wondering why we did not." Degtyarov gave them a minute to consider this.

"Q-fever[8] is a biological agent from the crack-up. You will begin to show symptoms about half an hour after exposure. Without immediate treatment, the prognosis is not good. Our battalion surgeon, Dr. Natasha Solchava-Snyman, has informed me that the mortality rate approximates 93 percent. I would add that she does not like biologicals and she will be exceedingly annoyed with me for using them, so I would appreciate it very much if you would surrender quietly. You have five minutes in which to decide." Degtyarov began walking away.

Van der Merwe tapped Cloete with his foot. "Please don't say things like that about the president where people can hear you."

De la Rey drew a deep breath and immediately thought better of it. "We can hold true to our principles. We will be the three hundred Spartans at Thermopylae or the three hundred Texans at the Alamo. We are still the vanguard of a nation!" The gas twisted at his intestines.

Cloete threw up, and Roelf Jordaan followed almost immediately.

Van der Merwe shook his head. "No, Klaes." He gestured. "It is over. The only thing left in our power to decide is whether our men walk out or leave feet foremost."

Jordaan carefully laid his weapon aside. A second or two later, Cloete copied him.

Van der Merwe shook his head and dropped his weapon on the floor. He walked over and touched the intercom. "Everybody, it's over! We are surrendering." He waited with De la Rey as his Silvershirts filed out the building's exits into the hands of the Johannesburg police.

De la Rey, whose stomach was weak, was too busy retching for a final speech.

As the police secured the building and bundled the Silvershirts into vehicles, Seibert Wild shoved a microphone under Tikhon Degtyarov's nose as he was about to leave in a Sparrow reconnaissance aircraft. "Seibert Wild, *Dagbreek*. Major, isn't there a danger of infecting the population with Q-fever?"

Degtyarov stared at him. "Heer Wild, I do not wish to be rude, but do you truly believe that Sergeant Moushegian and I carry biological agents around in our pockets? As it was, we had to borrow the tear gas from the police."

"But I heard you say—"

"Heer De la Rey and his people are rather credulous," Degtyarov explained in a bored voice. "As Colonel Coldewe is fond of pointing out, although the Devil is the father of lies, he neglected to patent the idea. Dr. Solchava would have been *exceedingly* annoyed if we had actually employed Q-fever." He climbed into the plane. "Now, I fear Moushegian and I must leave you. Although *Operasie Spuungslang* seems to have sprung a leak, there may be trouble with Silvershirts elsewhere."

It dawned on Wild that Degtyarov and Moushegian were the only soldiers he had seen, and his jaw dropped.

"I don't know why you are looking at me like that," Degtyarov said irritably. "There were any number of police to help."

"THAT CONCLUDES MY PREPARED REMARKS," STEEN STATED. "I endorse Heer De la Rey's actions to prevent the overthrow of our constitution, our laws, and our national existence."

The buzzing from reporters present was interrupted by a clear voice from the back of the room. "If President Steen is through, I have a few remarks to make."

Stepping through the crowd, Hans Coldewe walked up to the stage. Steen made a quick motion to kill the microphone, but Coldewe smiled and touched the collar of his battledress. "Thanks, but I'm wired for sound."

Reaching the stage, Coldewe leaned over the podium. "The Silvershirts occupying the Assembly building surrendered about ten minutes ago to the Johannesburg police. A couple of our people helped with negotiations, although Tikhon Degtyarov's idea of negotiation may leave something to be desired. The Lord Mayor of Johannesburg has formally declared a state of siege and his police are rounding up all of the Silvershirts they can find."

Coldewe pulled a rifle magazine out of his left pocket and tossed it to a reporter in the front row. "That includes the six choirboys who were standing outside when I arrived."

He reached into his right pocket and pulled out a handful of computer disks. "These are copies of what the police pulled off the computer in the Johannesburg chapter house. The public prosecutor told me it was okay to hand them out. President Steen neglected to mention that his party funds the Silvershirts, and the ones the police pulled out of the Assembly building claim that Steen personally ordered the attack two days ago. Now maybe I'm just a simple soldier, but to me, seizing the legislature to stop a coup sounds kind of silly."

Coldewe jammed his hands in his pockets to soften the image he was presenting on television. "I'll say this. Your president just lied through his teeth. We took an oath to defend this planet and its constitution against all enemies, foreign and domestic, which means that if President Steen orders his Silvershirts to overturn the constitution, we'd have to send a policeman to arrest them. But you people need to decide whether you want to bother having laws and a constitution in the future."

He looked at President Steen. " 'Flee from all prophets, from all those who are ready to die for the truth; for they will also provide the death of many others before their own.' "

He walked away whistling "The Yellow Rose of Texas."

Sunday (1173)

PROUD OF THEIR ACKNOWLEDGED ASSOCIATION WITH STEEN AND the Nationalists, most of De la Rey's men confessed to everything they had done and a few things they hadn't. The Johannesburg police cheerfully produced snippets of their confessions throughout the day.

A few tried to exculpate themselves; one member claimed to have been drunk at the time and asserted that he thought that they were driving to a beer hall. That remark and Coldewe's comment about sending a policeman both made headlines, and the one thing that no politician survives is ridicule.

Six Nationalist candidates for election met overnight and took the unusual step of purchasing a full-page ad in all eleven local newspapers denouncing Steen and distancing themselves from the Silvershirts. The Silvershirt district leaders also convened and hastily issued a statement to the effect that Klaes De la Rey was suffering from a disorder of the brain and was not responsible for his actions, which did their organization remarkably little good.

With a delicate taste for the jugular, in both major speeches for the day, Rikki Sanmartin chose to refer to Saturday afternoon's events as the "Beer Hall Putsch."

Monday (1173)

"THANK YOU FOR SHOWING ME YOUR PREPARATIONS NOW THAT it has become politically expedient to do so," Mutaro said as he walked the length of C Company's casern with Coldewe. He added with intended irony, "I understand that two of the men captured in the Assembly building were wanted by the police for murder. What a coincidence that President Steen adopted such an ill-considered policy on the eve of reelection, and how very strange that he only chose to communicate with Heer De la Rey by telephone."

Coldewe refused to be drawn. "Rikki's poll watchers are already scenting victory. Making Steen look like a villain was important, but making him look like a villain and a fool is so much more satisfying." He pointed to the landing strip. "That's Mika Hiltunen's platoon packing ammo into one-ton containers." He shaded his eyes. "And it looks like they're still ragging Uborevich about his girlfriend."

Mutaro clutched at Coldewe's sleeve, pointing to the two armored cars being worked on at the near end of the runway. "Please excuse me for saying this, but the soldier there looks like a woman."

"Oh. She is. That's Valeska Remmar. She is the gunner on armored car 14/3, and her father, Mikhail, with the limp, is the vehicle commander. Valeska's mother is a commo specialist now, so she's going, too."

Remmar was a tall girl with an uneven suntan and dark, kinky hair, some of which was peeping out from under her cap.

"Isn't this unusual?" Mutaro asked.

"I don't know. Mikhail's wife used to be his driver, and a female cousin was Mikhail's gunner for a few years before she got around to starting a family, so that crew has always been a family affair. Although, come to think of it, Valeska's brother went into forestry, so I guess it is a little unusual." Coldewe stared off into space. "We had four crews who wanted to come. They were all pretty much equally good, so we let them draw straws."

Sensing Mutaro's obvious concern, Coldewe took him by the arm. "The light attack detachment we're bringing along consists of two scout vehicles—the troops call them 'slicks'—and two

Type 97E4 'Cadillac' armored cars. We've made a few modifications since your government was kind enough to provide them—the slicks we're bringing have 12mm heavy machine guns in place of their original armament, and the Cadillacs have had their operating range extended. Mikhail can explain better than I can."

Out of the corner of his eye, Coldewe saw Mikhail snap his fingers, and his daughter popped the gum out of her mouth.

As they reached the two armored cars, Coldewe made introductions. "Commissioner, this is Section Sergeant Mikhail Remmar and his crew, Superior Privates Valeska Remmar and Rian Lange. Mikhail, this is Commissioner Mutaro. Where's Savichev hiding?"

Mikhail pointed toward the barracks. "Some things never change. He's arguing with Major Bukhanov about spares."

Mutaro looked up at the Cadillac's turret. "May I look inside, Section Sergeant?"

"Yes, sir," Mikhail replied, looking at Coldewe. "Please step around to the side with the little white gallows insignia. It's bad luck to climb up on this side."

Mutaro walked around, and Mikhail and his driver, Lange, helped him up.

From the hatch, the Cadillac's turret appeared incredibly cramped. Mutaro stepped onto the driver's seat, and Lange showed him how to use the handholds to lower himself. Valeska Remmar occupied the gunner's seat.

"This is a Type 97E4 armored car with a 90mm electromagnetic gun," Mikhail explained. "We, ah, picked up a few of them during the second rebellion."

Mutaro placed his hands on the wheel. "It appears very well preserved."

Mikhail nudged Lange, who was primarily responsible for the vehicle's maintenance and was slightly younger than the vehicle he drove. "She's had two refits since she entered service, so she is in very good shape, sir. Composites don't fatigue the way metals do."

Coldewe grinned. "Given the cost of shipping replacement items to colonial worlds, your government built its equipment to last."

"I have always wondered why we never employed tanks on colonial worlds," Mutaro commented, to see how Mikhail would respond.

"Well, sir, you know what it costs to push weight into orbit.

This vehicle weighs twelve tons loaded, and a tank weighs sixty." Remmar shrugged. "A tank drinks fuel like it was vodka, chews roads for breakfast, and needs at least sixteen man-hours of maintenance a day. Tanks belong on Earth."

Mutaro tugged on the wheel experimentally. "Colonel Coldewe was kind enough to tell me that this vehicle has been modified. Perhaps you could explain."

"Yes, sir." Mikhail looked at Coldewe. "The biggest problems with the type 97E4 were the lack of range and the increased maintenance. We haven't been able to do much to make them easier to maintain—keeping the electromagnetic gun working right is pretty much a full-time job—but we raised the deck four centimeters and added fuel cells there and under the seats to increase the range."

"Doesn't this pose an additional hazard of fire?" Mutaro asked.

Remmar nodded, silently complimenting Mutaro for choosing an intelligent question. "We have shielding and fire retardant, and the underseat cells are the first to empty, but it does pose an additional danger. What we found when we looked over the 97E4s we shot up during the rebellion was that if the crew compartment takes a solid hit, anybody who isn't dead already is probably going to get electrocuted when the electromagnetic sink discharges, so it doesn't much matter. A lot of our boys don't much like the 97E4s for that reason."

"I see," Mutaro commented. "Why did Colonel Coldewe select them, do you think?"

Remmar looked to Coldewe again. "A 97E4 generates a muzzle velocity of 1150 meters per second with armor-piercing ammo, which makes for a serious hole, and there's not much noise to it—just a pop when the shell passes the sound barrier. We figured out how to reduce the electromagnetic force when we fire high-explosive shells, which lets us use a thinner-walled casing without having it deform in flight, and you don't know you've been fired at until the shell blows up in your face. I expect Colonel Hans thinks that that might be useful on a trip like this."

Coldewe coughed. "An additional consideration is that we captured quite a few of them intact, and Sergei Okladnikov might not be too happy with me if I made him take a couple of his 97E1s out of service to make sure that the 97E1s we send along continue to run."

Mutaro nodded approvingly. "And I understand that you are

this vehicle's gunner, young lady. Perhaps you would be so kind as to show me how your cannon operates."

Her father nodded, and Valeska turned on her screen. "This joystick here, the left one, controls your sight. I can flip between visual and infrared by toggling left or right, and I can increase or decrease the magnification by moving forward or backward." She demonstrated.

"Unless the vehicle commander overrides, my right joystick controls the turret and the main gun. The red button under my thumb is my firing control. With this system I can get off a main gun round every four seconds."

"Thank you very much. I am most appreciative," Mutaro said. Lange helped him exit.

Coldewe explained as they walked away, "Mikhail was a rifleman before he lost his knee. He's actually the slowest gunner in the family, and they kid him about it a lot."

"His daughter is so much taller than he is," Mutaro observed.

"So is Mikhail's wife, which is another cross he has to bear. Valeska's kind of a tomboy, and Mikhail's given up on his son, so I guess he figures bringing her along is his best chance of having grandkids someday."

"I see." Mutaro's eyes twinkled.

"Come inside for a minute," Coldewe suggested, and Mutaro followed him into the main barracks. As he passed an object hung in an alcove by the door, Coldewe paused to rub it for luck. "This is our battalion crest, a white salamander on a sable field. He's looking backward—*regardant* in heraldic terminology—but the boys usually say he's chasing his tail, which is only fitting in a military organization."

Mutaro studied the beast's single, glittering green eye.

Coldewe explained, "Of the people we brought here, there is a solid core—Finns and Russians mostly—that never laid down roots. A lot of them are coming." In the evening when the Finns and Russians sang old songs together—the ones they made up and the ones from a home that didn't quite exist anymore—their eyes sometimes filled with tears. The older men had little to lose, except perhaps their spirit and their comrades.

Coldewe spotted Company Sergeant Isaac Wanjau. "Isaac, can you come here for a minute?"

Wanjau was very tall and very black, with a hint of gray in his hair. He patted the private he was talking to on the shoulder and walked over with an easy grace.

"I am showing Commissioner Mutaro around. Commissioner, may I present Company Sergeant Isaac Wanjau."

"*So desu,*" Wanjau said politely, inclining his head to the proper angle.

"My pleasure to make your acquaintance," Mutaro replied, returning the courtesy. "Your accent is quite superior."

Wanjau smiled genially. "I lived in Tokyo for a year."

"Indeed, what part?"

Wanjau's smile broadened, and Coldewe coughed. "Isaac went along on the Tokyo raid. He, ah, stayed behind to cover our retreat. It took us a while to get him back."

"Other than the food, your jails are very nice," Wanjau said politely.

Mutaro raised an eyebrow.

Coldewe grinned. "Jan was planning on fighting it out despite a bullet in his shoulder, and approving Isaac's leave was the last thing he remembers doing before Isaac popped a gas grenade under his nose and he woke up with a headache on the *Hendrik Pienaar*. After they let him go, Isaac went home to Nigeria on leave until he could get passage to Suid-Afrika."

Mutaro cleared his throat. "Perhaps I should not ask this, but it appears somewhat unusual for a person of your ethnic background to be a soldier on Suid-Afrika."

"That was Major Sanmartin's doing," Wanjau said, enjoying some private joke. "We met on a mountain."

"A mountain?"

"It was called the Jebel d'Aucune. It was on a planet called Ashcroft. Major Sanmartin was an Imperial soldier then, and I was a *caco*, a rebel. When he led C Company up the side of the mountain, I decided that I wanted to be a soldier, too. We met a few months later, and I became one."

Wanjau grinned hugely, but his eyes misted over. "At night, I tell recruits stories about the mountain, and about Tokyo and Krugersdorp so that they understand what it is to be a soldier. My wife complains about living in the barracks and not having any children, but the barracks is a fine place, and I have lots of children. They are all my children."

"Isaac's wife is a fine nurse," Coldewe added.

"I met her on leave. Although," Wanjau added wistfully, "it is sometimes difficult to get her to stop talking."

"And you decided to come back to Suid-Afrika?"

"I was the company sergeant," Wanjau replied, clearly viewing it as a complete answer.

Mutaro bowed. "Thank you, Company Sergeant."

Wanjau grinned. "Your hospitals are also very nice, Commissioner." He bowed correctly. *"Arigato."*

"Arigato," Mutaro said, tight-lipped but obviously amused.

As Wanjau strode away, Coldewe said very quietly, "People who do what we do are crazy as bedbugs, and company sergeants act even crazier to keep their people straight. After a while, it becomes a habit. Isaac is tolerably sane on most subjects."

He studied Mutaro's face. "When Isaac surrendered, the Imperial defense forces didn't quite know what to do with him. There was some question raised about his sanity because he responded to questions with his name, rank, and service number, including questions like, 'Would you like more tea?' " Coldewe coughed. "Anton says he learned his sense of humor from me."

"Please go on," Mutaro said politely.

"After about six months of this and a fair number of beatings, the prison authorities sent him to a hospital for observation. Isaac stayed insane until our local agent managed to let him know that the political climate had changed, whereupon Isaac had the most miraculous recovery in the history of psychiatry."

Coldewe looked away. "We left nine people behind—that never sat right with Matti Harjalo, although Matti knows he's not quite rational on the subject—and Isaac was one of the few we got back, so somebody, of course, was silly enough to interview him and asked whether he had fought to the last bullet. Isaac responded, 'Oh, no. Once we saw the shuttle off, it wouldn't have been fair to keep shooting those poor policemen,' which says worlds about why I'm keen to have him along. He and Jan Snyman are very close, and I think the two of them would flat out mutiny if I didn't take them both."

"I believe that I have seen enough," Mutaro said politely.

Thursday (1173)

"WELL, SERGEI, THE IMPERIAL SHIPS OUGHT TO BE HERE BY THE end of the week," Major Danny Meagher commented, "and they are tallying results as we speak, which means that you're a major again if Ssu miscounted, which, of course, he never does. Are you ready for the hand over?"

"Not until I can make the accounts balance *once*." Sleepless nights had affected Acting Lieutenant-Colonel Sergei Oklad-nikov's normally good humor.

Hans Coldewe gazed up at the ceiling. "Just tell Saki Bukhanov to take it out of the flower fund as usual. We've been cooking the books for so many years that it would be a shame to do things honestly."

Okladnikov tore the printout in his hand into confetti.

Friday (1173)

SUID-AFRIKA'S CONSTITUTION PERMITTED A NEW EXECUTIVE TO take office as soon as election results were validated. Andries Steen announced the results at midnight, and with the same painstaking care he gave to all of his endeavors, he cleared his office within the hour to make way for his successor.

HOPE

Some people dressed in silver with the money that they had,
*   They strutted in their costumes 'til they made the piggies*
*   mad.*
They made themselves a nuisance when they tried to legislate,
*   But pigs who like to whistle also like affairs of state.*
                                        —*"The Whistling Pig"*

Saturday (1173)

"HOW DOES IT FEEL TO BE HOME?" VERESHCHAGIN ASKED, PULL-
ing away a corner of the curtain to view the crowd beginning to
gather in Johannesburg's Vryheidsplain.

"Good." Hendricka Sanmartin took a deep breath. "Numb."
She ran her hand along the marble of the desk that had once belonged to her foster father. "What happens to Steen now?"

"He resigned his party offices at a party caucus early this
morning. So did his leading supporters. That was Christos
Claassen's price for picking up the pieces. The Nationalist party
knows that the party needs Christos more than he needs the
party."

She didn't ask him how he knew. "He could have been a very
good president. Steen, I mean." She stared out the window.
"Nothing about what he wanted makes sense to me."

"Even brilliant men sometimes allow their fears to rule them.
Andries Steen feared greatly. He chose not to be a good president." Vereshchagin asked, "Are you ready to go down?"

"No." Sanmartin took a deep breath. She said softly, "You
know it is my mother they want."

93

"No, not her. They want you." He squeezed her hand. "Or Joan of Arc."

"If you have visions, pass them along." She looked at her watch. "If my father could have been here, what would he have said?"

"Raul would have chosen Horace. *'Exegi monumentum aere perennius.'* 'I have raised a monument more enduring than brass.' "

She smiled wanly. "*Exegi?* I feel more like *exodium*, the farce that follows a tragedy."

"The quotation he used most frequently about me behind my back was *'Fortitur in re, sed suaviter in modo.'* 'Unflinching in principle, but gracious in method.' " Vereshchagin closed the curtain. "If your father and mother were here today, they would be very proud. Are you ready to go down?"

She took another deep breath. "Yes."

In accordance with the wishes of the candidate-elect, the minister who invoked God's blessing on Suid-Afrika, its people, and its new president took his text from the sixth chapter of Isaiah, which speaks of the wolf dwelling with the lamb, the leopard lying down with the kid, and the calf and young lion browsing together, with a little child to lead them.

Sunday (1174)

VERESHCHAGIN SET ASIDE THE BOOK HE WAS READING WHEN Gu entered. "What is it?"

"You have a visitor, Father Nick. You have time to see him." Gu made little secret of his likes and dislikes.

"Please show him in."

Born in Calgary of Croatian parents, Nicola Bosenac was a member of the small Franciscan mission in Upper Marlboro that ministered to the Catholics in the cowboy backcountry.

The 1/35th Rifle Battalion's original complement of Lutheran Finns and Orthodox Russians had thinned substantially over the years, and the battalion's Orthodox chaplain, Ivan Zakhariev, never fully recovered from a bad pelvic wound he took when A Company stormed the spaceport during the second rebellion. After Zakhariev died, Matti Harjalo persuaded Father Nick, an unassuming man fluent in four Slavic languages, to address the spiritual needs of the remaining Orthodox faithful.

With the muted and perhaps less than enthusiastic approval of Suid-Afrika's only Catholic bishop, Father Nick had performed Orthodox services once a month in what could accurately be described as an ecumenical spirit.

Vereshchagin rose when Gu ushered the priest into the room. "Father Nicola, how good to see you. Please sit. I can offer you tea, and I think that someone brought by a nut roll earlier this morning."

Bosenac dropped himself into a chair and patted his thickening middle. "No, thank you, Colonel. I'm still on my diet from Christmas." He glanced around the room. "I thought you might be too busy to see me."

Vereshchagin drew himself a cup of tea from the samovar. "Hans Coldewe is handling military preparations, and Simon Beetje is finding scientists for me. I learned years ago that the most effective way to prepare is to select good people and to stay away from them. Until Commissioner Mutaro's ships arrive, I really have very little to do."

This was a moderately transparent falsehood, but Bosenac allowed it to stand.

Vereshchagin looked around for the sugar. "What brings you to me?"

"I've spoken to Colonel Coldewe informally, and he advised me to see you." Bosenac leaned forward in his chair. "I would like to go with you."

Vereshchagin sipped at his tea. "I am severely constrained in the number of persons I can take. Our expedition has a place for God, but the physical space allocated is small."

"A lot of the old soldiers are going. You can hardly ask the Erixons to look after them—they're expecting another child next month—and I've noticed you don't enjoy the closest ties with the Dutch Reformed Church."

Vereshchagin chuckled. "This might have something to do with the number of Dutch Reformed ministers we shot during the first rebellion."

"I had hoped that you might consider me." When Vereshchagin made no immediate effort to reply, Bosenac went on, "I also feel that I can help. Religious faith plays an important role in human behavior, and human ethics and morality aren't easily separated from a belief in some form of god. I can't conceive of an intelligent species without some form of religious belief. I don't think you can understand the ethics and morals of this alien people without trying to understand their religious beliefs."

"The points you make are well taken, although I do not completely agree with your implied assertion that only a man of faith can adequately study the manifestations of faith in an alien species." Vereshchagin stared into his tea. "Your bishop is a charming man. I assume that you have spoken to him. How lukewarm is he about sending you?"

"He is excited about our encountering another intelligent species and agrees that I am the logical person to send." Bosenac stroked his thick black beard. "Although I think he feels that God might have exercised better care in selecting tools for His work."

Vereshchagin smiled wryly. "I appreciate your candor, and I owe you mine. I can only afford to take one chaplain, and in accordance with political realities, I have asked President Sanmartin and the legislature to suggest a suitable candidate."

For a few seconds, Bosenac sat without moving. Then he smiled and reached out to shake Vereshchagin's hand firmly. "I had hoped. I hope you won't mind when I say although I can't go with you, my prayers will go instead."

"Thank you. Your prayers will be greatly appreciated."

Gu materialized to see Bosenac out. A few moments later, he reappeared and eyed Vereshchagin reproachfully. "Why didn't you tell him the truth?"

"I did."

"When are you going to tell him the rest of it?"

"Never, I trust." Vereshchagin refilled his teacup. "I have his bishop to do that for me. Charming man, the bishop. He has not been here very long—I think he arrived seven or eight years ago—but I think he understands me quite well. I told him he should have been a Jesuit."

He took a sip of tea. "Our choices are limited. The cowboys, as is typical for a frontier community, have always been terribly short of educated clergy and lost some of their best when Reading was obliterated, while the dominees of this planet's Dutch Reformed Church were handpicked for their intransigence and have attempted to perpetuate it. Even the ones educated after Raul and Christos shook up the university are remarkably narrow-minded. The exceptions are, largely, married and unavailable."

Left unstated was Vereshchagin's conviction that the participation of the few open-minded Dutch Reformed ministers was essential to the shaping of Suid-Afrika's future, and that removing even one would be a serious error.

"After the legislature ties things in knots with help from Adriaan and Rikki, I will reluctantly drop my request for a chaplain and add a theological scholar at the last moment."

"You should add a request for a conscience," Gu scowled. "And what if one of the scientists coming from Go-Nihon turns out to be a theologian?"

"Religion is a blind spot of a sort for His Imperial Majesty's government. Both Shinto and Japanese Buddhism are so closely identified with Japanese nationalism that it is sometimes difficult for Japanese to think of religion as something other than a form of cultural identity. In Father Nicola's terms, obtaining a theologian from Go-Nihon would require a miracle."

"You still could have told him," Gu reproached.

"Unfortunately, Father Nicola's capacity for duplicity is limited." Vereshchagin stirred his tea. "We have enough lay ministers for the Calvinists aboard, but our Lutherans will be unrepresented. I should ask Pastor Erixon for an extra prayer book. It would be interesting to see just how far we can stretch Father Nicola's ecumenical principles."

Gu sniffed. "If you are finished being pleased with yourself, you should go over to Colonel Coldewe's headquarters. He says the Imp ships have arrived."

Vereshchagin sat upright. "When did this occur?"

"Hours ago." Gu put his hands on his hips. "I told him you couldn't come until you saw Father Bosenac. He laughed."

"You could have told me," Vereshchagin said mildly, perched at an unnatural angle.

"And give you hours to worry? My job is to look after you. The car will be here to pick you up in ten minutes."

"Thank you, Gu," Vereshchagin said with obviously mixed emotions.

At Coldewe's headquarters, he found Coldewe closeted with Commissioner Mutaro and a Japanese officer.

Coldewe took him by the arm. "Anton, this is Major Mitsuru Aichi, commanding No. 305 Independent Infantry Company."

Aichi was rail thin, with a prominent Adam's apple. He saluted stiffly. "Honored Vice-Commissioner."

"What ships are here?" Vereshchagin asked, returning Aichi's salute.

"My company is billeted with the scientists on assault transport *Zuiho*. Frigate *Aoba* has also arrived with two corvettes. We anticipate arrival of freighters *Singapore Maru* and *Miami Maru* within a few days." Aichi looked at Coldewe. "If the local situation permits, I would like to land my company. Shipboard conditions are never entirely pleasant."

Vereshchagin nodded. "President Sanmartin approved your request in advance, although she expects us to keep you as far from the local population as possible."

Mutaro said with a sly smile, "We were also discussing the company that Colonel Coldewe has undertaken to provide for the expedition. Major Aichi fails to see the necessity."

Vereshchagin raised one eyebrow.

"I believe my company is capable of undertaking all missions assigned to it, Vice-Commissioner," Aichi said with obvious pride. "In our most recent unit-readiness inspection, we were scored at the 105th percentile."

Coldewe smiled faintly.

"Have any of your men been in combat?" Vereshchagin asked.

"No, Vice-Commissioner. I regret not."

"Hans?" Vereshchagin asked.

Coldewe shrugged. "Fewer bad habits to unlearn. Shall we?"

Vereshchagin nodded. "I see no reason why not. Major Aichi, is your company equipped with mock combat equipment?"

"I regret that we did not bring it." Aichi began to look discomfited. "I regret that I did not anticipate the need."

"Hans?" Vereshchagin said.

"I'll put Karaev and Bukhanov onto it," Coldewe volunteered. "After they finish swearing, it should take them about an hour to assemble the stuff and get it to the shuttle strip."

Vereshchagin nodded. "Give them two hours, then. Major Aichi, an exercise will give you an opportunity to assess us, and it will give us an opportunity to assess you. Shall we try it?"

"Yes, Vice-Commissioner," Aichi said, looking at Mutaro, who was grinning.

"What role would you prefer, company in the offense or company in the defense?"

After a slight pause, Aichi said, "Company in the offense, Vice-Commissioner."

Vereshchagin nodded again. "Good. Hans, any suggestions for an objective?"

"Major Aichi's people aren't acclimated, so we don't want to spend too much time fooling around." Coldewe called up his electronic map and focused in on a map square in the continent's interior. "The forest all pretty much looks the same. Pick a hill. Any hill."

Aichi scanned the map carefully, clearly dismayed by the speed at which events were progressing. "Perhaps this one."

"Hmmm. Hill 410." Coldewe touched the radio at his temple. "Chiba point one. Break. Hello, Jan. This is Hans. Is No. 9 your ready platoon? . . . Good. Tell Hiltunen to get them into mock combat gear and out to defend Hill 410. We're going to throw an Imp infantry company at it. . . . No, wait an hour before you tell them. We don't want to give them too much of an advantage. . . . Same to you, Jan. Coldewe out."

He looked at Aichi. "I'll give you copies of our rules of engagement. Make sure your people understand them—we don't want any real casualties. Also, make sure your people carry three canteens. It gets pretty hot out there. Did you want to jump from the shuttle, or do you want me to lay on transport aircraft?"

"We will jump," Aichi said.

"Fine. How long will it take your people to get ready?"

"Perhaps twelve hours," Aichi admitted.

"Good enough." Coldewe shrugged. "I'll call Jan back and tell him to delay. If Hiltunen has twelve hours to dig into that rock, you'll never find him. Unless, of course, he wants you to."

"May I see to my command?" Aichi requested.

Coldewe nodded. "Poikolainnen will arrange a ride for you."

Aichi saluted and departed.

Vereshchagin watched him leave. "I suppose I should have chatted with him for a few minutes first."

Coldewe grinned. "I saw you stiffen when he said 'unit-readiness inspection.' " He told Mutaro, "We absolutely flunked our last Imperial unit-readiness inspection. None of our paperwork was in order. It still isn't."

"However, your soldiers can shoot," Mutaro observed.

"Well, yes," Coldewe admitted. "We're very good at that."

"There is an adage of venerable antiquity to the effect that no unit ready for inspection is fit for combat and vice versa," Vereshchagin explained. "Hans, what do you make of Major Aichi?"

"Green as all of Ireland, of course, but I think he'll do. He reminds me of Hiroshi Mizoguchi before we let Hiroshi wrestle with the tar baby."

"Hiroshi Mizoguchi was an excellent young officer who served with us until he was blinded, and Hans is referring to the process of breaking in a new officer," Vereshchagin translated absently. "We are going to have to take particular care with the transition. I suppose that we ought to think of this as an acquisition and merger."

Mutaro smiled. "A *shinchigun* is a company that buys out another firm. The word is also used for an army of occupation."

"It is appropriate, I think." Vereshchagin straightened. "Hans, with Commissioner Mutaro's permission, I think that I ought to introduce myself aboard *Zuiho* and *Aoba*."

"Say no more." Coldewe held up his hand. "I have Detlef Jankowskie and Nicolas Sery waiting to take you to the shuttle."

AFTER SPEAKING WITH MAJOR JAN SNYMAN, LIEUTENANT MIKA Hiltunen pulled No. 9 platoon together. "Gather, children." A hint of a smile graced Hiltunen's bony face. "It is metal music time."

In Suid-Afrikan Orbit

AS THE SHUTTLE ACHIEVED LOW ORBIT, VERESHCHAGIN METhodically studied a cutaway projection of His Imperial Majesty's assault transport *Zuiho*. Smaller than many newer ships, the hump of a shuttle bay marred her otherwise sleek, cylindrical lines. Vereshchagin had crossed paths with her once, years before during the Cyclade campaign.

Her consort, frigate *Aoba*, was even older. The Imperial Navy had added few ships since His Imperial Majesty's government had foresworn aggression.

Vereshchagin had known *Zuiho*'s captain as a junior lieutenant. *Aoba*'s commander would be the problem.

In the seat next over, Captain Detlef Jankowskie stirred. "Are you all right, sir? You've been very quiet."

Vereshchagin smiled and shut his computer off. "I am fine, Detlef."

Jankowskie had had nearly twenty years to learn the Variag and his moods. "Sir?" he asked, politely and pointedly.

"I cannot help wondering, Detlef. It has been so long since we fought a real opponent. Have we lost our edge?" Vereshchagin asked.

Jankowskie chuckled. "We won't answer that question for certain until the last and worst possible moment, but our people spend an incredible amount of time pounding on the reserve companies and each other. If it isn't war when C Company and A Company tangle, I don't know what is."

Vereshchagin smiled.

"Commencing docking procedures to board *Aoba*," the shuttle pilot announced in clipped English.

"The devil must be ice-skating," Nicolas Sery commented from the seat beside Jankowskie.

Jankowskie shook the fine blond hair out of his eyes, a grin on his absurdly boyish face. "It would be difficult to find three people less welcome aboard an Imperial Navy warship than the three of us. Plus Esko, who isn't welcome anywhere."

Senior Communications Sergeant Esko Poikolainnen snorted.

As the shuttle coupled, Vereshchagin waved farewell to Major Aichi, who was waiting for the shuttle to continue on to *Zuiho*. Aichi appeared lost in thought.

On board *Aoba*, a rating in coveralls led them forward to the bridge. Six officers were present, dressed in plain blue uniforms and saucer caps reminiscent of the uniforms worn by officers of Britain's Royal Navy in its years of glory. Three of the officers wore straight dress swords that marked them as ship commanders. They bowed in unison. Vereshchagin, Jankowskie, and Sery returned the courtesy.

"I am Captain Yotaro Kobayashi, captain of His Imperial Majesty's ship *Aoba*." Kobayashi was a tall, stocky officer with a broad, flat face. He eyed with distaste the battledress uniforms that Sery, Poikolainnen, and Jankowskie wore. "I have been instructed to place myself and my vessel under your command, Vice-Commissioner. May I present Commander Nitobe and Commander Mazaki, who command the two corvettes assigned to me; my executive officer, Commander Nagahiro; and my engineering officer, Lieutenant-Commander Iida."

"May I introduce Captain Detlef Jankowskie, commander of the *Hendrik Pienaar*; his chief gunner, Nicolas Sery; and my signals officer, Senior Communications Sergeant Esko Poikolainnen."

Kobayashi's eyes gleamed with an elfin light. "I confess that I had hoped to encounter you under different circumstances, Jankowskie-*san*."

Jankowskie grinned. "Through a targeting sight, no doubt."

"No doubt," Kobayashi agreed.

Observing the look that Kobayashi gave his corvette commanders, Vereshchagin said, "Captain Kobayashi, perhaps Captain Jankowskie and I could discuss arrangements with you in

private while Nicolas and Esko work out communications proto-
col with your people."

"My cabin would be best. Please come this way." Kobayashi
led Vereshchagin and Jankowskie from the bridge down to deck
A. "We will not be disturbed here," Kobayashi explained as he
shut the door behind them.

Vereshchagin studied the room to see what, if any, clues it
gave him to Kobayashi's personality. The walls were unadorned,
the desk in the corner empty except for a terminal. Kobayashi
remained standing. "Please excuse the awkward position I find
myself in. It is unprecedented."

"Having your ships placed under the operational command of
foreign—potentially hostile—officers?" Vereshchagin inquired
gently.

"Yes, honored Vice-Commissioner." Kobayashi's face tightened
almost imperceptibly. "I regret that I fail to share Commissioner
Mutaro's understanding of the situation."

"Allow me to sum up: you do not understand why Commissioner Mutaro chose me to lead this expedition, and you find
Captain Jankowskie's presence on your ship unsettling."

"My officers are quite agitated. I fail to see the necessity,"
Kobayashi said. "Although I am bound to obey the civil authority, which is Commissioner Mutaro, as an Imperial Naval officer,
I cannot allow Captain Jankowskie to issue operational orders
aboard an Imperial warship, if that is your intention."

"I assume that you shared your concerns with Commissioner
Mutaro."

Kobayashi returned a sour smile. "He declined my resignation. I did, of course, submit a formal protest through Navy
channels."

"Let me offer this compromise: Detlef and Nicolas will remain aboard your ship as my liaison officers and will offer you
advice, which you are free to accept or disregard. At a later
point in time, we will review this arrangement. Is this acceptable?"

Kobayashi bowed. "*Hai*, Vereshchagin-*sama*."

Jankowskie spoke up. "We still have a few days while the scientists and the ground forces are loading up. If you'd like, you
can try some maneuvers against the *Hendrik Pienaar* while
we're waiting."

"I think that my personnel would welcome the diversion."
Kobayashi examined Vereshchagin's face carefully. "May I ask
whether you consider such training to be indicated?"

"Are you asking whether I anticipate hostilities including space combat?" Vereshchagin responded. "The potential exists."

"Perhaps it does." Kobayashi studied the two of them. "Jankowskie-*san*, I will explain matters to my personnel. I would respectfully ask you to overlook any difficulties they may have in properly adjusting to the situation."

Slender and soft-spoken, with a hint of a potbelly, Jankowskie had been a lieutenant in The Iceman's company before Vereshchagin had selected him for ship command. In Hans Coldewe's words, Jankowskie was the mildest-mannered man who ever cut a throat or scuttled a ship. "Nicolas and I started out as infantrymen, so I can truthfully say that we have a fair amount of experience at hostile crowd control."

Kobayashi stroked his chin. "The admiral's cabin on board is unoccupied, and I would be honored if you accepted that. I had not considered where to billet Chief Gunner Sery."

"Why don't you put us both in there? I am sure there's plenty of room. I do, however, have a small request to make." Jankowskie pulled a little cylinder of spray paint out of his pocket. "We always paint a little white gallows insignia on vehicles and ships. For luck. With your permission."

Kobayashi nodded abruptly. "As you say. For luck. Have you brought your baggage?"

"Nicolas and I left it by the air lock," Jankowskie replied.

Kobayashi touched the intercom. "Officer of the deck, please have the foreign officers' dunnage brought from the air lock to the admiral's cabin."

"Detlef, why don't you find Nicolas and settle in?" Vereshchagin said. "Captain Kobayashi and I have much to discuss."

"All these frigates are laid out much the same," Jankowskie said. "The admiral's cabin is at the end of the corridor, right?"

"The door is not locked," Kobayashi acknowledged, with a rigid smile. He touched the intercom. "Officer of the deck, please arrange for Chief Gunner Sery to be escorted to the admiral's cabin."

Jankowskie and Sery arrived at the admiral's cabin at almost the same moment. A rating came by with their bags and dropped them on the deck.

"Let's unpack," Jankowskie said, trying the handle to the door.

Sery checked out the narrow bed folded up against the wall.

"Room for an army in here. Esko has things pretty much under control. The signals officer is pretty good." He unfolded the desk and looked through it. "I don't know how you feel, but I'd just as soon sling a hammock and let you take the bed."

"Fine by me." Jankowskie maneuvered to get by him. "I need to shave. Help me check out the bathroom."

They squeezed into the little stall that served as the admiral's bathroom, and Jankowskie switched his razor on. With the razor's modulated hum to drown out his words, he murmured to Sery, "You check for bugs?"

"Two. Not very well hidden."

"Bugging cabins isn't something the Navy does every day. Don't touch them. The Variag told us to be on our best behavior, and it would hurt their feelings." Jankowskie ran the razor over his chin. "This is a terrible razor for shaving with. How do you like the ship?"

"Kobayashi's people seem to know their stuff. She isn't home, but I expect I could get used to her. The layout is pretty much like the *Hendrik*."

"This one is a few years older, although I expect they've had a refit within the last five or six years. Did anyone ask you any battle questions?"

Sery's lip curled. "One ensign wanted to know how we took *Hendrik*. If you noticed, they scope cargos coming aboard, and the officers all carry sidearms. They've guessed how we did the trick, but they think we smuggled aboard about a hundred guys."

Jankowskie allowed himself a small chuckle. "A hundred guys wouldn't have had room to move. Twenty was overkill. You think anybody here has seen action?"

"Kobayashi, maybe. Maybe not even him. It's been a while since His Imperial Majesty's Navy has had anything much to shoot at."

"It's been a while for us, too," Jankowskie pointed out.

"Yes, but if you recall, we hang around the wrong kind of crowd when we're dirtside."

"I do recall, and I also recall, Nicolas, how you and those circus clowns in No. 9 left me hip deep in mud, and if you think I am going to forget anytime soon . . ." He listened to Sery giggle and lowered his voice even further. "So, if we had to, how long would it take?"

"To secure this ship? Just you and me?" Sery questioned in a soft whisper.

Jankowskie nodded as he used the razor to trim his sideburns.

"Fourteen minutes, stem to stern." Sery smiled, chillingly. "If we had to."

Jankowskie smiled, shutting off his razor. "It's always important to start things off in an atmosphere of trust."

Monday (1174)

STRETCHED OUT IN THE FOLIAGE BESIDE A CLEARING, SENIOR Private Denys Gordimer lifted one eyebrow. "What's up, Dolly?"

Assistant Section Sergeant Kalle Kekkonen touched his radio. "Chiba point one. Break. Kekkonen here. They're coming." He adjusted the setting on his night sights and quickly counted parachutes descending on the clearing in front of him. "Half a platoon just dropped in our laps."

Behind him, a relay switching node took his signal—weak to avoid detection—and channeled it through two other nodes to Major Jan Snyman, five kilometers away.

"What do you think, Mika?" Snyman asked Lieutenant Mika Hiltunen.

Hiltunen, a sleepy-eyed veteran, looked back at the hill they were supposed to be defending, partly visible in the distance. "They ought to jump into the trees. Aren't many clear areas, and they ought to know we have them covered. Has to be a feint."

"I don't know. Tree jumping is pretty wicked, and I'd hate to try it with a bunch as green as that." Snyman consulted his muse. A few seconds later his eyes refocused. He touched his radio. "Kalle, does it look like a feint?"

Kekkonen watched the Imperial soldiers for a few moments before replying. "They look serious."

"Good enough. Keep us posted. Snyman out." Snyman turned to Hiltunen. "Double or nothing?"

Hiltunen shook his head.

A corvette roared into the upper atmosphere over the hill. Snyman watched it pass and felt the hum of his radio.

"Coldewe here. Corvette *Jintsu* just simulated dusting the top of the hill with chicken seed. Major Meagher will assess casualties."

"That won't take long," Hiltunen commented. "You want me to start moving?"

"Yes, you have the farthest to go so you might as well get started. I'll call you if the Imps spring any surprises."

Hiltunen nodded and left.

A few moments later, Kekkonen provided a follow-up report. "The shuttle's back. They're opening chutes at about two thousand meters into a light crosswind and coming down all over the potato patch. It'll be another hour before they form up, maybe two. Hope you can work in some jump training for them. Kekkonen out."

TRAVELING JUST BEHIND HIS LEAD PLATOON, MAJOR AICHI paused to get a position reading from the warships overhead. Progress through the thick undergrowth that separated ridge lines was agonizingly slow, and his sections were finding it difficult to maintain their intervals. The heat and humidity of the forest was already causing problems, and Aichi paused to adjust the thermal controls on his battledress.

To Aichi's intense discomfort, Hans Coldewe, who had nominated himself as chief umpire for the exercise, scribbled yet another note to himself, all the while murmuring lines from *The Yeoman of the Guard.*

He was well into the second act.

Abruptly, Aichi came to a decision. Pulling in closer the two sections detailed as flank security, he checked his map and directed his men to walk down the spine of the ridge in the gaps that separated the towering fern trees. His point team entered a small saddle that separated the ridge from a slight elevation.

Seconds later, the point team was obliterated by an 88mm recoilless round, and the elevation erupted in a hail of s-mortar fire. As Aichi shouted orders into his radio, he felt a laser beam strike his shoulder. Immediately, his radio and weapon ceased to function.

Cursing, Aichi squatted and looked down to where the fabric of his battledress had turned itself red. Coldewe gestured sympathetically. Feeling stupid, Aichi checked his wrist mount, which registered 25 percent disabled.

A first platoon rifleman noticed his plight. He stopped trying to return fire at unseen enemies and crawled over to bandage Aichi's shoulder. As soon as the soldier taped an electronic "compress" over the "wound," Aichi gave Coldewe a hard look and ordered his second and third platoons into the low ground on either side of the ridge to flank the enemy ambush.

As they did so, hell broke loose from the dense vegetation. Aichi yelled, "Point Akita. Break. Aichi here. Platoon leaders, report!" A moment later, he realized to his horror that all three of his platoon leaders were down.

Firing intensified as he tried to make sense out of the situation. A moment later, he felt something touch him in the back.

Recognizing that he was "dead," Aichi stripped off his mask with numbed fingers as the No. 10 platoon soldier who had shot him went by in a low crouch looking for other targets.

The firing died away to a series of single shots.

Coldewe spoke rapidly into his wrist mount. Then he shook his head and looked at Aichi. "This one's over. You all right?"

Aichi replied, "Yes, sir," automatically. He picked up his face shield. Then he looked for his rifle and found it on the ground.

"There is something about walking into an ambush that concentrates the mind marvelously. Rest a minute, then round up your people. The sequence to unlock your radios is 34782." Coldewe glanced at his wrist mount. "I want the officers from both sides for a postmortem. Anton has been monitoring Jan's radio net, so he should be here in a few minutes."

"We went up against a company," Aichi said stupidly.

Coldewe nodded. "This was your introduction to the Neighbor task group. You were, of course, followed. These ridge lines are as good as trails—one of Suid-Afrika's peculiarities—and Jan Snyman knows it. Two sections from No. 9 platoon let you have it from the hill there. When you went for the cheese, No. 10 platoon and the rest of No. 9 fired you up from the low ground, and some people from the recon platoon rolled you up back to front when the people who were supposed to be providing you with rear security allowed themselves to be distracted. It's one of Jan's favorite stunts. It's about the only way you can ambush somebody from three sides, but it takes very, very good fire control to keep from shooting your own people."

He shrugged. "You have about a dozen privates left. Jan lost about half a dozen people, but judging from some of the things that his company sergeant is saying right now, a couple of them were 'own goals.' Somebody didn't shift fire, and Hiltunen is so upset he's stuttering. It's traditional for the loser in one of these to police up the battlefield, but you may have help."

Aichi was stunned. "A half a dozen," he repeated slowly, feeling disoriented.

"From what I saw, your boys were mostly shooting up treetops. That's another reason Jan arranged to hit you from below. Green troops tend to fire high to begin with, and you trained where, Go-Nihon?"

Aichi bowed his head.

"Go-Nihon has 104 percent of Suid-Afrika's gravitational pull and half the humidity, so the ballistics are different. Not much, but enough. I'll bet you didn't adjust for that on the trip over, did you? That's one of the tricks."

"I thought that we were to attack one platoon," Aichi said in a strained voice.

"And instead, I hit you with two platoons plus the recon platoon to scout. I wanted to see how your people would react to something unanticipated." Coldewe's eyes hardened. "One problem with taking on an entire planet with two companies is that you can't expect to have odds in your favor." He patted Aichi lightly on the shoulder. "Come on. We've got work to do. Put on an inscrutable face and get your people rounded up. As Suntzu used to say, a little self-knowledge is a useful thing."

A tilt-rotor transport aircraft appeared overhead. As Coldewe watched, the plane slowed and gradually tilted the engines on its wings from horizontal to vertical so that it could hover. An abseille rope appeared from the left rear door and fell between trees. Hooking himself to the rope, Anton Vereshchagin slid down, grunting when his knees absorbed the modest shock of landing. Piotr Kolomeitsev followed him down a few seconds later.

Coldewe walked over. "You really should leave this sort of thing to the younger generation." He handed Vereshchagin his notes as Aichi's company gathered itself, sullen and uneasy.

Vereshchagin read through them. "I see."

Aichi saluted stiffly. "Sir, I accept full responsibility."

Vereshchagin smiled. He took Aichi by the arm.

"Their confidence is shaken," The Iceman remarked to Coldewe.

"Jan's company hammered them pretty hard. He was a little too cute about it, which is something the two of us will discuss."

The Iceman, who had seen more combat as a company officer than any other man, allowed his eyes to smile. "If I know anything of my old company, money will change hands."

Although technically, the official language of the Imperial defense forces was English, Vereshchagin chose to address Aichi's men in Japanese. Coldewe observed him critically for several moments and shook his head. "He has them, Piotr. How does he do it?"

The Iceman didn't reply.

COLDEWE SAT BESIDE VERESHCHAGIN ON THE FLIGHT BACK. "Anton, an old lagg called last night with a tongue-tied request to come along."

Vereshchagin closed his eyes as if he knew what Coldewe was about to say. "Obviously, if this were a normal request, you would have simply made a decision."

Coldewe grinned. "It's Prigal, of course."

Formerly a driver in Paul Henke's light attack company, Prigal had left the battalion at the rank of recruit private having been promoted to the rank of superior private a total of fourteen times in his fourteen years of service.

"What is Prigal doing with himself these days?" Vereshchagin asked.

"He's a short-order cook."

"I thought he was driving a taxi."

Coldewe tried to maintain a straight face. "I asked. He didn't seem to want to discuss the details."

From the other side of the aircraft, Piotr Kolomeitsev, a silent witness to the conversation, eyed the two of them. "Prigal?" he inquired.

"Prigal!" Coldewe assured him.

"I trust you are not serious."

Coldewe held up one finger. "In the fullness of time, I have learned that you cannot make a sow's ear out of a silk purse, and there are some things in war for which an idiot is indispensable."

"Prigal is certainly that," The Iceman said.

"Besides," Coldewe added, "Jan Snyman wants him along for training purposes. Jan thinks he qualifies as an intelligent alien life-form."

Vereshchagin began tapping the bowl of his pipe against his knee in a rhythmic fashion. "Are you seriously suggesting that we take him?"

"Well, we haven't turned down any Tokyo vets yet."

"On your head may it be. Prigal has *baraka*. He will be our good-luck charm. In the fullness of time, he will once again be the galaxy's oldest recruit private. He may come. As a cook."

Although Vereshchagin had a well-deserved reputation for infallibility, he did on occasion make small errors. Although Prigal was employed as a cook, Coldewe hadn't told Vereshchagin that Prigal was a *good* cook.

"I suppose that this is as good a moment as any to bring up the subject of the puppies," Vereshchagin said.

Coldewe nodded. "I want to bring half our trained canines, which is eight pooches."

"I will trot out the obvious objections. This is an entirely alien planet, which is to say that from the moment they touch its surface they will be subjected to an overwhelming barrage of unfamiliar sights, sounds, and smells. The recon teams we dispatch will have little margin for error."

"Let me mention points in their favor. The logistical requirements are minimal—the fattest dog on my list weighs in at 2.1 kilograms—and it's a lot easier for a one-and-a-half-kilo dog to maintain surveillance than it is for a seventy kilo man."

As hundreds of Suid-Afrikan children looking for free pets had discovered over the years, Coldewe's standards were high. Even four generations into his breeding program, eight of every ten puppies tested were deemed unsuitable.

"Obviously, there is no way of knowing whether they can do the job on Neighbor," Coldewe continued stubbornly, "but my recon teams will sleep better with a third set of trained eyes along."

"And besides, it is good for morale," Vereshchagin concluded for him.

"Well, that too. Some of my guys don't realize that the dogs are dogs," Coldewe confessed. "Besides, you've got to take them if you take Prigal. They're at least as smart, and a lot better trained."

"Peace," Vereshchagin said, looking at Kolomeitsev.

When the aircraft touched down, Coldewe left Aichi and Snyman to organize retrieval of their remaining men and went to find Battalion Sergeant Beregov.

Still spry, although easily tired, The Iceman accompanied him. As they entered Beregov's room, Prigal hastily leaped to his feet and assumed a position of attention. Beregov looked at Coldewe indulgently.

Coldewe rubbed his hands together. "Prigal, I come as the bearer of glad tiding. The Variag has approved your plea, and you are once again restored to our bosom. How would you like to be a superior private?" He stopped. "Is something troubling you?"

"Well, sir, I don't know." Prigal looked at Beregov, "About being a superior private, I mean. It doesn't seem right somehow."

"I understand," Coldewe said, nodding his head.

Prigal blinked his eyes several times earnestly. "I'm not sure I want all that responsibility."

"I understand, Recruit Private Prigal," Coldewe assured him, conscious of the depth of humor in The Iceman's cold, gray eyes. "All right, Prigal, repeat the oath after me."

After Coldewe said the words and Prigal made appropriate responses, Battalion Sergeant Beregov laid a large, reassuring hand on Prigal's shoulder. "Welcome back, Prigal."

"Yes, Battalion Sergeant."

"A few words," Beregov whispered, leaning close. "You'll be aboard ship for a long, long time. And Company Sergeant Wanjau intends to make keeping track of you a duty and a pleasure."

"Yes, Battalion Sergeant."

"If you do anything that remotely resembles manufacturing a still, out the air lock you go."

"Yes, Battalion Sergeant."

"If you do anything that remotely resembles adjusting the temperature controls, out the air lock you go."

"Yes, Battalion Sergeant."

Coldewe and Kolomeitsev discreetly made their departure. Coldewe observed, "Bery is wasting his time. Prigal's beauty is that he never repeats mistakes; he finds new ones. He is a well of creativity, ever flowing."

"If you will keep him far from the control room and the fusion bottle, I will sleep better for it," The Iceman replied.

Esko Poikolainnen caught up with them in operations. "Colonel Coldewe, there is a woman here to see you."

"Dear gods—a scorned wife or an abandoned mother?" Coldewe touched his brow, hoping it wasn't Professor Dr. Anneke Brink. "I still need to talk with Simon. Is this something Jan can handle?"

Poikolainnen shook his head resolutely. "She's waiting in your room."

"All right," Coldewe said, understanding him. When he reached his door, he stopped and knocked.

A woman's voice, musical, answered, "Come in."

Coldewe walked inside. "Elise." He leaned over and kissed her lightly on the cheek. Then he held her hands. "I live here. Don't we have this backward?"

Elise Beckman, née Loux, laughed. Her dress was red, matching her hair, with green velvet trim. Her face was unmarked by lines, and her eyes were blue and clear.

"You're looking well. I like you in red."

"The dress or the hair?"

"Both, actually." Coldewe cleared his rucksack off a chair and held it for her. "Sorry about the wait."

"Not at all, your Sergeant Poikolainnen was very kind." Her eyes twinkled. "I wanted to surprise you."

Beckman accepted a seat from him. She folded her hands in her lap, clutching her green suede gloves tightly. "You're packing, I see."

"Yes, and I'm having the devil of a time figuring out what to take. I told Esko to burn anything I can't stuff in a rucksack." He spotted a black hat in his closet and reached down to pick it up. "Want a cowboy hat?"

She laughed and took it from him. "Charmer. I told Sergeant Poikolainnen about the night we met, when you blew up my house and asked for my phone number."

He grinned foolishly, remembering. "How is your family, Elise?"

"They're all well. I told my husband I wanted to see you off."

"Thanks. It means a lot. Tell me about everyone. How old is your daughter, now?"

"Babette just turned eighteen. She is at the stage where her parents are inarguably stupid."

"In a few short years she'll be shocked at how much they've learned. There is a boy involved, of course."

"Of course. The usual gawky, unshaven lout. She will grow out of it, and so will he."

Coldewe grinned. "I never did."

"I know. Peter, my husband, is well, and so are the twins." She looked up at him with a bright, unblinking stare. "I had almost caught up with you in age when you went to Tokyo. This time, when you get back I will be an old woman."

"Never!"

"What will you do when you get back?"

"I don't know. I've never really fit in here, you know, and I can't be a soldier all my life. Now that we're on speaking terms with the Imps again, maybe I'll look around for a planet that suits. Is Peter treating you well? You married him so—"

"Hastily, is this the word you are looking for? Two weeks and three days after our last stormy fight?" She laughed. "Peter is a dear. Without understanding me in the least, he loves me as much as any man can, and we have had eighteen good years together. There are times when I feel that I haven't been quite fair to him, but in my own way, I love him very much, and we make do. I suppose I haven't been quite fair to anyone."

"Good. Good. I'm very glad to hear that," Coldewe said, rubbing his hands together.

"I thought for a while that you and Marta were going to make a go of it."

Coldewe refused to meet her eyes. "A war got in the way."

"So I heard. I thought about coming to find you before you went to Tokyo, but the time was not right."

"Well, I'm glad you caught me here."

She smiled. "Would you have dropped me the way you dropped Marta?"

Coldewe shrugged. "Probably."

She laughed. "You were always honest." She fumbled with her purse. "Let me show you my pictures."

Coldewe examined the first few. "These are the twins? How old are they?"

"Eleven and twelve," she said with a perfectly straight face.

He raised one eyebrow. "I sent you a card, didn't I?"

"You did, and it was sweet of you." She handed him another. "This is Babette."

Coldewe looked and nodded. "Very pretty girl. She'll break a few hearts."

"She does favor you that way."

Coldewe's face froze.

"Peter has always known, but he loves her as much as if she had been his own daughter."

"Why didn't you ever tell me?"

"There wasn't any reason for you to know. But she has your eyes, and your temper. She was a little devil, if you must know. I have made my life and I am happy with it. Would it have made any difference if you had known?"

"I honestly don't know. Probably not."

"Probably not. Whether you believe it or not, there is a place for you here. Come back, when you are done. We Afrikaners are not very good at showing our emotions—"

"Three wars on three planets, and the only dent in my skull is the one you put there."

She smiled and continued, "But none of us have forgotten the handsome soldiers with funny names. The picture of Babette is yours, and I have another one of the five of us for you. I am sure you can find room for them in your rucksack."

He leaned over and kissed her on the cheek. "All right."

She stood and let him escort her to the door, in her red dress with green velvet trim.

Tuesday (1174)

JAN SNYMAN REVIEWED THE NEIGHBOR TASK GROUP. "THE UM-pires' results are in." He turned to Company Sergeant Isaac Wanjau. "The envelope please."

Wanjau handed it to him.

Snyman opened it with a flourish, "Coldewe states that some of you were inexcusably sloppy. The names of six individuals follow. You know who you are." He examined his assembled company balefully as they finished giving their weapons a final cleaning before taking them aboard ship. "Isaac and I will speak to each of you in private but loving detail."

He waited for the hooting to stop. "Hans also gave me the devil for springing a U-shaped ambush, which he thought was gilding the lily just a bit. And oh, yes, he says you won. Go collect on your bets. Quiet for a minute! I see a hand. What is it, Toivo?"

Corporal Toivo Virkki carefully set down the cocking handle from his 7.7mm general-purpose machine gun. "Sir, suppose the Neighbors are hostile."

"Yes?"

"Who do we shoot first, the Neighbors or the Imps?"

"Mother Elena" Yelenov, Virkki's section sergeant, smacked him on the back. "Neighbors, idiot! Business before pleasure."

"You people are bad! You people are truly bad!" Snyman said, trying not to smile. He examined the time display on his wrist mount. "I suppose this is as good a time as any to read you the riot act, as Colonel Hans calls it, on our relations with Major Aichi's company. In a word, beginning tomorrow, you *will* treat His Imperial Majesty's soldiers as friendly forces. I trust all of you remember what that means."

Virkki raised his hand again. "Sir, did you just say, 'starting tomorrow'?"

Snyman smiled. "Major Aichi and I have agreed to let you exchange pent-up hostility in the bars tonight. I trust you to limit yourselves to abrasions and contusions. When you are finished here, you are free for the rest of the day."

As he walked away, he remarked to Wanjau. "Time them. Let's see if we set a record."

Wednesday (1174)

VERESHCHAGIN GREETED COLDEWE, "WHAT IS THAT?"

Coldewe unwrapped the object he was carrying. "It's the battalion crest." He rubbed it for luck. "The battalion sergeant had a meeting—other ranks only, which is why I never heard about it—and they took a vote. The consensus was that it should come along. Sergei Okladnikov knows."

In place of battalion colors, the 1/35th Infantry Rifle Battalion had a battalion crest—a white salamander with green eyes and black spots on a black field. The ancient wood on which it was mounted was still slightly radioactive.

Vereshchagin took it from him and rewrapped it. "Please convey my thanks to the battalion. Tell Battalion Sergeant Beregov that I am touched."

"I'll do that."

"This is perhaps a foolish question, but what does Sergei intend to use in its place?"

"Do you remember the flag the Johannesburg ladies sewed for us that you were never able to get rid of? Well, Sergei says that his mother-in-law helped work on it, and since she's still years away from a nursing home, he figures he's pretty well stuck." Coldewe shrugged. "He says that if he can promote a battle and get it shot up a little, it won't look half bad. Of course, if he gets the thing anywhere near a battlefield, our people will make sure it gets shot up."

"How are final preparations coming?"

"Semiputrid." The circles under Coldewe's eyes bore witness to this. "Jan and I have agreed on a final list. Counting you and me, we have a grand total of just under two hundred people. Karaev is trying to make the freighter captains understand how to combat-load. He's not having luck, and there may be a few bodies on the deck plates before too long."

"I will intercede. How is Major Aichi?"

"He's still agonizing over Mutaro's request for a platoon for embassy security."

"Which platoon would you rather he leave behind?"

"His No. 3 platoon, although it's almost a toss-up between No. 3 and No. 1." Coldewe's expression was grim. "We had a twenty-kay route march last night, and forty people fell out. I notice you had Mutaro ask for an officer of suitable rank to command the detachment, so I'm going to use that as an excuse to get rid of his executive officer as well."

"Does Major Aichi suspect who generated the request?" Vereshchagin asked.

"If he does, I'll read him appropriate passages from the *Bjarkarímur*. We're going to be cutting corners on logistics as it is. We can't keep people in the icebox forever, and we can't afford to feed an extra forty people that I'm scared to use." Coldewe's face brightened. "Maybe I can talk him into using this as an excuse to comb out some of the screwups in his other two platoons."

"Do that, please. What do your spies say about their morale?"

Neighbor was six months ship time past Suid-Afrika, a planet already nine months ship time from Earth. Aichi's men had expected to return to Earth within a decade of leaving, with ample pay to compensate them for the difficulty of resuming lives in a world that aged while they were away. The expedition to Neighbor would destroy these expectations.

Coldewe meditated a moment before replying. "Aichi's boys are good boys. They'll obey their orders, but they weren't asked to volunteer and they aren't tremendously keen about spending a few years eating reconstituted rice balls on a transport light-years removed from wine, women, and song. Fortunately, some of the least well motivated manifested this by falling flat on their faces at about the fifteen-kilometer mark, which will make them easy to leave behind, but if I had to comb through Major Aichi's ranks for persons fit *and* enthusiastic, I might have trouble finding a foursome."

"They will do for our purposes," Vereshchagin said, remembering the old Imperial forces and a mutiny or two. "I would neither ask for nor expect more."

"Well, I can and will ask more for them than they've been receiving. Did Aichi mention that *Zuiho*'s captain had the ship on minimum spin on the trip over?"

When bones are subjected to a low degree of stress—during periods of weightlessness—calcium and apatite deposition decrease. Although a number of drugs had been developed to retard bone demineralization during spaceflight, the best and cheapest remedy for the problem was to maintain enough spin to provide an illusion of weight, despite the inconvenience this imposed on ship captains. Ground commanders who failed to inconvenience ship captains had to deal with the consequences, Vereshchagin reflected mirthlessly, remembering a battalion on Odawara that had suffered a stunning 19-percent casualty rate—

severe sprains and broken legs—during a routine parachute insertion.

Coldewe shook his head firmly. "We two had a long chat, and *Zuiho*'s captain repents of his evil ways, but you may want to look in on him."

"I will do that." Vereshchagin began methodically repacking the rucksack and bergen that Gu had packed for him. "Did you two also discuss artificial hibernation?"

"We have problems with artificial hibernation." Coldewe drummed his fingertips on Vereshchagin's desk. "*Zuiho*'s icebox consists of two 144-unit bays. Bad news is that one of the bays was mothballed eight years ago—the Imperial Navy hasn't been moving very many people around lately. *Zuiho*'s people spent the trip over fixing it up, and they still have a long way to go. I told *Aoba* and *Hendrik Pienaar* to send over what they have in the way of spare icebox circuitry over your signature, and I asked Meri Reinikka to go up there and roll up his sleeves."

Reinikka was a civil engineer by trade and a combat engineer by avocation. "What does Meri know about artificial-hibernation units?" Vereshchagin asked.

"Not a blessed thing," Coldewe said cheerfully, "but Meri expects to nap in one of those units, and *Zuiho*'s people don't."

Vereshchagin chuckled.

"After they finish sprucing it up, we'll still need to check that bay unit by unit," Coldewe continued, "so I don't expect to be able to use it for another two or three weeks."

"What do you propose?" Vereshchagin asked.

Coldewe passed across a list. "On D-plus-one, Aichi's first platoon, his biochem people, Jan's No. 1 platoon, aviation, the light attack crews, and third section of No. 9 go in the bay that's working. When we have the other bay operational, we'll put in Aichi's second platoon, the rest of No. 9, the recon, and a few odd bodies like you and Piotr. That leaves the scientists and the intelligence detachment awake to plan for eventualities, our support detachment to keep them from making too much of a mess of the place, and me and Esko to keep them from killing each other."

"I had planned on staying awake throughout," Vereshchagin said.

"You are not getting any younger, Variag-*sama*. Consider it doctor's orders; I spoke to Natasha. She thinks that the enforced rest will do the parts of you that need it some good. You'll have two or three weeks to snap the scientists into line, and after that any tangles that I can't unsnarl can wait until we arrive."

"All right, Hans." Vereshchagin scanned the list and scrawled his initials at the bottom. "How are things otherwise?"

Coldewe made a pretense of consulting his notes. "Surprisingly well, actually. Simon has scientists lined up, and Bukhanov and Karaev are moving the mountains and the heavens to get the supply situation under control. That, of course, leaves me free to discuss another important matter with you, which is the sauna."

"Pardon me, Hans. My age must be catching up with me," Vereshchagin found himself saying. "I thought you just said 'the sauna.'"

Coldewe plunged ahead. "The subject came up a few days ago—Valeska Remmar approached me, but I suspect she was put up to it." He cleared his throat. "I did a quick straw poll, and the vote in favor of retrofitting a sauna to our assault transport was a whole bunch to nothing."

"Hans, are you suggesting that we build a sauna on board an assault transport?" A deceptive calm suffused Vereshchagin's voice. "This is not something that people usually do."

"It doesn't have to be anything too fancy, and after all, we're probably going to be cooped up on board her for a couple of years. You know how our people love their sauna." Coldewe reached over to the terminal and called up a three-dimensional diagram of *Zuiho*'s interior. "I'm rather fond of it myself."

"Hans, we are extremely short of storage space as it is—"

"That's why I got Reinikka to work out the details." He pointed to two storage rooms near *Zuiho*'s outer skin. "We build it here—Mikhail found some real cedar panels to line the hot room, and insulating the cold room is no problem. Then we fill it up with food, and turn it on after we eat up what's inside. If anyone can build it, Meri can."

Vereshchagin shut his eyes. "What did the vessel's captain say when you discussed the matter with him?"

Coldewe pressed his index finger against his temple. "You may want to talk with him. He thinks I'm touched."

"I see," Vereshchagin said, trying not to laugh.

Esko Poikolainnen appeared. "Do you two have time to see Major Aichi?"

"Now is as good a time as any," Vereshchagin said.

Major Aichi entered and saluted. "Commissioner Vereshchagin, Colonel Coldewe, my company is prepared to reboard."

He hesitated. "Commissioner Mutaro has requested that I leave one platoon as an additional embassy guard detachment."

Vereshchagin looked at Coldewe. "Can we spare them?"

"I think so." Coldewe nodded. "It will simplify logistics."

Aichi inhaled deeply. "Subject to your approval, I have selected my No. 3 platoon to remain. In accordance with Commissioner Mutaro's instructions, I will leave my executive officer in command of them. Also, unless you advise me against it, I wish to exchange personnel between platoons."

Unsuccessfully masking the astonishment on his face, Coldewe nodded in agreement. "I think that's excellent."

Vereshchagin smiled. "I agree. I will leave you two to work out any details."

As he left, Coldewe shut the door firmly. "Major, I have something I need to go over with you, but first things first. Have you eaten?"

"No, sir."

"Here, try this." Coldewe picked up a combat ration on his desk. Taking a canteen from a shelf, he used the nozzle on the end to inject water into the ration. As soon as the plastic wrapper expanded, he popped the tab to heat it.

Aichi waited thirty seconds for it to heat and then opened it gingerly, stirring the contents. "What is it?"

"The label says ginger beef. Rate it, one to ten."

Aichi sampled it. Then ate a fair helping. "Perhaps a five."

Coldewe tried some himself. "Rusks and papaya must have been cheap this week. It's a five." He explained, "We have to produce our own arms, ammunition, uniforms, rations, and miscellaneous equipment. The legislature is a little tight with a rand, so we keep control to hold down costs. The company we use to produce rations is staffed by troopers' wives and they run it to suit themselves, which keeps the wives out of mischief, and if there's ever a problem with quality control, the production staff hears about it before I do."

"How interesting," Aichi said, beginning to think through the difficulties in maintaining a military force on an independent colonial world.

"Anjelica Degtyarov is the CEO, and basically, she buys up whatever the farmers are selling cheap, finds a good recipe that fits, and cranks out three or four years' supply with a little left over to sell on the civilian market. At the moment, we're running two shifts, and if we want to take any ginger beef with us, it has to be on the line by five o'clock this afternoon. Of course,

Anjelica says I have to eat the stuff before she puts it into mass production, which occasionally has its drawbacks. The cowboys celebrate a holiday called April Fool's Day, which is dedicated to the patron saint of pranksters, and after they served me up last year I thought I was going to die."

"I see, sir."

Coldewe leaned out the door and shouted down the hall, "Esko, tell Anjelica it needs more ginger." He picked a box up off the floor. "Next, Jan's people asked me to give your troops these berets."

"That is very kind of them." Aichi examined one of the silver berets, trying not to frown.

"Not especially. We took them away from some of the local thugs, although Jan's boys did pay to have them cleaned. They're probably hoping that I'll forget to rescind last month's order to nail anything in silver, which leads me to a delicate subject that I will attempt to discuss in a delicate way. Jan Snyman's company includes several dozen women—medical personnel, logistics personnel, even a few combatants. Your people need to be carefully briefed to understand that these women are fellow soldiers and need to be treated accordingly."

"Yes, of course," Aichi said, misunderstanding him, "this must go without saying."

"Major, if it goes without saying, I don't think it's going to go at all."

"I have utmost confidence in my troops," Aichi said stiffly.

"You don't sound convinced. Let me explain this differently. I was an Imperial officer a long, long time ago, and while I'm certain Japanese troops have changed since then, I'm equally certain that they haven't changed all that much. I've already looked over your roster and Captain Kobayashi's, and I see four individuals listed as nurses. While I don't doubt that these women have nursing skills, there's an 'and so forth' in their job descriptions, isn't there? In a word, they are comfort women."

Visibly embarrassed, Aichi nodded.

"The women that Jan is bringing aren't, and prostitution is not highly regarded on this planet. Soldiers being soldiers, your lads are going to think about testing the waters, and since these women are wives, girlfriends, and daughters, Jan's people are going to react very badly unless you make certain things absolutely clear to your people."

"Yes, Colonel Coldewe. However—"

"Major." Coldewe lapsed into obscure idiom. "Why don't we

make this the 'Come to Jesus' part of our little talk? To be quite candid, while Jan's people are well disciplined, if I took a poll tomorrow, some of them would describe your people as a waste of valuable rations, and on some of them, the veneer of civilization is decidedly thin. If one of your duller myrmidons were to utter a poorly phrased indecent proposal, or, God forbid, try the old grope with cash-in-hand approach, there would definitely be trouble right here in River City."

"Excuse me, please, sir?"

Coldewe smiled chillingly. "Mitsuru, your personnel presumably have mothers who would like them to come home someday. Ensure that your people treat female expedition personnel with the same courtesy that they extend to their mothers. Otherwise, hostilities will break out before we arrive."

Aichi saluted. "Yes, honorable Lieutenant-Colonel."

Thursday (1174)

FOR THE FOURTEENTH TIME, NATASHA SOLCHAVA-SNYMAN REviewed her list of pharmaceuticals, looking for something else to add to her already lengthy list of drugs. Frustrated, she switched her terminal off. Although, off and on, Solchava had more than a dozen years' experience as battalion surgeon for the 1/35th Rifle Battalion, she was uncomfortably aware of the difficulty in anticipating the medical needs of nearly four hundred men and women, counting ship crewmen, who would either be on or above a completely alien planet for a lengthy period of time.

Where Jan Snyman was golden-haired and had matured into a strikingly handsome man, his wife was plain and considerably older, and she showed it most convincingly in the frown lines in her face. The fact that Jan, who loved his wife dearly, never noticed and wouldn't have cared, alternately pleased and irritated her.

Anton Vereshchagin thrust his head through the doorway. "Natasha, may I interrupt?"

"You are not interrupting. I expected to see you at three, so you are only six hours early."

Despite having worn a military uniform for nearly twenty years, Natasha Solchava was the most thoroughly unmilitary person Vereshchagin knew. He shook his head and allowed her to thump and probe him. "And the verdict?" he asked.

She shrugged. "No different."

"I will not complain. I have not had the opportunity to thank you for coming along. I was not certain you would agree to do so."

"Jan and I discussed the matter and finally reached a decision in a calm, rational manner," she explained, methodically checking her instruments, "although I am sure that Jan would describe it differently."

"I believe that he has done so," Vereshchagin said diffidently. "You have been known to see things in a different light."

A momentary smile lit up Solchava's face, taking years off her age. "We only broke off our engagement three times."

"Jan says four." Vereshchagin's smile faded. "Natasha, you and Jan do not have to go if you do not want to. I could still take Degtyarov in Jan's place, and Commissioner Mutaro speaks highly of Dr. Miyagawa, who was his personal physician."

"And I am your personal physician. I thought about making Jan stay, but he would not have been happy. He and Hans are a little like small children these days." Her smile also dimmed. "The Tokyo mission was an opportunity for them like no other, but this is almost as important."

"At least as important."

"I think that he has always felt that he has had some special destiny, and he believes that this is it." She sighed. "His family had their annual gathering, and it was pathetic. He was like a caged bird."

"A caged falcon," Vereshchagin said, imagining the encounter.

"While I stood in the corner, talking to the wives, he did nothing but pace. He can't even be bothered to remember his cousins' names from year to year. I am always afraid for him, you know."

"Yes, I do."

"And now that fear is back." She closed her eyes.

"Have you spoken with Dr. Miyagawa yet?" Vereshchagin asked, changing the subject.

"He appeared mildly surprised to find that he would be sharing his facility. Although it was a struggle, we managed to work matters out. You know how disorganized civilians are." Although not known for her sense of humor, Solchava winked solemnly. "There was, however, a serious matter on which we failed to find agreement. Normally, one takes no special precautions against importing alien diseases. Although I am not aware of any instances here, I do know of instances where pathogens have ravaged various animal and plant species on other worlds. While the risk of direct transmission is somewhat remote, bacteria exchange plasmids of all types during conjugation, and Earth microbes occasionally exchange genetic material with alien microorganisms. This sometimes results in rather deadly new strains." She paused. "Even healthy human beings harbor huge reservoirs of microorganisms. While I do not foresee any substantial risk to expedition personnel—the body's defense mechanisms are quite effective—I do see a possibility that we might unintentionally infect Neighbor's inhabitants. The results would potentially be devastating."

Vereshchagin frowned. "What do you suggest?"

"I recommend that all expedition personnel undergo a ten-day treatment with an antimicrobial and a wide-spectrum antibiotic. This would significantly reduce the number of organisms to which we play host. The quarantine procedures for equipment brought back from the planet's surface should also be applied to equipment sent down."

"The last will drive Karaev to distraction, but it should not represent a major difficulty," Vereshchagin said, thinking aloud. "What was Dr. Miyagawa's objection to the ten-day treatment?"

"A significant check on the reproduction of antibiotic-resistant strains of pathogens is competition with other microorganisms. There is a small risk that in attempting to avoid an epidemic on Neighbor, we may in fact cause one on board ship. It will also occasion logistical difficulties in that we will not be able to place soldiers in artificial hibernation until the treatment is complete."

"Can it wait until we arrive?"

"When stressed, bacteria increase the rate at which they absorb scraps of DNA and patch it into their cells. Delaying until arrival would increase the risk to personnel sent to the planet's surface."

Vereshchagin frowned. "Can we shorten the treatment?"

Solchava shook her head. "Shortening the treatment would increase risk and provide little or no benefit. While the risk of causing a pandemic on Neighbor is slight, flushing our systems would reduce it. I have convinced myself that it would be unconscionable to expose the people there." She closed her eyes.

"You always had a strong streak of idealism in you. All right then. Go ahead, and tell Hans to adjust his schedule accordingly. We need our idealists desperately."

Solchava opened her eyes. "Anton, you are a complete fraud.

Despite your cloak of hardheaded pragmatism, you are the most confirmed idealist I know." She reached for his arm. "I might as well get you started."

Friday (1174)

IN THE COURTYARD, A SMALL FIRE WAS BURNING, AS SOLDIERS leaving sorted through the possessions they had accumulated: to be burned, to be given away, to be stored, and a precious few to be taken along.

Meri Reinikka and Piotr Kolomeitsev watched. "How are matters aboard *Zuiho*?" The Iceman asked.

"The ship's chief engineer and I keep having minor professional disagreements. He keeps using words like 'impossible' and I keep saying, 'Just let me show you,' and adding, 'you silly little pip-squeak' under my breath." Reinikka had given up command of one of the reserve battalions to come. He shook his head. "And now, I am a staff officer of all things."

"It is a job rarely done well. We will do it well, I think."

Reinikka gave him a curious look. "Is it true on Ashcroft you offered a three-day pass to anyone in your company who accidentally shot a staff officer?"

"Certainly not," The Iceman replied, scandalized. "I would never reward someone for shooting anything accidentally. In any case, the story originated on Cyclade."

Reinikka laughed and leaned his weight on the railing. "I still remember my old engineer platoon—what a thumb-fingered bunch they were. The only thing they did well was football, and fifteen years later, I still love them all."

"Despite dilation, time has a way of catching us short, Meri. Why did you agree to come?"

"I suppose I got tired of building roads designed by idiots for people I didn't much like, which includes my wife's family. I didn't want to end up like Lebanik, who is working to become a full-time lush. I'm not sure I'll have a home to go back to after this mission. It frightens me to think that things will go so smoothly that I might as well have stayed."

"I suspect you have little need to worry," The Iceman said distantly.

"Piotr, you were married once, weren't you?"

"Ages and ages ago. I carry her picture, but the only time I can see her anymore is when I am in space," Kolomeitsev said, vouchsafing some private secret. He looked at Reinikka. "Is she married?"

"What?"

"The one you left your wife for. We are not skilled at keeping secrets from one another."

Reinikka looked shocked. Then he laughed. "Yes, she is."

"Do you have regrets?"

"None."

"The best thing about time dilation," The Iceman said, "is that by the time we return, no one will remember."

"Or care," Reinikka added.

"I sometimes think to myself how anachronistic it is to travel to a far-off star with men carrying rifles, but men are territorial creatures, and stripped to its essence, war is a little man with a rifle sitting on a patch of ground until politicians finish arguing over who it belongs to. Because any place where we have a man with a rifle is ours," The Iceman said, "until someone wishes to pay the price for taking it away."

Saturday (1174)

IN THE EAST WING OF THE STAATSAMP, MATTI HARJALO PROPPED an assault rifle in the corner and threw a blanket over it to avoid offending visitors, and then began unloading items from a box. Ornate bookshelves trimmed in brass covered one wall of his new office.

The young student who had appointed himself Harjalo's secretary stuck his head inside. "Matti, there is a Captain Karaev here to see you."

"Ship him in."

Karaev—whose prename was Gennadi, which he hated—had straight, black hair and vaulted cheekbones that made him look strikingly oriental. He looked around the room. "Fancy place you have. What will you do with those bookshelves?"

Harjalo reached into the box and pulled out an old football. "Center right." He dropped it on the floor and followed through. "Swish! And score." He caught the rebound off the wall.

Karaev nodded. "I like it."

"When are you leaving?"

"Late tomorrow, if nothing else runs amuck." Karaev took the ball and tried a shot. "I have decided that I have no intention of being an intendance officer in my next life. I am beginning to see sacks of freeze-dried rations in my sleep."

"I haven't talked to Saki Bukhanov in years, but I'm still surprised he isn't going."

"Saki would have been Anton's first choice, but his wife now prefers murder to divorce, and either of the two to leaving." Karaev added wistfully, "I would have preferred a combat assignment, but combat assignments belong to younger men."

He unzipped a brown leather case he was carrying and pulled out a lutelike musical instrument. He pulled away the protective plastic and ran his hands over the smooth wooden surface. "My grandmother was a Khant, from Siberia. I inherited my strikingly good looks from her, as well as a *sankvyltap*, a sound maker."

"It looks like a Finnish *kanatele*," Harjalo said, taking it and handling it reverently.

"Finns and Khanty are distantly related, although a sea of Slavs separated them millennia ago. There is little left of my grandmother's people, which is why it came to my father and eventually to me. It is old, very old. The Mansi—another forgotten people who merged with the Khanty—used them for their bear festivals. It should be strung with reindeer tendon," Karaev explained. "I also have these." He pulled out a pair of *kees*, soft boots, ancient and stiff, made from reindeer skin and similarly encased in protective plastic. "I thought of giving them to a museum, but museums are for dead things."

"What do you want me to do with them?" Harjalo asked, accepting the items.

Karaev smiled, a secret smile. "Keep them for me. I do not think they should go with me, and I cannot think of anyone else to give them to. If I don't come back, burn them."

Harjalo nodded slowly. "If that's what you want. What about your umbrella?" As a platoon leader, Karaev had carried a battered black umbrella with six carefully patched bullet holes, which had earned him a reputation for eccentricity in very eccentric company.

"You never know when it might rain on one of these ships." Karaev stretched out a hand. "This is good-bye."

"For a while, anyway." Harjalo took Karaev's hand limply, with all a Finn's distaste for displays of emotion.

Karaev laughed and wrapped him in a bear hug. "I would love to stay and chat, but I'm not going to get any sleep tonight

as it is. Besides, you have another visitor waiting to see you."
He called through the door, "Anton?"

Vereshchagin walked through the door. Karaev said, "I will
leave you two," and left.

"Have a seat." Harjalo looked around. "Somewhere. It's been
a while."

"It is good to see you. I like your bookshelves."

"You came to say good-bye?"

"Among other things. I would like to make peace with you
before I go. I am also in hiding for the moment." Vereshchagin
picked the ball off the floor to read the names written on it.
"Maria and Simon Beetje have separated—at least Simon thinks
so—and I just approved Maria's request to come along."

"Simon is going to be very surprised."

"To say the least."

"They're both in the same field, so they're going to have to
work closely with each other. A transport is a pretty awkward
place to have a war break out. Are you sure they're not going
to try to kill each other?"

"Not entirely, but Natasha Solchava and I interviewed Maria
at some length, and I consider the risks acceptable."

"And you need her, I imagine. I remember Rikki telling me
that Simon's lab technique is terrible."

"This is correct."

There was an awkward silence. "I suppose I should say that
history is repeating itself," Harjalo said. "You're flying off to
glory, and I'm here picking up the pieces."

"Is that really the way you feel, Matti?" Vereshchagin asked
quietly.

"No, not really." Harjalo thought for a minute. "I've decided
that the problem with saying horrible things you can't take back
is that even after other people forget, you don't."

"I did not wish to leave without seeing you. I am glad that
you are willing to see me. How are you and Rikki getting
along?"

Harjalo snorted. "Better than you might expect. I made her
promise to go out on a date."

"What did you promise her in return?"

"That I'd go out on a date. Apparently one of the campaign
workers I ran through the grinder took a liking to me, although
for the life of me, I can't put a face to her name."

Vereshchagin allowed himself to smile. "Does Rikki have
plans for you?"

"She asked me to take over the interior ministry until she finds someone else for the job."

"Is she looking for someone else?"

"I suppose not." Harjalo grinned, then his face grew serious. "I spoke to Betje Beyers. You knew that Rikki was one of the few people I couldn't say no to, and you put Betje up to pushing my name forward."

"I suggested you, yes. Are you sorry that I did?"

"No. But you use people damnably hard, Anton, and you know it."

"Yes, I do."

"You used Hendrik Pienaar. You used Raul and Hanna. And now you're using Rikki, which makes three generations of the same family. Isn't that a bit much, even for you?"

"Matti," Vereshchagin said, suddenly tired, "I have asked Sergei to watch over her. I would ask you to do the same. I do have a conscience."

"Too much of one sometimes. I'll do it." Harjalo reached over to embrace the man who had been his closest friend. "Take care of yourself, Anton. Take very good care of yourself."

Sunday (1175)

AS SIMON BEETJE MOVED FORWARD TO FIND A SHUTTLE SEAT, HE jumped when he felt a hand on his shoulder. "Oh, hello, Hans. You surprised me."

Coldewe patted him on the back. "Sit here with me. We only let really green herring sit in the first two rows. Fewer people get thrown up on that way."

Feeling really green and fishy, Beetje obediently strapped himself into the seat beside Coldewe, who gave him an odd look. "That's right, you were born here, weren't you? Is this your first flight?"

Beetje nodded. "Are there other novices on board?"

"Not many. We try to send all of our people up to practice drops as often as we can arrange. I did notice one of your colleagues up there stuffing himself with motion-sickness pills."

"That would be Connie Marais, professor of linguistics." Beetje swiveled his head around. The soldiers in the seats behind him were relaxed. Many of the older veterans were already asleep.

"Anton and Piotr ought to be along in a minute. Try and relax, we still have more cargo to load, so we'll be here another fifteen minutes."

"I am all right. I didn't expect us to be delayed."

"Final departures are never on time—it's a long way to Tipperary." Coldewe grinned. "An attractive young woman from the landrost's office came by in a black dress cut down to her navel to take testamentary instructions. I'm not sure she realized it, but her dress was loose and every time she bent over to apply her seal, you could see her knees and points in between. I think some of our lads had their laundry lists sealed and may have gone through the line more than once. Are you sure you're all right?"

"Oh, I am fine," Beetje lied, as his wife left her seat and sat down in the seat to his left with a stony expression. "There are diamonds in stardust, so I was thinking about plucking a few as we go by."

Coldewe opened his eyes. "Eh?"

"Tiny carbon motes crystallized by the heat of a sun. Of course, they're only about twenty-six angstroms across, so we aren't exactly going to get rich from them," Beetje babbled.

"I suppose not." Coldewe looked up and snapped his fingers. "Father Nick, over here! I want you to meet someone."

Father Bosenac elbowed his way forward.

Coldewe made introductions. "Father Nick, this is Dr. Simon Beetje and Dr. Maria Beetje, two of our biologists. Father Nick is our specialist in comparative theology. He also plays a good hand of skat."

Bosenac blinked his eyes. "I'm still a little stunned to be here."

"I should have warned you. Although Anton almost always tells the truth, he never tells all of it." Coldewe assured Simon and Maria, "You'll like Father Nick. Good skat players are hard to find." He turned his attention back to Bosenac. "Insofar as we have a table of organization, you belong to Simon."

Simon reached into his briefcase and pulled out a folder. He selected a piece of paper from it and handed it to Bosenac. "These are directions. When we arrive, please go straight to your cabin, log yourself on to the computer, and read through the ship's instructions. Hans has assured me in great and colorful detail that the ship is going to be an absolute madhouse, and he asked me to especially emphasize the fact that the fewer people we have wandering around, the better off we will be until things get settled." He looked at the sheet. "It says here that you will be by yourself, so I'm afraid your cabin won't be very large."

"That's all right," Bosenac assured him as the red check light came on.

"You might also want to skim through the capsule summaries on the other scientists aboard."

"The light means to strap yourself in," Maria Beetje interjected, silencing her husband. Bosenac did so. Moments later, the shuttle took off.

When the shuttle docked, Simon and the rest of Suid-Afrika's scientific contingent went down a deck, turned left, and went aft to find their cabins.

As Simon stopped to check the number on his door, the door to the cabin on the opposite side of the corridor opened, and a stocky man with a fringe of beard almost ran over him. From the printed directory Coldewe had given him—and directed him to leave behind because of the weight—Simon recognized the man as a physicist from the Go-Nihon contingent.

"Ah, Dr. Ferenc Szuba? I am Simon Beetje from the University of Suid-Afrika."

Szuba grabbed Simon's wrist and clung to it like a drowning man. Hovering behind Szuba, Beetje saw the physicist's diminutive wife, Pia, the expedition's lead sociologist.

"Beetje, Simon? Yes, someone spoke of you! I am Ferenc. This is Pia. It is outrageous! You are from Suid-Afrika—you know these military people, no?"

"Yes, I know Colonel Coldewe, and Commissioner Vereshchagin, a little." Beetje tried to pry his arm loose, without success.

Connie Marais and a genial geologist named Johan Hartlieb squeezed past them as best they could.

Tightening his hold with his right hand, Szuba pulled Beetje into his cabin and waved his left arm for emphasis. "Perhaps then you can reason with them! This Commissioner Vereshchagin, I just saw him." Szuba's swarthy face burned with indignation. "And when I tried to explain the matter, I was turned away! Turned away! Can you believe this?"

Conscious of Pia Szuba's unblinking gaze, Beetje permitted himself a small lie. "Perhaps the commissioner didn't understand. What, ah, is the problem?"

"Pia and I were moved out of our cabin into—this cubicle!" Szuba snapped his fingers. "Like that! Like that! Can you believe it?"

Beetje nodded. "Yes, Dr. Hartlieb and I have the cabin across from you."

"Then you are outraged, too!" Szuba gestured at the interior of the cabin to emphasize the depths of his outrage. "This is an affront!" He released his grip. "Where is Dr. Hartlieb? We will remedy this injustice!"

Dimly recollecting the dictum to try logic when all else fails, Beetje tactfully tried to explain. "We are moving over two hundred soldiers and scientists on board right now, and a lot of space is being taken up with supplies for them. Accommodations are a little cramped, I'm afraid." A sudden flash of inspiration struck him. "Did you see Commissioner Vereshchagin's cabin?"

"Eh?" Szuba was slow to switch gears.

His wife tugged at his sleeve, speaking for the first time. "That is what I was saying to you, Ferenc. It looked like a broom closet."

"A lot of soldiers—Suid-Afrikans and Imperials—are moving into cold sleep, and the rest are stringing hammocks in the forward areas. They are pretty well packed in there." Like cocoons in a mulberry tree, Beetje thought, remembering his father's greenhouse.

"Smaller? But—he is the commissioner!" Szuba said plaintively.

"Ferenc," Pia Szuba said.

Ferenc tilted his head. "Yes, sweet?"

"You are making a fool of yourself."

His shoulders slumped. "Yes, sweet."

She stretched out a delicate hand, which Beetje took. "Ferenc and I are pleased to make your acquaintance, Dr. Beetje." She gave him a quizzical look. "You say you are with Dr. Hartlieb? I thought I saw your wife's name on the roster."

Beetje choked. "Ah, it is a . . . complicated situation for me to explain."

"When you and Dr. Hartlieb are free, come by and see us and we will open a bottle of wine." She dug her elbow into her husband's well-padded ribs. "We are most anxious to hear about Suid-Afrika. And about Commissioner Vereshchagin." Pia rewarded Beetje with a smile that transformed her face. "Right, Ferenc?"

IN VERESHCHAGIN'S BROOM CLOSET OF A CABIN, HANS COLDEWE leaned back in his chair and whistled for approximately the thirtieth time. "Could we have accidentally gotten on a cruise ship?"

"There are comic-opera overtones to this," Vereshchagin agreed.

"Who's next to see?" Coldewe asked. He qualified this statement. "Who *haven't* we seen?"

"Mutaro's deputy, Dr. Seki," Vereshchagin said equitably.

"That's right." Coldewe raised one eyebrow. "What do we want from Seki, and how did you keep him away this long?"

"When I spoke to him, I explained the handicap I was working under in taking control of the expedition at this juncture, and I asked him to prepare a confidential appraisal on all of the scientific personnel from Go-Nihon for me."

"That will flatter his ego."

"Even if it does not tell me very much about the scientists on board, it will tell me a great deal about Dr. Seki."

Coldewe closed his eyes for a second. "I turned Kasha loose in the galley. I heard lots of bad language. We may or may not get dinner."

"I wonder how Prigal is adjusting."

"By now, he probably wishes he was back driving a taxi. What did Commissioner Mutaro say when you bid him farewell?"

Vereshchagin stretched out. "He said that he had met several great men in his lifetime, and that he hoped it would not go to my head."

"That makes two of us."

"He also said that he hoped that various gods would guide my footsteps. Under the circumstances, he did not wish to leave it up to just one."

Coldewe laughed. "He's a nice old gentleman, a brave one, too, and he's going to go home in an urn when all this hits the mud."

"Yes, Hans, all that is true and more. When His Imperial Majesty's ministers hear of my appointment, they will collectively have hysterics."

They heard a soft knock at the door, and Esko Poikolainnen entered. "Dr. Seki is here to see you."

Inagi Seki was a short, thin man dressed in a rumpled gray suit and a white shirt. Although his hair was almost completely gone from the top of his head, he wore it long around the back and sides.

Vereshchagin nodded. "Please, take a seat. As Commissioner

Mutaro perhaps explained, Colonel Coldewe will be commanding the military contingent."

"I am pleased to make your acquaintance, Colonel Coldewe." Seki's expression was fixed, and his bright, unblinking eyes were strangely birdlike. "Nevertheless, I earnestly hope that your special services will not be needed."

"Given the disparity in forces, so do I."

"Would you care for some tea?" Vereshchagin asked.

"Decaffeinated tea, if you please."

Coldewe reached around to the samovar and drew him a cupful.

"Colonel Coldewe, are you Suid-Afrikan?" Seki asked.

Coldewe shook his head. "No, I am originally from Tübingen, Germany."

"How interesting. At one time, I corresponded with a colleague in that city." Seki sipped at his tea and then passed Vereshchagin a hefty written report. "I hope that this appraisal fulfills your requirements, Vice-Commissioner."

Observing Vereshchagin's slight look of dismay, Coldewe vaulted himself back into the conversation. "You were an academic before you became Commissioner Mutaro's deputy. Isn't this an unusual progression?"

"Yes, this is correct." Seki's face relaxed slightly. "Although a colonial posting of this nature may strike you as unconventional for a person with my academic qualifications, I became dissatisfied with the caliber of decision making in public life and determined that the most effective use of my talents would be as a ministry official."

Vereshchagin set Seki's report aside. "At the outset, perhaps I should make my objectives and your role clear. In accordance with Commissioner Mutaro's directive, I intend to study and establish contacts with Neighbor's inhabitants, evaluate the possibilities for trade and technology exchange, and assess the planet's military potential. Lastly, should these people prove hostile to mankind, I intend to take appropriate action of a military nature."

Seki took a sharp breath. "I should mention that I am not completely in agreement with Commissioner Mutaro's emphasis on military measures. History teaches that where one looks for hostile intent, one finds it. Mankind is outgrowing warlike pursuits. As a scholar, I believe that it simply is not rational for another intelligent species to manifest hostile feelings toward us so long as we demonstrate our peaceful intent and explain the benefit that would accrue from peaceable cooperation. Nevertheless, I earnestly hope to work with you in a fully cooperative spirit."

Vereshchagin caught Coldewe's eye. "I appreciate your bringing your views to my attention. Although military officers are professionally required to assess military potentialities, I assure you that Colonel Coldewe and I both hope that military preparations prove unnecessary."

Seki bowed his head.

"I intend to utilize you as my bridge to the scientific community. Please convey to the scientists on board my further hope that in working together, we can establish the proper spirit of cooperation in all of the personnel assigned to the expedition," Vereshchagin concluded.

Seki studied first Vereshchagin's face, then Coldewe's, then he again bowed his head. "I am most gratified." He looked at Vereshchagin curiously. "Have you lived in Japan? I cannot help thinking that you have a curiously Japanese spirit for a foreigner. Perhaps this was a factor in Commissioner Mutaro's decision that I was not aware of."

"Yes," Vereshchagin said, controlling his expression, "I attended war college there and I have also visited on other occasions." He added as an apparent afterthought, "We will have to integrate our Suid-Afrikan scientists into the various scientific working groups, once they are settled. I think it would be helpful for me to sit in on working-group meetings over the next several days."

Seki nodded thoughtfully. "I will speak to the working-group chairmen and arrange this. I would be honored to accompany you."

"Excellent." Vereshchagin's face grew pensive. "I would like to keep this as informal as practicable. Perhaps we should attend separately."

"Ah, yes, that would appear to be an excellent solution, honored Vice-Commissioner."

"A second matter that concerns me is water usage," Vereshchagin continued. "Recycling is never completely efficient, and *Zuiho* had to load six tons of water on arrival, which is far too much. As a measure to curb wastage, I intend to turn off the taps for six hours each day."

Seki bowed his head. "As you wish, Vice-Commissioner."

"Are there any matters that you wish to raise?" Vereshchagin asked, not quite hopefully.

"If I may comment, Commissioner Mutaro's decision to bring

nuclear weapons particularly concerns me. I do not foresee any circumstances wherein we would use such weapons, and leaving them behind would eliminate any possibility of accident. It is a matter of some concern to myself and to the scientists on board."

"I understand your feelings in this matter, but I concur with Commissioner Mutaro. Nuclear weapons give us a possible means to avert more serious conflict," Vereshchagin said politely.

Seki accepted the decision gracefully. "There is one matter I have been asked to bring to your attention. During the voyage over, the kitchen staff prepared individual meals to order, which was very convenient for the scientific personnel aboard. A number of scientists have asked whether this service will continue."

Hans Coldewe saw Vereshchagin flinch as if stuck with a needle.

"I regret not." Vereshchagin carefully measured his words. "As you are perhaps aware, we have only a small fraction of the support personnel considered necessary for a force this size, and I do not deem it appropriate to divert personnel to perform catering duties. The dining facility will serve meals at appropriate hours. Tea and soup will be available at other times. It is, of course, traditional to wheedle the cooks occasionally."

"But Commissioner Vereshchagin, really!" Seki persisted. "Experiments and creative thinking cannot be confined to set hours. Surely my scientists are entitled to the same considerations as your officers receive."

"I am not aware of any ongoing experiments that require constant attention," Vereshchagin said, with a studied absence of emotion, "and my officers will eat with everyone else at the appropriate hours, as I will."

Perhaps sensing his mistake, Seki bowed. "Thank you, Vice-Commissioner. I look forward to working together with you." He bowed again and left.

Coldewe stared at Vereshchagin, trying not to laugh. "I can see why you wanted me in here instead of The Iceman."

"You can mimic youth and naïveté, whereas with Piotr it is readily apparent what one is dealing with, which many people find unsettling," Vereshchagin said absently, tapping his pipe against his thigh. "What is your impression of Dr. Seki?"

"A nice man, a true scholar." Coldewe's eyes glittered. "He

seems to possess all the virtues that one associates with academics and bureaucrats, as well as all the vices."

"And what is your definition of a scholar?" Vereshchagin asked dryly.

"If you ask a scholar why Indians put dog manure on the corn plants, he'll start you off with the Creation myth, drag you through the religious observances of several generations of remote maternal ancestors, and finally opine that it is undoubtedly a purely symbolic rite rooted in clan connections. Unless, of course, he's had psychiatric training, in which case he will attribute it to subliminal Oedipal urges."

"I see." Vereshchagin smiled. "And why do Indians put dog manure on the corn plants?"

"It scares off the rabbits."

"And the moral of the story?"

"I don't know why the Neighbors shot at the probe, but five will get you ten it's because they're not very friendly. And if that's the case, it might be nice to have nukes. *And* chem, *and* bio."

" 'The fact that slaughter is a horrifying spectacle must make us take war more seriously, but does not provide an excuse for gradually blunting our swords in the name of humanity. Sooner or later, someone will come along with a sharper sword and hack off our arms,' " Vereshchagin quoted.

"Clausewitz," Coldewe guessed, and Vereshchagin nodded.

Coldewe tilted his head. "Is the tea?"

"Is the tea what?"

"Decaffeinated."

"No."

Coldewe consulted his wrist mount, which he had remembered to reset to ship's time. "What's next?"

"Piotr and Captain Yamawaki are discussing the first law of transports, which is that the crew expands to occupy any and all underutilized space. When they fail to reach a meeting of minds, I will intervene. I also have to prepare my oration about our mission." Vereshchagin stared at the far bulkhead. "Has Aksu told you the interesting part? He believes that a small band of Major Aichi's noncommissioned officers are planning to assassinate me on the voyage over to redeem the honor of Imperial Japan. Major Aichi has not said anything, but he appears worried."

"We're a happy ship, aren't we? Anton, take a nap. You could use one," Coldewe urged. "Piotr can handle Captain Yama-waki."

"I will do that," Vereshchagin said dreamily. His eyes began to close.

Coldewe's eyes widened. "Not here!" he announced. "All of the unscheduled callers who wish a moment or twenty-two of your time would be scandalized to find you here asleep. Go to my cabin." He pulled out his *kukri* and began toying with the blade. "I can handle things here."

Vereshchagin smiled and followed his advice.

Hours later, from atop an ammunition box in the ship's gymnasium, Vereshchagin explained to assembled soldiers, scientists, and ship's crew that humanity would come to an alien planet bearing an olive branch outstretched in one hand, with a sword prudently concealed in the other.

Monday (1175)

HANNES VAN DER MERWE, FORMER SILVERSHIRT AND ONETIME terrorist, cleaned his apartment for the last time. Packing a lunch and a few personal items in a knapsack, he wrote out a short note that was, in effect, a last will and testament. In it, he left no apologies for what he had done with his life. After thinking for a bit, he wrote another note to his current girlfriend. He placed the first note neatly on his bed and posted the other. Then he got in his car and drove to the resort town of Roodepoort, on the shore of the Tethys Sea.

Greeting a few old friends at the marina warmly—much too warmly, some of them recalled later—he sailed his boat out a few kilometers, took in his sails, ate lunch, and waited.

The sea, empty of edible fish and boats to catch them, was calm and glassy. Van der Merwe trailed his fingers in the water.

A Sparrow reconnaissance plane materialized almost directly overhead. With its odd angles, forward stabilizers, and an extremely quiet, eight-bladed adjustable-pitch prop, a Sparrow was bizarre in appearance, but extraordinarily difficult to see. Molded from sheets of thin, radar-absorbing composite material, the plane had tiny sensors in the skin to gauge ambient light, allowing a computer-driven network of photoelectric cells to match the light coming in and even, to a degree, the background coloration on the opposite side. Used as a utility aircraft, a Sparrow could carry two men easily, and a third in a pinch.

Taking advantage of the sea breezes, the pilot, Flight Sergeant Ivan Kokovtsov, throttled back almost to stalling speed and adjusted his stabilizers to literally hover over the boat.

"Well, you took your sweet time," Van der Merwe told Kokovtsov over the hum of the engine. Slinging his knapsack, he went down and opened the boat's sea cocks. Then as Kokovtsov skillfully rested the plane almost on the boat's deck, Van der Merwe climbed on board.

He watched his boat sink into the Tethys Sea. Her name was the *Seebodem*, as if Van der Merwe had always known in his heart that the sea bottom would be her resting place. "I'll miss her a little," he told Kokovtsov. He might have been talking about the boat, and he wasn't sure himself.

When Kokovtsov made no reply, he said, "I'm sorry I had to bring De la Rey down. He was the only honorable one of the bunch, you know."

"I don't follow politics," Kokovtsov admitted, breaking his habitual silence when flying. "What name do you want to use? Aksu says that with the Imps and scientists around, you might as well get used to it on board ship."

"I'll have to give it some thought," Van der Merwe confessed, sorting through the possessions he had brought away. "Something Finnish, I think."

Late in the evening, the final shuttle took off for *Zuiho*.

Transit (Day 1), HIMS *Zuiho*

REVERTING TO OLD HABITS, VERESHCHAGIN'S PRIVATE COUNSEL of war met at 5 A.M., ship's time, over tea in his cabin. As The Iceman rubbed ointment into his hands, Hans Coldewe asked, "How did your scientific group meetings go?"

Sipping his tea, Vereshchagin involuntarily rolled his eyes. "We added the Suid-Afrikan scientists to the working groups yesterday. Although I would prefer to wait before initiating changes—"

"How bad was it?" Kolomeitsev inquired.

"Bad. In addition to the initial contact team, we have four working groups; linguistics, social sciences, biological sciences, and physical sciences. I suggested to Dr. Seki that integrating the Suid-Afrikan scientists had increased the size of the groups to awkward levels, and that we should create an interdisciplinary group to investigate specific issues."

The Iceman chuckled. "And you will stuff the recalcitrant and stupid into the interdisciplinary group in the hope that they will merely annoy each other instead of keeping everyone else from getting anything done."

After a moment's silence, Vereshchagin said, "I sincerely hope, Piotr, that no one else on board knows me as well as you do."

Coldewe smiled and stirred sugar into his tea. "Of the five groups, who takes the palm?"

"The linguists," Kolomeitsev guessed.

Vereshchagin shuddered, remembering. "They had a presentation of sorts for me. As they carefully assured me, English has a chaotic sentence structure and is replete with synonyms, homonyms, and words that convey very little meaning. Accordingly, they recommended against using English as our mechanism for communicating with Neighbor's inhabitants."

"Did they suggest a substitute?" Kolomeitsev asked.

"They advanced several, which is to say that they offered no solution at all. Doctor Marais, who was sitting in for the first time, suggested teaching the aliens Afrikaans because it is a 'purer' language; I think he was making a joke. Someone else mentioned Japanese."

"Japanese often fail to comprehend what is being said in Japanese," The Iceman reflected. "What was the final verdict?"

"The team piously suggested that we consider developing an artificial language to facilitate communication."

Coldewe's hand shook, spilling some of his tea. He pulled out a handkerchief and began dabbing at it. "Dear God. I've tried reading *Finnegan's Wake*."

"Exactly. I told them politely that if some sort of lingua franca develops, well and good, but that we do not have the time—"

"Or talent—" The Iceman commented.

"To create a new language from scratch. I firmly suggested that we use English supplemented by standard English sign language for the deaf as an additional means for conveying meaning." Vereshchagin shook his head. "I confess that I had the devil's own time making them think it was their idea."

Coldewe grinned. "I assume we have someone on board who knows how to sign."

"In that we do not know whether the aliens communicate as we do, we have two of the best available on Suid-Afrika. They appear to be nice women. One has never been married and the other was recently divorced. Both of them knew Hanna Bruwer-Sanmartin in her teaching days. I reminded them of this and of the fact that they would be two unattached women on a ship full of bachelor scientists and soldiers without shame, Hans, or hesitation."

Coldewe laid his head on Vereshchagin's desk and laughed himself silly.

The Iceman commented, "You realize that on Earth, there is a complete plan for how to contact an alien species in some bureaucrat's drawer."

"Where it has moldered for the past fifty years." Vereshchagin shook his head wryly. "Can you imagine what it must read like?"

Coldewe slapped the top of the desk. "Can we get a copy? It would liven up parties for decades."

Vereshchagin set his cup down. "I hear footsteps. That must be Dr. Seki." He looked at Kolomeitsev. "Apparently, it did not initially dawn on Dr. Seki that our curbs on water usage would also apply to scientists. Last night, the good doctor told Simon Beetje and others that my decision to turn off the taps was nonsensical and should be reversed, so I think that I am about to throw a fit."

"Oh, dear," Coldewe said.

Vereshchagin raised his voice. "Dr. Seki, please, come in."

Seki opened the door and looked around. Even with Vereshchagin's hammock neatly rolled and hung, the cabin did not seem large enough to hold five chairs, a small table, and a field desk.

Vereshchagin waved him to an unoccupied seat. "Doctor, this is my operations officer, Major Piotr Kolomeitsev. I do not believe that you have met."

"My pleasure," Kolomeitsev said politely. Kicking the door shut, he pulled a fourth cup from a receptacle in the wall, which he handed to Coldewe to fill.

"Yes, of course," Seki replied, clinging to his chair.

"We were just discussing the difficulties inherent in contacting an alien species," Vereshchagin explained.

"Yes, Dr. Iwao mentioned your interest in this problem." The tea steadied Seki. "Dr. Iwao appeared quite disturbed by the interest you took. Indeed, he mentioned that the linguistics group reached an important decision to use spoken English and English sign language as the primary means of communication, but he felt that your interference with the discussion nearly prevented them from reaching this conclusion."

"Excuse me." Coldewe coughed, pointing to his throat. "Something got stuck."

"Dr. Iwao would be an excellent choice to head the interdisciplinary team," Vereshchagin said. "Perhaps there are a few matters I should clarify." His manner changed perceptibly. "Our resources are severely constrained. As I understand it, the art of science consists of framing problems, proposing solutions, and gathering information to prove or disprove these solutions. Although I will solicit advice, it is fair to state that the problems that I deem essential to completion of our mission will receive priority, and that ultimately, I will decide how we will allocate resources, including scientists' time."

Seki swallowed hard.

Vereshchagin laid his cup aside. "Regrettably, a few scientists regard data as personal property. Yesterday, I even noticed researchers taking what appeared to be a proprietary interest in lines of inquiry. The computer system on board currently allows researchers to restrict access. I have asked Senior Communications Sergeant Poikolainnen to remove these restrictions, and I would direct you to subtly make each researcher aware of my strong feelings."

He paused. "To better regulate such matters, I would like you to chair a three-person committee to promulgate standards and review complaints on data sharing and similar matters. The committee will have the power to impose sanctions. I will hear appeals from the committee's decisions. Please think about this overnight and let me know who you would propose as committee members."

"The committee will handle minor infractions," Kolomeitsev explained, amused by Seki's reaction, "and operate as a safety valve for personality clashes."

"Honored Vice-Commissioner, indeed, we cannot do this!" Seki protested.

"Indeed, we can, Doctor." Vereshchagin stared at him coldly. "Failure to do this could ultimately cost lives, and this I will not allow. To avoid misunderstandings about what I can or cannot do, I will ask each person not already subject to military law to sign a form consenting to the imposition of military discipline." He passed one across. "The Suid-Afrikan scientists have already signed."

"Vice-Commissioner, one simply does not court-martial scientists and throw them in jail!"

"An assault transport has no jail," The Iceman pointed out. "In space, we shoot people who give us adequate cause."

Dr. Seki clutched at his chest.

Vereshchagin smiled very slightly. "We appear to have basic differences in assumptions, which leads me to a different point. Soldiers and scientists are often ignorant of each other's professions. Soldiers will gather much of the data that the scientists will interpret. For this expedition to succeed, the military personnel and scientists aboard must work closely together and understand each other's cultures. To this end, I intend to assign the personnel on board to discussion groups. Hans, would you care to add anything?"

"Yes, my people know a lot about staying alive under hostile conditions, and discussions will allow them to pass along survival skills." Remembering some of the truly fey spirits from old No. 2 platoon, Coldewe added, "For example, certain scientists on board ought to know what observations about soldiers are likely to get them half killed."

Vereshchagin nodded. "Doctor, as a final matter, inasmuch as there is a military dimension to our first contacts with the aliens, I have selected Company Sergeant Wanjau to be the military representative on your initial contact team. Please provide him with copies of committee minutes and any other relevant documents."

Isaac Wanjau was a special kind of soldier, and Vereshchagin intended to convey a very subtle message to Neighbor by his presence on the team.

He inquired politely, "Would you care for more tea?"

Seki bowed his head, visibly shaken. "No, thank you, honored Vice-Commissioner. Indeed, if I might be excused."

Vereshchagin nodded his head. "Certainly, Doctor."

The Iceman poured himself another cup of tea. "I think he understood."

Transit (2), HIMS *Zuiho*

PERHAPS MORE WORRIED ABOUT THE FEY SPIRITS FROM OLD No. 2 than he was willing to admit, Vereshchagin scheduled the first discussion group after supper and asked Simon Beetje, the new head of the biological sciences working group, to be the moderator. Beetje and Dr. Seki agreed to select Dr. Tomomi Motofugi, a linguist on the contact team; Pia Szuba, head of the social sciences team; a graduate assistant, Takanobu Ohkata; and chemical technician Ijo Kumata. Coldewe, in turn, picked Lieutenant Mika Hiltunen, Section Sergeant Dmitri "Bory" Uborevich, Assistant Section Sergeant Kalle Kekkonen, Superior Private Brit Smits, and Corporal Makato Omori from Major Aichi's company.

After introductions, Beetje explained, "I really do not have a set agenda. Today, I would just like for us to talk before I go back to Dr. Seki and Colonel Coldewe with specific recommendations as to how to structure future discussions."

Hiltunen nodded. "That's fair."

Beetje looked around the table. "Would anyone like to hazard an opinion as to why we are here?"

Motofugi, staring at the far wall, allowed himself a smile.

"Anyone?" Beetje repeated.

Hiltunen, the archetype of a dour Finn to all outward appearances, scowled. "Colonel Hans likes to call it citizenship training. I guess we're here to see if you're worth dying for."

Dr. Motofugi smiled. "But the mission of this expedition is to establish peaceful relations with Neighbor's inhabitants, the naturales, so obviously there is no question of anyone dying."

Dr. Seki had selected the name "naturales" for Neighbor's inhabitants. The soldiers had accepted it with a carelessness that suggested their devotion might prove insincere.

"They shot at the probe. Might shoot at you, too," Hiltunen pointed out.

"But because we are there to reach out a hand in peaceful friendship, there is no reason for them to do so once we establish our peaceful purpose," Motofugi said, obviously believing that he had scored a point.

Hiltunen looked down his long nose at the linguist. "You been shot at, Doctor?"

"No, however—"

"I have. Often. Don't like it much. Do know that when human beings shoot at you once, they tend to do it again."

Motofugi appeared annoyed. "But these are not humans!"

"Don't know that that matters. I do know that their shooting at the probe gives me a better reason to say they might shoot at us than it gives you to say that they won't." Hiltunen bared his teeth in what was intended to be a pleasant manner. "Colonel Hans said to be polite, so I won't argue, but there are different ways to make these people want to establish peaceful relations. If your way works, I play a few hands of tarok and catch up on my reading. If it doesn't, we have ours."

Simon Beetje intervened to keep the discussion alive. "Dr. Seki suggested that we might talk a little about how each of us perceives authority."

Pia Szuba laughed nervously. "Subroto writes, 'Within the military tradition there exists the general belief that, heedless of difficulties, all problems can be overcome if the right orders are given.' "

The soldiers present looked at one another. Hiltunen said, "Bory, you've been unusually quiet."

Uborevich leaned back in his chair. "If it's the Variag or Colonel Hans giving the orders, this Subroto might be right. I can't say I'd trust just anybody."

Kalle Kekkonen laughed. "There speaks a cautious man. You've been hit, what, twice now?"

"Yeah, once on Ashcroft and once on Suid-Afrika." Uborevich's lean Kalmyk face appeared troubled. "It's worse getting shot the second time—then you know they meant it the first time. Sometimes I have dreams." He shrugged. "It's my body telling me that I don't want to get killed, right?"

Motofugi stared. "Is this true?"

"Of course, it is!" Uborevich said, with heartfelt indignation. He looked around for support. "Colonel Hans said that you academic types were naïve and credulous folk, and that if I didn't stick to the truth, I'd be eating soggy rice balls." Uborevich shuddered at the prospect and glared at his colleagues. "And these people would tell him, too!"

Mika Hiltunen nodded solemnly, with a certain light in his blue-gray eyes. "Oh, *ja*. It would be too much fun not to."

"Now, the way I look at it," Uborevich continued, "most people like to fight, unless they think they're going to get their tails kicked doing it—it's in their genes or something—so why should these people be different?"

Motofugi folded his hands in front of him and said sharply, "To say that human beings act out aggressive behavior patterns that are encoded in their genes is attributable to a paradigm that smacks of biological determinism; indeed, this paradigm appears to have racist overtones."

Simon Beetje cleared his throat, taken slightly aback.

Hiltunen shrugged. "Kalle, it's your turn to say something."

Kekkonen grinned. "I wouldn't know about that biological

determinalism stuff—I took engineering courses when I went to school nights. But people have been bashing each other with stone clubs for a long time and haven't stopped yet, so it wouldn't surprise me too much if Neighbor's people turned out to be unfriendly."

Pia Szuba gave Dr. Motofugi an irritated look. "I believe what Dr. Motofugi is trying to say is that mankind is capable of rising above the need to kill, and we would hope that the naturales are capable of doing the same."

"Yes, I hope so, too," Corporal Omori said.

Ohkata, the graduate assistant, said, "I believe that many of us are not too certain why soldiers had to come at all if our purpose is to establish peaceful relations."

"I can't say for sure," Hiltunen said slowly, "but Simon, did Captain Sanmartin ever tell you the story about the kiwi?"

"This all sounds very interesting, but I fail to see—" Motofugi began to say.

Hiltunen's expression stopped him. "Captain Sanmartin was a professor for a while, and I can't remember him ever talking to us like we were idiots."

"Yes, I heard the story from him," Simon Beetje said hastily.

"A kiwi's a kind of bird. On New Zealand where they live, there weren't any animals to eat them, so they lost their wings and ran around on the ground," Hiltunen said, impatient to make his point. "The ones that laid the biggest eggs survived best, so after a while, you have two kilogram birds laying eggs weighing half a kilogram."

Motofugi opened his mouth, but Pia Szuba laid a hand on his arm.

"When people came to New Zealand, some of the dogs they brought went wild and pretty much wiped up the kiwis because they couldn't fly and couldn't lay enough eggs to replace their losses. Captain Sanmartin said that it wasn't healthy for a species to adapt to not having predators around. I think he meant that this applies to people, too."

"I can envision two equally unfortunate tendencies," Technician Kumata said unexpectedly. "The first is the belief that mankind is morally superior to the naturales because we possess the fusion drive and they do not. The second is that because humans are frequently a violent species, the naturales are morally superior to us. Some men are good and wise, but many are not, and I suspect in my heart that the naturales may be much like us in this regard."

"I think that you are on to something there," Hiltunen said slowly.

"Why do men become soldiers?" Pia Szuba asked, taking her cue from Beetje.

"Brit, how about you?" Hiltunen asked.

Smits shook his head. "No story here, sir."

Hiltunen was silent for a moment. Finally, when no one else spoke, he said, "Funny, everybody knows how much I hate talking, and I'm doing most of it. I knew one boy in Helsinki, a friend, with the usual things—a fiancée, a university degree, a job. He didn't get along with his family, but people don't. He met the wife of one of his firm's partners, a young wife, and somehow—it doesn't matter how—he ended up being her lover. Not her first, but he didn't know."

Szuba nodded, watching the movement of Hiltunen's hands. Although far more cosmopolitan than most Finns, Hiltunen was not one to "laugh, cry, or kiss," as the Finns say. Nevertheless, the emotion there was easy to read.

"Something went wrong. She got pregnant, which was awkward because her husband's tubes were tied. He found out, fired the boy publicly, and went home to confront her. He collected antique guns. Nobody knows who said what, but he shot her and shot himself. Finland isn't a very big or violent country, so it was a nine-week sensation, and when it was over, the boy emigrated to a world called Esdraelon."

Kekkonen and Uborevich, who both knew the story, kept quiet.

"New colonial worlds take building up, and there are worse things than soldiering. Our battalion had ties there, and when some people he knew joined, the boy did, too. Time dilation being what it is, when you join the colonial infantry, there's no point in going back, so he stayed. Now, I don't know two such stories, but I do know one."

"Two lives taken," Pia Szuba said, "and the baby's as well."

Hiltunen's face never changed. "It came out at the inquest that the boy wasn't the baby's father, but as I said, he was just a boy. We mostly came along to do recon work—finding out facts for you scientists without anyone knowing we're there. If we can accomplish our mission without killing anybody, so much the better." He allowed himself a small joke. "It isn't as though we're paid at piecework rates."

Transit (3), HIMS *Zuiho*

AN UNFAMILIAR MAN OPENED VERESHCHAGIN'S DOOR WHEN Nicola Bosenac knocked. "Father Bosenac, please enter. Anton should return shortly. We have not met. I am Piotr Kolomeitsev."

Although The Iceman was deft in his movements, Bosenac registered the gun he had held in his hand and was disturbed by it.

Music was playing inside the room. Kolomeitsev shook Bosenac's hand with unexpected strength in his long fingers and waved him to a seat.

When the piece ended, Bosenac acknowledged it. "Very nice."

"Tchaikovsky. It lacks strength. For that one needs the German, Beethoven. I like it, nonetheless. Anton appears to be delayed. May I assist you?"

"Perhaps you can. The ship's calendar says that it is Saturday. I would like to hold services tomorrow."

"Of course. Hans or Jan should have gotten with you, but we are all pressed for time. Can you be ready at seven?"

Bosenac nodded. "Bread and wine?"

"We have both available, although a great deal less of the latter than the former. You know our esteemed chief cook, Kasha Vladimirovna? Speak to her."

"Thank you. Where is Gu these days?"

"We have him on the night shift. That is his chair you are sitting in. I will be sure to mention your service to him."

The Franciscan studied The Iceman. "Perhaps you would care to attend."

"I am no longer a Christian."

Bosenac looked dismayed, and The Iceman chuckled. "Forgive me, Father Bosenac. I am not an atheist. Atheists, I have found, have a touching devotion to their own creed." He leisurely studied Bosenac's face. "I am not hostile to the idea of God, merely indifferent. To become a believer, I would have to repent of killing a considerable number of people, and at this stage of my life, I find the idea risible."

Recovering slightly, Bosenac sensed Kolomeitsev's desire to fence. He responded carefully, "I have learned that what may seem folly to man is not necessarily folly to God."

"I am told I have my own god to worship, and I understand

he is a vengeful god, ever vigilant and filled with wrath."
Kolomeitsev appeared to be watching to see Bosenac's reaction.

"One of the minor poets?"

"Very minor. Hans Coldewe does not drink, but when he
does, his muse slips forth, although equally befuddled."

"I see."

"Perhaps you do," The Iceman conceded. "I met your bishop
once. We had very little to say to one another."

"My bishop is very sure in his faith. He fits people into cat-
egories. Some keep Christ's law and await salvation, others do
not." Bosenac did not know why he was explaining this to a
man he hardly knew. "I am not nearly as certain of what God
wants."

Kolomeitsev smiled. "My profession rarely lends itself to cer-
tainties. Although Anton admires your bishop, he would not
have welcomed him. Anton needs a conscience, you see."

"Excuse me?"

The Iceman chuckled. "Anton can weigh military and political considerations to an uncanny degree, but now he feels that
the rules he has learned may not apply. It is, of course, very unsettling to have to learn new things at our age."

"I will help as well as I can, as well as God can guide me,"
Bosenac said, his mind racing. He noticed that Kolomeitsev's
face was scarred. "There is a God. I believe, with all my heart
and soul. And his mercy is infinite."

"Perhaps there is," The Iceman said indifferently, "but very
far away. On this planet, I think that we will find that the Devil
is much closer."

Before Bosenac could fill the silence, Vereshchagin opened
the door and walked inside. "Father Nicola. How good to see
you."

The Iceman raised one eyebrow. "I have been keeping him
amused for you." He stood. "Father Nicola, it has been a pleasure."

Kolomeitsev left, and Vereshchagin found himself a seat. "I
trust that Piotr was polite to you."

"I have no complaint," Bosenac replied.

"I am encouraged. Piotr is an excellent actor, and he enjoys
playing to the image people have formed of him. There is more
to him than is apparent."

"I'm certain of that," Bosenac replied dryly. "We discussed
scheduling services at seven tomorrow. I hope you can come."

"I will attend." Vereshchagin smiled. "We may have the makings of a choir. I trust the singing of our reconnaissance platoon did not offend you."

"No, I rather like 'Jesus Was a Recon Trooper.' But you're quite right, there is something else I'd like to discuss with you. I've been doing some reading, of history mostly, and listening to my parishioners." Bosenac drew in his breath. "I noticed a pattern to the European voyages of discovery. The ships would kidnap a few natives, to Christianize and train as interpreters."

"Please continue."

"Few of them returned home. Some forgave their captors and taught them much, but most died of disease and homesickness. I know how important it is for us to know how the naturales see, how they hear, what they think, but as ignorant as we are of their physiology and psychology, taking a few of them prisoner would be little short of murder."

Vereshchagin smiled very, very stiffly. "I assure you, Father, this is not a flying saucer and I am not a little green person from Mars. We will do no extraneous kidnapping. At most, a little grave robbing."

Bosenac bowed his head. "Thank you, Commissioner." He hesitated and spoke again, "When I came to the door, it troubled me that Heer Kolomeitsev answered it with a gun in his hand."

"This is not something I would prefer to discuss, Father," Vereshchagin said quietly. "Nevertheless, it is not always necessary to travel to a faraway star to find enemies."

Transit (4), HIMS *Zuiho*

"HOW VERY NICE FOR YOU TO SHOW ME AROUND, COLONEL Coldewe." Deltje Brink, the younger of the two sign-language interpreters, had a mischievous light in her eyes. "Can you spare the time?"

"If I didn't, my officers would schedule me for a physical, so it saves me time in the long run." Coldewe hesitated. "You wouldn't have a relative—"

"My cousin Anneke. She mentioned you. You never asked her out." Deltje winked. "It shows good taste on your part. Your soldiers won't mind me?"

"You haven't been around soldiers very much, have you?" Coldewe knocked on the door to the compartment where the intelligence detachment and the soldiers designated for the contact team were billeted. "Anybody home?"

Corporal Kobus Nicodemus opened the door. "Come on in, sir. Company Sergeant Wanjau and Lieutenant Aksu aren't back yet, so we are swapping lies with each other."

Brink looked past them at the wall. "What is that? It is very pretty."

"It's an icon. Kobus paints them," Coldewe explained. "Fedya Venedikov taught him how. He's really quite good."

"Thank you, sir." Nicodemus tried not to smile. "That's not what you usually say."

"A foolish consistency is the hobgoblin of little minds. With consistency, a great soul simply has nothing to do. Everyone, this is Juffrou Deltje Brink, one of our sign-language interpreters. I brought her here to meet some students." Coldewe made introductions all around. "What is that you're drinking, and are you going to offer us any?"

"Would you like some beer, Juffrou Brink? We made it ourselves," Nicodemus asked politely, plinking the flask twice with his index finger.

"You just got here," Brink exclaimed, accepting a mug.

"Major Reinikka set it up for us when he went aboard to work on the icebox bays," Superior Private Brit Smits, a contact team member, assured her. "This is our test batch."

Coldewe sampled the brew. "I'd age it another hour if I were you. So whose war story are we interrupting?"

The story was Intelligence Sergeant Paavo Heiskanen's, and more followed. Aksu appeared, grinned, and left again.

After three or four more, Brink rose to her feet. "I'm not used to sitting cross-legged like this."

Coldewe pointed. "This batch is kind of strong. Down the corridor, first door on your left."

As the compartment door closed behind her, Nicodemus asked hesitantly, "Sir, is, ah, she here with you?"

Coldewe spread his hands. "Kobus, as far as I know, the lady is unattached."

Nicodemus, Smits, and a third Afrikaner, an intelligence specialist named Kelly, produced coins. "Odd man out gets to ask her out first," Kelly suggested. Heiskanen, a phlegmatic Finn, almost choked.

The three of them tossed. Nicodemus peered at his. "Heads."

Smits had tails, and all eyes turned to Kelly who intended to see which response suited him best.

"It has to be one or the other," Smits said in a severe voice. He then asked Colonel Coldewe and Intelligence Specialist

"Hanno Toernvaenen," who bore a remarkable resemblance to one Hannes Van der Merwe, to please stop laughing.

The door opened. "It was occupied," Brink explained breathlessly. Her eyes took in the tableau. "*What* is going on?"

Transit (5), HIMS *Zuiho*

JAN SNYMAN RHYTHMICALLY SLAPPED HIS HAND AGAINST HIS thigh several times. "Maybe if we run through this one more time, I can pretend I understand." Snyman was deliberately being obtuse during the first read through of the tentative operations plan The Iceman had drafted, as he usually was when he thought something was calculated to get his people killed unnecessarily.

"Certainly, Jan," Coldewe assured him.

"If the naturales suspect that we have recon teams roaming around, our people may end up dead, but you want to insert them using an Imperial shuttle that is *not* adequately masked against detection, and you don't want to use any tricks to conceal the shuttle's departure from *Zuiho*. The happy natives will see the shuttle coming and going." Snyman threw his hands up. "Why don't I like this?"

Kolomeitsev intervened. "Jan, the first task that we have assigned the teams is to set up projectors broadcasting a message of peace and goodwill. Neighbor's inhabitants will know we have landed. I want them to think that we set up the projectors and left. With Kokovtsov exercising his usual skill at low-level insertion, I do not expect them to be able to track the actual drops. If they spot Kokovtsov leaving *Zuiho* and returning, they will believe that they can observe our shuttle departures. This will allow us to resupply the recon teams without their presence being suspected."

"We need to work a mild deception here, Jan," Coldewe explained. "In the words of the prophet, you can fool some of the people all of the time, and you can fool all of the people some of the time, but you can't fool all of the people all of the time. We want to mislead the naturales into thinking they can spot all the shuttles leaving *Zuiho* so that they won't be tempted to improve their detection capacities to the point where they actually can spot all shuttles leaving *Zuiho*. This way, the only shuttles they'll see are the ones we *want* them to see."

Snyman conceded the point. "All right." His company sergeant, Isaac Wanjau, smiled.

Coldewe looked at his other officers. "Everybody take the plan back and see if you can pick it apart. We'll take another look at it when we arrive and update our data."

As the compartment cleared, he asked Major Aichi, "So, what did you think?"

With the bulk of the recon platoon committed in two-man teams and Snyman's No. 9 and No. 10 platoons assigned as the reaction force, Aichi's men had been relegated to a general reserve.

"I had hoped for a greater role for my personnel," Aichi confessed. "If places could be found for even one or two of them, it would help in maintaining morale."

The Iceman nodded, and Coldewe sighed. "All right, pick out a few people who can operate independently, and we'll see what we can do."

Aichi smiled, like a sunburst. "Apart from this, I found the concept of operations entirely fascinating. Very few of the details would have occurred to me."

"So little has changed over the past few decades and so much," Kolomeitsev said, almost to himself. "Hans, may I speak with Major Aichi for a few moments?"

"Of course."

The Iceman took a vacated seat and Aichi did the same, almost by reflex. "I assume you have read about us."

"Yes, sir. I have," Aichi said, bowing his head slightly. "It would have been derelict for me not to do so."

"Once there were, what? Two hundred twenty combat battalions in the Imperial defense forces?"

"Yes, sir, twelve years ago. Now there are far fewer."

The Iceman's eyes drifted and then captured Aichi's. "Of those 220 battalions, no more than eighteen were true colonial battalions—the battalions that left Earth and never returned. Ours was the last. The rest were all disbanded a generation ago. On Earth, the handful of officers who understood the colonial infantry are retired or dead. Many things occurred on the fringes of empire that Earth only dimly understood. Different rules apply." The Iceman asked Coldewe, "Hans, is Hiltunen still out in the corridor?"

Coldewe nodded. "It sounds like him. Want me to get him?" He smiled at Aichi. "You know you've been at this too long when you know your people by their footsteps." He opened the door. "Mika? Can you come in here for a minute? We are discussing the colonial infantry."

Coldewe guided Hiltunen into the room. "Mika was a rifleman when I first came to the battalion."

Hiltunen bared his teeth in what passed for a smile. "We made his first two weeks miserable."

"Mika, for Major Aichi's edification, what possessions do you own?" Kolomeitsev asked.

Hiltunen reached into a side pocket. Pulling out a leather purse, he tossed it on a chair.

Aichi raised his eyebrows.

"What do you spend your money on, Mika?" Coldewe asked, half humorously.

"Good meal, sometimes. A restaurant meal is nice, sometimes. Don't tell Kasha. Sometimes on a woman." Hiltunen looked wistful, remembering some of Suid-Afrika's matrons. "I go listen to music sometimes."

"Thank you, Mika." Kolomeitsev returned Hiltunen's billfold. When Hiltunen left, he explained, "Kasha Vladimirovna has been the C Company cook for nearly thirty years and is now the expedition's chief cook. It would wound her feelings to know that Mika voluntarily dined elsewhere."

His eyes were half-slitted. "Mika deposits nearly every rand of his pay in the battalion bank. He has been doing it for twenty years. He receives interest on this money, and I know that he is a fairly wealthy individual, although I would wager that he neither knows or cares how much he has. He fixes up a barracks room or a fighting position as well as any man, and when the moment arrives, he leaves it without a backward glance. In the universe, there are very few men like him. Think of a monastic order, and you perhaps will understand the colonial infantry better. For many of us, the battalion has been our home and our family. In a true sense, the men we have brought with us are the last, the very last. The battalion that we left behind is an excellent fighting force, but its home is now Suid-Afrika."

"We've never been very good at spray painting the brown grass green, but the best-dressed army usually loses anyway." Coldewe grinned. "About the only bad habit we allow our people is shooting foreigners."

The Iceman closed his eyes. "Major Aichi, Anton and I have looked at your file and discussed you. If things go well on this expedition, you will become an admiral someday."

He smiled at Aichi's small gasp of astonishment and opened

his eyes. "The colonial infantry is something very special. It is something that Earth needs very much. When you become an admiral, make them understand this."

"*Hai*, Kolomeitsev-*sama*," Aichi said.

Transit (6), HIMS *Aoba*

"DOOR'S OPEN," DETLEF JANKOWSKIE SAID, WITHOUT LOOKING up from his computer, "not that there's a lock on it." He looked up. "Captain Kobayashi."

"Jankowskie-*san*." Kobayashi shut the door and flourished a bottle of whiskey. "May I interrupt?"

Jankowskie shut down his terminal. "If you can't, the bottle in your hand can. Sumitomo?"

Kobayashi nodded.

Jankowskie looked around the cabin. "Nicolas is familiarizing himself with your night shift, so he won't be back for hours yet. I have some dirty glasses here somewhere. Pumping me for information?"

Kobayashi nodded. "It would seem indicated. It would also be better if we understood each other more."

"Suits me well," Jankowskie said, reaching for a pair of glasses. "On a long voyage, one has to get along."

Several hours later, Kobayashi lifted the bottle and stared critically at what was left of its contents. "I have another bottle in my cabin." His speech was slightly slurred.

Jankowskie waved his hand. "I wouldn't want to drink up your last bottle. Besides, we've got at least a year ahead of us, and all I brought was a bottle of brandy."

Kobayashi considered this. "The supply ship might bring more."

"We're also running out of lies to tell each other."

Kobayashi considered this. "True."

"Anyway, where were we?"

"You were telling me to tell Commander Nitobe that he is completely wrong."

"Right." Jankowskie used his hands to demonstrate. "Two corvettes against a frigate is not a fair fight if they separate for an anvil attack. I'm going to wreck whichever one is closest and then go after the other one at my leisure."

Kobayashi grinned and poured himself another finger of whiskey. "Nitobe insists he could withstand your fire long enough for the other corvette to engage."

"What's he base that on, computerized damage projections?" Jankowskie shook his head. "Computer's only as good as whoever programmed it. I've seen a corvette go up."

"So you have reminded me," Kobayashi replied dryly. "Commander Nitobe is an exceptionally brave man."

"That's something you never know about until people start shooting." Jankowskie shut his eyes to clear his vision and then focused them. "It's funny the things you remember. First rebellion, there was a lieutenant-colonel named Higuchi, a nervous little guy—passed over for promotion. You wouldn't think much to look at him." Jankowskie shook his head. "When the spaceport was about to get nuked, he stayed to get the aircraft off. He did, too. The Variag wanted to name the new spaceport after him and got talked into calling it something else, which is something he regrets."

Kobayashi took a gulp from his glass. "I find the first rebellion interesting."

"We had a terrible time getting Admiral Lee and his people to believe that the pot was boiling."

"I hope we will not encounter similar difficulties on Neighbor."

"If anyone can sniff out trouble, it's the Variag," Jankowskie averred. He laughed as Kobayashi reached awkwardly for the bottle. "Here we are, with absolutely nothing in common."

"Except age, temperament, and a love of ships." Kobayashi shook his head. "We have much in common." He checked the level of the bottle. "Although not as much liquor as before."

"There's no trusting coincidences around the Variag, but I don't see how he could have planned this." Jankowskie stretched his legs across the floor and leaned back against the bulkhead. "You know, Nicolas and I were the last members of the ship's original crew. Excuse me, the ship's original Suid-Afrikan crew. My officers probably thought they'd retire before I did."

"A ship command is all I ever wanted. And yet were it not for this expedition, I would be on my way to Earth to retire."

"What did you plan on doing?" Jankowskie asked with renewed interest.

"Marry. Look for a salaryman's position. Were you ever married?" Kobayashi tried to splash some more whiskey into Jankowskie's glass.

"I considered it once. Her name was Suzanne. Here, give me

some more of that." Jankowskie took a sip from his glass. "In the colonial infantry, you only marry if your spouse can find a place. Suzanne didn't, and I'm not sure she wanted to. I asked Colonel Hans for permission anyway, and he said no. I said a few things to him."

"This would have been after your battalion had settled on Suid-Afrika."

Jankowskie stared down at his hands. "I'm not sure I ever expected us to deploy, but someone did, and Hans didn't think I'd be available tied to Suzanne. He was really quite nice about it, he arranged for me to take command of one of the reserve companies and lined up a job for me. But when the time came, I couldn't go through with it." He looked up at Kobayashi. "You understand, don't you?"

"Yes. I understand completely."

"She married an engineer. She sent me a picture when her first kid arrived. And you?"

"My own circumstances were distressingly similar." Kobayashi examined his glass. "I find it painful to discuss. Did the same happen to Sery-*san*?"

Jankowskie laughed. "Not Nicolas. Nicolas married the *Hendrik Pienaar* and scrapes the other girls off like dirt on his shoe if they get clingy."

A thought occurred to Kobayashi. He leaned forward. "Could you take this ship? The way you took the *General Hendrik Pienaar*?"

"Not until I sober up." Jankowskie tried to make a joke out of it. "Excuse me, not unless I sober up."

"We found your submachine gun."

"Gods." Jankowskie tried to clear his head. "Karaev, our intendance officer, is old school. No nonsense. We were lieutenants together. I hope you didn't steal the firing pin. He'd take it out of my pay."

"We did not." Kobayashi flashed a smile. "As you say, on a long voyage, one needs to get along."

Transit (7), HIMS *Zuiho*

COLDEWE SPOTTED DR. SEKI EATING ALONE WITH A READER propped up in front of his nose. He picked up his tray and walked over. He cleared his throat. "Is this seat taken?"

Seki looked up, momentarily bemused. "Oh, Colonel

Coldewe. I did not see you. Please join me." He turned off the reader. "I apologize for my lack of sociability, but one sometimes falls into bad habits. I was reading *Frequency of Paedomorphosis in the Origin of Higher Taxa.* I sometimes enjoy things from outside my field."

"I do, too," Coldewe confessed, who was rereading *Old Surehand* for the eleventh time.

"Are we eating Finnish or Russian, today?" Seki inquired.

"This is Russian," Coldewe explained, digging into his buckwheat porridge.

In a Solomonic decision, Vereshchagin had directed Kasha Vladimirovna to serve Japanese food three days a week, and Russian, Finnish, and Suid-Afrikan meals the remaining four. After most of the military contingent went into the icebox, the ratio would change.

Bemused, Seki pressed down much too hard on his plastic fork and broke a tine.

"Must have had a bubble," Coldewe said, passing his across. Because power tapped from the fusion drive was the one thing that a transport never ran short of, after food scraps went to the fish and plants in the hydroponic section, dishes and tableware were melted and remolded, rather than washed.

"I often dine alone," Seki said.

"I do, too. Too often." Looking around to make sure Kasha the cook wasn't watching, Coldewe pulled a tube of hot sauce out of his pocket and squirted it onto his piroshkis. "Pardon my manners; would you like to try some?"

Seki put a few drops on his plate. Coldewe noticed that he didn't ask for more.

"So, Colonel Coldewe," Seki said, "I presume that you wish to discuss artificial hibernation."

"The first group goes under four days from now, and Meri Reinikka tells me we'll be ready to fill the second bay a week later. Anton is going with the second group, which leaves me with only a handful of cells to fill—eleven to be exact. The question is who we put in."

"All of the scientific groups are working diligently. We have barely scratched the surface of the probe data. Is it possible to leave the final eleven cells unfilled?"

"Possible, yes. Practicable, no." Coldewe smiled. "As Karaev, my intendance officer, reminds me on a constant basis, for planning purposes, every day, a man or woman requires 3.08 kilograms of food, 0.12 kilograms of medical supplies, 0.76

kilograms of personal-demand items like toothpaste, 3.47 kilograms of assorted ammunition—I forget the rest, but you get the general idea. Plus an additional 4.6 percent for packaging."

He finished his lunch and pushed his tray away. "Eleven spaces times 180 days adds up to a reasonably tall mountain, and we don't have anywhere near the reserve we'd like in the event that a supply ship is late. I've been on half rations, and I can truthfully say that I don't like it much. Filling those spaces might mean the difference between staying and going home just when things are getting interesting."

Seki smiled. "How can I possibly resist such eloquence? May I give you the names tomorrow?"

"Tomorrow is fine."

Seki took a deep breath. "The ship will seem quite empty with nearly everyone in hibernation."

"Eh? Yes, it will."

"At such times, it often becomes difficult to recall one's purpose." Seki removed a small wallet from his coat pocket and toyed with it.

Something struck Coldewe. "Are you married, Doctor?"

"Oh, yes. I have three very fine children. I carry their pictures with me." He pulled them out and passed them across. "Bringing my family with me on this expedition was considered, but ultimately it was decided that it would be best if they remained behind. As you must imagine, ensuring that children receive the proper schooling is a matter of importance."

He took the pictures from Seki, knowing as Seki undoubtedly did what effect separation and time dilation would have on his marriage and his children, and for the first time, he felt a degree of respect—and pity—for Dr. Inagi Seki.

Transit (7), HIMS *Zuiho*

WHEN HIS DISCUSSION GROUP ENDED, SIMON BEETJE FOUND JAN Snyman waiting for him in the corridor. "How did it go?"

"It was very interesting."

The crease of a smile altered Snyman's face. "So have you and Dr. Motofugi sold Mika on intergalactic peace and beinghood?"

"I doubt it."

Snyman smiled and began singing a verse to "The Whistling Pig" in a clear tenor voice.

Someday, there won't be fighting, they'll put the guns away,
*   Men will love each other, and join their hands to pray.*
Peace will come forever, men won't get shot and die—
*   And on that day, the pigs will spread their wings and*
*   learn to fly!*

Beetje winced. "I am glad that hasn't come out in our discussions."

"It would have been wasted. 'Blessed are the peacemakers,' " Snyman quoted, " 'for theirs are the labors of Sisyphus.' "

"If that is one of Hans's better lines, please spare me his worst." Snyman and Beetje had once been classmates in school, although Beetje now felt inexpressibly older. He gestured. "What do you need from me?"

"I need you to sit down with my recon teams and tell them what kind of flora and fauna you want us to provide."

"Most of them know already." Beetje stopped when he saw a note taped to his door. "Damn. That must be from Maria."

"Waste of paper," Snyman said sympathetically.

Beetje took the note and thrust it carelessly in his pocket. "You know, Jan, what I'd really like right now is a cold bottle of beer."

Snyman gave him a strange look. "Come on."

He walked Beetje to the compartment he shared with Isaac Wanjau and took a vacuum flask from a storage receptacle. "Here. There's about half a liter left. It's not bad. My sergeants make it. If you want more, go down to A43, knock twice, and say that I sent you. A refill will cost you three rand or the equivalent in yen."

Beetje raised both eyebrows. "What if Colonel Vereshchagin finds out?"

"Who do you think sets the price?"

Beetje blinked hard. "But why the 'knock twice' and 'Snyman says'?"

"Tradition, Simon, tradition." Snyman waved his hand. "Anton is very keen on tradition. Besides, it keeps the soldiers occupied during the voyage, and it's actually kind of fun. Oh, if they ask you for the password, say 'Elandslaagte.' "

Beetje shook his head. "It still seems rather strange."

"I asked Hans about it once. The best I could get out of him was the observation that the science of economics is based on the fundamentally flawed proposition that human beings in a given situation will choose to behave in a rational manner."

Transit (8), HIMS *Zuiho*

MAJOR AICHI TOUCHED THE INTERCOM. "AICHI HERE. COLONEL
Coldewe, could you come to the ship's gymnasium? We have
had an accident. I regret to say that one of my noncommissioned
officers is dead." Although outwardly calm, Aichi felt himself in
a state of shock.

"What happened?" Coldewe's voice was cold.

"It occurred during training. I am afraid that it was my fault
entirely. We have initiated changes to ensure that such a tragedy
does not recur," Aichi replied, sidestepping the question neatly.
"The man was a fifteen-year veteran. In his own mind he served
his emperor well. I wish to give him full military honors."

"Certainly. Is everything under control there?"

Aichi could sense the slight confusion in Coldewe's voice.
Conscious of the soldiers watching him, Aichi willed himself to
remain upright. "Yes, Colonel. I am in complete control of the
situation."

The Iceman turned his pistol in to the armsroom.

Interlude

AS *ZUIHO* SETTLED INTO A ROUTINE, A FRIENDLY DISPUTATION
developed between Father Nicola Bosenac, who maintained that
it was inconceivable that an intelligent species could exist without a conception of God, and Ferenc Szuba and Tomomi
Motofugi, who maintained with equal vigor that it was inconceivable that two intelligent species could independently dream
up something that idiotic.

Partisans of both points of view proliferated until "Snack Bar"
Meier earned himself a certain grudging respect by prudently in-
vesting enough money on both sides of the proposition to guarantee a profit regardless of the outcome.

Two months into the voyage, Maria Beetje traded cabins with
Dr. Hartlieb, Simon Beetje's roommate. No one in the scientific
community quite had the nerve to ask Simon what he thought of
the swap, and life pretty much continued as it had before.

Transit (171), HIMS *Zuiho*

"WELL, DEKE, ANOTHER PLANET. YOU UP FOR A LANDING?" Kalle Kekkonen stopped and whistled softly. "Look at those people in line."

DeKe de Kantzow pulled up beside him. "Frosting hell! We'll be here half an hour before we get fed."

Men come out of extended artificial hibernation painfully thin and hungry as hamsters, and most of Major Aichi's first platoon was already lined up out in the corridor waiting to get into the ship's cafeteria.

"They could have spaced us out of the icebox better."

"Frosting transport crewmen never change," de Kantzow grumbled. He thought swiftly. "I got an idea."

Kekkonen shook his head emphatically. "Oh, no. Oh, no!"

De Kantzow stepped to the end of the line. Suddenly, he let out a piercing whistle and followed it with a whooshing sound from deep in his lungs that seemed to emanate from the corridor walls.

"Meteor strike! Meteor strike! Up there! Clear the compartment! Clear the compartment!" Kekkonen yelled, reluctantly acting out his role.

The line of startled Japanese soldiers parted like the Red Sea and raced each other for the rear exit.

"Not bad," de Kantzow murmured, checking his time display. "Twenty-six seconds. Nimble little buggers, aren't they?"

"Just how long do you think we're going to get away with this, anyway?" Kekkonen asked as they walked into the cafeteria, which was mostly filled with No. 9 platoon.

"Long enough to eat." De Kantzow rubbed his hands together. "Smells good. Kasha frosting did herself proud. You know, some things about this frosting business never change." He squinted. "Who's she chasing back there? It looks like Prigal. He's pretty nimble, too."

None of the other diners evidenced concern. Kekkonen nodded. "The old lady still has good wheels."

As *Zuiho* made her final approach, Hans Coldewe converted her forward storage area into a football field, and the supply echelon and each of the five platoons set about putting together teams. Arguing that most of his people were scheduled to deploy with the first lift, Lieutenant Wessels, Snyman's reconnaissance platoon leader, was permitted to recruit players from the light attack personnel and other odd bodies aboard.

The scientific community also formed a team. As the rest of the ship duly noted, they had wonderful arguments on their way to last place.

Planetary Approach, HIMS *Zuiho*

AS *ZUIHO* SHED SPEED TO MAKE HER FINAL APPROACH, Vereshchagin quietly asked, "Can we obtain a visual image?"

Captain Yamawaki gestured, and Neighbor appeared as it was being seen from *Aoba*. The planet's surface, bathed in water, held a shimmering, ethereal beauty.

"Probe pictures didn't do it justice," Coldewe commented.

The inland sea nestled between the two halves of the planet's great world continent was a glimmer of light blue beneath the froth of clouds.

The Iceman nodded slowly. "As large as Eurasia."

"Larger," Coldewe retorted. "Besides, Eurasia is mostly Siberia and if you melted the permafrost, Siberia would fit in my bathtub."

Vereshchagin pointed to a great river that ran nearly the length of the eastern half of the supercontinent. Immense lakes caught behind dams graced its length like blue pearls. "On Earth, the first signs of man's presence that one sees from space are his irrigation works. Here, as well."

Yamawaki pulled his headset off. "Honored Commissioner, *Aoba* detects small quantities of orbital debris."

"We expected it, didn't we?" Coldewe gestured. "If the people down there didn't learn anything else from the probe, they assuredly learned that fusion bottles and spaceflight are possible, which eliminates two or three thousand dead ends."

"We will see what else they have learned," Kolomeitsev said.

"Captain Yamawaki, please advise Captain Kobayashi that he may move into sensor range and commence medium-altitude mapping passes." Vereshchagin added, almost as an afterthought, "Begin broadcasting the welcome tape."

The welcome tape, prepared by Esko Poikolainnen at the direction of Dr. Seki and Simon Beetje, was a twenty-two hour tour de force intended to convey the rudiments of written and spoken English. While Dr. Seki narrated slowly, pointing out objects and demonstrating actions, a split screen flashed the written text, with a light bar illuminating each word as Seki uttered it. Poikolainnen had done his best to ensure that the visual images were recognizable well into the infrared and ultraviolet wavelengths. Hologram imagery gave the finished project as much three-dimensionality as possible.

"What are the odds that they'll be able to decrypt your transmission?" Coldewe asked Poikolainnen, who was watching quietly.

"The audio shouldn't pose them too many problems." Poikolainnen shrugged. "As for the video, we'll see."

"We will, won't we?"

In Orbit, HIMS *Aoba*

ABOARD *AOBA*, THE HOURS SPENT MAPPING THE MAIN CONTInent's features with corvettes *Chokei* and *Jintsu* passed glacially slow. Periodically, *Aoba* disgorged a small, solar-powered reconnaissance satellite in a geosynchronous orbit as part of a growing network.

While the maps based on the probe's data were accurate, the warships could provide infinitely greater detail, and Vereshchagin was most interested in what had changed since the probe's visit.

At the twelve-hour mark, *Jintsu* docked to change crews, and *Aoba*'s second shift came on. Kobayashi, Jankowskie, and Sery remained on the bridge. To pass time, Jankowskie was playing solitaire. "Any increase in radio traffic?" he asked the signals rating for the fourth or fifth time.

"No increase since our arrival, sir. However, we do not have a sufficient baseline to determine whether this represents an increase over normal traffic." The rating reviewed his instruments. "It would perhaps also appear that a statistically significant percentage of the signals we are intercepting are random."

Jankowskie threw in his cards. "Ask a foolish question."

Sery, who had been napping in the sensor second seat, opened one eye. "Isn't it quiet enough for you?"

"Too quiet, perhaps."

Kobayashi pointed to the dull glow of lights. "We are coming over a thickly inhabited portion of the main landmass."

"Big cities, aren't they?" Sery commented.

"*Big* cities," Jankowskie agreed. A brilliant white pinpoint suddenly appeared on the darkened surface of the supercontinent below. "Oh, my sweet God. They just fired at us."

Kobayashi slapped the panel to sound action stations.

The petty officer manning the sensor sang out, "One missile." He checked his instruments. "At our current course and speed, I estimate impact in seven minutes, twenty seconds."

"Contact *Zuiho*," Kobayashi instructed his signals rating. "Commissioner, we have just been fired upon."

"Yes, we see it, too, *Aoba*," Vereshchagin's voice replied. "Can you evade?"

"Liquid fuel, most likely. From spectral analysis, it appears to be simple hydrogen-oxygen. We have the legs to run away unless it's a nuke," Jankowskie said soberly, leaning over Sery's shoulder to read the instruments himself, "but it is an awfully big puppy."

"*Chokei* requests orders," the signals rating said crisply.

"Give us standoff distance," Kobayashi instructed his navigator. "Tell *Chokei* to conform to our movements." He said to Vereshchagin, "Commissioner, I request permission to engage."

There was a slight pause. "I imagine Seki is telling Anton not to start ourselves off with these people by shooting back," Jankowskie said mirthlessly.

"It could conceivably be a scientific probe," the sensor operator volunteered doubtfully.

"The last one wasn't," Sery said.

Vereshchagin's voice replied. "*Aoba*, you have permission to fire. Vereshchagin out."

Kobayashi looked at Detlef Jankowskie. "Captain Jankowskie, please assume tactical command."

Jankowskie nodded appreciatively. "All right, Nicolas, you take over weapons station one, and I'll take navigation." As he pulled the ship into a parabola, he said conversationally, "Let me know if the missile alters course."

Seconds later, the sensor operator confirmed his suspicions.

"Nicolas, that's your cue. I will continue on this course and heading. Lay down a chicken-seed pattern and see if they run into it." For Kobayashi's benefit, Jankowskie added, "It looks like a modified launch vehicle, or maybe a modified long-range ballistic missile. I see a nose cap to protect it during reentry, but the rest of it doesn't look hardened. I don't think it's being controlled from the ground, so I want to try two-gram composite particles first. It isn't likely to recognize them as a threat, and even a couple of hits ought to wreck its circuitry."

"Firing," Sery reported, having run his calculations. "Two minutes twenty seconds to impact if it holds its course." Canted at an extreme angle, the composite-particle dispenser under his control spewed out several thousand tiny particles imbued with fusion energy from the ship's engines.

"The range is rather extreme for composite particles," Kobayashi reasoned.

"I know." Jankowskie said apologetically, "we wouldn't have tried manure like this on you." Two minutes passed.

"On target," the sensor operator said excitedly. "Hits."

Several seconds later, the missile's fuel leaked out just behind the second stage and erupted in a gout of flame. The missile's pieces began cartwheeling in odd trajectories.

"Missile destroyed," the sensor operator reported.

"Reassuming tactical command," Kobayashi ordered. "Have *Chokei* resume station. Prepare *Jintsu* for launch." He eyed Jankowskie. "Let us send out a pig and see if we can collect up some of the debris."

"Better tell them to watch for leaking radiation," Sery said, vacating his seat.

The sensor operator looked up, his eyes unnaturally wide. "Honored Captain, another silo is opening."

"Are there more silos at that site?"

"Four more, Captain."

The signals rating automatically patched Kobayashi through to *Zuiho*. "Kobayashi to Vereshchagin. Missile destroyed. Another launch appears imminent. Request permission to engage launch site."

Before Vereshchagin could reply, the second silo began to close.

Kobayashi didn't realize that he had been holding his breath. After a moment he said, "Dispatch corvette *Jintsu*. Prepare to recover debris."

In Orbit, HIMS *Zuiho*

"HARDLY THE RED CARPET," HANS COLDEWE COMMENTED, sweeping the tension from *Zuiho*'s bridge.

Vereshchagin rose from his seat. "That would seem to be all the fireworks for now. Hans, I wish to see an analysis of the destroyed missile as soon as practicable."

Dr. Seki also stood. "Commissioner, I would interpret the launch as a warning gesture. I am of the view that we should suspend mapping passes, and I respectfully request permission to go to the planet's surface immediately. I feel it to be vitally important for us to assure the naturales of our continued peaceful intentions."

"If their intention was to convey a message by firing at us, Doctor, I will pretend to be deaf. I would prefer not to encourage them to repeat the gesture. I will take your suggestion to initiate contact under advisement," Vereshchagin said, expressionless.

Captain Yamawaki bit his lip. "Is it possible that the planet's inhabitants may not have realized that our ships were manned until we fired?"

The Iceman chuckled. "How devastated they must feel!"

Seki played his final card. "Commissioner, even if the naturales are xenophobic as we now surmise, it merely heightens the need for immediate contact. In the long view, the only cure for xenophobia is prolonged contact and understanding."

"Or genocide," The Iceman noted.

"As I have said, I will take your suggestion under advisement," Vereshchagin repeated.

When Seki left the bridge, Vereshchagin reproved Kolomeitsev gently. "That was unkind of you, Piotr."

"I dislike substituting sentiment for logic."

"All right, Piotr," Vereshchagin said. "Both of us are very tired. I suggest that we both get eight hours sleep, and then we will see how Aksu is faring at gathering intelligence."

The task group had two distinct systems for analyzing the intelligence gathered by the network of reconnaissance satellites that *Aoba* was laying down.

The first was statistical. With little or no human assistance, *Aoba*'s computers converted masses of raw data into statistics on such disparate subjects as number of aircraft sorties, kilometers of paved road, and hectares of arable land. Initially, of course, many of these programs were useless; from a computer's point of view, few objects on Neighbor bore any resemblance to their human equivalents. The program measuring food production dutifully combed incoming images for the signatures of certain plants and animals, found none, and reported Neighbor's average daily caloric intake as zero. An ensign named Arita had already begun the delicate and laborious task of realigning the program parameters.

The second system was interpretive. Although *Zuiho* lacked *Aoba*'s sophisticated sensors, Esko Poikolainnen had set up a continuous short-range data link to feed raw imagery directly to Lieutenant Resit Aksu's eight-man intelligence detachment, which was augmented by four Navy analysts and two enthusiastic but inexperienced volunteers from Major Aichi's first platoon.

In truth, Aksu would have needed an army of analysts to review and interpret the mass of images *Aoba* was recording, but computer screening, refined over decades, winnowed most of the chaff, rendering Aksu's task of providing accurate, timely, and comprehensive information merely impossible.

Unable to analyze activity in more than a small fraction of Neighbor's thickly populated supercontinent in detail, Aksu obtained Vereshchagin's permission to focus his team's attention on the cities and villages along a hundred kilometer stretch of the Great River, and the landing zones where Vereshchagin tentatively planned to insert teams. Two team members were given responsibility for reviewing occurrences of extraordinary interest on the rest of the continent.

Aksu smiled and tugged at his graying mustache when Vereshchagin and Kolomeitsev entered his sanctum. "Welcome, honored Vice-Commissioner. Nothing has broken down. Yet."

The Iceman's gray eyes gleamed as he took station behind two operators, Heiskanen and Kelly.

Kelly's monitor was split to display visual and infrared images side by side, with radio and microwave signatures to provide perspective. As The Iceman watched, Kelly hit the same button to transmit the current clip to Heiskanen for detailed review. "Judging from the traffic, people are pretty excited down there," he commented.

The Iceman nodded.

"It will take another thirteen hours for our ships to complete mapping passes," Aksu explained. "We are now reviewing the southeastern corner of the delta where the Great River runs into the inland sea. What we are seeing are large numbers of villages of thirty to sixty dwellings each. They are separated by what appear to be dikes, with roads running along the top connecting one village to another."

The Iceman pointed to a series of lines. "What are these?"

"They are probably irrigation channels that connect to the river, but I am not going to say for certain until we have had a chance to examine them further," Aksu replied. "Spectrum analysis shows a monocrop growing in the diked areas."

From his terminal on the other side of the compartment, Pihkala called out, "Five desserts says they're irrigation channels."

Kelly shook his head emphatically. "No bet."

Vereshchagin asked Aksu in a quiet voice, "How are your volunteers from Major Aichi's company working out?"

Aksu shrugged. "Ask me in a week." He pointed to the Japanese corporal sitting at Pihkala's elbow to observe. "Gradually we will let them assume greater responsibility."

Kolomeitsev asked, "Could you use more?"

"More newcomers would overwhelm us. We spent three months training these two. They are very bright, but there is a certain knack to this work, and it remains to be seen whether they will prove out." Aksu smiled. "If you were training Major Aichi's men for A Company, how many would make it?"

"Have you and Hans discussed where to insert teams?" Vereshchagin asked.

"Yes, honored sir. He dropped by an hour ago." Aksu called up a map of the eastern half of the supercontinent and narrowed the focus to the mountain ranges fronting the inland sea. "I see nine potential drop zones, and of the nine, Colonel Coldewe and I would recommend zones seven and eight. We will study them over the next week, and prepare recommendations."

"Why these two?" Kolomeitsev asked.

"The two zones are situated together, which simplifies resupply. The terrain along the land bridge joining the two halves of the supercontinent is quite rugged and appears to be sparsely populated, which would allow us to fly shuttle missions with small fear of detection. The mountains there also shield us from some of the effects of the jet stream."

As the probe data had indicated, deep, uninterrupted seas north and south of Neighbor's equator and an absence of high mountains gave the planet savage winds.

Aksu framed the rocky north shore of the inland sea and pointed to a small, urn-shaped body of water that the team had designated Jug Bay. Although the only thing Irish about Kelly was his name, he had already named the small river flowing into it the Shannon. "This is zone eight. As you can see, the villages along the coast here abruptly give way to knife-edged ridges that are thickly vegetated and are likely to provide the teams with a safe haven. It also appears to be a good place to collect zoological and botanical specimens for the scientists."

Aksu shifted to zone seven. "Zone seven abuts on the northern arm of the river delta. The delta itself is extensively cultivated and densely populated." He pointed to several long, white streaks along the water's edge. "These are almost certainly seawalls, and it would appear that land here has been reclaimed from the sea. Despite the supercontinent's large size, arable land does not appear to be common. Zone seven would appear to be the only place where our reconnaissance people can approach the cities and villages along the Great River with any degree of security. We will, of course, take a closer look over the next six or seven days."

"Piotr, what do you think?" Vereshchagin asked.

"We will want to send a team to investigate the missile site, but it is likely to be heavily guarded, and I would recommend holding off until we have had a chance to snoop around to obtain a better notion of what we are up against," The Iceman said judiciously. "Seven and eight would appear to be adequate for our purposes."

Vereshchagin patted Aksu on the shoulder. "Carry on."

Interlude

NEIGHBOR'S SMALLER MOON WAS A TINY MOTE IN SPACE, TOO small to have an atmosphere and almost too small to have a gravitational pull. It looped around the planet in an eccentric orbit with one side continually pointed toward space.

Freighter *Singapore Maru*'s cargo of ammunition, bottled oxygen, water, and dry food had been selected and placed in tough, insulated bags so that it could be unloaded in space. While the rest of the task group concentrated on collecting data, *Singapore Maru* stationed herself half a kilometer from the moon's backside, where small working parties anchored rods into the moon's dusty surface and tethered the ship's cargo to allow *Singapore Maru* to return to Go-Nihon and resume doing what freighters are designed to do.

The work crews operating the engineering vehicles affectionately named the tiny moon Supply Dump. This, of course, was immediately shortened to Dump by everyone else.

Although expected to last five days, the operation lasted seven after one particularly industrious crew misidentified forty-three bags.

In Orbit, HIMS *Zuiho*

AS HE WAS PLACING HIS PERSONAL POSSESSIONS IN A STORAGE
bin with the other members of the recon platoon's first section,
Superior Private Denys Gordimer noticed Simon Beetje appear
in the doorway. "Hey, Dr. Beetje's here!"

"Which one?" Superior Private Blaar Schuur yelled back.
Alariesto, the section sergeant, gave him a friendly poke in the
ribs to remind him of his manners.

Gordimer went over, and Simon took him by the hand.
"Hello, Denys, I came to wish you luck."

Gordimer's face broke out into a smile. "Nice of you, Doc."

"Are you still with Kalle?"

"No, I'm partnered with Blaar Schuur, now. Kalle is with
DeKe de Kantzow. We're dropping twelve two-man teams, half
moles, half lizards. I'm a mole, he's a lizard." Observing
Beetje's blank look, Gordimer explained, "Moles stay put. Lizards move around."

Kekkonen and Roy de Kantzow joined them. "Frosting good
to see you, Simon," The Deacon said.

"Nervous?" Beetje asked.

De Kantzow shook his head. "Old Frippie used to say, 'Yea,
though I walk through the valley of the shadow of death, I will
not fear because I don't plan letting the frosters know I'm
here.' "

"That's pretty close to what Frippie used to say," Kekkonen
explained, "although his rhyme scanned better."

Beetje looked around. "Major Aichi said that two of his men
were going."

"Yeah, those are Aichi's buggers over there. Nikoskelainen
hurt his frosting arm, so Colonel Hans decided to send them instead." De Kantzow shook his head. "They'll probably get
caught straight off."

"They're moles, too," Gordimer explained. "Of course, being
a mole isn't easy. People know the place where they live. It's
like trying to hide in somebody's bedroom—they notice if something isn't right."

Kekkonen laughed. "DeKe and I were moles once upon a
time. Amphtiles and Afrikaners aren't real smart, so Colonel
Harjalo used to send out fighting patrols to keep us awake.
No. 2 platoon found us once. They said they were pouring fuel
alcohol down the hole, the miserable, lying scum. It took me

thirty seconds to realize what was trickling in my shoes wasn't alcohol."

Cognizant of Alariesto's paternal glare, Gordimer wandered off to finish up. Beetje whispered, "Is there some problem with Major Aichi's men?"

Kekkonen lowered his voice. "They're good kids, but they barely know the basics. We all have at least two specialties—I have tracking, dog handling, and medical. DeKe has sniping, demolition, and aerial resupply."

"Colonel Hans made me frosting requalify in everything," de Kantzow mourned.

"We all know jungle, and quite a few of us know xeric, which is desert." Kekkonen shrugged. "Aichi's boys have never even seen a jungle. Hope they do okay."

From the other side of the cubicle, Thys Meiring, another lizard, said, "Hey, grandfather, show Simon your s-mortar." A ripple of mild laughter accompanied the remark.

"Is that what you plan to carry?" Beetje asked.

"DeKe doesn't think a silenced submachine gun is rugged enough." Kekkonen patted his own affectionately. "He carries an s-mortar stuffed with fléchette rounds, with a sniper's rifle in his bergen."

"I want something that'll fire dipped in pig shit," The Deacon explained tersely.

Kekkonen laughed, his soft brown eyes shining. "With an s-mortar, the propellant charge you need to kick fléchettes out at a reasonable velocity is hell on the weapon as well as your arm. Three fléchette rounds is maybe too much of a good thing."

"With fléchettes, what I hit goes down," de Kantzow explained.

"With fléchettes, what you hit usually has sunshine showing through it," Kekkonen retorted.

De Kantzow slipped away to help a trooper with his bergen, and Beetje murmured without thinking, "I'm glad DeKe decided to come, but all the same, it seems a little horrible that he left his wife like that." Appalled at what he had just said, he put his hand to his mouth.

Kekkonen took Beetje's sleeve and unobtrusively steered him out into the corridor. "I suppose I should explain before you say something." He spared a glance back over his shoulder. "Do you know The Deacon's wife? She's kind of an idiot. A looker, but really kind of dumb. We warned DeKe about that. You can imagine the good it did."

"Not a great deal," Beetje said, recalling similar advice.

"Less. DeKe won't say much, of course, but the two of them had been having their fights, and DeKe is pretty self-sufficient; he just ignores people if they try to fight when he's not in the mood. Anyway, Lara—that's her name—started feeling ignored, which of course she was, so when she began shopping her troubles around and her friends stopped listening, she started sharing them with one of the neighbors. He was about her age and not much smarter, so I suppose one thing led to another."

"DeKe must have been deeply hurt," Beetje reflected.

"Not especially," Kekkonen confided, "but the two of them weren't real discreet, and after everybody started talking, she felt so guilty she treated DeKe like dirt and the neighbor lost his head. He was sure DeKe was going to come around and break him in half, so he bought a gun and barricaded his house until his wife got fed up and threw him out."

"Oh, dear." Beetje tried to maintain a straight face.

"I suppose the guy would have felt better if DeKe had gone and winged him or something, but shooting people for frivolous civilian reasons would have hurt Jan Snyman's feelings—DeKe likes Jan a lot more than he lets on; he kind of took Jan under his wing when Jan was just a kid—and besides, the police would have confiscated his rifle. He really loves that rifle."

"I see."

"He's happy to be here now, but he's pretty sore about the whole thing and maybe a little embarrassed." Kekkonen shrugged. "To tell the truth, your coming by to wish us luck means a lot to him. One or two of your scientists seem to think we're going on vacation."

"Eh?"

Kekkonen stared down the corridor. "If the naturales suspect we're there, how long it takes them to hunt us down will tell the Variag something."

"Kalle, you shouldn't say things like that!"

The gentleness in Kekkonen's eyes frightened Beetje. "Hey, Simon, everybody dies sometime."

PROTECTED BEHIND ARMORED GLASS, VERESHCHAGIN AND SEKI watched from the tiny, cramped observation platform overlooking *Zuiho*'s shuttle bay—a tiny extravagance in so large a ship—as the shuttle transporting the reconnaissance teams awaited takeoff. "It is time," Seki said.

Zuiho's captain agreed. Almost as he finished speaking, taped music played out over the ship's intercom and died away.

"Such mournful music," Seki exclaimed as the haunting bugle notes ceased.

"It is the Krakow 'Hejnal,' " Vereshchagin responded. "Kokovtsov asked Captain Yamawaki to play it to commemorate Stanislaus Wojcek, who completed half a mission."

"Please excuse me?"

"He was shot down by ground fire during the second rebellion," Vereshchagin explained patiently, "which is half a mission."

"Yes, I see. The second rebellion." Seki looked at him oddly. "May I ask you why you rebelled?"

Vereshchagin fixed his eyes on the shuttle below. "I once heard an Iranian story about a running fox. To the man who asked why he was running, the fox said, 'The people of the town are conscripting camels.' 'But you are a fox,' the man said, to which the fox replied, 'There is no justice there, so they would take me if someone said I was a camel.' On Suid-Afrika, the Imperial Security Police and the director of a company called United Steel–Standard saw rebels to be punished, but all I saw were foxes, and the uniform I was wearing shamed me."

He stared as the hangar doors opened and the shuttle glided forward. "A few months from now, ask me if I see camels or foxes."

Landing Day [4-wind Rain 13]

DIPPING INTO THE PLANET'S ATMOSPHERE, THE SHUTTLE LEVeled out about thirty kilometers above the surface of the main continent. As the clamshell doors opened up in back, twenty-four men and twelve equipment bundles spilled out and began falling.

Breathing oxygen from a small sack, de Kantzow pulled his arms and legs in to speed up his descent for the first twenty kilometers or so and watched the planet's surface gradually rise to meet him through the night-vision lenses in his face shield.

He glanced up to check the position of the equipment bundle he was responsible for, using the transmitter strapped to his wrist to adjust the bundle's tiny paravanes. De Kantzow had to land the bundle close enough to eliminate the discomfort of searching potentially hostile countryside for a hundred kilos of missing toys—but not too close. From de Kantzow's point of view, the only thing worse than landing a bundle on his head would be living through the experience and having the rest of the battalion find out.

He patted the hard plastic case strapped to his chest. The dog inside whimpered. "It's okay, Dolly," he murmured in a soft voice he rarely used on people. Suspended in her harness inside the padded case, the dog barked appreciatively.

At four-tenths of a kilometer, de Kantzow popped his parachute and the chute on the bundle. Although Senior Quartermaster Sergeant Vulko Redzup had personally looked over the photos with a microscope and hadn't spotted so much as a log buried in the thin vegetation, de Kantzow methodically began examining the field below for obstructions.

Two minutes later, he landed uneventfully on reasonably solid ground, took his roll, and bounced to his feet, rubbing the soreness out of his muscles. He took a deep breath, mercifully filtered by the mask he was wearing, and rolled his chute. A few seconds later, he began walking downwind. As the heat of the day radiated from the baked soil underfoot, the circuitry in de Kantzow's battledress uniform began cooling him, reducing his need for water. Kalle Kekkonen was sorting through the equipment bundle when he arrived.

"How's Dolly?" Kekkonen demanded.

De Kantzow patted the case gently. "How's the frosting projector look?"

"Looks okay to me," Kekkonen replied, examining the item.

De Kantzow nodded. The geopositioning device on his belt read a signal from Jankowskie's ship overhead, and he used it to check their position. He said in a mildly surprised voice, "You know, we're actually where we're frosting supposed to be. The frosting road is a kilometer east of here."

Kekkonen grinned.

They redistributed the equipment, stuffing their chutes inside the equipment bundle. Pulling tiny bicycles out of their bergens, they snapped the wheels in place, and with Kekkonen precariously balancing the equipment bundle behind him, they rode away, the faint hum of the bicycles' tiny alcohol-fueled engines almost inaudible in the darkness.

The little bicycles were made from the same lightweight composite materials that formed a Cadillac's armor and weighed less than a kilogram. Helped along by the motor, in an evening, a skilled rider like de Kantzow could cover thirty kilometers cross-country without undue effort, an important consideration in extended operations. With freeze-dried rations and the fuel alcohol in their bergens, de Kantzow and Kekkonen were as mobile and self-sufficient as infantrymen could be.

Stopping at a pond, they weighted the bundle with stones and watched it sink. "Ready?" de Kantzow asked.

Kekkonen shook his head and pointed to some small creatures splashing around in the shallows. De Kantzow uttered a thoroughly blasphemous oath and began patting down his pockets. "You bring a dip net?"

Kekkonen grinned. Removing his gloves, he waded knee-deep into the water and gently cupped his hand under one of the small swimmers. He quickly brought up his free hand to keep the animal from escaping. "It's all in the wrist."

The Deacon pronounced another thoroughly blasphemous oath as he produced a bag for Kekkonen's find. They carefully obscured their footprints and left.

Eleven minutes later, they reached the road. Cautiously watching for traffic, they set up a projector and screen to broadcast Dr. Seki's videotape.

"Okay, the delay is set. The thing will start broadcasting in twenty minutes," Kekkonen said cheerfully in a whisper.

"If the first frosting truck doesn't knock it over."

Kekkonen kicked at the road surface. "Funny kind of road. It almost feels like porcelain."

"Use your frosting knife to pry a piece loose and we'll see what it looks like in the morning."

"Hey, DeKe!" Kekkonen pointed to a thin rail, seventeen or eighteen centimeters square, that snaked along parallel to the road and almost unnoticeable in the darkness about three and a half meters above the ground. Round supports spaced every twenty meters or so held it aloft.

De Kantzow rubbed his chin. "What do you frosting make of it?"

"I'll bet it's a power line. Those little things on top of the supports must be insulators. Think we ought to get a sample of that, too?"

Filthy DeKe stared at him in disgust. "You ever try cutting into a frosting power line someplace else?"

"No, that's a good way to get fried," Kekkonen said artlessly, then laughed, realizing what he had said.

De Kantzow pointed one long finger at him. "You frosting get yourself killed, not only does Colonel Hans piss on me from a great height, but I also got to lug your anemic carcass around."

He stared up at the putative power line. "The frosting egg-heads can think on it. That's what we frosting pay them for."

Inside her case next to his chest, Dolly whimpered. De Kantzow opened it and reached inside to pat her. "It's okay, girl. The hard part's over. Now, we'll go find some place to eat and go potty."

Kekkonen grinned. "How come you don't talk to me as nice as you talk to our dog?"

"You frosting aren't as good at what you do."

TO THE SOUTHWEST NEAR THE DELTA, DENYS GORDIMER AND Blaar Schuur were busy putting the finishing touches on a hide site on the crest of a high, barren ridge line. Their hole, wedged into the thin topsoil and framed with plastic tubing, was a little over two meters long and eighty centimeters wide. The "village" or "town" or "estate" they were observing was about two kilometers distant, clearly visible through the high-powered, wide-angle telephoto lens peeping out of the front.

"I'll set out the sensors so we don't get any unexpected guests," Gordimer offered.

Preoccupied with sculpting the surface of the hide to make it indistinguishable from the surrounding landscape, Schuur merely nodded. "See if you can find a spring."

Unlike the "lizards" like de Kantzow and Kekkonen, "moles" were expected to remain stationary, observing one location for weeks at a time. Suid-Afrika's Karoo, where Gordimer and Schuur had spent considerable time, was mostly dry, and as they both knew, a spring nearby would obviate the need to choose between shaving in the tea or making tea from shaving water. Even among recon troopers, not everyone was cut out to be a mole. The strain of remaining motionless in a coffin-sized hide in hostile country for a day—or days—at a time was hard on many people.

"I still think I'd make a better lizard," Schuur confided.

His partner grinned. "As Colonel Hans likes to say, 'Thousands at his bidding speed. And post o'er Land and Ocean without rest: They also serve, who only stand and wait.' "

Schuur flipped a pebble at him. "University dropout. Go find water."

TWO HOURS BEFORE SUNRISE, SECTION SERGEANT MARKUS Alariesto skidded to a stop and looked at his partner, Superior

Private Chris Heunis. "This spot looks good. We got enough samples?"

Heunis dismounted and used his submachine gun to flip over a stone. He nudged a small invertebrate with an indeterminate number of legs into a plastic vial, which he sealed securely. "We got dirt, all kinds of plant matter and creepy crawlies, and a few broken artifacts. I make our haul about three kilos."

"That's plenty." Alariesto reached into the side pocket on his bicycle and pulled out a small square of plastic. Unfolding it into a transparent balloon, he hooked it to a plastic cylinder of pressurized helium and inflated it rapidly.

"Three point one seven kilos," Heunis said crisply, packaging his bundle. "I'll set the transmitter to start signaling when it gets three kilometers up."

"Hope there isn't too much of a breeze up there." Alariesto looked up. "Coconut won't like having to chase it down."

As the planet's inhabitants measured time, it was the fourth of nine days of "wind," in the thirteenth year of "Rain."

In Orbit, HIMS *Zuiho* [5-wind Rain 13]

HANS COLDEWE JOINED VERESHCHAGIN ON *ZUIHO*'S BRIDGE TO study the face of the planet below. "All twelve teams have reported in, Anton. So far no serious problems. We set up two of the three projectors. The third one seems to have landed hard, and I told Salchow to abandon it. Most of the active teams have collected samples, and I'm ready to send Kokovtsov to pick them up. That should be enough to keep the scientists happy for a day or two."

"And the relay node?"

Coldewe nodded. "It's up and running, and Esko thinks that our transmissions are secure. The first pictures came through about half an hour ago."

Vereshchagin turned his head. "I had forgotten just how hard it is, to send them off, and wait."

L-Day plus 5 [9-wind Rain 13]

IN THE VALLEY OF THE GREAT RIVER, FIELDS FOR A FOOD CROP nicknamed the "water potato" fitted one into another in a mosaic of shapes and colors. While seedlings in some fields barely pricked their way through the water's surface, adjacent fields shone an iridescent bluish green, the plants springing from the water in regimented lines, each a precise distance from the next. From above, the bold, brown lines of the ditches looked like scrawled handwriting as they carried silty, chocolate-brown water released from the dams upriver. Thatched stone shelters for tools dotted interstices where the dikes joined.

Schuur elbowed Gordimer. "Siesta time's almost over. Get the camera ready."

From their hide on the mountain, the two had noticed patterns in the activities of the inhabitants of the village in the great valley below. Rolling on his stomach, Gordimer rubbed his eyes.

"If they do the upland fields again, see if you can get a clear shot of the harrow before it starts kicking up dust," Schuur urged. Although the vehicle was awkwardly put together by Earth standards, with the engine mounted directly under the steering column and the driver perched on top, Schuur, farmborn, knew harrowing when he saw it.

Gordimer obediently rested the video camera on his shoulder and adjusted the telephoto lens. "Why do they have two ponds?"

"One for water, the other for garbage. And for night soil, unless they spread that on the fields. Better pay attention to which one is which, city boy." Unconsciously, Schuur looked up. "Rains are coming. Monsoon season's almost here."

Gordimer jerked Schuur by the arm. "Hush! Listen!"

From the slope behind them they could hear voices like the chirping of birds. Gordimer turned on the video camera without focusing it to capture the sounds on tape. Then he cautiously adjusted his mirror to look through the hide's rear peephole.

Schuur propped himself up on one elbow and ran his hands over his submachine gun, checking the magazine and the safety. "Five, maybe six of them," he whispered.

"Too small for adults. Kids. Just kids," Gordimer replied.

As they watched, a child scampered into view with a cloth wrapped around its loins and a baggy cap on its rounded head. The blue down covering the child's skin, long spindly arms, and large, luminescent eyes gave it a curiously angelic appearance. It ran with its knees flexed and pointed backward, which made Gordimer think of a boy with a bird's legs.

It paused to watch the glittering mothlike creatures buzzing around a rotting branch. As Schuur and Gordimer waited with drawn breath, the child carefully uncoiled a pink rope from around its waist and began moving it gently. Suddenly, the child snapped the thong at one of the moths. The elastic line stretched, and the moth found itself stuck to the end. Reeling its capture in, the child peeled away the wings and ate it with obvious relish.

As the child refastened the line around its waist, it stopped and began looking directly at the hide, swaying its head from side to side in apparent indecision. Although the hide had been skillfully crafted, with the extra dirt carefully scattered in the ravine below, some minor alteration in the contour had betrayed them. A long moment passed. Then voices from farther down the hill attracted the child's attention. Without a backward glance it ran down to rejoin its companions.

Schuur exhaled. "That felt too close." He flipped on the safety; somehow he had released it without thinking.

The plan was to capture anyone who discovered the hide and try to arrange for a night pickup, but the two of them both knew how difficult that would be; the odds that this world's inhabitants would recognize a submachine gun for what it was and react accordingly were not especially good.

Schuur rolled from his side to his back. "You think he noticed anything?"

The child's sex was indeterminate, but somehow Schuur knew it was a boy.

"We'll know if he comes back with his father." Gordimer turned his head. "If we don't see anybody before nightfall, I'd say we're all right."

Schuur nodded. "We'd best tell the Variag to tell everyone to be extra careful; the kid knew something wasn't quite right, he just couldn't put it together. Did you see the legs on him? I wonder if we can teach them to play football?"

Gordimer giggled. "You see the way he gobbled up that bug?"

"What of it? Eating bugs got you into recon, didn't it?"

L-Day plus 17 [3-rain Rain 13]

AN HOUR BEFORE DAWN, KEKKONEN AND DE KANTZOW VENtured out from the campsite they had set up in a rocky cleft to check the wire snares they had laid along small animal trails.

Moving slowly downhill toward the sounds of running water, Kekkonen, the point man, suddenly held up his hand. "Recon point one-two-one. Break. Kalle here. I hear something, DeKe," he murmured into his radio.

Next to him, Dolly, acclimated to Neighbor's sights and smells, whimpered.

De Kantzow moved up to join him in slow, patient steps.

Kekkonen listened for a minute. "It sounds like a bunch of monkeys." Ahead of him, one of the bushes moved. "Whatever they are, they've got to be better than the blue mouse deer Salchow saw."

"Don't let Simon kiss you if we catch one," The Deacon advised gruffly.

In Orbit, HIMS *Zuiho* [4-rain Rain 13]

SIMON BEETJE, MARIA BEETJE, AND A THIRD BIOLOGIST, Kantaro Ozawa, assessed the photographic images Kekkonen and de Kantzow transmitted from the planet's surface. Ozawa ran the film backward and froze it. Although his specialty was plant succession, he had spent two years studying rhesus monkey groups on Earth. "It is astonishing that they were able to get this close."

Simon Beetje nodded. "DeKe and Kalle are both very good."

For the biologists, Neighbor's first surprise was the discovery that most of Neighbor's trees had lacelike internal skeletons of calcium carbonate, which presumably better protected them from predation and the planet's fierce winds. The second was the apelike creatures Kekkonen and de Kantzow had found.

"The animals are wary, but they have no reason for identifying humans as predators," Maria Beetje pointed out.

"They'll learn," Simon commented, tapping his front teeth with the end of a light pencil.

The lemur-apes were blue-gray. The chloroplasts in Neighbor's vegetation reflected far more blue light than their Earth counterparts, and Beetje's team had already noticed that the larger fauna tended to patterns in shades of blue, gray, and black.

"My first thought was that the creatures are gibbon analogues, from their generally slender build," Ozawa said judiciously, "but they are not arboreal at all."

"Walkers—look at the structure of the hips and feet. Tailless lemurs," Maria commented brusquely. "We'll need to assess their social interaction to determine how advanced they are."

"We should call them lemur-apes for now," Ozawa temporized.

Simon smiled. "We'd better, before Filthy DeKe thinks of something else. Pia Szuba has been pushing me for an analysis of the water potato, which appears to be the only intensely cultivated food crop other than that thing that looks like a purple yam. Did we get that done?"

Ozawa nodded. "The plant is quite interesting. It has an extensive system of air passages from the leaves to the roots, which allow it to grow well in saturated, anaerobic soils—under such conditions, the plant respirates aerobically—and both the biological value, indexing the absorbable nitrogen, and the protein content appear to be exceptionally high. Field flooding avoids leaching of nutrients through the subsoil and frees soluble phosphorus and trace elements such as iron, aluminum, manganese, and calcium for the plant to utilize, so a flooded cultivation system would appear to be well suited to very intensive, very sustained production, but that would be Dr. Szuba's specialty more than mine."

Ozawa's elfin face grew serious. "The closer the lemur-apes are to the naturales in evolutionary terms, the more I think we should learn from them. I recommend that we draft a written request for Sergeant Kekkonen's team to continue studying them."

Simon froze the record again to study one particular individual. "Anton agreed to that at dinner."

L-Day plus 23 [9-rain Rain 13]

EVEN ASLEEP, DEKE DE KANTZOW FELT THE KICK BEFORE IT landed and rolled to avoid it.

Kalle Kekkonen grinned. "You're slowing down, DeKe." He pointed. "It's almost dawn." The lemur-apes were crepuscular, most active at dawn and dusk to avoid the sun's fierce heat, and the troop was beginning to stir.

De Kantzow began folding the space blanket he had wrapped around himself against the evening chill.

The troop they were studying numbered thirty individuals: five adult males, thirteen adult females, and a dozen juveniles. The four subordinate males, a third again as large as the females, occupied individual nests of tree boughs in a loose perimeter around the central nest. Invariably, they were the first to awaken. The two reconnaissance men had sensibly shortened the name the scientists had chosen to "lemps."

If the troop held to its pattern, it would move out in formation at first light to forage.

"Five rand says they go play in the frosting creek again," de Kantzow murmured.

"You're on, grandfather," Kekkonen replied as he methodically filmed the troop, "and I'll go you one better: the loser has to scrape up the dung samples for the rest of the week."

Picking up food and fecal samples was part of the team's job, but not necessarily a favored part.

"Did Simon say when he wants us to take the net and give the little frosters a ride?"

"Not yet." Kekkonen admitted, "That's the part that bothers me. They're almost like people, women and kids, you know?"

"Too much like people, if you ask me," de Kantzow agreed, "the big bastards are frosting mean, and the little ones aren't much better." The previous day, the alpha male had nearly jerked the arm off a female who had been a little slow to let him climb her back.

De Kantzow squeezed water into a ration, expanding the plastic membrane wrapped around it. A few seconds later, the ration began cooking itself.

The Japanese were smart little buggers, de Kantzow observed sourly to himself. On the new rations, the only thing you couldn't eat was the wrapper. Unfortunately, diced squid was still diced squid.

An hour passed. "I wonder what's keeping them?" Kekkonen asked, puzzled.

A chorus of shrieks from the lemur-apes punctuated the silence of the forest.

"I'll be frosted." De Kantzow looked at Kekkonen. "We're going to need to think up another frosting name. Tiny little bugger, isn't it?"

A moment later, Kekkonen grinned. "Looks like twins at least. Keep thinking up names, Deacon." He nudged de Kantzow. "You ready to pay up?"

"We'd frosting better let the Variag know," de Kantzow growled.

An hour later, the female gave birth to two more.

Around local midnight, a second female went into labor.

L-Day plus 25 [2-hexagon Rain 13]

VERESHCHAGIN PACED THE LENGTH OF HIS CUBICLE WITH A CUP of tea in his hand, lost in thought. Coldewe and Kolomeitsev waited for a question to bubble to the surface.

The Iceman cleared his throat to break the spell.

Vereshchagin's eyes refocused, and he turned to look at Coldewe, wedged into the far corner. "How are we doing with communications intercepts?"

"Oh, we've got tons of stuff—mostly audio, but a fair amount of visual—now that Esko's crew has the knack of distinguishing goodies from background noise. The problem is that we don't have the slightest idea what any of it means. Our scientists all have theories, of course. In the words of the great Samuel Clemens, 'There is something fascinating about science. One gets such wholesale returns of conjecture out of such a trifling investment of fact.' " Coldewe saw Vereshchagin surreptitiously look down at the time display on his wrist mount. "Is it that time, already?"

"Two minutes and counting."

A moment later, they heard a knock on the door. Coldewe grinned. "He's early."

Esko Poikolainnen stuck his head inside. "Sir, Dr. Seki is here."

Vereshchagin nodded, and Seki awkwardly followed Poikolainnen through the doorway.

"Good morning, Doctor. What may I do for you?" Vereshchagin inquired politely.

"On behalf of the scientific community, I respectfully request that you consider dispatching the initial-contact team," Seki said stiffly, as he had on each of the previous three mornings.

Vereshchagin looked up at Seki. "I have considered it, Doctor. We will dispatch the team, today."

"It is the considered opinion of each of my subject-matter experts that continued delay is purposeless and that we have reached a point of diminishing returns . . ." Puzzlement formed in Seki's eyes. "Excuse me, what did you say, honored Vice-Commissioner?"

"I said that we will dispatch the initial-contact team, today. Please advise the individual team members," Vereshchagin said without turning a hair.

Seki bowed. "Thank you, Vereshchagin-*sama*." He cocked

one eyebrow. "As a further matter, the physical scientists respectfully request—"

"The recon teams to take core samples." Vereshchagin folded his hands. "No."

Seki bowed again. After he left, Hans Coldewe said admiringly, "You are truly evil, Anton. When did you decide?"

"Last night. Everyone concerned will be better for having had a full night's sleep. Especially Dr. Seki."

"This is it, isn't it?"

"Yes, we will put our tents down, and see who passes within. The welcome tape gave us a few weeks grace, but it is time to establish a dialogue. Before somebody there becomes impatient and initiates a dialogue with missiles."

AS COMPANY SERGEANT ISAAC WANJAU FLOATED TO THE ground, wearing coveralls over an outlandish uniform largely of his own devising—khaki, with a maroon beret and a silver aiguillette over his left shoulder—he looked up to assess the progress of the civilians, most of whom were making their first parachute jump. For once, Kokovtsov, piloting the shuttle, wasn't concerned about being seen or wasting fuel, which made this particular jump unusually easy. Food and equipment would follow on Kokovtsov's second pass.

The initial-contact team consisted of three scientists and two soldiers. If all went well, more would follow.

In the fields below, startled Blues stared upward with their mouths open.

By the time Wanjau reached the ground, they were gone. Unperturbed, he grabbed Corporal Kobus Nicodemus to help him set up the team's tents and get the equipment unpacked as half-ton supply pallets gently impacted the ground.

Two hours later, the contact team's camp consisted of four tents erected side by side with breakaway pallets for flooring. The flags of Imperial Japan and the Republic of Suid-Afrika flew from improvised flagstaffs, and from Wanjau's point of view, although a lot of important work remained, the store was open for business.

L-Day plus 26 [3-hexagon Rain 13]

PRECARIOUSLY SEATED ON A FIELD CHAIR, SEKI WATCHED ISAAC Wanjau and Kobus Nicodemus erect a shower stall with help from Dr. Connie Marais, whose fair skin was already reddening.

Solar panels on the slanted roofs of the contact team's tents provided power to run the generator that pumped water from a nearby irrigation canal to supply the campsite. Of the four tents, two housed personnel, another the kitchen, and a fourth the generator and supplies.

The aroma of rehydrated meat and vegetables sizzling in a wok wafted through the still air as the team's second linguist, Dr. Keiji Katakura, worked at preparing dinner.

Dictating data on the campsite vicinity, Seki became aware that he was being watched. Turning his head, he saw two beings standing beside the open tent flap.

The aliens were tall, a little over two meters, and heavily muscled around the shoulders and thighs. They wore multicolored kilts belted at the waist, and brown cloaks fastened with green clasps at the left shoulder. They stood tilted slightly forward with knees bent, their lower legs strikingly slender. A fine bluish brown down covered the visible parts of their bodies, thickening on top of the head and around the shoulders and rather long necks, and disappearing around the delicately inhuman faces. Their ears were small, down free, and cupped.

"Hello, I am Dr. Seki," Seki said, fumbling through signs.

Seki read astonishment in the eyes of the nearer being. He was conscious of a slightly sweetish odor. A second later, both of them were gone.

Hours later, an official delegation arrived, dressed in cloaks of a fiery red.

In Orbit, HIMS *Aoba* [4-reed Rain 13]

LEADING CREWMAN MAEDA SHOOK ENSIGN ARITA'S SHOULDER lightly.

Arita stirred. "What?" He lifted his head.

"Sir?" Maeda said with a worried look in his eyes. "Are you all right? Did the statistical analysis run?"

Arita sat up straight. "Unfortunately, it would appear that we will again need to readjust our programming."

"Sir?"

"The analysis for estimated population fails to accord with the analyses for food production and transportation links. I would be remiss in sending our inadequate efforts on to the flagship."

"But sir, it is possible—"

Arita smiled, touched by Maeda's concern. "All things are possible under heaven, Maeda. Yet our analyses indicate that the population level of upland areas is exceptionally low, and that estimated food production and the transportation network are clearly inadequate to maintain the observed level of culture. This would appear to be due to flaws in our methodology. No other theory would appear to account for the discrepancies."

Arita closed his eyes and laid his head back down for a moment. "I will, of course, report our continued failure to achieve acceptable progress to Captain Kobayashi and accept responsibility."

L-Day plus 38 [6-reed Rain 13]

THE EARLY MORNING MIST HUNG IN STRIPS. MOISTENED BY THE vapor in the air, the mossy filaments clung to the trees like great, gray cobwebs, and rubbery vines hung beneath them almost to the ground.

Dolly whimpered softly, and Kekkonen elbowed de Kantzow awake. "They're coming."

De Kantzow rolled over, growled, and checked the time. "Greedy little bastards are coming earlier every day."

As bait for the ambush, as de Kantzow liked to call it, for the fourth day running, Kekkonen had filled small containers near the edge of the clearing with a variety of choice arthropods.

"Colonel Hans said he wanted a male and a female," Kekkonen repeated.

De Kantzow nodded.

In advance of the rest of the lemp troop, a male outrider and a lower-ranking female galloped toward the pails to grab morsels before their social superiors snatched them away. "Perfect," de Kantzow whispered. Seconds later, he sprung the trap, and bent saplings vaulted upright.

As the two netted lemps writhed in the meshes, the rest of the troop raced off in panic.

De Kantzow and Kekkonen went forward carrying cages. Dolly trotted obediently at their heels.

"Love of money is the root of all evil," Kekkonen admonished their first screaming captive as they plopped her into a padded plastic container, "but love of food ranks a close second."

Similarly disposing of the second victim, he touched his radio. "Command point one. Break. Kekkonen here. Two lemps coming in separate packages. When can you effect pickup? . . . Good. Kekkonen out." He told de Kantzow, "He'll be overhead in about an hour."

"Good, I thought we'd be stuck with the little frosters until nightfall. Is Coconut flying?"

Kekkonen lifted his face shield and spat. "No, it's some Imp, which means we have to prepare a manifest. The Imp Navy has its regulations."

While Kekkonen prepared the balloons, de Kantzow pulled a marker from a side pocket and swiftly scrawled his name, the date-time group, and a summary of the cage's contents on the side. They waited forty minutes to be on the safe side, then de Kantzow inquired, "First balloon ready?"

"Set." Kekkonen had secured the two-meter balloon to a thick log to inflate it, and he whipped the free end to de Kantzow, who locked it to the cage and slipped the knot free. The cage followed the balloon into the air. A few seconds later, the second lemp followed.

De Kantzow and Kekkonen paused to watch. "Off they go," Kekkonen said, "flying high into the sun."

"I listed the little buggers as recruits for the Imp Navy," de Kantzow confessed.

L-Day plus 40 [8-reed Rain 13]

SUPERIOR PRIVATE BRIT SMITS SHRUGGED OUT OF HIS PARACHUTE harness and went to meet his welcoming committee, Corporal Kobus Nicodemus and six Blues. "Hello, Kobus. You taught these people English yet?" He glanced up at Dr. Tomomi Motofugi and Dr. Teruzo Ando, who were parachuting down after him.

Nicodemus laughed. "No, but we're working on it. I'll get your chute. Go on inside."

Six members of the original Blue delegation had immediately paired off and attached themselves to Seki, Marais, and Katakura. The role of the other delegation members was not immediately apparent, and by now everyone on the contact team realized that it would probably take weeks or months to establish the meaning of complex concepts like "We come in peace and friendship."

Feeling slightly foolish wearing khaki, Smits grabbed his bergen and walked into the kitchen tent, where he found Dr. Connie Marais seated around a table with two Blues.

Marais had positioned a computer terminal running a standard stenographic program so that the two Blues could see his spoken English displayed in written form. Over The Iceman's objections, Vereshchagin had permitted Dr. Seki to supply the Blues with several computers set to run modified, interactive English-language tutorials; Kolomeitsev was concerned that computers would teach the Blues more about Earth's technology than about Earth's languages.

Marais lifted his head. "Oh, hello, Brit! Sit down." A blond beard was coming in to cover some of his sunburn. He said very slowly, "Brit Smits, the person to your left is Ekpalawehud and the other is Meniolagomeka."

"Bri Smi-sez," Ekpalawehud repeated.

"Sorry, Doctor, I didn't mean to interrupt," Smits stammered, taking a seat.

"No problem. We were at an impasse. We often get there." Marais laughed. "We spend a lot of time just staring at each other when we run out of things to say. No, don't try shaking hands. They don't do that."

Two of the Blues with Nicodemus followed Smits inside and awkwardly perched themselves on the edges of the two remaining camp chairs.

"So how are things aboard ship?" Marais asked.

"Oh, very well." Feeling confused, Smits tried to remember to speak slowly and make the correct signs. "Everyone is just a little disappointed that we aren't making better progress teaching the Blues English and learning their language."

Marais smiled. "It may not seem like much, but we are making progress. Consider the problems." He held up a finger.

"First, humans and naturales do not have the same speech organs. Humans have the larynx, which allows sounds to be voiced or unvoiced, the soft palate, which controls nasal sounds, the lips, the tongue root, the tongue body, and the tongue tip." As he spoke, he pointed to the various organs.

"Without ever thinking about it, you perform a whole series of gymnastics with these speech organs to form phonemes, which are bits of words, like the three phonemes that make up the word 'cat.' English uses about forty phonemes." Marais grinned. "Of course, one particular problem we have is that none of us are native English speakers. My English consonants and vowels sound Afrikaans, Dr. Seki's sound Japanese, and Isaac's sound like God knows what. At first, the naturales weren't sure we were all speaking the same language."

Ekpalawehud and Meniolagomeka listened diligently.

"Ekpalawehud and Meniolagomeka can't reproduce English phonemes any more than a parrot can—their vocal apparatus isn't built that way—but with practice, they can mimic sounds that our brains can recognize as English."

Meniolagomeka said something to Ekpalawehud in a language that clearly wasn't English—or human.

"As you can see," Marais continued, "we have even more trouble mimicking the sounds their language uses."

Smits nodded. "Is there a reason why we have to say everything so slowly?"

"Try listening to yourself sometime. At normal speaking speed, words flow seamlessly into each other. The human brain can decode up to forty-five phonemes per second, which gives us the illusion that we are hearing a string of separate words, but in reality, the boundaries between words only exist in our minds." Marais laughed. "When you first begin to learn a foreign language, what do you say?"

Smits smiled. "Please speak slower."

Marais nodded. "Despite millions of years of evolution to help you in decoding human vocal sounds, with a strange language you need help breaking the sounds into discrete words." He placed his fingers around his voice box. "Yet another problem is the fact that human speech isn't a series of pure tones with a single frequency, but rather a wave with vibrations from a hundred cycles per second all the way up to four thousand cycles per second. When we speak, what the naturales hear is a buzz."

"With all these difficulties, how do they manage to understand us at all?" Smits asked, as Dr. Motofugi poked his head through the tent flap, followed by Dr. Ando.

"We don't know enough words to discuss this yet, but I am sure that they do what we do, which is to record everything, study the noises at night, and have computers try to break them down and make sense out of them. It is going to be a very slow process."

In Orbit, HIMS *Zuiho* [9-reed Rain 13]

LOOKING TIRED BUT HAPPY, MARIA BEETJE DROPPED A PRINTOUT on top of Simon Beetje's computer. "Here it is. I checked my results over twice to be certain."

Simon glanced through it. "The female lemur-ape's karotype is 2N equals fifty-eight: sixteen macrochromosomes with median or submedian centomeres, ten macrochromosomes with terminal or subterminal centomeres, and thirty-two microchromosomes. Absolutely ordinary. I was hoping for something outlandish."

Many of Neighbor's small mammal analogues sent up for examination possessed combinations of three sex chromosomes—X, Y, and W—rather than the usual two, with the W chromosome suppressing the Y chromosome in the WY combination to leave an otherwise male animal female. Simon was quite sure that this would result in a permanent but stable imbalance between the two sexes.

"How closely are they related to the naturales?" he asked.

"Find me a naturale to dissect, and I will tell you." Maria straightened. "The specimen was pregnant and would have given birth to quadruplets within a few days. Didn't Kalle say that all of the births have been quadruplets?"

"So far."

"Interesting. This one would have done the same. The fetuses appeared very immature. Eleven centimeters on average. Three were female, one was male, which does not surprise me given the mother's low social rank. What really strikes me as interesting is the genotypes. Although all four are the same age, only two of them share the same father."

Simon put the printout down and began thinking aloud. "Huh, that is interesting! Although they appear to have a fixed breeding season triggered by the onset of the rains, Kalle says they mate at any time."

"The females either store sperm or delay implantation of fertilized eggs, I haven't decided which yet."

"Clearly either delayed fertilization or delayed implantation," Beetje agreed, half to himself. "If the lemur-apes do this, I wonder if the naturales can, too?"

"Females that don't need males for years at a time," his wife said, teasing him.

Simon said nothing.

L-Day plus 49 [8-mist Rain 13]

"YES, I KNOW WE NEED TO FIND ANTON A LARGER OFFICE," Coldewe said apologetically, as Pia Szuba, Simon Beetje, and Dr. Naoki Kita, head of the physical sciences working group, struggled to find seats, "but moving him to A deck would interfere with football practice." He thought a few seconds longer. "Maybe we could use the sauna."

The Iceman merely grinned.

Although Vereshchagin allowed all five scientific working-group leaders to attend staff meetings after Dr. Seki's departure, he was politely intolerant of idle chatter, and two of the five had asked to be excused with a fair degree of alacrity. The head of the interdisciplinary group, Dr. Iwao, only lasted one meeting.

"Shall we begin with you, Simon?" Vereshchagin asked.

"Oh, sorry." Beetje rubbed his eyes. "We dissected the first lemur-ape. We're observing the other for the time being. Dr. Ozawa, Maria, and I all agree that they are likely to be closely related to the naturales, but there is no way to verify this until we have a tissue sample for comparison."

Jan Snyman shrugged. "We're still looking for a cemetery."

Beetje continued, "We've given linguistics details on the respiratory and nasal structure, which will help them understand the range of sounds that the naturales are capable of."

Szuba interrupted, "Did this include an analysis of the auditory structure?"

"We will have that ready in a day or so," Beetje admitted.

"Please provide the rest of us with a copy as well, Simon," Vereshchagin ruled.

"And a translation," Coldewe added.

Beetje went on, "We examined the eye structure very closely, and it would appear that the lemur-apes have excellent color vision. In fact, where humans have three types of color-detecting cells in the eye—blue, red, and green—lemur-apes have four."

"Very impressive," Major Aichi murmured.

"To a degree." Beetje folded his hands. "Some Earth birds have seven. In any case, we are running tests on the male, and Esko Poikolainnen is helping me design a computer model. In a few days, I should be able to tell you what the lemur-apes see, and by extension, what the Blues see."

"Please do. We need this as soon as practicable," The Iceman commented.

Dr. Kita said politely, "Excuse me, please?"

Coldewe fingered the battledress he was wearing. "It could affect our operations. The camouflage we use is designed for human eyes. The individual threads of my uniform reflect different wavelengths of light, which allows me to blend into a variety of backgrounds. I wouldn't want to find out the hard way that this makes me stand out like a Christmas tree to a Blue. Similarly, our reconnaissance aircraft—the Sparrows, which are manned, and the Hummingbirds, which are not—are fitted with panels that match the ambient light. If the Blues see color differently than we do, we need to make adjustments."

"Until we do so, it would be very dangerous for us to use our reconnaissance aircraft," Vereshchagin explained. "Hans, you are next."

Coldewe nodded. "Maintaining covert surveillance is either nerve-racking or boring, and usually it's both. Salchow has found a good safe zone in the limestone cliffs by the head of the bay. As soon as Simon comes through on the vision, I want to set up a permanent camp so I can land some aircraft and start rotating teams in to rest before some of our moles start killing each other."

"I concur, and I would also suggest changing some of the hide sites," The Iceman interjected. "In our observations of the peasantry, we may be reaching the point of diminishing returns."

"Agreed," Vereshchagin said. "Next, I would like to address the issue of the motive power of local motor vehicles. It would appear that vehicles run on stored electric power in some manner, but the precise mechanism is unclear and appears potentially worth knowing. Dr. Kita's committee examined the pictures that Alariesto's team took and passed the problem on to the interdisciplinary team." He gave Kita a sharp look. "The interdisciplinary team has requested a vehicle engine to examine."

"Last week," Jan Snyman complained, "they wanted us to take a close look at a truck. This week, they want us to *steal* a truck."

"Just the engine, Jan," Simon Beetje said jocularly.

"Better and better," Snyman agreed. "They want us to disassemble the truck and steal selected portions. Has anyone on the interdisciplinary committee ever tried to lift a truck engine?"

"Hans?" Vereshchagin asked.

Coldewe spread his hands. "No promises. We'll toss the idea back and forth and see if anyone has any ideas."

"Thank you, Hans." Vereshchagin turned to Szuba, who spoke

for the linguistics working group, stripped to staff the contact team, as well as her own. "Pia, where are we with language?"

"We are beginning to progress in teaching the naturales English. We have had less success learning their language. We anticipated difficulties. May I explain?"

"Please do."

Aichi interjected, "I recall how I first learned English. I wonder if there is some way to immerse the contact team in the culture more."

Szuba smiled. "I wish it were that simple. Just as songbirds inherit the ability to learn bird songs, thousands of generations of natural selection have produced an innate capacity to learn human language in humans."

"True," Aichi conceded.

"This ability to learn human language does not necessarily relate to the ability to cognate, as many people assume," Szuba continued didactically.

Coldewe grinned. "People who can talk can't necessarily think."

Szuba nodded. "I should mention examples. Williams Syndrome is caused by a defect in chromosome eleven. Although children with the syndrome are severely retarded, they absorb words readily and converse loquaciously, although their discourse is empty of meaning." She smiled impishly. "Some people call it 'party-conversation syndrome.' The reverse is also true. Persons born with any of the various types of specific language impairment have perfectly normal intelligence, but are only able to string words together with extreme difficulty."

"How does this affect our ability to converse with the Blues?" Kolomeitsev asked.

"Every human being shares a common, however distant, ancestry and a certain basic way of looking at language. In a crude sense, we humans have a certain operating system for language built into our genes, like the operating system on a computer. The naturales have a different operating system, which is similar to ours—indeed, we appear to share many basic assumptions about the nature of language—but it is designed to a different standard."

The Iceman continued to probe. "This fails to explain why they seem to be picking up more English than we are able to pick up of their language."

Szuba hesitated. "The linguistics team has not yet arrived at a suitable consensus on this matter."

"I understand," Vereshchagin said. "What do you think?"

Again Szuba hesitated. Finally, she said, "One factor appears to be that the naturales are superb at mimicking sounds and tonal qualities, while most human beings are not, myself included. A second factor may be that the naturales have an entire continent from which to select personnel. Had we assembled the contact team on Earth, I am sure that we could have gotten persons more talented." She paused. "It is also possible that the naturales have an aversion to allowing us to learn their language, for reasons that we cannot comprehend as yet."

Vereshchagin turned to The Iceman. "What is it that we need to know in their language?"

"I would like to know the word for 'missile,'" Kolomeitsev replied.

Coldewe leaned back in his chair and hammered on the door. A moment later, Esko Poikolainnen stuck his head inside.

"Esko, please establish contact with Dr. Seki," Vereshchagin said in a soft voice.

Poikolainnen nodded, and a moment later, Seki's image appeared on the wall behind Simon Beetje's head.

"Hello, Doctor," Vereshchagin said. "I am calling to ask whether you have made any progress in learning local equivalents for the words on the list I gave you."

"Not as yet, Vice-Commissioner," Seki replied. "Indeed, we do not know whether these people even have a word for war."

"We know very little, Doctor. Whether or not these people have a word for war, they do know how to wage it," Vereshchagin said quietly. "Please show them pictures of the missiles and insist upon being told what they are called."

"Commissioner, I beseech you. Whenever we bring out pictures of weapons, the naturales turn their backs and refuse to speak with us. We have made such a promising beginning that I implore you not to place it in jeopardy," Seki said, clearly anguished by the thought. "What possible purpose would this serve?"

"It would be helpful to know what a missile is called the next time they fire one at us," Vereshchagin explained patiently. "Please pursue the matter. Vereshchagin out."

He looked around the crowded and suddenly silent room. "Is there anything else we should discuss?"

Beetje spoke up. "I would ask you to keep de Kantzow's team in place as long as possible. In fact, I would ask you to consider sending Kantaro Ozawa down to study the lemur-apes firsthand."

Vereshchagin lifted one eyebrow. "Pia?"

"I concur. He tells me that he is a skydiver, so jumping from a shuttle should not be a problem for him," Szuba explained.

"The Blues don't seem to go up there, so it seems safe enough for now," Coldewe admitted, "and it would free up DeKe and Kalle once they have Ozawa broken in."

The Iceman frowned. "Ozawa is not trained as a soldier. His presence places the recon teams at risk. I also trust that he understands that if he goes in, there is a distinct possibility that we will not be able to get him out."

Vereshchagin nodded. "Simon?"

"Oh, sorry. I was daydreaming." Beetje hesitated. "I think that the lemur-apes have something important to teach us. I understand that there is a risk, but I think the risk is worth it."

Szuba had sense enough to keep quiet.

Coldewe spoke slowly. "I'd like to move DeKe and Kalle— our teams are stretched so damned thin—but I don't recommend sending Ozawa in alone. Maybe we could send one of Aichi's men along as a bodyguard."

Vereshchagin turned to The Iceman. "Piotr?"

"I think it would be a mistake, Anton. I also think that sending down the rest of the contact team will prove to be a mistake. The Blues are not nearly as pacifistic as Dr. Seki believes."

Dr. Szuba started to speak, but a look from Vereshchagin silenced her. "Hans, do you agree?"

"Oh, I agree with Piotr," Coldewe said distantly. "I just think we need to find out as much as we can before things blow up in our faces."

As the meeting broke up, Coldewe looked for Simon Beetje. "What's wrong, Simon? You seemed a little out of it in there."

Beetje shook his head. "I am all right. I truly hope that you are not right about the naturales."

"A man may choose his friends, but God chooses his enemies. Simon, let me try asking this as a friend. Is the strain of working with Maria getting to you? How are you and she getting along?"

"Everything's fine between us, Hans. We've never had any trouble separating our professional concerns from our personal lives."

Coldewe raised an eyebrow.

"Actually, it's awful." Beetje ruminated about first causes. "I still can't believe how much she changed after we got married."

"You and a few hundred million others," Coldewe said politely. "You notice God never got married."

"She became obsessed with our careers, with the house. I just didn't expect her to change like that, Hans."

"I've noticed that a woman marries a man expecting him to change, and he doesn't; while a man marries a woman expecting her to stay the same, and she doesn't."

"I should have seen it coming when I didn't even get to pick what I wore at our wedding. But it absolutely shocked me when she decided to come along. I never expected that. Not ever," Beetje announced. "Why did Anton let her come?"

"The same reason he let you come. He needed her enough to put up with the inconvenience."

"It is crazy, Hans. Now for once, I need her less than she needs me, and it is as though she's suddenly changed back to the girl I married." Beetje shook his head. "Does this surprise you?"

"Not a bit. Marriage is an institution for the commitment of the criminally insane."

"Joke about it if you want to," Beetje said bitterly.

"Sorry, Simon. Go on," Coldewe coaxed. "How are you making things work?"

"To be truthful, I am not. Maria is more interested in me than I am in her, so I play a game with Pia as my collaborator. I pretend to be interested in Pia, and Maria coos like a turtledove." Again, he shook his head. "Is this any way to live?"

" 'Married life' may be an oxymoron. Simon, forgive me for asking, but if you feel like this, why did you let her move back in with you?"

"Well, it's not that bad, Hans." A spasm of truthfulness tugged at Beetje. "The sex is great. Better than it has been in ten years."

"There's a price you pay for that sort of thing," Coldewe declared. "Remind me to send flowers. They always add a festive touch to funerals."

After Beetje wandered off, disconsolate, Coldewe explained to Intelligence Sergeant Lasse Pihkala, who was passing through, "Man's desire is for the woman, but the woman's desire is rarely for other than the desire of the man. That's Coleridge."

L-Day plus 51 [1-zephyr Rain 13]

ALTHOUGH DE KANTZOW IDENTIFIED EACH LEMP BY NUMBER IN field reports, he, of course, christened each of them, naming males after Imperial admirals the 1/35th had served under and choosing flower names for the females. Kekkonen knew he hadn't liked any of the admirals and had his suspicions about the origin of the flower names.

Resting on his belly with the video camera poised on his shoulder, he nudged de Kantzow. "Look at Buttercup there."

The troop's lowest-ranking female, habitually nervous, was down to one infant, which she clutched possessively throughout the day. As Kekkonen and de Kantzow watched, three older juvenile females marched up to her.

"Isn't that cute? They want to hold the baby," Kekkonen observed.

De Kantzow grunted, "Bossy little bitches."

The three were all obviously daughters of the alpha female, and they clearly weren't about to accept a rejection from Buttercup.

"This must be how they learn to care for their own infants," Kekkonen commented as Jasmine, the eldest of the three, cuddled the infant and brushed aside Buttercup's ineffectual effort to reclaim it.

"They frosting need to," was de Kantzow's rejoinder.

"I met Ozawa aboard ship. He's maybe twenty-nine or thirty. A nice kid. You'll like him," Kekkonen predicted confidently.

"I hope somebody told this nice kid what happens if he's frosting dumb enough to get himself spotted," The Deacon growled.

As they watched, Jasmine's sibling, Daisy, snatched the infant away by the neck and scrambled off with the body dangling.

De Kantzow commented a few minutes later, "We'll grab the corpse when the frosters move on. Make the frosting eggheads happy." He added cheerfully, "This frosting planet is a great place for a nice kid."

Kekkonen grimly recorded the sequence on camera.

For half a day, Buttercup carried her dead infant. When she finally laid it down, Horii, the lowest-ranking male, picked it up and carried it into the bushes.

This time, Kekkonen refrained from surmises. As de Kantzow observed indignantly when they finally found the tiny carcass, "The bastard bugger ate the best parts."

L-Day plus 58 [8-zephyr Rain 13]

SEATED AT THE RICKETY LITTLE TABLE IN THE KITCHEN TENT, Connie Marais sighed, "Beer! That's what we need. You can't run a scientific inquiry without beer."

"Kirin beer," Keiji Katakura specified. "On ice."

Marais, dressed in lemon-yellow shorts and sandals, slapped at the blond fur covering his chest. "On ice," he agreed. "Where is Isaac?"

Tomomi Motofugi said sharply, "He is outside with Dr. Ando, I would imagine. How long until siesta time is over?"

"A few moments more, perhaps," Katakura said, making a show of examining his watch.

"I will go to the latrine, then." Motofugi rose to his feet.

As soon as he left, Marais and Katakura exploded into laughter.

"I wonder what Dr. Seki will make of his complaint," Katakura said as soon as he recovered.

"A longing for beer is obviously evidence of a frivolous and unscientific attitude." The Afrikaner philologist locked his hands over his head and stretched. "He probably thinks that if he complains about us enough, Seki will ask Vereshchagin to send a shuttle to pick us up."

"Would the commissioner do this?"

"I asked Isaac Wanjau what he thought, and he said that in his 'professionally scientific opinion,' first, pigs would fly, and the salamander on the battalion crest would eat its tail. Isaac also mentioned that there is money in it for us if we can tell the odds-makers aboard ship how the Blues accomplish sex."

"I do wish we could persuade the naturales to spend less time learning English and more time teaching us their language," Katakura said wistfully.

Marais shook his head. "It wouldn't help. They don't talk—they sing. My ears can't pick up the differences in tone, and the computer isn't helping. Half the time we can't make sense out of what we're saying and signing to each other. It's very frustrating."

"These things take time, Connie, as you keep saying."

As Katakura spoke, they heard a single pistol shot. "Oh, my God!" Marais exclaimed. He grabbed Katakura by the arm, and they raced outside and looked around.

Motofugi was lying on the ground, trembling, with his head over his arms.

Another three shots rang out.

"This way!" Katakura said.

As they climbed a small rise, they spotted Isaac Wanjau and Kobus Nicodemus next to a dozen Blues. Wanjau had a 9mm pistol in his hand and was demonstrating the trigger action. A piece of broken plastic was sitting on a rock as a target.

"Hello, Dr. Marais, Dr. Katakura, I was showing my friend Kikhinipallin how to fire a pistol. He is a soldier, too, you know," Wanjau said matter-of-factly, speaking slowly with discrete intervals between words.

Katakura and Marais exchanged glances. "You can talk to him?" Marais questioned.

"One manages these things. As I was saying, the Nakamura pistol fires an 8mm-by-18mm round at an initial velocity of 350 meters per second." He held up a round and then extended his fingers precisely a meter apart. "This is a meter." He then pantomimed the flight of the bullet and used his watch and a pocket abacus to elucidate, although with little apparent success.

Dr. Seki appeared a moment later.

Kikhinipallin chirped something and made arm motions downrange. Isaac took the pistol from him, pulled the empty magazine, and demonstrated how the spring worked by feeding in fresh rounds, naming the parts as he did so.

"How did you know he was a soldier?" Katakura asked, looking to Dr. Seki for encouragement.

"One knows these things. There are a few dozen of them camped out in the forest there," Wanjau said in the same disinterested tone as he reloaded the pistol.

Kikhinipallin reached for the pistol again, and Wanjau shook his head, grinning. Tucking it into his holster, he pantomimed shooting downrange and pointed toward the forest emphatically.

Kikhinipallin turned toward an older individual and chirped something. The other Blue made a movement with his head, and Kikhinipallin scampered off at a run toward the forest, returning minutes later with something that looked like a stockless air rifle, which Wanjau immediately recognized as an advanced bullpup design.

Dr. Seki's eyes widened considerably.

Wanjau, who had learned a disconcerting amount about what it meant to be Japanese during his stint in a Japanese jail, paid no attention to the three scientists. He took the weapon, which was obviously meant to be fired resting against the hip, and waited for his friend to demonstrate how the safety worked.

Within ten minutes, Wanjau had learned the words for recoil, gas operation, and the weapon's various parts. He also cleared up an outstanding problem concerning the conversion of numbers when he discovered that the magazine held thirty-six rounds, which is the number forty in base nine, and learned the word for "pretty toy," which tickled him to no end, dovetailing as it did with his own notion on the value of a pistol as a weapon.

It wasn't so hard to communicate, Wanjau explained later; while there may be any number of languages, there are only four ways to supply the working force to an automatic rifle.

Marais and Katakura returned to find a jug on the table with their names scrawled on the side.

Marais picked it up and sniffed at its contents. "It's beer."

Katakura glanced toward the kitchen where Superior Private Brit Smits was working. "I think this place is haunted."

L-Day plus 59 [9-zephyr Rain 13]

ILLUMINATED BY STARLIGHT, DE KANTZOW SAID, "OKAY, YOU say Ozawa's going to fall in the frosting forest, and I say he frosting lands in the ravine."

"Loser has to fish him out." Kekkonen looked up. "Looks like more rain tomorrow. There's a chute now."

"He's about five hundred meters too high," de Kantzow growled.

Kekkonen grinned. "What do you expect from a civ?"

A second chute opened a few seconds later.

Both jumpers steered into the middle of the small clearing. "He missed the forest and he missed the frosting ravine," de Kantzow sighed. "I guess that means Dolly wins."

Dolly barked appreciatively.

"We did have a second bet on," Kekkonen observed.

Closely followed by his bodyguard, Dr. Kantaro Ozawa clumsily gathered up his chute and began walking toward them with a beatific smile on his face. "Not a scratch," Kekkonen observed.

"Little froster bounced once, that ought to count for something," The Deacon grumbled.

At daybreak, when they went to introduce Ozawa to the

lemps, Ozawa finally interrupted Kekkonen's well-meaning flow of dialogue. "Goodness, I did not realize that you were so interested in primate research!"

"He's just frosting happy he's got somebody else to talk to," The Deacon commented from the shelter of a tree as the morning rains pelted them. The fourth member of their party, a corporal from Major Aichi's company, hung back, still a little uncertain of his bearings in a strange land.

"You had some questions about the lemps' diet?" Kekkonen asked.

"More shit to collect," de Kantzow groaned.

"There are certain aspects that are puzzling," Ozawa explained, oblivious to the remark. "For example, the fecal samples contain a high percentage of indigestible vegetable matter."

As he spoke, a male lemp quit grubbing for grubs and left his position on the troop's perimeter to confront them.

Kekkonen immediately backed off a few steps. "That's Ishizu, Doctor. Don't get too close."

Ozawa held his ground. "I do not believe that I will frighten him." He moved a step closer.

Kekkonen shrugged. De Kantzow smiled.

Ishizu squared his shoulders. Grasping something from the ground, he whipped his left arm forward in an underarm motion and flung a chunk of quartz that impacted on Ozawa's battledress. Stunned slightly, the biologist stepped backward and landed on his rump.

"The frosting little son of a bitch is a demon with a rock," de Kantzow explained.

In Orbit, HIMS *Zuiho* [1-lake Rain 13]

"ANTON, I HAVE A CONFESSION TO MAKE," COLDEWE SAID AS HE and Vereshchagin waited for everyone else to arrive. "I'm getting awfully tired of tea. Do you think anyone would notice if I switched to cocoa?"

Vereshchagin tried unsuccessfully to maintain his composure. "I think it might have a deleterious effect on Kasha's morale."

"The heavy burden of tradition." Coldewe brightened. "Maybe I can talk Natasha into writing me a prescription. She does consider me a mental case. Are you set for your meeting with Hokiundoquen? Or is it *the* Hokiundoquen? Seki didn't seem too sure whether it was a personal name or a title."

"There is very little preparation I can make. I will see his image on a view screen and he will see mine, we will exchange a few words in mutually incomprehensible languages, and we will carefully avoid discussing issues. High-level negotiations seem to be much the same everywhere. Nonetheless, Dr. Seki believes that this is an important bridge to build, however tenuously, and I am inclined to agree."

Piotr Kolomeitsev appeared and squeezed between the chairs to draw himself a mug of tea. "Good morning. Hans, you are early."

"Before everyone else gets here, I want to talk about sneaking a team into the missile site that fired on us."

The Iceman digested this information. "Whose team?"

"Zerebtsov's, of course."

For a dozen years, Section Sergeant Vsevolod Zerebtsov had asked for and received the toughest missions the reconnaissance company drew.

Coldewe continued, "I think we have enough data to have a good shot of pulling it off. There is a decent drop zone not too far away. I've checked the distance from the airhead, and if he and Kemp travel light, we can squeeze them into one Sparrow to pick them up. Anton?"

"I agree." Vereshchagin tapped the bowl of his pipe against his thigh. "It is time."

AFTER ELEVEN HOURS SPENT PORING OVER THE PHOTOGRAPHS and other data that Aksu had lovingly compiled, Zerebtsov and his partner, Superior Private Coenraad Kemp, sought out Coldewe, with Jan Snyman to referee.

Coldewe settled back and projected a map on the wall. "How do you want to go in?"

"On foot." Zerebtsov superimposed an infrared photograph of the site. Five low buildings were grouped in an irregular pentagram and surrounded by a low wall. A building on the north side was the source of the missile launched at the task group.

Coldewe could see no pattern to the structures. "Why not a drop on the target?"

Zerebtsov enlarged the image of the buildings to the east and west and pointed to twin superstructures occupying the slanted roofs. "Either those things are radars, or the Blues cook with microwave."

"They're radars; they've just not been active." Coldewe said. "I don't want to find out how good those radars are."

Zerebtsov put the map back up. "Coen and I will drop here and cycle in. I want pickup at LZ Ehime Gifu unless we get in trouble."

"How much trouble do you expect?" Snyman asked.

Zerebtsov reached up and patted Kemp on the shoulder affectionately. "Nothing this big bullock can't pull me out of. The only thing that bothers me about going in is that I can't spot any ground defenses. Just the wall, which isn't much of a wall."

Coldewe sighed. "Just remember, if you run into trouble, pull out. This is just a probe. If we want to go in and disassemble everything movable, we'll do that later. Right now, it's more important to keep them oblivious to our snooping."

"If we have to shoot anybody, do we bring them back?" Kemp inquired.

Snyman looked at Coldewe helplessly. "Hell, yes."

L-Day plus 63 [4-lake Rain 13]

"IT LOOKS PRETTY OVERCAST," SECTION SERGEANT MARKUS Alariesto commented. "Tonight would be a good night to get close-ups from the village and maybe some more plant samples."

The village in question was a small one with twenty houses and outbuildings, and perhaps two hundred souls. Alariesto and Chris Heunis had spent enough hours on the village's fringes to assume a proprietary interest.

Heunis rode his bike over a rock and skillfully leaned his weight forward to clear it with the least amount of effort. "Collecting sick plants, and more peeping in windows. My father caught me peeping in windows when I was twelve, and after he finished whipping me, he swore I was going straight to hell. You know, I would hate to live as close to my neighbors as these people do."

Alariesto snickered. "I grew up in a fifth-floor flat in Turku. You'd have really hated that." Turning his bike into the forest, he noticed three well-nourished shrubs growing beside a shallow depression, and a memory tugged at him. "Hold on."

"What is it?" Heunis asked. Hansel, the team's scout dog, trotted to the edge of the depression and whined softly.

Alariesto put his bike aside and knelt down. Pulling out his *kukri*, he shoved it into the soil to test its texture and then began scraping at the surface. "Remember what Colonel Hans said about finding a cemetery?"

Heunis nodded. "I'm beginning to think the Blues don't have cemeteries."

Alariesto gouged out a chunk of dirt and pointed to a weathered object whose tip had been resting almost unnoticed on the surface. He tapped it with the heavy Gurkha knife. "Leg bone."

Heunis frowned. "You don't think it's an animal bone, do you?"

"You don't either." Alariesto grinned mirthlessly.

Heunis solemnly unstrapped his camera and recorded the image on a laser disk. "This is worth a balloon. You dig. I'll take pictures. The big brains up top are going to want us to record the position of every bone to help them figure out how the skeleton got here."

"Skeleton, huh?" Alariesto's grin widened as he began scooping away at the humus overlaying the shallow grave. On Cyclade, where Alariesto had served, the Provisional Army concealed bodies of people they murdered as a neat exercise in psychological warfare. He remembered quite a few graves in odd corners. "I think I know how it got here. And what makes you think there's only one?"

L-Day plus 66 [7-lake Rain 13]

"WHAT'S WRONG?" COEN KEMP ASKED SECTION SERGEANT Vsevolod Zerebtsov as they crouched together in the darkness observing the missile complex.

"I don't know. Something is, that's all." Zerebtsov took a reading from the portable sensor unit he was carrying and spent a few seconds obliterating a stray boot print.

"Colonel Hans said—"

"I know what Colonel Hans said, but this is important. All right, here's what we'll do. You stay here. I'll try to get close up to the buildings. After I take a quick look around, we'll both get out of here and come back another night."

Without waiting for Kemp to reply, Zerebtsov began moving forward, spider fashion. About fifty meters from the building, he gasped and fell on his face. He didn't move.

Kemp keyed his radio. "Battalion point one. Break. Kemp here. Zerebtsov looks dead, and I am aborting. I don't think we're compromised. I'm pulling his body out, but I'm going to need pick-up at LZ Akita Chiba." Uncoiling a length of rope to loop around Zerebtsov's ankle, he hesitated for a second. "To save you from asking, I have no idea what killed him."

L-Day plus 72 [4-brook Rain 13]

"WHAT WORK DOES YOUR FATHER PERFORM?" MARAIS ASKED Meniolagomeka, the junior of the two naturales who had assigned themselves to him. He made the appropriate signs.

Ekpalawehud and Meniolagomeka discussed the question in a series of short trills, then Ekpalawehud, who always spoke first, replied, "Meniolagomeka is scholar."

"Yes, but is his father also a scholar?" Marais asked.

Although nearly as proficient as Spoagusa or Nessenletam, who had attached themselves to Dr. Seki, Ekpalawehud was either confused or irritated by the question. "He is scholar. Father am scholar."

Marais still wasn't sure whether the word *father* meant the same to the Blues as it did to humans, but he sensed that he was on to something. "My father is a farmer. He grows food plants."

Ekpalawehud appeared agitated. "Are you farmer? Do you grow food plants?"

"I am a scholar. My father is a farmer." Marais mentally crossed his fingers. "Is Meniolagomeka's father a scholar?"

The down on Ekpalawehud's neck and shoulders rose—a gesture Marais had learned to associate with irritation—and he made a gesture to keep Meniolagomeka from responding. "Pochteca decides." Ekpalawehud clicked his teeth together with a finality that Marais had come to loathe. The Pochteca was an undefined governmental authority, and the response "Pochteca decides," accompanied by a click, was intended to end discussion.

"Drink to friendship. Why must Pochteca decide?" Marais asked bluntly. "I am a scholar, my father is a farmer."

Clearly disconcerted, Ekpalawehud reached for Marais's mug instead of his own, gulped from it, and immediately spit up. Choking, with foam flecking his nostrils, he ran from the tent.

Spilled beer dripped to the tent floor. Marais half rose to follow, appalled. Meniolagomeka watched with no expression that Marais could read. "Why you come here?" he asked suddenly.

"To meet with your people. To establish friendly relations,"

Marais said automatically, realizing that this was the first time he had ever seen a naturale alone.

"Doctorseki state. Doctorseki the wrist, Wanjau the hand. Variag the brain," Meniolagomeka said without moving his eyes from the entrance to the tent. "Pochteca not believe Doctorseki." He turned his head slowly, moving his hands as he spoke. "Doctorseki state you have many spheres."

"Planets," Marais corrected automatically.

"Plan-ets," Meniolagomeka repeated, storing the word away. "We have one planet. No changes. Why. You come. Changes." Meniolagomeka searched for more words than he knew. "You come."

"We don't mean to change things. We want to exchange ideas, exchange technologies. Learn things about you and your planet."

Meniolagomeka trimmed Marais's explanation with a brusque gesture. "Not understand. Why. You come," Meniolagomeka repeated. "Pochteca not understand. Not believe Doctorseki."

The conversation terminated abruptly as Spoagusa and Nessenletam both entered the tent.

The following day, a naturale named Kanyase replaced Meniolagomeka. Ekpalawehud refused to say why.

In Orbit, HIMS *Zuiho* [7-brook Rain 13]

"THE SKELETONS WERE DISARTICULATED. FROM THE BROKEN ends, Dr. Solchava and I think someone used an ax," Simon Beetje explained to Coldewe, Kolomeitsev, and Pia Szuba as he laid out the graying bones for examination. "I am not a pathologist, but judging from the sizes, we probably have a male and two females here, although it is conceivable that the females are actually juveniles."

"Is it possible that the disarticulation is part of a ritual?" Szuba asked, with a fraction of her usual assurance.

Hans Coldewe handed her a skull and pointed to a hole. "Occam's razor being what it is, I know where I'd put my money. Poor Dr. Seki has himself half-convinced that the naturales are inherently peaceful. As Raul Sanmartin used to say, so many wonderful theories are ambushed by nasty little facts."

"Perhaps we should not try to make too much of a single grave," Pia Szuba said, replacing the skull on the table.

"That's true," Coldewe agreed, "however, statistically speaking, if we found one grave, there are probably more of them out there. This could be how the Blues normally dispose of their dead, or it could be something else, which, upon reflection, is not a reassuring thought."

Using echolocation and the dogs, a team had found an underground cable at the spot where Zerebtsov died, and Coldewe was less than pleased at the progress the physical sciences working group was making in unraveling its mysteries.

"Have you spoken with Commissioner Vereshchagin? How did his meeting with Hokiundoquen go?" Szuba asked.

"I think that he is of the opinion that Hokiundoquen is a personal name," Coldewe commented. "Apart from that, I don't think he came away with a great deal."

Szuba nodded. "I will study the recording."

"Simon," The Iceman inquired crisply, "are you ready to explain what these bones tell us about the Blues?"

"I'll try. Like lemur-ape bones, the pieces have an unusual composition. Under a microscope, they look more like mineralized cartilage than true bone." Beetje took an arm bone in his hand and bent it in a very slight arc. "A lot of strength and a fair amount of flexibility, but less rigidity than I would have expected. Pia, did you want to say something?"

"How much of this mineralization preceded death? Can we tell how long these bones have been in the ground?"

"I wish I could. They aren't fresh, and based on the comparison of the lemur-ape bones, about 15 percent of the original calcium phosphate has been leached out. I asked Dr. Takanobu, but he refused to even speculate. These bones could have been five years in the ground, or fifty."

Coldewe gestured. "Can't you do tests? Carbon^{14} dating and that sort of thing?"

· Beetje smiled. "Even if I knew how to do radiocarbon dating, I'm not entirely sure how much carbon^{14} there should be in a normal sampling here. Besides, even under ideal conditions, the best margin of error I could hope for in a test like that would be plus or minus fifty years."

"Were there any traces of clothing or other artifacts?" Kolomeitsev asked.

"None. I would have to speculate that the bodies were stripped before being buried." Beetje continued, "Maria is comparing amino-acid sequences to see how closely DNA from the skeletons corresponds with lemur-ape DNA."

"Just how does that work?" Coldewe asked.

"The technique is actually fairly simple. She first runs the samples through an enzyme solution and through electrically charged gelatin to fragment the DNA. She bathes the fragments in water laced with phosphorus[32] and exposes X-ray film, which she can then use as a guide in selecting DNA strands to replicate. So far, she is seeing a 90 to 94 percent correlation, which suggests that lemur-apes and naturales shared a common ancestor eight or nine million years ago. I'm glad. I would have had some serious explaining to do otherwise." He laid out a handful of finger bones.

Coldewe looked at Szuba. "It's probably a little late to ask this, but shouldn't we be a little hesitant about handling these? The rule I learned on alien microbes is that anything indiscriminating enough to attach itself to a human is likely to be seriously fatal."

Beetje smiled. "I wouldn't worry. These have been pretty thoroughly sterilized—irradiated, exposed to hard vacuum, and what have you. Maria was rather put out."

Coldewe rubbed his head. "Your esteemed once and future wife can go put her head in a bucket of water and count to a hundred. What did you tell her?"

"To put her head in a bucket of water and count to a hundred."

Coldewe laughed. "Simon, we're going to make a soldier out of you yet. Now, what are we looking for here?"

"A couple of things." Beetje held up four small bones. "This is a thumb. As you can see, the end of this bone is rounded, and it fits into this piece, which I'll call the central hand bone for want of a better term, like a ball and socket."

Coldewe tried to appear interested. "Of course, you're going to tell us what that means."

Simon held out the central hand bone for Coldewe and Kolomeitsev to examine. "While the central hand bone is fairly rigid, the fingers—especially the thumb—make up for it by being flexible. Now look at the fingers, see how broad the ends are. Do you see these little ridges? That's where fairly powerful muscles attach. So instead of holding things with the fingertips, the naturales prefer to hold things between the sides of two fingers, or between the thumb and the side of the index finger, which corresponds with the contact team's observations."

Next, Simon picked up a long leg bone. "This is a femur. Legs are generally sloppy affairs, a couple of bones slapped together with some muscles, but this is very neat." He held up the narrow end. "There's no patella. Instead, the shaft of the tibia fits neatly into the groove between the two condyles—the bony bumps on the end here. Very nicely engineered."

He picked up the larger of the two skulls. "I haven't had time to examine the skulls in detail, but this looks like an auditory tube running underneath what I will call the mastoid process, for the sake of argument." He showed them an opening on the skull's lower left side. "Humans hear sounds vibrating at frequencies ranging from 20 hertz to about 20 kilohertz, with greatest sensitivity between 1000 and 4000 hertz. Computer modeling suggests the Blues have a similar range."

Coldewe grinned, seeing the bored look on The Iceman's face. "Simon, this is all fascinating, but is there anything actually useful in this?"

"Oh, useful." Beetje blew some air through his lips. "What the skeletons really do is show that some of our conclusions about the lemur-apes may also be applicable to the Blues." He pointed to a pelvis. "The pelvic bone, which consists of six other bones fused together, is essentially a scaled-up version of a lemur-ape pelvis. You see how narrow the birth canal is. It suggests that the Blues also give birth to infants that are basically in a larval state. Before I commit myself, I'd like to see some sociological data if I can, but that's where my tentative conclusions lead me."

"Pia, how are your own inquiries coming?" Coldewe asked.

Szuba shook her head. "Much of the data we have been getting from the contact team is incomplete and confused. Even basic facts about the social and political structure appear to elude us. I cannot help but think that the naturales do not trust us."

"Having been around people all your life, would you?" Coldewe asked.

Concern etched lines into Szuba's doll-like face. "Failure to convince the naturales to lay aside their suspicions may make it impossible for us to carry out our mission."

"Of greater concern," The Iceman observed, "it may get us killed."

L-Day plus 76 [8-brook Rain 13]

"LET ME SEE HERE." SUPERIOR PRIVATE DENYS GORDIMER punched numbers into his wrist mount. "I make it 1,207,630 rand you owe me. Excuse me, that isn't right. One million, two hundred seven thousand, six hundred thirty rand and fifty cents. Want to play another hand?"

"You're just shot full of luck," Blaar Schuur complained, his eye glued to the telephoto lens.

Gordimer rubbed his fingernails against his breast and blew on them. "It comes from clean living."

"Clean living? Someone in here smells like a goat, and it isn't me."

Gordimer tilted his head with evident interest. "You know, that's an excellent idea. We could bet on which one of us smells the worst when we get to camp. Sergeant Alariesto can judge."

Schuur grinned. "You *know* what Alariesto is going to say."

The two of them echoed in chorus, "*Both* you moles smell like pig manure."

"You still counting the hours until we get out of here?" Gordimer asked.

"Eleven hours, thirty-six minutes, and fourteen seconds," Schuur stated without lifting his eyes.

"You know, you really could try to improve your outlook on life," Gordimer said, scratching his left shoulder blade against the framework of the hide. "I mean, if you think about it, most people have to commute to work."

"Hush up, Denys!" Schuur hissed, waving him to silence. "The peasants are restless." He began recording.

Gordimer elbowed forward.

The noon sun illuminated the village in the valley with a harsh light. In the far distance the surface of the Great River shimmered.

Normally quiescent at noon, family by family, the village's inhabitants, tall males draped in red cloaks and petite females carrying infants and trailing toddlers, were spilling out into the diked fields.

"Look at them all," Gordimer murmured.

"What are they doing?" Schuur asked the rocks and stones.

Carrying white cloths, the Blues were tossing what looked like handfuls of dust into the air.

"What are they *doing*?" Schuur repeated, lost in wonder.

"Don't ask me," Gordimer replied, to which the rocks and stones gave silent assent.

The scene was repeated elsewhere, in cities and villages across the continent. Although committed to a rigorously behavioralistic and integrationalistic approach devoid of "value preferences," Pia Szuba's social sciences working group carefully reviewed the gestures employed and concluded that the phenomenon represented a religious ritual. Rather testily, Szuba stood by her opinion when questioned.

At midnight, ship's time, the backers of secular humanism threw in the allegorical towel and paid off at an average of seven to six.

L-Day plus 78 [9-brook Rain 13]

"THERE WAS A SMALL FIREFIGHT IN THE WOODS SOUTH OF HERE last night." Company Sergeant Isaac Wanjau spooned his cereal. "I intend to visit the site if the Blues will allow it."

Dr. Connie Marais was making orange juice. He set the pitcher down. Thinking better of the impulse, he picked it back up and resumed stirring the mix. "Dear God! Are you sure?"

Nicodemus roused himself from his early morning stupor. "He is a company sergeant."

"Oh. Right." Marais thought for a moment. "What would the naturales be fighting about? Not us, surely."

"One wonders," Wanjau said.

Dr. Motofugi entered the tent, looking sleepy. Marais set a bowl of miso in front of his nose. "Tomomi, Isaac heard shooting last night."

"He must be mistaken. I slept well and heard nothing." Motofugi poured himself tea. "Someone in the shower is singing that pig song again."

Pigs whistle when they lose, and they whistle when they win,
'Cause when the shooting's over they scrub off and start again.

Nicodemus grinned. "Well, that is a matter of opinion." Although Brit Smits was very popular despite—or perhaps because of—the harassment he took for being vain about his looks, he was moderately tone-deaf.

Motofugi carefully put his spoon down and held his hands to his ears. "If I hear another verse, I will scream. Is Dr. Seki awake?"

"He and Dr. Ando are reviewing their notes." Marais reached for a rice cracker and spread peanut butter on it. "We found out yesterday that the naturales have a money economy."

"We, of course, have our own little economy based upon scarcity of desserts," Wanjau observed.

Motofugi, who didn't have much of a sweet tooth, ignored the dessert issue. "This is a wonderful breakthrough. How did you get them to talk about money?"

Marais gestured with the butter knife. "I couldn't get Kanyase to discuss it, so I turned Isaac loose on the problem."

"The Blues reckon prices in hypothetical units of electrum," Wanjau explained modestly.

"Electrum?" Motofugi appeared dumbfounded.

"It is an alloy of gold and silver." Wanjau kept a straight face.

Marais tried to eat and speak at the same time. "I think he wants to know how you found out."

"Why, yes," Motofugi amplified.

"When the Blue soldiers pump me for information, they often tell me things without meaning to. I explained to them how I met my wife and what I had to pay for her, and then Lupwaekoawuk explained what his wife cost. He is an officer, and he is hoping to afford another someday. None of the privates spoke much, but I think they are all hoping that they will be able to afford a wife someday."

Dr. Motofugi's eyes bulged.

Wanjau patted Motofugi's arm. "I told them that humans have differing customs, and that instead of a bride-price, most men pay for being married in other ways."

"Ekpalawehud admitted some of it when I questioned him directly." Marais put peanut butter on another cracker and bit into it.

"Wanjau-*san*, you do not appear to comprehend." The Japanese linguist trembled with suppressed excitement. "This is truly an important breakthrough. The insight this will give us into their speech patterns and into the origin of words is very important."

"It might also give us insights into their society," Wanjau wondered aloud with seeming innocence.

"Oh, someone may wish to look into those aspects." Motofugi nodded to himself, to all outward appearances already lost in thoughts appropriate to his discipline. "Language is, of course, a mirror to society."

Marais cursed softly. Wanjau grinned, then said, "And we're having pudding tonight."

"I learned a great deal about human nature during my stay in Japan," Wanjau said, still grinning.

Smits entered the tent with his towel over his arm. "Kobus has the shower next, but after that it's free."

Wanjau moved his head up and down slowly to get a better look at him. "Your top shirt button is undone. Showing yourself off to the native women? What would your good friend Miss Deltje say?"

Smits blushed to the roots of his hair and hastily buttoned the offending button. He then placed a wad of wet hair in the cooker set aside for that purpose and watched it incinerate. A slight odor filled the tent.

"It is my view that the directive concerning disposal of hair and nail clippings is especially senseless," Motofugi complained.

"It is bad luck to let an enemy have a part of you," Wanjau replied calmly.

"I wish that you would not refer to the naturales as enemies," Motofugi said peevishly. "And what would they do with our hair? Make voodoo dolls?"

"Extract the DNA," Wanjau replied.

In Orbit, HIMS *Zuiho* [3-cloud Rain 13]

"THIS IS THE *DIABELLI VARIATIONS*," PIOTR KOLOMEITSEV EXplained to Nicola Bosenac.

Although unlike in every other way, the Franciscan and The Iceman shared a love for music. Perhaps lonely, Kolomeitsev had made an effort to cultivate Bosenac, professing to regard him as the keeper of Vereshchagin's conscience.

Bosenac searched for an appropriate phrase. "It is interesting."

Kolomeitsev chuckled. "It is perhaps not among Beethoven's finest works. I have seen it described as 'an act of artistic aggression,' but I enjoy it. To me, it is a challenge, taken up and hurled back."

Bosenac recalled the tape of a discussion that a Blue named Tapakoase had with Dr. Ando over the nature of poetry. Perhaps speaking for a consensus of Neighbor's inhabitants, Tapakoase had asserted, insofar as Ando was able to follow, that the essence of poetry is aggressive, feverish expression, and that beauty lies in violently forcing the unknown to bow before the mind. It was a sobering and in some ways revealing argument, one of the few that the contact team had managed to elicit. "Have you always loved music?" he asked.

"Until I retired, the lives of individuals were in my hands, and I did not develop interests apart from fishing."

The piece ended. "I spoke with Commissioner Vereshchagin today," Bosenac said.

"He mentioned your frustration."

"I read everything that comes through from the contact team." Bosenac clenched his fists. "To be so near and not understand these people—their feelings, their beliefs."

"Most of us are equally dissatisfied."

"Are you?"

"I am patient." The Iceman scrolled to find Mussorgsky's *Pictures at an Exhibition.* "I believe that there is a universal human nature, one that is recognizably the same as it was millennia ago. The motives and feelings of the personalities in *The Tale of Genji* or *Henry V* are thoroughly and idiosyncratically human, as recognizable now as when these were written. The Blues are people like us. But they are not human."

"But we don't know that. Whatever the Blues are, they hide it from us, Piotr. I know that they are not like us in every respect, but I believe that the essence of what makes them people is very human, and in every important way, they are people just like ourselves." He almost added, "with souls." He reflected, "I find it fascinating that although a technologically advanced stage is the merest blink of an eye in all the thousands of years of their history, we reached them just at this time."

The Iceman gave him a sour look. "If you deity had a hand in this, he plays with weighted dice. Unfortunately, in the examples at hand, technologically advanced civilizations tend to be destructive ones." Kolomeitsev studied Bosenac's face. "You have been thinking your way to a question or questions all evening."

Bosenac laughed. "Yes, I suppose I have." He paused. "What is it about war that so fascinates people?"

"War," The Iceman said solemnly, "is murder and destruction on a grand scale. And yet it is the most powerful catalyst for change, both good and ill, that human societies know. The unlamented Vladimir Ilyich Lenin, who factored so prominently in my nation's troubled history, viewed an army as the ideal organizational model because of its power to impart a single will to millions of people. Waging modern war and preparing to wage it have shaped nations and their governing institutions, and unending war, which atomizes potential internal opposition and generates powerful pressure to enlarge the authority of the state, is the textbook recipe for successful totalitarianism."

"I would like to think that yours is a cynical view of human history."

"Unfortunately, I find myself looking for parallels here, and in a thoroughly unscientific manner, perhaps finding them."

"I pray that you are wrong." Bosenac ruminated.

The Iceman paused. Then he said, "I was intensely religious once. Before my wife died. It took her three months to die." He reached into his breast pocket and pulled out a photograph, encased in plastic for permanency.

Bosenac looked at it. The woman in it was in no way remarkable.

"I read what has been written to explain why people suffer pain and die," The Iceman said, "and no explanation I have read suffices. Your church teaches that your God suffered and died for man, but I have seen many men suffer and die."

"You are surely a unique man," Bosenac said quietly and carefully, "to have borne so deep an anger so calmly for so many years."

"So I have been told," The Iceman replied.

L-Day plus 82 [5-cloud Rain 13]

"I SUPPOSE IT'S A LITTLE LATE TO ASK THIS," SENIOR QUARTERmaster Sergeant Vulko Redzup commented idly as he stared out the opened shuttle door into the darkness, "but I wonder whether the line is going to hold."

"Of course, it will," the engineer in Meri Reinikka responded. "The composite fiber of the cable has roughly 123 times the tensile strength of LV^8 steel of equivalent diameter. The airframe will tear loose before the cable breaks."

"Oh?" Redzup raised one eyebrow.

"As a safety precaution, the winch mounting will go before the airframe does."

Redzup, a resupply specialist for most of his life, turned his head around and braced himself against his safety line. With the shuttle's cargo bay darkened, the only light came from the starlight magnified fifty thousand times by the night goggles he and Reinikka wore. "I hope Alariesto has sense enough to pick a truck that isn't loaded."

"Statistical probabilities and the ancient law of Murphy being what they are, the vehicle will be full of lead."

The problem with stealing a motor vehicle lay in getting it off the ground without landing a shuttle and wheeling it on board, which was something that Coldewe felt the Blues might notice. Trucks, as a rule, do not fly, and the magnetized arresting wire that a shuttle lowered to snag balloons was clearly not up to the task of snagging flying trucks. The problem remained unresolved until Section Sergeant Markus Alariesto reported that the Blues parked vehicles overnight in an unfenced area on one of the south coastal mesas.

With the precipitous drop-off from the mesa to the sea and a heavy night wind blowing out, Redzup and Reinikka surmised that a low-flying shuttle might be able to jerk a truck off the mesa and pull it in, and Flight Sergeant Ivan Kokovtsov was eventually persuaded, with some difficulty, to fly the mission.

Redzup grinned wolfishly. "Lead might prove embarrassing."

Kokovtsov interrupted. "Final course alteration. Bearing 178 degrees. Altitude 120 meters. Winds gusting at thirty-two to thirty-five kilometers per hour. Alariesto reports green."

Reinikka punched the intercom. "Green here."

"Estimate one hundred seconds to contact. Kokovtsov out."

"Coconut is getting almost talkative in his old age. You know, I wonder if anyone has tried this before?" Reinikka mused. A moment later, he said, "It wasn't *that* funny."

Redzup wiped his eyes. "Meri, you missed your calling in life becoming an engineer, you really did."

"I said it wasn't *that* funny."

Kokovtsov broke in. "I see the balloon. The wind is pushing it out to sea at a 45-degree angle." He checked his instruments. "A 44-degree angle."

Reinikka glanced at his calculations and hit the intercom. "Still green." He looked at Redzup. "Ready?"

Redzup nodded.

A second later, the shuttle's airflow jerked the balloon alongside the open cargo bay. "Pull it in!" Redzup said.

Reinikka powered the winch. The shuttle jerked, then thrust forward as Kokovtsov increased power. Reinikka found himself breathing in short, ragged gasps. "Did it work?"

"Yes and no." Redzup braced himself and leaned out to take a better look. "It was loaded. Which end of a Blue truck has the engine, do you think?"

"I hope the fishes are okay," Kokovtsov commented laconically.

Within hours after their safe return, an anonymous rhymester posted a poem in the style of Tennyson, which opened with the immortal line, "Half a truck, half a truck, half a truck onward," and concluded, "When can their glory fade?/Oh, what a gaff they made/Honor the shuttle brigade/Gallant half dozen."

"You wouldn't know who wrote that poem, would you?" Reinikka asked Coldewe suspiciously.

"Of course not. But it was good for morale, wasn't it?"

"Most people's."

L-Day plus 175 [4-flint Rain 13]

"INFANT G-3 DIED TODAY, LEAVING ONLY FIVE SURVIVING INfants, including one born to the dominant female and given to another female to nurse. Lack of food due to increasingly arid conditions has induced the lemur-apes to make their closest approach to civilized areas. It will be important to assess whether the next breeding cycle reflects a similarly high mortality."

To the dismay of Omori, the Japanese trooper assigned as his bodyguard, Dr. Ozawa spoke almost continuously into his recorder as he worked.

Ozawa followed the lemur-ape troop up a ridge line, plunging through a thorn thicket. "The local year, which is twenty-three days longer than a standard year, appears to be well suited to a generally slower growth rate among higher animals, due to what are both objectively and subjectively harsher environmental conditions than are found on most similar worlds."

Omori struggled after him.

Unnoticed, the thorns took Ozawa's spare recorder from his belt. Hours of searching failed to locate it.

L-Day plus 182 [2-dust Rain 13]

IGNORING THE ASH FROM THE MINE'S SMELTERS, SECTION SERgeant Thys Meiring nodded at his partner, Superior Private Pieter Kriel.

With a small dog and a portable sensor as insurance against traps, Meiring cautiously poked an optical fiber around the small building's door. Satisfied there were no alarms or unpleasant surprises, Meiring, son of a mining engineer, went to work on the surprisingly familiar-looking padlock with his cutting bar, sawing through it in short, careful strokes. He disappeared inside to fill his bergen with local explosives.

"Just like home," Meiring remarked as they fled the scene of the crime.

"You know, Thys," Kriel commented, "I like blowing things up as much as the next man, but working with funny detonators makes me nervous. I know *Zuiho* will look over this stuff six ways from next Tuesday, and if the Blues analyzed residue from our stuff they might raise some eyebrows, if they had any, but still—"

Meiring grinned. "Pieter, you talk too much."

Following an exhaustive series of tests on the explosives in space, Meiring and Kriel obtained pieces of ceramic railway and a ceramic power line, disguising their work as local sabotage.

As Dr. Kita's working group discovered, both fragments had layered, ambient-temperature superconductive cores. The power line excited particular interest. The working group estimated that it would dissipate a tenth of a percent of conducted energy per hundred kilometers, which meant that the Blues effectively had a continentwide power grid.

The finding helped explain the trap that killed Zerebtsov and ended any talk about the Blues being backward.

LOVE

The pig got bored with football, and he wanted something new,
So he found himself a planet where the folks were colored
· blue.
The pig put on his manners and he wore a tie and suit,
And the people were so friendly that they almost didn't
shoot!

—"The Whistling Pig"

In Orbit, HIMS *Zuiho* [6-wind Rain 14]

COLDEWE ROLLED OUT OF HIS HAMMOCK WITH PRACTICED EASE.
"Hello, Simon. What can I do for you?"

"Kantaro Ozawa broke his leg." Beetje looked around for a
chair in Coldewe's cabin.

"Yes, it sounds like a compound fracture. Wessels is going to
bring him back to base camp after dark."

"It is an exceedingly awkward time for him to be injured,
Hans. This year's breeding season data is crucial to the lemur-
ape study."

"I have most of the recon platoon sitting around base camp
eating their heads off. How about if I put DeKe de Kantzow and
Kalle Kekkonen back on the project?"

Beetje shook his head impatiently. "I need to go, Hans. We've
spent nearly thirteen months on this, and I have to be sure that
I have good data for two seasons to support my conclusions."

"Good data is something we're short of all around. Captain
Kobayashi and Detlef Jankowskie are still trying to match population density to food production for their statistical analyses,
and there still seems to be more Blues than food to feed them.
To put it bluntly, they've lost considerable faith in the values
your people have given them to work with."

Arita, the young ensign whose job it was to rewrite the statistical programs *Aoba*'s computers used to translate raw sensor data into usable information, had suffered a nervous breakdown, and Coldewe had been forced to send Esko Poikolainnen over to *Aoba* to try to crack the problem.

"I'm sorry, Hans," Beetje apologized. "Short of cutting up a Blue, I'm not sure what we can do." Except for holdouts like Dr. Seki, all of the expedition's personnel had fallen into the habit of calling Neighbor's inhabitants Blues.

Coldewe yawned. "In theory, the problem ought to be easy. The Blues don't have maize fields, rice fields, wheat fields, or amber waves of grain. All they have is that silly water potato and that silly purple yam, two root crops."

"This planet never developed an analogue to grasses, and all major human cereal crops are grass species."

"Then apart from potatoes and yams, which appear to be the staff of life to them, what do these people eat? They don't have many meat animals. Although they appear to get some of their vegetable fiber and a lot of their protein from the sea, Kobayashi insists that the numbers simply don't add up."

Beetje looked puzzled. "They have orchards and gardens."

"There aren't many calories in rabbit food. As I see it, the Blues got badly shortchanged by Mother Nature—they don't have much in the way of domesticated plants and animals to work with, no horses or oxen, and because this continent hasn't been glaciated in a long, long time, they don't have very good soil, either." Coldewe reached over and used Beetje's computer to call up an encyclopedia. "According to this, in nearly every human society, over 50 percent of all calories come from cereal plants. And in preindustrial human societies, the figure is closer to 80 percent. It makes me wonder how the Blues managed to build a technological civilization in the first place, if you know what I mean."

Beetje thought for a moment. "Ozawa has a theory that the planet's higher animals have a resting state where normal metabolic activity shuts down almost completely."

"Like being asleep?"

"Yes and no. With mammals—people sometimes forget that human beings are mammals—about 90 percent of caloric intake goes to maintain body temperature. Even sleeping, mammals still expend a lot of energy this way, although some bats and marsupials are exceptions. Our studies indicate that some of Neighbor's animals allow their body temperature to fluctuate as much as 10 or 15 degrees in the course of a day. The Blues may do so as well."

"It doesn't sound like much."

"It is, Hans. Believe me, it is."

Coldewe went over to make himself some tea and offered Simon a cup, which he declined. "Then finish studying the issue and give Kobayashi some numbers. What's Dr. Seki have to say this morning? Are our on-again, off-again relations with the Blues back on track?"

"Dr. Seki really is mystified this time. Usually, the Blues will try to explain why they are cutting off contact—although you know what their explanations are worth, even when we understand what they're saying, which isn't always—but this time they didn't say anything at all. It's been what, two weeks now?"

"Closer to three. I'd like to move the contact team somewhere else and try and do business with a different set of Blues."

Beetje shook his head. "They've threatened to kill our team if they move to a different location. They were very emphatic about it."

"As I say, I'd like to deal with a different set of Blues. Even Anton is getting annoyed with them, and Anton has oceans of patience compared to me. We still don't know whether the Blues have one nation or dozens, or even whether the Blues have nations in our sense. So much for political data from the contact team."

He gestured. "It takes the Blues an awful lot of stoop labor to maintain the canals and dikes for the water-potato fields. Anton knows more history than any three people I know, and he says that human societies organized to do this tend to be village oriented and thoroughly authoritarian."

"We can't assume that the Blues think like human beings, Hans," Beetje cautioned.

"Simon, I don't know how they think, and I don't much care. Prior to mechanization—and maybe even after it—there simply isn't any place for a family farm here. Unless a hundred or so of these people work together on a given plot of land, they don't get the crops in. That strongly colors social organizations. To get the kind of massive levies you see along the Great River, you need a centralized state. Look at the results—the capital that fueled industrialization here got pooled somehow. How did the Blues get from there to here?"

"You can argue this with Pia, Hans. I'll stick to animals, thank you," Beetje said forthrightly.

"Arguing with Pia can be fun." Coldewe cradled his cup and drank from it. "When she gets really excited, her mind moves faster than her mouth, and the words get stuck coming out. Of course, her team is driving everybody crazy with their 'myth and symbol' approach to Blue culture. Pia tells me that evading questions is culturally shaped behavior that indicates a strain on traditional leadership and tension within a cultural idea. Just once I'd like to hear a sociologist call the Blues liars."

"I'm noticing you're willing to discuss everything and anything except laying on a shuttle flight and sending me down to fill in for Kantaro."

"Simon, I am miserably short of fuel for shuttle flights. Absent a genuine emergency, I need to reserve what I have to make sure we can get our people off Neighbor if our supply ship doesn't show up soon. And I hope that little tin gods reminded Mutaro to send the next supply ship by way of Suid-Afrika, because I'm tired of eating rice."

"Hans, in a way this is an emergency."

"There's also another reason, which has to do with whether you've looked in a mirror lately. You're not young, you're built like a twig, and you haven't been exercising."

"Hans, I had to reconstruct two months of data we lost when Kantaro dropped his recorder," Beetje protested.

Coldewe shook his head, thinking how much he'd like to find Ozawa's lost recorder. "Simon, even if I thought that your reasons for keeping yourself in rotten shape were wonderful, it doesn't alter facts. Now, I really would like you to make yourself useful by talking to Captain Kobayashi about this resting-state business and any other little facts and surmises you've been hoarding so we can get our statistical-information gathering on track. This is military intelligence, not science, and it doesn't have to be 100 percent right the first time. In fact, military intelligence never is."

"Hans, I'm sorry I mentioned the resting-state hypothesis. We really don't have enough data to say anything about it yet."

Coldewe grinned. "Simon, do you remember what you told me the last time I asked you a question about amphtiles?"

Beetje looked puzzled.

"You said, 'I don't know. I only have seventeen years' data.' "

Beetje blushed scarlet.

"Simon, in civilian endeavors, people who publish data before they know what they're talking about are usually called idiots.

Military people who wait until they have complete data to operate from are usually called corpses."

"All right, Hans." Beetje steadied himself. "I will see what I can do."

L-Day plus 399 [6-sand Rain 14]

SUPERIOR PRIVATE CHRIS HEUNIS USED THE BLADE ON THE LITtle engineer vehicle to build a wall in front of the recon platoon's supplies before the monsoon rains came washing into the cavern.

Someone had named the recon platoon's base camp the Tabun Bogdo, and the name stuck. With the arrival of a new monsoon season, in accordance with military custom, Section Sergeant Markus Alariesto solemnly assured his young Afrikaners that *tabun* was Mongolian for "mud," while *bogdo* meant "more mud."

Alariesto walked up and pitched a clean uniform into Heunis's lap. Heunis turned off the engine. "I thought we had to conserve."

"Supply ship is headed in." Alariesto punched him very lightly on the arm. "Get yourself dressed—we're celebrating. Boerewors on the grill."

Aboard *Zuiho*, with three platoons in hibernation to reduce consumption, the imminent arrival of fresh food and new movies had touched off an impromptu saturnalia.

"Super!" Heunis exclaimed. Something dropped to the cavern floor as he unfolded the uniform. "There's a note here."

Alariesto read it. He passed it across. "Colonel Coldewe should stop reading old books. It says, 'Help, I'm being held prisoner in a Chinese laundry.' "

In Orbit, HIMS *Zuiho* [9-sand Rain 14]

POIKOLAINNEN KNOCKED TIMIDLY ON VERESHCHAGIN'S DOOR. "Sir, you, ah, have a visitor."

The same sixth sense that had kept Vereshchagin alive as a soldier gave him just enough warning to retain his composure. "Rikki! What are you doing here?"

Hendricka Sanmartin found herself a seat. "I arrived on the supply ship. Aren't you going to say hello?"

"Forgive me," he said dryly. "I thought you were safely back on Suid-Afrika, being president."

"I was. It took me six months to piece together what you had done, and another month to work out details of my resignation."

"I see." He contemplated this. "I had hoped to cover our tracks."

"You covered them very well. You took along everyone who could tell me anything, and the key witness, Hannes Van der Merwe, vanished, quite literally into thin air as we later deduced. But having Silvershirts seize the Assembly building under orders from Steen seemed to be just the sort of coincidence you would arrange for yourself. You did arrange it, didn't you?"

"Yes. Hannes calls himself Hanno now, but he still works for Aksu. Your father recruited him originally."

"It was not right. I would have liked you to have let me win fairly. Incidentally, the people on Go-Nihon are annoyed with Commissioner Mutaro. He has had to divert their shipping to keep you supplied, and it is having an effect." She eyed him speculatively. "Aren't you going to ask who is president?"

"Christos Claassen?" Vereshchagin guessed.

She nodded. "He is making very sure that Steen's friends never grasp control of the Nationalist party again, which left me free to follow you—Matti tried to talk me out of it, but I did not see a place for a young, unemployed ex-president."

"How much of your program were you able to carry out?" Vereshchagin asked quietly.

"Enough. We still control the Assembly. My people were quite dismayed when I told them I intended to resign—I pushed through some nice legislation, and they thought they would have a full four years to collect the political debts I owed them in return—but they warmed to the idea very nicely when I offered to let them resign in my place or to live with the voters when the scandal finally broke." She turned her head. "I thought about it very carefully. It would not have been right for me to continue."

"What about the young people who helped with your campaign?"

"Matti is still interior minister, and I left them in his care. The better ones have ministry positions, and Christos will leave them in place. By the time we get back, I think that they will be a surprise to the politicians in both parties. I even found a spot for your friend Eva in the finance ministry." She smiled. "As it is, the politicians who cannot do higher math are scared silly at the thought that I might return in time for the next election."

Vereshchagin smiled. "Maybe the one after that."

"I may even win. Steen and his people are snapped reeds; there is no way for them to deny what they were planning to do, even though they received a helpful push from you."

"What, may I ask, gave us away?"

"De la Rey maintained vehemently that Steen had ordered him to execute the takeover, and Steen maintained with equal venom that De la Rey had acted on his own." She curled up in Vereshchagin's old spider chair. "At the inquest, both of them loudly trumpeted their version of events. I also found it extremely curious that the men who murdered campaign workers were part of the group that invaded the Assembly. Something was not quite right, so I made Timo Haerkoennen dig through your computer files. When I discovered that the presumably drowned Hannes Van der Merwe was one of your people, things began to fall into place. I pardoned everyone concerned, including you, before I resigned. You synthesized Steen's voice, didn't you?"

Vereshchagin nodded. "After you resigned, what explanation did you give for coming here?"

"None, of course. I merely reiterated my campaign promise to be sure that Suid-Afrika came in on the first floor if there was money to be made trading things with Neighbor. According to the two theories I enjoyed the best, I am either madly in love with you or your secret illegitimate daughter."

Vereshchagin chuckled. "Has anyone on board questioned you?"

"I did field a few inquiries about the football standings."

He paused. "How did Betje take your decision to come here?"

"She said that she would be waiting for me and as I am still her little girl, the time dilation will not be as hard for her."

"And do you believe that?" he asked quietly.

She shook her head. "No. She will be dead before I get back, won't she?"

"It is possible."

A tear trickled down her cheek. "Oh, God. I promised myself I wouldn't cry about it anymore, and here I am already." She wiped her face. "Abram van Zyl died in his sleep—his heart, they said."

"Some ways to die are less painful than others. Someone once told me that bullets were kind, and for a time, I believed it."

Vereshchagin looked away. "For years, I never let it touch me, but lately, the faces keep coming to me—Raul, Hanna, Yuri Malinov, Rudi Scheel, Rhett Rettaglia—many more that you have never heard of."

She looked at him, and then reached over to embrace him.

"Gu knows my secret. And now you. Did you actually get Matti to go out on a date?"

Her eyes lit up as she sat back down. "Oh, he was awful, the excuses he made! And when Janine finally got him on the dance floor, oh, how he blushed! He was so prim and so horribly embarrassed, it was funny. Growing up, I never noticed how shy he is around women."

"Finland does have the lowest birthrate in Europe."

"He just thinks that he is old," Rikki said confidently. "Janine had him well in hand when I left. How are matters here? Things are not going well, are they?"

Vereshchagin shook his head. "They are not. The Pochteca, which is a governing authority, has again suspended relations. Aksu has been monitoring matters with increasing disquiet, and he is certain that they are implacing missiles at a feverish pace."

"Has anyone discovered the recon teams you planned to send?"

"Some of the people of the mountains are seemingly aware of our presence. Thys Meiring and Pieter Kriel found books propped up in a forest clearing. They, of course, had to assume that the books were booby-trapped, so it made for an interesting morning. The books are like artists' portfolios, and the writing is a continuous script—you hold them with the spine facing away from you. Unfortunately, the planet's inhabitants are reluctant to allow us to learn their languages, and we have no way of deciphering them. Although at least one of our sociologists affects to believe that leaving the books is a religious act of propitiation of some sort, I suspect that there are elements in Blue society that have their own message to impart to us."

"I will get settled and see Simon to be brought up to date so that I can talk to you about what is happening without feeling an utter fool." She stood up and kissed him lightly on the cheek. "You didn't really think you could keep me away forever, did you, Uncle Anton?"

"No, I suppose not."

Piotr Kolomeitsev appeared after she left. "Was that Rikki I just saw? I told you that she would eventually figure it out."

"I had sincerely hoped it would take her much longer."

"She knows you." The Iceman examined Vereshchagin's face. "Simon will want her to study the lemps, and she will want to go. What will you say?"

Vereshchagin sighed deeply. "Do I have a choice, Piotr?"

"Out of curiosity, Anton," The Iceman asked with an air of indifference, "who knows about your heart condition besides Dr. Solchava and Gu?"

Vereshchagin stopped. "How did you know?"

"I know you, too. That was why you brought Hans along, so that you would have someone who was capable of finishing what you began." The Iceman examined Vereshchagin's face with all that was in him of compassion. "You really should tell him."

L-Day plus 411 [9-rain Rain 14]

"DR. MARAIS, DR. KATAKURA." SUPERIOR PRIVATE BRIT SMITS stuck his head inside the tent. "They're coming."

Connie Marais put down the sock he was mending and grabbed his recorder, and he and Katakura hurried outside.

One of the two remaining members of the original delegation, Spoagusa was leading, clearly recognizable by the yellowish cast to the skin around his face. Blue etiquette was precise and unvarying: seniors always walked in front of their juniors. There was a carefulness about each of them, a poise and a balance, as if every gesture and footstep was calculated not to disturb a delicate equilibrium.

Marais noted absently that three of the Blues, the "People," assigned to the contact team had been replaced by new faces and that Ekpalawehud had moved up two places. In Blue society, each individual was defined by his relationship to others, literally "where he sits," and based on stray remarks, Marais and Katakura were both convinced that the eleemosynary—or pauper—class was very large. For Marais, the most unpleasant discovery was that the Blues used not one language, but several, all seemingly different, to address persons of differing social ranks.

Humans, by definition, had no social rank.

With a glance toward Keiji Katakura, Marais turned on his recorder to play the correct tones. "*Nyaiikymylyieea*, Spoagusa."

The language was "low" language, inferior speaking to superior. The "ny" was a marker indicating that the word was a focal point. The "a" was a gender marker; the Blues recognized nine—singular, dual, plural, extended objects, paired or clustered objects, body parts, diminutives, abstract qualities, and locations.

The "ii" was a tense marker; the Blues recognized eleven tenses—"now," "earlier today," "yesterday," "earlier than yesterday," "in the remote past," "habitually," "continually," "hypothetically," "in the future," "at an indeterminate time in the future," and "never." The "ky" was an object-agreement marker, the "my" a benefactive marker indicating the gender of the object for whose benefit the action was taking place.

The "lyi" was the verb "to welcome."

The "ee" was an "applicative" marker. The "a" was a terminal vowel, indicating indicative mood.

A rough English translation of Marais's remark would be "I welcome you for our benefit, Spoagusa."

To indicate he had heard, Spoagusa touched his own recorder, a copy of one Dr. Seki had given him. The Blues were quick to adopt Imperial technology that did not interfere with the ordering of their society, and equally quick to reject technology that did. Keiji Katakura had been testing them, offering them driblets of fact to see what they would digest. Marais hoped that the pattern was not becoming too obvious.

Spoagusa pointed to Ekpalawehud, who stood back from Marais to allow him a comfortable fight-or-flight distance and attempted to make eye contact out of courtesy. "Doctorseki is where?"

It piqued Marais's professional interest that the Blues made no effort to distinguish names from honorifics, but no explanation for the mystery appeared forthcoming. He replied, "Doctor Seki is present. I will get him."

"Do so, Conniemarais," Spoagusa said politely, speaking to Marais directly. "I am not displeased to view you."

Inwardly, Marais let out a sigh of relief as he went to fetch Seki. Although Spoagusa was even more addicted to litotes—affirmatives expressed by negatives of the contrary—than other Blues, making his remarks maddeningly obscure at times, his polite acknowledgement meant that the Blues would not insist on preconditions for resuming contact.

This, in itself, was not necessarily a good sign.

In Orbit, HIMS *Zuiho* [2-hexagon Rain 14]

"I PICKED GERRIT MYBURGH AS RIKKI'S BODYGUARD," COLDEWE explained to Simon Beetje. "I'm still not happy about this. Having Rikki appear right after Ozawa breaks his leg is a coincidence, and I don't like coincidences I haven't planned."

"We really should have a trained professional on the ground to avoid invalidating our results, not that DeKe and Kalle are not doing good work," Beetje assured him hastily. "Besides, Rikki really wants to go."

"And Maria probably really wants Rikki to go, too." Coldewe grinned. "Myburgh is a good, pious lad, and he already has a girlfriend, which should keep him in line. I hope it does. Valeska Remmar masses what I do, and she can shoot."

"Abject fear of one's girlfriend is a strong motivating force," Simon mused, flushing very slightly. "There are, however, dangers to the approach. To Myburgh, of course. Are you familiar with the phenomenon of copying?"

"I assume this has nothing to do with cheating on exams."

"Females of many species tend to be attracted to males who are already courting other females. On Earth, for example, they've run experiments with male black grouse, which stake out part of a field as a lek and try to attract as many females as possible. Placing a stuffed female bird in a male's territory causes other female birds to gravitate toward that male."

"I remember school dances like that," Coldewe agreed, "and the girls there probably put as much thought into it as the grouse." He raised one eyebrow. "Why are you telling me this?"

"To play with your mind. There is an inherent amusement value."

"I see. I thought about trying to talk Anton into letting you go instead, but having two broken-down biologists on the ground struck me as too much of a good thing." Coldewe thought for a moment. "Did you know that the interdisciplinary working group is looking at Blue art?"

"Oh, no."

Coldewe nodded. "Dr. Iwao." A gifted linguist, Dr. Iwao spoke nine languages, often continuously. "One of the teams found a wall painting—between the two of us, I think it was a beer advertisement—and Dr. Iwao told me that he was of the view that the paratactic ordering of the figures in the composition was extremely significant, and that this significance was profound if it represented a school of art, so I, of course, made myself a note to look up the word 'paratactic' and asked him what he meant by profound. He told me that it was difficult to say without reviewing a wide range of other compositions for comparison. I, of course, told him that I'd ask Wessels to stop and take pictures if he found himself inside an art museum. By the way, did you notice the pumpkin on the end of Pia Szuba's nose?"

"Yes. She said she walked into a door."

"Simon." Coldewe tapped his foot. "You believe in elves and fairies, don't you?"

"You don't think—"

"I think. You're Pia's closest friend, and you're also her husband's friend, and someone needs to sit down and have a friendly talk with Ferenc Szuba and ensure that there's no repetition. I have Jan Snyman sitting down with the third party involved."

"You don't think Pia and *Mika*—"

"Simon, the two of them are big children, and while I don't think anything much happened given Mika's past, I don't much care. What does concern me is that getting smacked around by Ferenc affects Pia's work, and I want it to stop."

Beetje thought. "Hans, you don't think that Ferenc might try to go after Mika?"

"No, but another thing a little voice might mention is that Mika is death on crooked legs. There might be three people on board who can take him, but Ferenc assuredly isn't one of them."

"I will do that," Beetje said dully. He looked at Coldewe. "Hans, you are not very comfortable about sending Rikki off, are you?"

"No, but with all the new missile silos Aksu keeps showing me, I'm not very comfortable about keeping her aboard ship, either. Simon, I'm not much into dreams and portents, but last night I dreamed that my fingers were bleeding and I couldn't get it to stop, so that everything I touched had blood on it."

"What do you think it means?" Beetje asked seriously.

"I hope it means I need to lay off eating those miserable pickled beets before bedtime, but I'm getting just a little bit nervous here, Simon."

"So is Maria." Beetje shook his head. "I still don't know why Anton let her come."

Coldewe grinned. "There was an inherent amusement value."

SUPERIOR PRIVATE GERRIT MYBURGH, A PLEASANT LAD WITH sandy hair and a blunt, round face, set down his Bible and stood to attention. "Ma'am, Colonel Coldewe detailed me as your escort."

"Please sit down, Gerrit." Sanmartin found herself a seat and watched to make sure Myburgh would do the same. "Did Colonel Coldewe explain what that would entail?"

"Yes, ma'am. He said that you were going to study monkeys so we'd know what to expect from the Blues, and that I am to keep you from getting shot while doing it or die trying."

"You may relax, Gerrit. And you do not need to call me ma'am. It makes me feel like someone's maiden aunt."

"Yes, ma'am."

Sanmartin wrinkled her nose. "What else did Colonel Coldewe tell you?"

Myburgh looked embarrassed. "He, ah, told me to think of you as the president of the republic and the Variag's niece." Myburgh appeared to equate the two in terms of importance. "He, ah, warned me that if I think an improper thought, he'll tell Valeska so that my blood won't be on his hands."

"How kind of him," she murmured insincerely. "Valeska?"

"Valeska Remmar, my girlfriend. She is a gunner on an armored car. She says we will get married at Christmas."

An impish thought entered her head. "I take it that you know better than to argue."

Myburgh nodded solemnly. "Yes, ma'am."

"And what does your family think of me?"

Myburgh smiled. "My brother Kurt told me that when he teased Father about you, all Father would say was, 'That snip of a girl!' Kurt often does things to— What is the English word?"

"Rile people?" she suggested.

"That is it. I do the same sometimes." He shrugged. "I have no head for politics or book things, but I think that I know a bad man or woman when I see one."

She smiled. "What would you like to ask me?"

Myburgh's eyes lit up. "Is it true the Springboks finished second?"

Rikki asked Coldewe later, "Are you really going to have a wedding aboard ship?"

" 'The Whistling Pig' makes a fine wedding march."

She reflected, "Uncle Matti told me that my mother had her heart set on being married in Witfontein, and he swears the minister exorcised the church afterward. You did not really threaten to burn it down if he refused to perform the ceremony, did you?"

"Of course not. Don't be silly. There wasn't a scrap of wood in the place. I told the minister I had fourteen people who could drop the bell tower into the vestry easy as walking a field, but to achieve combustion, we'd have had to soak the place in artillery propellant, which would have taken hours."

He thought of the pictures Aksu had shown him of what looked like a Blue rebellion being suppressed. Some of the victims had been impaled. "DeKe and Kalle are looking forward to your arrival. I think the way DeKe phrased it is that he's looking forward to introducing you to his friends. But you watch yourself down there."

"I will." She added quietly, "You know, until I became president, I never understood what you were doing—to me it was Uncle Hans playing the clown."

"It's funny. People naturally fall into routines. This last decade has been hard in some ways. How do you keep good soldiers—the best of the best—from resting on their laurels when there isn't even a hint of a war to prepare for?"

She understood. "You shake them up."

Coldewe nodded. "Even here, the thought that I might take it into my head to launch a raid on A deck to dye everyone's underwear blue keeps them all from going cabin crazy."

"Did you?"

"What?"

"Raid A deck to dye everyone's underwear blue?"

"Of course not! Something like that would create hard feelings." Coldewe grinned. "We did do some preliminary reconnaissance. So what did you think of Gerrit?"

"He told me how much he wanted to come on the expedition and how lucky it was that his girlfriend won the lottery to come. I think that my lovable relatives, who amuse themselves by toppling empires and fixing elections, would not find it difficult to rig a lottery." Sanmartin tapped the end of her nose with a forefinger. "Uncle Hans! You are blushing."

Coldewe, who rarely found himself at a loss for words, replied, "It's my modest nature."

L-Day plus 429 [9-reed Rain 14]

"IT WOULD BE NICE TO HAVE A FIRE," HENDRICKA SANMARTIN remarked, seated on a log, sorting her notes. "I know," she added, seeing the expression on Myburgh's face. "Bad security."

"Ma'am, it is much too hot for a fire," Myburgh protested, wishing Kekkonen and de Kantzow hadn't left.

"I know." She looked up to see if she could make out the moving dots in the night sky that were *Aoba* and *Zuiho*. "But it would still be nice. Gerrit, what made you decide to be a soldier?"

"Papa never trusted the Imps, so all of us did reserve service. I found I liked it. It gave me a chance to get away and see things, and Sergeant Kivela says that I have an aptitude."

"I imagine you do. You said your father owns a farm." She shook her head. "I am sorry. I have difficulty picturing you as a farmer. Is that what you plan to go back to?"

"Not really, ma'am. Papa planted trees, dipterocarps, when my oldest brother was born—that's Kurt—and he planted more after the land reform. Last year, we cut some to let the wood season. I love to carve things. I am good with my hands." He held them out for inspection. "Kurt says they are craftsman's hands. Kurt will get the farm, you see, and I will inherit the trees to make into furniture. People want that sort of thing, and it's much too expensive to ship real wooden furniture from Earth."

Animated by her interest, he continued, "Plastic and metal furniture is nice enough, but furniture really should be wood. When you look at the grain of a log, you can almost see the pieces waiting to be let out." He smiled shyly. "I think that the business will do well. People around Krugersdorp know me, and some of them have already placed orders for when I get back."

He had, Sanmartin recognized, a quiet confidence in his abilities, both as a cabinetmaker and as a soldier.

"And what made you decide to come to Neighbor?" she asked, setting her notebook down.

"I always wanted to travel off planet, just a little bit. And I always wanted to do something important in my life." He shook his head regretfully. "I had to argue with Papa to make him see. And while I am gone, the trees will grow and the cut wood will season." He asked hesitantly, "Did you enjoy being president?"

"Every minute of it." She smiled demurely, "It is almost enough to turn a girl's head. And now I am here."

"I wish I understood why everyone thinks the lemps are so important," Myburgh said wistfully.

"Lemur-ape babies are extremely altricial—they are almost completely undeveloped—and are born four at a time. The females lactate—it isn't milk in the mammalian sense, but it

serves the same purpose—but in an average year, which this
year seems to be, a mother can only nurse two of her offspring,
which means that half of the infants born die immediately. Judging from the subadults in the troop, less than 10 percent survive
a year, and virtually all of the survivors come from high-status
mothers. Do you follow me so far?"

Myburgh shook his head regretfully. "Not really, ma'am."

"Let me try to make it simpler. If Blue women give birth to
four babies at a time and have to choose which of the four babies survive, as is quite possible, it says unpleasant things about
the society they have."

He frowned. "Does Colonel Vereshchagin know about this?"

"With two breeding seasons behind us, as far as I am concerned, we have enough data. I told Simon and Maria to stop
dithering and tell him," Sanmartin said distantly.

In Orbit, HIMS *Zuiho* [1-mist Rain 14]

"ALL RIGHT, SIMON," VERESHCHAGIN SAID, "WOULD YOU CARE
to begin?"

Beetje ignored the puzzled look Dr. Kita gave him. "Maria
and I have prepared a preliminary summary of our lemur-ape
data." He passed out paper copies and gave everyone present a
few moments to study it. "I would like to discuss the possible
implications."

Szuba set her copy aside and quietly sat back to listen.

"Let me begin with first principles. All animals, including humans and Blues, reflect the cumulative impact of mortality and
female selection over thousands of generations, and in general,
males act as a genetic sieve—only the best males get to breed,
and the incremental elimination of genes belonging to inferior
males purges bad genes from populations. The greater the degree of complexity in behavior patterns, genetic mechanisms, or
physiological structures, the clearer it becomes that natural selection shaped these to an end. Human reproductive strategies
are both complex and environmentally conditioned, but unlike
most of Earth's other mammals, humans are basically monogamous animals with a predilection for adultery. Can all of you accept this as a starting point for discussion?"

"I might reverse the order of your last point there," Coldewe
responded, "but I think we're in agreement."

"Lemur-apes are not monogamous. In lemur-ape troops, genetically unrelated males share access to harems of females, with the alpha male dominating. In the troop we are following, every adult female not already burdened with young gave birth to quadruplets during the breeding season. Most of these infants died or were killed almost immediately. There are a number of interesting details, but the point to be made is that while lemur-apes are capable of explosive population growth when food resources permit, in normal times, only offspring of high-ranking mothers and fathers survive."

Beetje took a deep breath. "I am convinced that lemur-apes and Blues share a common reproductive strategy. I say this despite the fact that human reproductive strategy differs significantly from that employed by man's closest relatives—chimpanzees, gorillas, and bonobos—and despite current theory that holds that monogamous pair-bonding is an essential step in the development of intelligence."

Intrigued, Dr. Kita asked, "What do you base this on, Simon?"

"Male lemur-apes and Blues are 42 percent larger than females on average. This is a significant difference, roughly double the disparity in size between male and female human beings. Lieutenant Aksu's observations also show a significant decrease in the number of Blue females working in the water-potato paddies after the onset of the monsoon, which suggests that the Blues also have a fixed breeding season. Moreover—"

The Iceman interrupted. "Perhaps you can discuss the details with your colleagues later, Simon. What conclusions have you drawn about the Blues?"

Beetje wiped his brow, thankful for Pia Szuba's quiet support. "Frankly, the implications are a little frightening. A fixed breeding season implies that the Blues have harem arrangements rather than pair-bonds, and even in an intelligent species, gross overproduction of infants would almost certainly compel infanticide."

Kolomeitsev closed his eyes then opened them. "Exposing unwanted infants is an ancient practice on Earth."

"I am straying out of my field here, but all sorts of possibilities suggest themselves," Beetje declared. "The Blues may kill infants based on sex; they may kill infants belonging to lower-class mothers and give them higher-class infants to nurse."

"The absence of a pair-bonding instinct could have a substantially negative impact on the development of Neighbor's ethics and morals," Pia Szuba said, "although it is possible that the data are inadequate to support such a sweeping premise."

"Hypotheses should be constructed from the best available evidence and tested rigorously," Vereshchagin ruled. "Let us attempt to validate or disprove this particular hypothesis. Hans, I see you stirring."

Coldewe said promptly, "If circumstances compel the people here to snuff out infants casually, it's going to leave an imprint on them. As Goethe put it, 'A man, even the best, who accustoms his spirit to cruelty and finally even makes, from that which he detests, a law; and from that habit becomes hard and almost unrecognizable.' I've been telling Simon for a while now that I thought that Mother Nature shortchanged these people.

> 'So runs my dream: but what am I?
> An infant crying in the night:
> An infant crying for the light:
> And with no language but a cry.
> So careful of the type she seems,
> So careless of the single life.
> The world's great altar-stairs
> That slope thro' darkness up to God.
> Man . . .
> Who trusted God was love indeed
> And love Creation's final law—
> Tho' Nature, red in tooth and claw
> With ravine, shrieked against his creed.'

'Nature, red in tooth and claw,' " he repeated. "So careful of the type, she seems. So careless of the single life. That's Tennyson by the way."

Afterward, Simon told his wife, Maria, "I just presented them with facts, didn't I?"

Looking at his face, Maria Beetje choked off her reply and used her shoulder to support him.

L-Day plus 441 [3-zephyr Rain 14]

"LET'S SEE," SUPERIOR PRIVATE DENYS GORDIMER SAID, ENGAGED in his second-favorite pastime, "I make it 3,227,630 rand and fifty cents."

Without lifting his eye from the telescope, Blaar Schuur tossed a pebble at him. "Here's the fifty cents."

"How about a hand when we get back? You know you could try and work off your debt, bringing me breakfast in bed and things."

"Shut up." When Gordimer failed to respond, Schuur turned his head and looked at his partner. "Denys?"

"All of a sudden, I feel dizzy." Gordimer set his submachine gun down and took his face shield off. "I feel sick."

Schuur reached across in the darkness and felt Gordimer's throat. "Oh, God!" He touched his radio. "Command point one. Break. Schuur here. Denys is burning up. He's running 3 or 4 degrees of fever. I am going to walk him back to the spring on Hangman's Hill. I will take blood and tissue samples and send them from there."

He refastened Gordimer's face shield. Strapping their submachine guns to his webbing, he looked to see if they had left any other signs of their presence. Then he wrapped Gordimer's arm around his neck. "Colonel Hans, if you don't hear from me, that is where you will find us. Schuur out."

He squeezed Gordimer's hand. "It's all right, Denys."

"No, it's not!" Gordimer protested weakly. "It's frosting damned bad."

"I know," Schuur admitted.

In Orbit, HIMS *Zuiho* [5-zephyr Rain 14]

VERESHCHAGIN PROJECTED DR. SOLCHAVA'S IMAGE ON THE WALL where everyone present could see. "Natasha, what can you tell us?"

Solchava brushed the hair from her eyes. "Gordimer's blood and tissue cultures contain heavy growths of *Staphylococcus aureus*. The growths appear resistant both to antibiotics and to the body's natural defenses. In some manner, alien genetic material appears to have been incorporated in the staphylococci nuclei. This is quite extraordinary. I hope that I am mistaken." Solchava appeared tired. "I have sealed my lab and will examine samples using category-two procedures. Until we know more, I strongly recommend restricting contact between the planet and *Zuiho*, and between *Zuiho* and *Aoba*."

"How could nonterrestrial genetic material end up in a terrestrial bacillus?" Pia Szuba asked.

"Natasha, please explain for those of us who are not scientists," Vereshchagin asked quietly.

"I have reviewed the literature. It is not unknown." Solchava shrugged carelessly. "Bacteria are notorious for scavenging stray DNA and plasmids from each other. It would appear that the staphylococci absorbed the organelles in some manner and have discovered a use for them. However, the mechanism here is different than any I have seen described in the literature."

"And Denys?" Coldewe asked.

Solchava shook her head helplessly. "In a sense, he is being killed by his own body's defenses. Reacting to the staphylococci, his body is producing huge quantities of leukocyctes. The leukocytes are not, however, recognizing the altered staphylococci. Instead, they are aggregating in clumps, causing severe capillary blockage, and are releasing large amounts of lysosomal enzymes and pyrogen, which is inducing fever and causing tissue damage. I think. The actual process may be far more subtle. It may take us months to discover an effective treatment. Or years. I will want to see blood and tissue samples from every individual on the surface. Until we know a great deal more, we have to assume that they may be carrying something quite deadly."

"The naturales may be able to help us. With men's lives at risk, I think we should solicit their assistance," Szuba urged, looking around the room.

Vereshchagin smiled thinly. "Telling them may be a greater risk to the people we have operating on the surface. I am afraid that this is one of the risks inherent in our situation." He paused. "Please stress to everyone that information about this is not to be disseminated to the contact team."

Szuba challenged him. "And if they become ill?"

Simon Beetje laid a hand on her arm.

L-Day plus 446 [8-zephyr Rain 14]

DENYS GORDIMER DIED TWO HOURS AFTER SUNDOWN. BLAAR Schuur packed his body in a plastic bag, heat sealed the edge, and lofted it skyward so that a low-flying shuttle could haul it in.

Schuur sat down on a rock and played a few hands of solitaire, waiting. "Troubles usually come in bunches," he said to himself.

Around dawn, a little sheepish, he went back to his hide site.

In Orbit, HIMS *Zuiho* [8-zephyr Rain 14]

"IT IS, OF COURSE, VERY DISCOURAGING TO SPEND SO MUCH TIME here and not be able to set foot on the planet's surface," Senior Technician Tsuyoshi Kodama told Coldewe over yet another cup of tea.

"Yesterday, I had four platoons who would have loved a little time down below, although that was yesterday," Coldewe replied. "Unfortunately, they may get some."

The soft-spoken senior technician, a specialist in his own arcane field, took Coldewe's meaning immediately.

" 'Scale of dragon, tooth of wolf,/Witches' mummy, maw and gulf/Of the ravin'd salt-sea shark/Root of hemlock digged i' the dark,' " Coldewe reflected. "Last time I came down here, you said you might be on to something."

"It is, of course, very premature for me to say so without more complete testing than we are presently able to carry out. Under normal circumstances, my team would only be expected to disburse existing agents, and one must expect failures in the course of developing new agents." Kodama sipped his tea.

This was, of course, a slight exaggeration. The biochem-warfare unit assigned to watch over Suid-Afrika was theoretically the best such team in the employ of His Imperial Majesty's government, and Coldewe knew Kodama never would have opened his mouth if he hadn't been reasonably sure he had a winner.

Coldewe toyed with his cup. "How long would it take you to give me something that *looks* good—it doesn't necessarily have to *be* good—along the lines we were discussing?"

Kodama's face grew thoughtful.

"It always helps to know how Anton thinks," Coldewe explained obscurely.

L-Day plus 448 [1-lake Rain 14]

REPISKOSHAN STRAIGHTENED HIS CLOAK.

"I am sorry," Connie Marais told the Blue. "I do not understand."

Ekpalawehud, who probably understood quite well and certainly spoke English better than his new compatriot, maintained a distant and lofty silence.

"Soh-ree. Vite do-awn vord plesh," Repiskoshan said in labored and barely comprehensible English. His signing was scarcely better. The daily monsoon shower gave the tent a vile odor.

Marais suddenly tired of the effort of breaking in a new contact. "Stop. I must go. Enough for today. *Neaikimmyiia.*"

Ekpalawehud stiffened. He chirped something to Repiskoshan that Marais missed, threw his cloak over his head, and strode from the tent, with Repiskoshan scurrying after him in an almost comical fashion.

Marais went into the kitchen area and found Isaac Wanjau drinking tea. "Hello, Isaac."

Wanjau inclined his head. "Dr. Marais. You look discouraged."

"Annoyed and discouraged. Kanyase stopped coming today. Ekpalawehud brought someone new instead. It's so frustrating. I asked why, but you know how those discussions go. And it happened just when I thought we were finally beginning to establish a rapport." Marais shook his head. "Oh, have you seen Brit Smits? He was supposed to work on my computer."

Wanjau carefully set his cup down. "He did not do so?"

"No. In fact, I haven't seen him."

Wanjau touched his radio. "Contact point three. Break. Wanjau here. Brit, where are you?"

There was no response. Wanjau put his beret on his head and walked through the rain to check the other tents. A moment later, he touched his radio again. "Command point one. Break. Wanjau here. Smits is missing. I say again, Smits is missing."

With a heavy heart, Dr. Seki obeyed instructions to suspend relations until Smits was returned.

During the night, a single missile arched into the sky. *Aoba* destroyed it.

In Orbit, HIMS *Zuiho* [2-lake Rain 14]

"ARE WE READY TO DISCUSS A RESPONSE?" VERESHCHAGIN INquired.

"Are we not perhaps being precipitous?" Dr. Kita inquired. "The naturales have expressed concern and promised to make an investigation to find Smits, and they have assured us that the missile was an accident."

"I believe that we can assume that Smits did not wander off," Hans Coldewe replied, outwardly calm. "And where missiles are concerned, I don't believe in accidents."

Simon Beetje held his breath, and Dr. Kita looked uncertain. "We should consider all possibilities. Could Private Smits have defected?" Pia Szuba asked.

The Iceman smiled coldly. "What would they have promised him, a harem of native women?"

"Could he have come down with the same disease that killed Private Gordimer and wandered off?" Szuba persisted.

"It is possible, but in that event his body should be easy to find," Vereshchagin said.

"Surely Dr. Seki has promised his best efforts in resolving this crisis," Dr. Kita said, attempting to defend Seki's viewpoint, despite obvious personal qualms. "Of course, this is very serious, but do we really wish to cut off relations merely because of one man?"

"I have met Brit's sister. She did not want him to come," The Iceman said softly. "Admittedly, one man counts for very little in the universe's grand design, but Brit Smits is one of ours, and I would like to think that this makes a difference."

"I think that we are being tested," Vereshchagin said.

"Shouldn't we send a shuttle to pick up the contact team?" Simon Beetje asked.

"If we're right about the Blues, it would cost us a shuttle," Coldewe explained coldly.

"Get me Dr. Seki," Vereshchagin told Esko Poikolainnen. When Seki's face appeared, he said, "Good morning, Doctor."

Seki appeared haggard. He bowed. "Good morning, Commissioner."

"Has Superior Private Smits been returned?"

"No, Commissioner. However, we must reopen discussions with the naturales. The situation is fraught with danger. We cannot simultaneously prepare for war and prevent war." He made a final effort. "Surely an intransigent attitude is a grave danger to the overall success of our mission." Aware that he was not on the firmest ground, he added, "I have been assured that the missile was launched in error, and it clearly was not intended to harm any of our ships."

"No, it wasn't intended to harm us," Coldewe said grimly. "It struck me as an experiment."

"I fail to understand."

"The Blues wanted to see us maneuver. They wanted to see us fire. In layman's terms, Doctor, the Blues are peeking at our cards, and I'm wondering what they plan on doing when they think they've got a winning hand."

"Dr. Seki," Vereshchagin said, calm and detached, "in light of circumstances, I consider it appropriate to name Company Sergeant Wanjau head of the contact team. I would ask you to accept this change in a constructive manner."

Seki appeared stunned. Finally, he said, "Yes, Commissioner."

"Thank you, Doctor. Vereshchagin out." Vereshchagin terminated the contact.

"Funny," Coldewe remarked, "I thought the *only* way you prevented war was to prepare for it."

"So Vegetius said. Hans, do you remember Dr. Devoucoux?"

Coldewe thought for a moment. "Yes. Yes, I do. Dapper Claude. He was Natasha's predecessor. We lost him when the Brothers nuked Reading. He used to like peanuts. Kept them in his pocket all the time. Strange what you remember after twenty years."

"Yes, it is."

"We took him out on patrol once, and Vijer—you remember Vijer, he had the worst luck—Vijer had abdominal pains, so Dapper Claude wanted to do laparoscopic surgery right there in the middle of the desert. He was miffed we hadn't brought the proper equipment. Bery was rolling around in the sand, he thought it was so funny. Poor old Dapper Claude. We've lost so many over the years, it's sometimes hard to remember them all."

"We have to, Hans. No one else will." Vereshchagin looked away. "Claude once said a profound thing about Suid-Afrika. He called it 'a land God gave to Cain.' I think that that may be more true of this world."

"These people aren't evil, Anton."

"No, they are simply people, which means that they can be monumentally stupid sometimes." He thought aloud, "We could pull *Zuiho* and *Aoba* out of orbit, but that would make it impossible for us to play our little games with the shuttles and perhaps even precipitate the conflagration we seek to avoid."

"How much time do you think we have? Should we pull back our covert people?"

"We have a few months, perhaps. No, it does not appear necessary to pull in our people. We have no reason to believe any of them are compromised," Vereshchagin said, hoping he was right.

In Orbit, HIMS *Zuiho* [5-lake Rain 14]

JAN SNYMAN AWOKE. HE SAT UP GROGGILY.

Deltje Brink peered at him from a few meters away. "Major Snyman?"

"Oh, hello, Juffrou Brink."

She sat down on the deck across from him. "They told me I would find you here. Why are you sleeping on the floor?"

Snyman patted the door next to him. "My wife, Natasha, is in quarantine. We see each other by computer, but being here makes her that much closer. I haven't seen much of you since sign-language classes ended. How have you been?"

The banal question amused her. "Oh, I have been fine."

Snyman hesitated. "Hans mentioned that you knew Hanna Bruwer."

"Yes, I was one of her students." Brink smiled. "When she was speaker, she sometimes used to ask us what we thought about important issues. We were all terribly young, and it made us feel terribly important. I think that we all loved her."

"Everyone did." Snyman stretched. "What may I do for you?"

"I did not want to disturb Colonel Coldewe, but no one seems to be able to tell me anything about Brit Smits."

"He's missing," Snyman said hesitantly. "How well do you know him?"

"Oh." She brushed back her hair. "He asked me out to see a movie—so have a lot of other soldiers on board."

He nodded. "That is not surprising."

"I don't think that he realized how much older I am than he is, but it turned out that I knew his sister quite well. We were friends. She used to complain about him horribly." Brink smiled nervously. "Please. Can't you tell me the truth? Was it the disease? There are so many stories. I don't know what to believe."

Snyman looked for a graceful way to evade the question and

found none. He shook his head. "It probably wasn't disease. So far, everyone else's staphylococci appear normal, even Blaar Schuur's. We think the Blues took Brit. It's possible they have found a way to keep him alive, but not likely." He did not burden her with his personal belief that Smits had been killed for dissection. For a moment, he thought she hadn't heard him, and then he saw her rub her eyes fiercely. "Juffrou Brink?"

"No," she said. "It is all right. I am all right. I knew ... I suppose hearing it makes a difference."

"Until we find a body, there's always hope," Snyman said lamely.

She tried to smile. "But not very much hope, you mean. He really was a sweet boy."

"He was."

"People's lives are like a cloth." She locked her fingers together to try to show him. "They all tie together. Cut a thread, and the cloth is weaker."

"Juffrou Brink, are you all right? If you want to sleep, my wife could prescribe a sedative for you."

"No, thank you, Major. I am all right."

L-day plus 458 [2-brook Rain 14]

HENDRICKA SANMARTIN FELT HER ARM BEING SHAKEN. "WE need to move fast," Myburgh said.

"It's still dark out. Are the lemps moving?"

"No, the Blues are." Myburgh was already rolling her space blanket as the rain dripped down. "*Aoba* reports truckloads of them heading here. Maybe an entire division, twenty thousand."

Sanmartin sat upright. Myburgh began painstakingly replacing the forest litter to obscure their campsite. "Lieutenant Aksu thinks the Blues may have found the recorder Dr. Ozawa lost." He began assembling the two tiny bicycles he carried in his bergen. "We have to get moving."

In Orbit, HIMS *Aoba* [2-brook Rain 14]

"HEADS UP, CHILDREN. A CLOUD OF MISSILES RISING—I MAKE out fourteen, with more still launching," Sery sang out from the console. "Target appears to be *Zuiho*."

Detlef Jankowskie slammed the panel to sound action stations. "Somebody wake Captain Kobayashi." Jankowskie and Kobayashi had begun alternating watches after the last missile.

Jankowskie opened a channel to *Zuiho*. "Jankowskie here. We're being fired at. Fourteen missiles and counting. It looks as though they plan on swamping our defenses, and the missiles probably have nuclear warheads. Put some distance between your ship and those warheads."

Zuiho acknowledged.

"They'll never clear," Sery announced.

"Open a line to corvette *Jintsu*," Jankowskie said curtly. "Commander Nitobe, this is Jankowskie. Make an oblique firing pass and scatter some chicken seed across the missiles' path. We'll interpose and act as goalkeeper for the ones you miss."

"I will comply. Good hunting, *Aoba*," Nitobe replied.

Tatekawa and Kawabe, manning the firing positions, were running check sequences without waiting to be told to do so.

"I hope the Blues hired the lowest bidder," Jankowskie joked as he began maneuvering the ship into harm's way.

Lieutenant-Commander Nagahiro, the ship's executive officer, reached the bridge and took a seat next to him.

"Jankowskie-*san*, perhaps we still have time to launch corvette *Chokei*," Kawabe said hesitantly.

Jankowskie shook his head impatiently. "They were waiting to catch us like this, and we haven't got ten minutes. We'll have to dance with who we have."

"Fast little buggers," Sery commented as his sensors measured the missiles' speed. "Total of twenty-seven fired."

No one else had much to say.

As the missiles reached the hundred-kilometer mark, *Jintsu* came in at a sharp angle. Nitobe skillfully steered his ship to scatter a cloud of chicken seed in the path of four missiles and twisted to engage four more.

"All right. Mark the stragglers, and prepare to clean them up," Jankowskie said.

"Captain! *Jintsu* missed!" Kawabe said excitedly.

"Hits. No damage," Sery reported. The fusion-charged chicken seed was gouging small dents in the ceramic casing of the missiles without penetrating. Sery looked up. "The missiles are dropping their third stages now. Don't count on running them out of fuel."

Jintsu ineffectually engaged with a laser. "*Aoba*, our fire has no effect. We are preparing to engage with five-hundred-kilogram projectiles," Nitobe reported.

Ignoring little *Jintsu*, the missiles continued to streak toward *Aoba* and *Zuiho*.

"They have speed and we do not," Lieutenant-Commander Nagahiro said quietly. "This is most awkward."

"Kawabe, launch the five-hundred-kilogram projectiles we have fused for impact at forty-second intervals," Jankowskie said to fill the deadly silence. "When we run out of those, launch whatever else we've got loaded."

"*Jintsu*'s first projectile is a clean miss. It looks as though their electronic countermeasures aren't too shabby either," Sery said.

Captain Kobayashi appeared. "Twenty-seven missiles," Jankowskie told him. "We're luring them into rifle range."

"Launching five-hundred-kilogram projectile," Kawabe said, his voice unnaturally shrill.

"*Jintsu* is making another firing run," Sery said.

Jankowskie slapped the intership frequency. "Nitobe, sheer off. We're launching."

"So very sorry, honorable Captain. I cannot comply. Please tell Commissioner Mutaro and Vice-Commissioner Vereshchagin we did our duty."

Seconds later, *Jintsu* impaled herself on a missile in the middle of the swarm. The missile's nuclear warhead and the ship's fusion bottle went up together in a horrific explosion.

"Launching second projectile," Kawabe reported.

"Discontinue launching," Kobayashi told him.

The blast overtook the lead missiles. Half a moment later, it engulfed *Aoba*.

"Sensors down," Sery reported.

"I can no longer track," Kawabe reported. "I greatly hope that *Jintsu* got all of them." Tatekawa, who had banged his head, hung limply in his seat with a bruise on his temple.

"We will know in a minute," Kobayashi observed.

Sery shook his head. "Hell of an O-Bon festival."

"We lose more corvettes that way," Jankowskie commented. "Radiation count is up. I hope nobody was planning on children."

An hour later, hanging off at a safe distance, it was clear that *Aoba* had suffered major damage. *Jintsu* continued to exist as a cloud of stripped atomic nuclei in an area about a hundred kilometers in diameter.

Before returning command to Captain Kobayashi, Jankowskie

entered a scrap of verse he had once heard from Hans Coldewe into the ship's log:

"Nail to the mast her holy flag/Set every threadbare sail/And give her to the god of storms/The lightning and the gale."

L-Day plus 459 [3-brook Rain 14]

CONNIE MARAIS SAT AT HIS WORKSTATION, PUZZLING OVER A poem Kanyase had left him. He had studied it for two months and felt no nearer to unlocking its riddle. In translation, it read:

In the sky two moons	In your face one mouth
In the sky many stars	In your face only two eyes

Hearing Kobus Nicodemus calling, he turned off his computer and stepped outside to see Isaac Wanjau and Dr. Seki returning from a meeting with the Blues. Marais was shocked at the change in Seki's appearance. Never robust, Seki now appeared careworn.

Seki addressed the team. "Company Sergeant Wanjau and I have been informed that there is concern over our security here. For this reason, the Pochteca have asked us to move to the city of Cuextla. Although there are many disadvantages attendant upon this course, it will provide us with an opportunity to see a city and perhaps understand the naturales better."

"We have perhaps ten minutes to pack," Wanjau said gruffly. "Stuff your pockets with food and a change of clothes. If any of you have records or data files from the ship that I have not personally approved, destroy them now."

Marais felt as if he had been punched in the stomach.

Wanjau looked at each of them in turn. "I asked Dr. Seki to try to put a polite face on things."

HIMS *Zuiho* [3-brook Rain 14]

"DO WE KNOW WHAT IS HAPPENING DOWN THERE?" NICOLA Bosenac asked.

"We activated a relay station on the smaller moon, which allows us to make contact with our reconnaissance platoon twice a day." Vereshchagin paced the compartment. "Markus Alariesto flew east in a Sparrow to try to extricate Gerrit Myburgh and

Rikki Sanmartin, but Blue soldiers are occupying the area in force, and he was not able to land. The contact team is being held. Natasha Solchava has had to sedate Isaac Wanjau's wife."

"But why would the Blues attack like this?" Bosenac knotted his hands. "It seems senseless."

Vereshchagin paused before responding. "Many months ago, Dr. Marais reported a fragmentary conversation to the effect that the Pochteca mistrusted us, that we represented change. This would seem to be our only clue."

"It seems a terribly thin reason to go to war."

"As little as I understand the Blues, I do not believe that their society would survive open contact with us without being changed. If the contact team is correct, they have no word for 'religion' because the word implies that there can be more than one set of beliefs."

"The one fact about them we seem sure of is that they kill their infants. My church would view this as a terrible sin."

"Perhaps the Blues believe us incapable of overlooking this. Hans often takes me to task for violating the great law of living, which is 'Thou shalt not offend against the notions of thy neighbors.'" Vereshchagin tried to smile and gave up the effort. "Father Nicola, I sometimes wonder whether I accomplished anything on Suid-Afrika and what I can hope to accomplish here."

"Commissioner, God can't keep men from folly, and folly is something that Suid-Afrikans are unusually good at." Bosenac shook his head ruefully. "As for the Blues, it's astonishing how little we know about them and how much less we understand."

"The converse is also true," Vereshchagin said absently.

"Eh?"

"The Blues know more about us, and understand less." Vereshchagin paced the cabin a few more times. "Sun-tzu said that leadership in war requires intelligence, trustworthiness, humaneness, courage, and sternness. Trustworthiness and humaneness are perhaps the most difficult to cultivate."

He paused. "Soldiers share expectations, a moral sense of what is right and wrong. This is the common thread underlying the traditions, the stories we tell, and the trust my men have in me and each other is rooted in it. It gives meaning to deaths and suffering. Now, I am about to do something my men will find incomprehensible." He checked the time. "I must leave you now, Father. If you wish to be a good chaplain, pray."

Entering his cabin, Vereshchagin saw that Aksu and Reinikka

were squeezed in next to his usual conferees, and that Esko Poikolainnen had set up a view screen so that Kobayashi and Jankowskie could also participate. He accepted a cup of tea from Piotr Kolomeitsev and held it, feeling the warmth seep into his hand. "Hans? Shall we begin?"

"You know how I feel. Twenty-seven missiles qualifies as hostile intent." Coldewe gestured. "Detlef tells me that the Blues are trying to knock down our satellite network as we speak. I'd like to sugar the Blues' tea for *Jintsu*, and I *want* our people back, even Dr. Seki, bless his pacifistic little heart. The Blues have twenty-nine days worth of food to feed the contact team, after which things get sticky. We have an even larger problem looming, which is the strong possibility that the Blues will shoot down our next supply ship when it wanders into orbit, fat, dumb, and happy to be a target drone. If we lose that ship, we lose our ability to maintain ourselves here."

Kobayashi and Jankowskie looked at each other. Kobayashi amplified Coldewe's remarks. "We do not know precisely when or where the next supply ship will arrive, and we will have a limited ability to communicate with the ship before it enters orbit. I regret that I consider it necessary to strike."

"Will we use nuclear weapons?" Simon Beetje asked.

The Iceman's explanation confused Beetje. "I somehow doubt that obliterating cities with the forty nuclear warheads we possess would influence the Pochteca—the Blues appear somewhat callous about loss of life. It would also seem to be a fragile foundation upon which to build a lasting relationship."

Kobayashi said stiffly, "Captain Jankowskie and I have discussed employing ship-launched munitions to damage the planet's industrial base. Lieutenant Aksu has convinced me that we lack the capacity to obtain lasting results, and that the attempt would almost certainly result in the loss of *Aoba* and *Chokei*."

"Indeed," Pia Szuba volunteered unexpectedly, "identified industrial plants do not account for the level of industrial activity here. Significant subcomponent production is carried out at the village level. Attacks on industrial plants would merely force the Blues to further disperse their industry."

Jankowskie added, "People think a big meteor strike helped finish off the last dinosaurs, so Yotaro and I kicked around the idea of moving about fifty kilometers worth of asteroid onto a collision course with the planet."

"There are inherent difficulties in taking orbital material in tow," Kobayashi said, "and there does not appear to be any extraneous planetary matter that could be induced to strike the planet anytime in the near future, the near future being defined as within the next hundred years."

"Dr. Kita, Dr. Beetje?" Vereshchagin asked. "Would you care to add anything?"

Beetje said in a weary voice, "We have to do something, but what can we do?"

Vereshchagin asked, "Piotr?"

The Iceman smiled. "Anton, you have already determined the course of action we will follow, and the sole responsibility is yours."

Vereshchagin looked at the faces around him. "Although our relations with the Blues are unfriendly, waging war in earnest is not calculated to improve them. Our objective is to prevent the Blues from becoming a threat to Earth and the colonial worlds. Until—and unless—they evidence a desire to leave their home world and move into space, I do not view them as a threat."

"Even if inaction results in sacrificing the next supply ship and curtailing our stay?" Kolomeitsev asked.

Vereshchagin nodded. "Hans, I would like to see a plan for rationing."

Coldewe shrugged. "You'll have it by tomorrow."

Jan Snyman could not contain his astonishment. "Sir, it sounds like we're just going to do nothing." Mitsuru Aichi wordlessly echoed his sentiments.

Kolomeitsev said nothing, but smiled, perhaps recalling admirals who made careers out of doing nothing.

"Commissioner," Kobayashi said, "we are almost finished with our repairs. The Blues have a rudimentary satellite network on the water side of their planet. Destroying this network would temporarily reduce the danger to ourselves and the supply ship."

Vereshchagin considered briefly, then nodded. "Take it out."

"What about the hostages?" Coldewe asked. "I want them back and I want Rikki back, but if we pull them out, we let the Blues know we can sneak shuttles into their airspace."

Detlef Jankowskie started to suggest taking Blues as hostages to trade before the futility of this impressed itself on him.

Vereshchagin made no reply for a long while. Finally, he said, "Hans, see if you can come up with a plan that allows us a reasonable chance of bringing out our people."

"Even if this plan risks compromising future operations?" The Iceman asked.

Vereshchagin nodded. "Even so."

"All right," Coldewe said.

"Are all of you comfortable with this policy of nonaction?" Vereshchagin asked. He looked directly at Mitsuru Aichi. "Are you, Major?"

Aichi swallowed hard. He recalled a phrase from the *I Ching*: "The inchworm shrinks so as to be able to gain faith." Just as the worm has to pull its ends together before it can stretch out and move forward, a person must bend and yield in order to grow. "I am satisfied, honored Commissioner."

Vereshchagin nodded. "Thank you all," he said with finality.

As the meeting broke up, Jan Snyman said to Coldewe, "Our people aren't going to like this much."

Coldewe said slowly, "Anton gets paid to make decisions people don't like. We get paid to make them like it."

L-Day plus 510 [4-brook Rain 14]

"I THINK WE SHOULD GO BACK INSIDE," SUPERIOR PRIVATE Myburgh said apologetically, studying his pitifully thin sensor array. "They will begin looking for us again at daybreak."

"I feel like a lizard." Hendricka Sanmartin made no immediate move to comply. "Scuttling into a hole at the approach of the sun."

"Please, ma'am." Myburgh tugged timidly at her sleeve. "Getting shot at makes me nervous."

"What are our chances of escaping?"

"Not very good," Myburgh admitted.

The Blues had found enough evidence of human presence to convince themselves to keep looking. Although the forest was far too wet to set ablaze, they were combing it carefully, and the hide site Kekkonen and de Kantzow had prepared was not intended to withstand prolonged scrutiny.

Sanmartin shook her head. "If I give myself up, they will be so pleased at having found me that you can sneak away."

"Ma'am, these people aren't people." There was considerable fear in Myburgh's eyes. "Finding you might make them look even harder. And if I let you get caught, if *they* don't shoot me, Colonel Hans *will*. He ordered me to take care of you."

She reluctantly crawled in after him. "You must pardon me. I seem to be a little bit out of my depth here."

"To tell the truth, ma'am," Myburgh said with feeling, "so am I." He held up a tarok deck. "Want to play a few hands?"

"Are you sure you want to play?" She turned onto her left side and tried to make herself comfortable. "You don't seem to win very often."

Myburgh shuddered.

She grinned. "I suppose keeping me occupied is the lesser of two evils."

"Yes, ma'am," Myburgh said with real feeling.

HIMS *Zuiho* [5-brook Rain 14]

"I AM TELLING YOU, PIA, I AM REACHING THE POINT WHERE I can't live with the situation anymore." Simon Beetje brushed his hair back. "I feel as though I am living a lie."

"Maria appears happy. She is even wearing makeup, now."

"But the pattern hasn't changed." Beetje tried to think of examples. "She assumes that because I love her, I will do whatever she wants, and if I balk, it is because I'm too stupid to understand. It's maddening—" He caught his breath. Pia wore a high-buttoned blouse, and he found his eyes straying. "It is particularly maddening because I *don't* love her anymore."

Szuba's shoulders slumped, ever so slightly. "Is there anything new about Miss Sanmartin?"

He shook his head. "Hans keeps me informed. The Blues are still searching, which gives us hope that they haven't found her yet." He tried to redirect the conversation. "Pia, there is something I have been meaning to say to you for a while, now. You've been incredibly patient, listening to me—"

"But the important thing is that you still care about Maria, and she cares about you very much," Szuba said dogmatically, staring at him with an unwavering and disconcerting gaze.

"But that is just the point . . . I don't care about her anymore. I only recently realized what I do care about. Pia—"

"But you do care about Maria still, and love ends with one thing, which is indifference." Szuba let her hand rest lightly on his arm. "Simon, don't you see? You cannot leave Maria. The two of you care for each other. That is what is important."

"Pia, there is nothing left of what we had. For weeks now, I feel as though I've been living a lie."

"Simon." She stared at him. "You have been together twenty years. Maria won't have very much of a life if you leave her now. Sometimes both persons in a marriage have to do insane things to hold it together. And that is what matters."

Before Beetje could explain what he was attempting to say, the door to the compartment swung open and Ferenc Szuba stood in the doorway, panting. He bellowed, "I see you! With my wife! I will kill you!" Shaking his fist menacingly, he took a step inside. "I *will* kill you!"

Simon looked at Pia. "This is very embarrassing."

"Excuse me for interrupting." Hans Coldewe put his head through the doorway. "Ferenc, your assistant called; he's rather worried about you. I know where Mika is, so I thought I might find you here."

"You!" Ferenc shouted.

Coldewe looked puzzled. "Who else were you expecting?"

Pia Szuba said sharply, "Ferenc!"

Ferenc recognized the note of command in her voice. "Yes, sweet?"

"This has gone on long enough!"

Ferenc's shoulders slumped visibly. "Yes, sweet."

"I am tired of your jealousy, and I am through putting up with your ill humors."

"Yes, sweet."

"Simon is our friend, and he needs our help."

"Yes, sweet."

"Now take me home." She sniffed. "You have embarrassed me quite enough."

As the door closed behind them, Beetje looked at Coldewe. "He was beating her."

Coldewe nodded.

"This is not the way things happen in real life. I mean—" Beetje said, remembering the secret and often not particularly secret sins of his university colleagues. "People don't act this way."

Again, Coldewe nodded.

"You don't have a clue either, do you?"

Coldewe kept nodding.

"I almost—" He stopped himself. "I almost made a complete fool of myself. Ridiculous." He eyed Coldewe. "I was pretty pathetic, wasn't I?"

"I missed that part."

"I almost—" Beetje started to say. Then he shook his head. "Simply incredible. Is Pia crazy, or are we?"

"Simon," Coldewe said, "I'd rather see a farce than a tragedy any day. Come on. We've shut down the brewery, but I'll find you a beer."

"I need to see my wife."

Coldewe shook his head to clear it. "Make that two beers. Why?"

"I seem to have forgotten that Ferenc is my friend." Beetje stared at the door. "You know, the trouble with looking for something that isn't there is that sometimes you think you've found it."

Coldewe wrinkled his nose. "Come again?"

"Hans, Maria isn't the only woman in the universe, but she's the only woman for me. On this ship."

Coldewe often wondered whether Cupid used a bow and arrow or a machine gun. "Now that you mention it, there's a reason why Eve was Adam's one and only."

"Maria has been trying to patch things up. I'd better talk to her before the rumor mill begins churning."

"And before we get Rikki back," Coldewe observed, beginning to understand.

"That, too." Beetje shook his head in resignation. "Come on, I could use that beer."

Planetary Approach, HIMS *Aoba* [6-brook Rain 14]

SCREENED BY THE SMALLER MOON, *AOBA* AND *CHOKEI* MATERIalized out of the sun into the upper atmosphere on the water side of Neighbor.

"Tracking satellite Noto Yamato," the sensor operator, Noma, announced. "Eight-seven-zero point three kilometers altitude, ascending sun synchronous orbit."

"You may fire," Kobayashi told Sery.

Sery did so, shattering the satellite's solar array and ripping through a series of antennas and pinwheel louvers.

"Tracking satellite Beppu Mutsu," Noma said. "Eight-six-six point four kilometers altitude, descending sun synchronous orbit."

"You may fire," Kobayashi directed.

Long before Blue missiles could creep over the horizon, the two ships seared every satellite on the water side of the planet. Hours later, two follow-up passes decimated Neighbor's surviving satellites as they made the dangerous transition from the planet's land face to its water face.

L-Day plus 512 [6-brook Rain 14]

ALTHOUGH THE BLUES HAD STRIPPED THE CONTACT TEAM OF
the metal objects in their pockets, they allowed Corporal Kobus
Nicodemus to keep the paint set and brush he used for his icons.

Finding a wall in the room where they were imprisoned to his
liking, Kobus had begun painting a kneeling woman surmounted
by a lightning flash. With little to occupy them, the rest of the
team watched.

The door opened, and six armed Blues escorted Dr. Seki back
inside.

After the door closed, Connie Marais asked, "Spoagusa?"

Seki nodded, for a moment too spent to respond. Spoagusa
was perhaps the canniest of the Blues, and it was becoming
more and more difficult for Seki to learn more from Spoagusa
than Spoagusa learned from him.

"Now?" Nicodemus murmured as he executed a brush stroke.

Wanjau shook his head.

Dr. Motofugi, mildly subdued by his incarceration, studied the
image beginning to emerge under Nicodemus's brush. "Who are
you depicting?"

"St. Barbara." Nicodemus stepped back to gauge the effect.
"Patron saint of captives."

HIMS *Zuiho* [7-brook Rain 14]

"DESPITE THE BEST EFFORTS OF HANS AND JAN, YOUR OSTRICH
policy is wildly unpopular," The Iceman commented, resting in
a chair. "Captain Kobayashi and Major Aichi have their hands
full, although *Aoba*'s attack on the satellite network drew off
some of the venom, and the raid to free the hostages, once we
locate them, will also have a salutary effect."

Vereshchagin sipped his tea. "You expect trouble?"

"If you will recall, Admiral Horii's junior officers all but mu-
tinied under less egregious circumstances."

"Until I see evidence that the Blues mean to break into space,
it is the correct decision."

"Perhaps." The Iceman held up a pistol. "Gu will be watching
you as you sleep, and I have this. I have also suggested to Father Bosenac that he should consider carrying one." He laughed
at the horror on Vereshchagin's face. "The thoughtless will reason that someone on board is exercising a malign, pacifistic in-

fluence on you, and to resolve the problem, they may strike at the supposed source."

"Is this what we have come to?" Vereshchagin shook his head.

"There are worse things," The Iceman said.

L-Day plus 514 [8-brook Rain 14]

"WATER IS FINE IF IT KEEPS RAINING." MYBURGH HAD CARE-fully poked holes into the surface of the hide to capture some of the water striking it, at the risk of noise as the dripping water landed in the containers he and Sanmartin had improvised. "Food is a problem. I think we should cut back to one ration a day."

"It is not fair," Sanmartin pointed out. "I weigh less than you, so I should eat less."

"We train for this." Myburgh changed the topic. "I spoke with Alariesto; he flew over in a Sparrow while you were asleep."

A momentary hope touched her and died.

"He couldn't land. Wet, unhappy Blues are still camping in all of the clearings. The reconnaissance platoon has a tilt-rotor concealed at base camp, but Lieutenant Wessels will not dispatch it. It makes noise, and he is sure that with Blue soldiers so near, they will hear it. I think he is right about that."

Vereshchagin had brought three tilt-rotor transport aircraft sheathed in the same radar-absorbent materials the Sparrows used, but little could be done to make them quieter.

"What did Alariesto say about the shots we heard yesterday?" she asked.

Myburgh replied reluctantly. "He thinks the Blues found the rest of the lemps. He saw skins."

Rikki lay back, trying to banish from her thoughts the smell of chemical-treated urine. "I suppose the Blues are hungry, too."

"We will just have to wait and hope that the Blues give up." Myburgh shook his head. "Ma'am, I am amazed at how calm and brave you are about this."

"No braver than you." She almost added, "In fact, I am terrified right now."

"It is part of my job to be brave." He sighed deeply.

She sat up. "Gerrit?" Sometimes Myburgh's complexity perplexed her.

"Ma'am, it is just that I am wondering why we came to

Neighbor." He refused to meet her eyes. "I mean, the people here don't want us. Couldn't we have left them alone?"

"You miss Valeska," she perceived.

He nodded vigorously. "I should not ask you, but I thought that being so smart, being a president and a scientist and all, you would know the answer."

Hendricka Sanmartin wished she felt that smart. "The simplest explanation is to say that we have a great deal to learn from these people and a great deal to teach them, once they learn better manners." She warmed to her task. "The universe is a smaller place than we once thought, and people, even blue people, must get along with each other."

"Even if they don't want to?"

"Especially if they don't want to. Sometimes the first stage in such a discussion is to say, 'If you hit me, I'll hit you twice as hard,' and it takes time to move past this."

"I don't know," Myburgh said doubtfully, "it seems like a very simple answer."

She laughed. "I will think about it for a day or so and try to give you a better one." She saw him trying to summon up the courage to ask a question. There was one question she hoped he would not ask.

"Ma'am?"

"Yes."

"Will you come to our wedding?"

"Of course," she laughed, trying not to let her relief show.

He thought for a minute and then asked timidly, "Ma'am, did what you said about people having to get along also apply to being married?" Remembering his half-wistful, half-apprehensive description of Valeska, his blushing bride-to-be, she laughed quietly until the tears ran.

HIMS *Zuiho* [9-brook Rain 14]

SNACK BAR MEIER SUDDENLY THREW DOWN HIS CARDS.

"Terrible hand?" his buddy, Eloff, inquired.

"This is crazy, sitting here doing nothing while our people on the ground are being killed," Meier stormed. "I think maybe Colonel Vee has lost it."

Dead silence greeted his outburst. The other card players in first section, No. 9 kept playing. Platoon Sergeant Kaarlo Kivela lazily opened one eye. "Snack Bar, your mother really should have stopped drinking when she got pregnant."

"I don't understand, Platoon Sergeant," Meier stammered.

"Don't we all know," Kivela said brutally, closing his eyes.

"How many wars have you won?" Section Sergeant Uborevich inquired. He slapped the cards down in front of Meier. "It's your deal."

An even uglier scene played itself out farther aft. In the compartment where half of Major Aichi's first platoon was billeted, Aichi's first platoon leader, Lieutenant Aritomo Tsukahara, declared belligerently, "Fully realizing my impertinence, I am forced to state my impression that the present course of nonaction is far short of expectations. It has become a matter of honor. Someone must explain what is being done!"

Lieutenant Tsukahara was suddenly aware of another presence in the room.

Major Aichi looked at his men. "I am responsible for safeguarding His Imperial Majesty's honor. I am also responsible for obeying orders and enforcing discipline." He loosened the flap on his holster and half lifted his 8mm pistol, as if to reassure himself that it was present. "Does anyone else have something he wishes to say?"

His first platoon withered beneath his silent contempt.

"Platoon Sergeant Joshima," Aichi said quietly. "You now command first platoon."

Tsukahara was placed under guard in an empty storeroom until he begged to be released.

L-Day plus 517 [2-cloud Rain 14]

"YOU EACH ONE ARE WELL? YOU EACH ONE EAT?" Ekpalawehud asked as he walked Connie Marais back to his cell.

"Ekpalawehud," Marais said, "you have to let us go. Tell the Pochteca they cannot keep us here like this."

One warder opened the door while others covered the contact team with their weapons. Ekpalawehud stood by the door with his forearms folded, knowing that the Pochteca could.

Marais glanced at the other members of the contact team huddled around the table, seemingly unconcerned with the conversation, but in fact listening intently. "Ekpalawehud, can we have our computers?"

"Pochteca will consider," Ekpalawehud said, which meant no. Marais's eyes pleaded. "Why is this happening?"

With few, if any, mobile facial muscles, the Blues were a singularly expressionless species, but Ekpalawehud's posture softened slightly. "You are change," he said. "You block us."

Marais was instantly aware that Ekpalawehud had advanced two separate reasons. "From space?"

"You each one are well? You each one eat?" Ekpalawehud repeated.

"Yes, we are well. We are eating," Marais replied.

"Best," Ekpalawehud said. He left.

Isaac Wanjau waited a moment, checking the time, then swept the tarok cards together and handed them to Nicodemus. "I need to go to the bathroom. Dr. Marais, would you take my place?"

Inside the "bathroom," he checked for surveillance devices. Unhooking the aiguillette on his shoulder, he bent it into an antenna and coupled it to the plastic pieces backing his epaulets. Two battle ribbons containing microprocessors, a raised metal button, and the power unit from his razor completed the radio. Holding his breath, Wanjau tapped out an initializing sequence: dot-dot-dot, dash-dash-dash, dot-dot-dot, break.

The relay picked it up and boosted it to the moon overhead, where a second relay would transmit it to *Zuiho*. A second later, Wanjau heard a short click and exhaled slowly.

Then he began tapping out a detailed message, which his radio would transmit as a single pulse, after which Vereshchagin would know the contact team's situation and location.

Eleven hours later, Lieutenant Resit Aksu's team fortuitously confirmed Wanjau's assessment of Blue intentions with the discovery of a building which appeared to be, and probably was, a pilot fusion project.

HIMS *Zuiho* [3-cloud Rain 14]

"IT WOULD APPEAR THAT THE BLUES NOW POSE A THREAT," Vereshchagin said without preamble. "What are our objectives?"

"We wish to free the contact team and to cajole our blue friends into decommissioning their missiles and halting work on spacecraft." The Iceman's gray eyes glinted. "Terror bombing lacks elegance and aesthetic appeal. It seems to me that the last time we had a similar discussion, Raul Sanmartin had a plan tucked away against a rainy day. Hans?"

"First things first." Coldewe unfolded his arms. "We need to spring Rikki and Myburgh. The Blues have been going over that forest centimeter by centimeter, and it's a miracle they haven't been found."

"What do you propose?" Vereshchagin asked.

"Something suitably crack-brained. Now that we have some privacy until the Blues launch more satellites, I want *Aoba* and *Chokei* to provide a diversion so the recon platoon can pull them out."

"If I may suggest," Major Aichi said, watching Coldewe intently. "In that we intend to free the contact team, perhaps we could permit Miss Sanmartin and Private Myburgh to surrender. Surely, they would be taken to the same place."

Coldewe shook his head emphatically. "I don't want to admit that we have people on the ground. The Blues are almost sure or they wouldn't be taking the woods apart twig by twig, but there's oceans of difference between being almost sure and being sure. More to the point, they've never seen a woman. If they grab Rikki, they may want to open her up to see what she looks like on the inside."

The probable fate of Brit Smits hung like a pall over the discussion.

"Captain Kobayashi?" Vereshchagin asked.

"It might be practicable," Kobayashi said stoically.

Vereshchagin nodded. "Are we ready to discuss other matters, Hans?"

Coldewe nodded. "Cajoling the Blues into reasonability is best accomplished by placing a thumb over their windpipes and squeezing—they do have windpipes; I asked Simon."

"I take it you have a plan," Snyman said.

"The key to this society is food production. If we show we can touch that, we'll have their attention. To that end, Kodama's biochem people have spliced the working parts of tobacco mosaic virus onto a native pest of the water potato."

"As a threat to draw the Blues to the bargaining table, infecting an isolated planting of water potato with Kodama's cultured virus has much to commend it," The Iceman commented. "However, it lacks immediacy. If these people are human in the way they react, it is not the threat of famine that will compel their leaders to accommodate us, but threat of the disorder that an impending famine would inspire. A few spectacular touches would help."

"We need sparkle," Snyman agreed. "Something else to grab attention."

Noting Aichi's bewilderment, Coldewe explained, "It's quite all right, Mitsuru, we've done this before." He spread his hands. "Any ideas?"

"One, I think," The Iceman said, after a brief silence. "The monsoon season is filling the reservoirs along the Great River. Destruction of the dams there would cause extensive flooding downstream, and the loss of hydroelectric power and water needed to produce dry-season crops would strain the Blues economically. Collapsing a few dams should attract serious attention."

"Drowning a few million people generally does," Snyman commented dourly.

"A few tens of thousands, maybe," Coldewe said. "The people downstream will have a fair amount of warning. We'll need to do some computer modeling."

Kobayashi spoke. "Destroying dams with shipborne munitions would appear to pose an unacceptable degree of risk."

Jankowskie amplified his remark. "We're talking about targets hundreds of kilometers apart in the middle of the continent. We can probably get one dam, but after that, the Blues will probably get us."

Kolomeitsev appeared nonplussed. "I assumed that we would place detached nuclear warheads or conventional charges by hand."

"Have we ever blown up a dam before?" Snyman asked.

"It is always nice," The Iceman said, "to try something new for a change."

Synman shook his head. "Those dams are *big*."

"The second dam from the sea, dam B, is approximately 211 meters thick at the base and 318 meters high," The Iceman agreed.

Guessing who The Iceman had discussed the idea with, Coldewe turned to Meri Reinikka. "Meri, how feasible is this?"

Reinikka reached over to turn on Vereshchagin's terminal. "We can't exactly carry around nuclear warheads in our rucksacks. Bear with me if this starts out sounding insane. We fit some of our assault boats with extra flotation cells, mount charges inside, and then drop the boats in the reservoirs with the rig we use to airdrop armored cars."

"You're right, it did start out sounding insane," Coldewe commented. "It also ended up that way."

"I worked it out." Reinikka projected a diagram onto the wall. "For dams B and C, which are arched masonry, I'd use six point two tons of tetramethylene tetranitramine—there are better explosives for the job, but that's what we brought—shaped into a big plate charge. Dam A, the one closest to the sea, is a large, earth-fill gravity dam. That one will take a nuke."

"Six point two tons times two—do we have that much explosive?" Snyman asked thoughtfully.

Reinikka nodded. "And more. Karaev and I *know* you people."

Coldewe grinned. "All right. Back to the plan."

"We hook the boat to the top of the dam, extend the hydroplanes to give us enough standoff distance for the planar jet to form, and deflate the flotation cells back to front so the boat slides down the water face of the dam. We'll need two people at the top to reel out line, and some people in diving suits to make sure nothing snags. Water is relatively incompressible, and water pressure increases the deeper we go, which will concentrate the shock wave. When we reach a good depth, we bolt the boat to the dam using some of *Zuiho*'s tools for working in vacuum, trigger the timer on the detonators, and get our people out of there." Reinikka added with a perfectly deadpan expression, "Boats are the most efficient way to move the charges around, unless you want to steal a truck."

"How much damage will destroying these dams cause?" Aichi asked.

"The gradient energy of a river is dependent on slope. In the highlands between dam C and dam B, there is a slope of approximately 3 percent. This increases to 5 percent between dam B and dam A as the highlands drop away, and when we reach the plain, it goes back to a 1 percent slope between dam A and the sea." Reinikka turned his projection of the Great Valley on its side to show a cutaway view. "You see this in the river's sinuosity; it's fairly straight until it hits dam A and then it starts to meander. When you consider the roughness coefficient, which is the hardness of bed and bank material—"

"Ah, Meri?" Coldewe asked.

"Oh, excuse me, Hans." Reinikka grinned. "I got caught up in the poetry in the language of fluxial geomorphology."

The truck engine "plucked from the precipice" had turned out to be a rather ordinary rotary, which may have had something to do with a slight grudge that Reinikka held against poets.

Reinikka projected images of the three dams, side by side. "A couple of days ago, I had Aksu bounce some signals off the bottom to measure reservoir depth. As you can see, the monsoons are filling the reservoirs almost to the top, and another week or so of rains should do it. Between the three dams, we are talking about something like 150 billion cubic meters of water pent up. The Blues have twenty-six-meter levees running the length of the river. If we touch off the dams sequentially, by the time the massed water from the three dams reaches the lowlands and begins to spread, it will be travelling at better than forty kilometers an hour and most of it will be going over the top of those levees."

Reinikka switched to a three-dimensional view of the Great Valley and began coloring it blue to show how the river would rise. "To answer Major Aichi's question in words, with the river running close to bank full, if we take out two dams, the Blues are deep in mud. If we blow three, they are deeper than deep."

Vereshchagin considered. "All right then. We have the virus, the dams, and the contact team." He looked to see if anyone had anything to add. "Are we agreed?"

The three civilians present were silent.

"Hans, please get with Piotr and work out a plan." Vereshchagin turned to Pia Szuba. "Dr. Szuba, please prepare an ultimatum for me to transmit."

Szuba colored, and Simon Beetje came to her rescue. "I am not sure that we know the words for that."

Vereshchagin smiled. "Let us keep it a simple message then. Unless they return our people and blow up their missiles and the fusion plant, we will attack."

"I think that we can convey the sense of it," Szuba said. "Do you anticipate they will comply?"

Vereshchagin smiled. "On Earth, it was once deemed appropriate to issue declarations of war. I wish to introduce the custom here."

"Capital," The Iceman said with savage good humor as the meeting ended. "We really should have one of these planning sessions every twenty years."

As the people in front of him began to leave, Simon Beetje whispered to Pia Szuba, "He was so calm about it." He felt a hand on his shoulder and turned to find The Iceman looking at him.

"For Neighbor's sake, I hope that this plan works," Kolomeitsev said amiably. "Occasionally in this business, one is allowed to have personal feelings. Anton feels responsible for

Rikki, and there will be the absolute devil to pay if we do not get her back." The Iceman recalled the ratissage Vereshchagin had ordered on NovySibir that sent most of that planet's gunmen to the wall. "Anton can be a very unforgiving person if provoked."

HIMS *Zuiho* [4-cloud Rain 14]

ALTHOUGH NICOLA BOSENAC NORMALLY DID NOT CARRY A ROsary, for some reason he had slipped one into his pocket. "Are we at war now?" he asked.

"First, we will issue an ultimatum," Vereshchagin replied. "In a few days, we will be certain."

"On Earth, they are writing books about you," Bosenac said carefully, wondering what was in Vereshchagin's heart. "There is even a play."

"Hans reviewed it. He described it as 'putrid.' " Vereshchagin fingered his empty pipe. "One would-be biographer even made his way to Suid-Afrika. My people stuffed him with lies, including a particularly egregious one involving cutting a cherry tree."

"Myths are often more comforting than the truth."

"I am so tired of the myths," Vereshchagin said dejectedly. "I have made many mistakes in my life, and I seem to have made most of them here." He thought for a moment. "Nicola, what made you become a priest?"

"I prayed over it until one day I reread something St. Augustine wrote, 'To myself, a heart of steel; to my fellow man, a heart of love; to my God, a heart of flame.' Then, somehow, I knew." Bosenac shook his head wondering. "No moment has ever been so clear to me, before or since."

"You are wedded to your vocation, and in a sense, I became wedded to mine. Perhaps only Piotr remembers, but I wanted to be a teacher. I sometimes look at Simon and wonder how I would have been." Vereshchagin fell silent.

"Commissioner," Bosenac said hesitantly, "is it necessary for us to attack?"

"The things one does, or does not do, have consequences. In my judgment, it is necessary."

"I am told we will destroy three dams on the Great River."

"Yes. We will inundate as much as two hundred thousand square kilometers of farmland and forty-three cities."

Bosenac found himself speechless for a moment. "Dear God."

"We will disrupt transportation and power generation, and we will destroy an incalculable amount of property. We will kill as many as a hundred thousand people." Vereshchagin's face appeared inhumanly calm.

"Anton, do you know how horrible this sounds?"

"Father Bosenac," Vereshchagin said softly, "we can only strike once with any assurance of success, and I must accurately calculate how hard to strike in order to persuade the Blues. The cost of failing is impossibly high."

Some trick of the lighting framed Vereshchagin's head so that for a single irrational instant Bosenac thought he was seeing Lucifer before the Fall. "These are civilians we are speaking of. Aren't there rules to war?"

Vereshchagin stared at him sadly. "My people tell me that the first rule to war is to stay alive, and the second is insure that people shooting at you do not. We often break the first rule, but the second one rarely. I cannot afford to misjudge. I must be as certain as I can."

"Anton, God never demands what we are incapable of, and certainty is something that belongs to God, not men."

"I am sorry, Father Nicola. In Finland, we would say, *Ei se myt toida sopia*. It does not appear to fit." Finnish, like Japanese, is a very polite language, and the expression was as polite a way as any to say no.

When he left Vereshchagin, Bosenac prayed for several hours. Then breathing deeply, he made his way forward to the ship's armsroom.

"Father Nick," Rytov, the armorer, greeted him. He patted his workbench. "Sit down."

Bosenac did so. White-haired and serene, Rytov continued fiddling with the electronic sight to a trooper's rifle, extracting one microchip and replacing it with another.

No one professed to know Rytov's age for certain. He had witnessed the crack-up as a child and had refused retirement four times. Bosenac guessed he was at least seventy, even with time dilation, although he looked the same as he had when Bosenac first met him a dozen years ago.

Hans Coldewe refused to make him go as long as he could pass a physical and do his job. Coldewe might have left him behind, but virtually all the people Rytov knew were going, and the battalion's other armorers, veterans Rytov had trained, asked him to consider it. Rytov had accepted the mission and the notion of a planetful of blue aliens with the polite disinterest he gave to nearly everything outside his chosen world of weapons, ammunition, and battlefield electronics.

Seeing that Rytov was unmoved to speak further, Bosenac cleared his throat. "How are things going?"

"Busy. The usual. Mission coming up." Rytov freed a hand. "It is always the same. You hand out live ammo, and people suddenly find things that need looking after. Reminds me of what you said about foolish virgins." In the course of a long life, Rytov had taken many things in stride, including a Catholic priest masquerading as an Orthodox pope. He looked up. "You need something, Father?"

Bosenac swallowed hard. "Yes, I was hoping to sign out a pistol."

Rytov's eyes narrowed. "The Imps?"

Unwilling to speak, Bosenac nodded.

Rytov relaxed, and pointed to the shelves in back. "Find something you like."

Wandering the aisles, Bosenac reached for a back plate and a battery pack and what looked like a modulation unit. Aware that Rytov was oblivious to his activities, he filled his pockets with a motley collection of electronics before finally selecting a small pistol. He returned and showed the pistol to Rytov, who nodded. "You find ammo for it?"

"I'd rather wait until someone can show me how to use it safely," Bosenac stammered. "Thank you, very much."

Rytov nodded, once again lost in the task at hand. "Go with God, Father."

Bosenac curtly acknowledged and took his leave from the armsroom, bitterly ashamed of his deception.

L-Day plus 469 [5-cloud Rain 14]

"NERVOUS?" SECTION SERGEANT MARKUS ALARIESTO ASKED HIS pilot, Corporal Erasmus van Rooyen.

"Maybe just a little," van Rooyen admitted. Although a good pilot with ten years service, van Rooyen was new to being shot at.

"Good. People who don't know enough to be a little nervous make *me* nervous." Alariesto checked the tilt-rotor's position. "In another five minutes, we ought to see *Aoba* and *Chokei* over the mountains. We promised the Blues an attack." Alariesto shook his head sadly. "You know, in the old days, the Variag wouldn't have done this."

Van Rooyen peered at him. "You think?"

"Think about what happens if the Blues plaster us. We're using most of our fuel reserve—getting more is a problem—and risking two warships, all for two people." Alariesto chuckled. "Although if the Blues are sharp enough to do some plastering, Colonel Hans may need to rethink his plans. Anyway, he says rescuing Rikki will appease Captain Raul Sanmartin's manes, and that if we had ever read a story called 'The Luck of Roaring Camp' we would understand."

Van Rooyen shook his head. "We *got* to get Colonel Coldewe to stop reading those old books." He scanned the summary instrument display hanging in front of his right eye, then glanced over at Alariesto. "Think the Variag is making a mistake?"

"Don't know what to think anymore. Look at poor Simon."

"Beetje?"

"Yeah, Simon. He drops his wife and comes with us to get away. She follows, they spend a year dancing around each other, and he finally goes back to her. Now she kicks him out of her bed. Go figure."

Van Rooyen shook his head. "Isn't love grand?" He slowed his airspeed to better time their approach. "Looks like another bad storm brewing. We ought to just beat it."

"Every pilot's dream, flying treetop high, on a dark night on a strange planet in bad weather. Of course, I'm for anything that keeps the Blues from looking up when we're flying overhead."

Alariesto spoke to the two recon platoon machine-gun teams, who were preparing to act as door gunners. "You awake back there?"

"All set," Assistant Section Sergeant Luoto Saloranta assured him.

Van Rooyen throttled back. "I see camp fires on the ground."

The plane's radio clicked, indicating receipt of an incoming transmission. "Kobayashi here. Preparing to commence firing pass. Sergeant Alariesto, please respond."

Alariesto touched the transmit button. "Alariesto here. We will follow you in, *Aoba*." Seconds later, he got a fix on Myburgh's beacon signal. "Locking on to beacon, five point eight kilometers on a bearing of 277 degrees."

"Commencing firing pass. Kobayashi out."

Whipping in from the sea over the mountains that joined the two halves of the supercontinent, *Aoba* and *Chokei* began launching chicken seed when they were still thirty kilometers out. As the two ships made a high-speed run over the Blue encampments, the deadly rain of fusion-charged particles hit, followed by the lightning flashes of the ships' lasers.

"God sy dank," van Rooyen whispered as he watched the deadly fireworks display.

"That is our cue," Alariesto shouted as the transport slipped into position and began tilting its engines skyward. All around them, the trees lay burning, except for a small patch centered around the beacon. The smoke eddied skyward, and van Rooyen struggled to hold the plane steady in the updraft. The plane's computer automatically adjusted the fuel mixture.

As the machine gunners in back dropped lines on either side, Alariesto could see flashes of light in the smoldering forest. "We're taking fire! Take them out!"

For two long minutes, the recon platoon machine gunners dueled with surviving Blues who were firing at the plane or the sky or the warships, which were already riding a towering rain squall back out at sea.

"We have them hooked. Pulling them in," Private Heunis reported coolly. "One casualty back here."

At a nod from Alariesto, van Rooyen lifted the tilt-rotor straight up and began leveling his engines.

"Doors secure," Heunis said.

"Get us out of here fast," Alariesto told van Rooyen, who didn't argue.

Moments later, Alariesto caught a white flash to the northwest out of the corner of his eye and counted seconds until the shock wave hit. "I think we're all right," he told van Rooyen who was unnaturally pale.

Rikki Sanmartin collapsed getting off the plane after it touched down at the camouflaged landing pad the recon platoon had hacked out on the Tabun Bogdo. She woke up smiling nine hours later, starved and utterly spent. Ozawa, still on crutches, talked her into helping identify vegetation zones on the mountain after the vigil over Luoto Saloranta.

Saloranta, struck by a stray round that went through his face shield, never regained consciousness.

Chokei also suffered. Following the raid on the satellite network, the Blues had refined their technique, fusing their missiles to explode at a distance. Portions of the unlucky little corvette, with only a fraction of *Aoba*'s external shielding, were exposed to the leading wave of gamma radiation from a blast just when it seemed that both ships had escaped unscathed. Four of her primary crew died, including her captain, Commander Mazaki, and much of the vessel was declared unfit for extended occupation.

Aoba's executive officer, Commander Nagahiro, quietly assumed command when the lieutenant-commander who headed up *Chokei*'s alternate crew began exhibiting signs of nervousness.

HIMS *Zuiho* [6-cloud Rain 14]

JAN SNYMAN RAISED HIS ARMS AND LET THEM FALL. "HANS, running four separate operations hundreds of kilometers apart is completely insane."

Coldewe thought this through. "You're right. It is."

Snyman nodded meekly. "Just checking."

"All right, we have two shuttles we can use, each of which can carry a tilt-rotor. Plus we have four Sparrows, three of which are flyable, and a transport on the ground with the recon platoon. The recon platoon drops teams to scout the dams a few days ahead of time—" Coldewe broke off. "Karaev, what are you doing?"

"Figuring fuel consumption for the flights you want the recon platoon to make." Karaev punched numbers into his wrist mount and saved the result. "Please continue."

"All right. The night we go in, the recon platoon lands two Sparrows to cover two shuttle landing zones. That leaves the rest of the platoon with a Sparrow and a transport to spring the contact team. Does this work?"

"We have a total of thirty-four people alive on the ground, counting Blaar Schuur and the two biologists," The Iceman commented. "If we place three men in each of the Sparrows we send to the shuttle landing zones, we can get everyone out."

Coldewe nodded. "We use a section from No. 9 platoon at each dam—we have the shuttles drop one four-man team in the water with a boat, and three more teams around the dam to keep the natives from interfering. Jan, who do we have who can use underwater gear?"

"We have a few people," Snyman conceded. "Now, how do we get everybody out?"

"Good question," Coldewe conceded.

Snyman called up computer images of the three dams. "We

do what we did for Tokyo. Each shuttle carries a transport. The first shuttle drops off people at dams B and C, the second shuttle lands people at dam A, then they both land somewhere on one of the highways."

"There are three parallel roads that run straight as an arrow for six hundred kilometers, so there's no problem finding convenient places to park shuttles." Reinikka shrugged. "The problem will be finding landing zones that aren't going to be underwater when we want to use them."

"The transport from the first shuttle picks up the people from dams B and C. The second transport provides taxi service for dam A. What about the contact team?"

Karaev put his fingers on the map. "If we land the second shuttle somewhere near here, the recon platoon has enough fuel to fly on to the shuttle. Barely."

"That helps," Snyman acknowledged. "We use half of No. 10 and half the light attack—a Cadillac and a slick—to provide security for each shuttle while the tilt-rotors are in the air. Can we get by with using half sections to blow dams B and C? That way, the first transport can fly from dam C to dam B and back to the shuttle instead of having to make two complete trips."

The Iceman shook his head. "We have to anticipate resistance at each dam. A half section is insufficient."

"A full section, then." Snyman looked at Coldewe. "That means two round trips for the first tilt-rotor. At best, we're talking about keeping that shuttle on the ground for two hours. That's a long time."

"Maybe if we keep the shuttle loads light, we can have the shuttles take off and fly around a bit while they're waiting for the transports to come back. They'll be less vulnerable that way," Reinikka suggested.

"Makes sense to me," Coldewe agreed. "Piotr?"

"We will need more security on the ground," The Iceman said, looking directly at Major Aichi, who had remained silent during the discussion. "I recommend using No. 10 to secure the second landing zone, and Major Aichi's platoons to secure the first. Shipboard conditions have not permitted us to train Major Aichi's men properly, but if they are not adequate for the mission, we share in the blame for this."

Aichi bowed his head.

Coldewe grinned. "I was afraid you'd say that. All right."

"Perhaps Jan and Meri can flesh out details to the plan so that the rest of us can kick it to pieces," The Iceman said.

"There is another thing I have been waiting for someone to mention," Snyman commented. "Lange broke his hand playing football, so Mikhail Remmar's Cadillac is going to need a substitute driver."

Coldewe was struck by a ghastly thought. "Oh, no. Not that!"

"You were the one who convinced us to bring Prigal along," Kolomeitsev pointed out. Briefly, there was silence.

Snyman looked around soberly. "Think we can pull this off?"

Coldewe spoke, and for once, the humor left his voice. "Anton stuck Isaac Wanjau on the contact team to take a close, personal look at the Blue soldiery. Isaac says we can take them."

He put his arm around Esko Poikolainnen. "Esko, why don't you work up a computerized attack simulation so we can identify gross errors before we actually commit them." He waved a finger and added sweetly, "Oh, and Esko? No option G this time."

The attack simulation worked up for the Tokyo raid included an option G, wherein a large green monster trampled the city.

HIMS *Zuiho* [7-cloud Rain 14]

WORKING FROM A SHELF THAT FOLDED OUT INTO A DESK, Nicola Bosenac's fingers began tripping over themselves as he tried to fit an amplification module into place.

Bosenac, trained in electrical engineering years before, grew more and more detached as the work progressed. He knew enough to adjust the frequency modulation for the distortion of Neighbor's atmosphere, but the details seemed to elude his memory. Finally, he set down the half-completed radio. Moments later, his mind registered that someone was knocking at his door.

"Father Bosenac?"

Bosenac realized it was Gu on his nocturnal rounds. His answer caught in his throat. Wetting dry lips, he reached for the radio and succeeded in knocking it to the floor.

Hearing the noise, Gu threw his body at the door and sprung the lock.

"Hello, Gu." Bosenac tried to keep his eyes from straying to the floor. "I wasn't expecting you."

"Father Bosenac," Gu repeated, this time in a reproachful tone. He punched the intercom. "Colonel Vereshchagin. Gu here. Please come to Father Bosenac's cabin."

Gu folded his arms. He made no effort to speak, and perhaps no speech was necessary.

Tired, Bosenac left the pieces where they were. Anton Vereshchagin appeared a few minutes later. He looked at Gu and Bosenac, then he quietly shut the door.

"I wanted to warn them. I couldn't quite make myself go through with it." Bosenac willed himself to relax, and his voice assumed a semblance of normalcy. "I thought of all those people dying. I'm sorry." His eyes strayed to his handiwork. "I suppose I should have tried harder."

Vereshchagin said nothing.

"I prayed over it. Believe me, I prayed. I prayed it was God's voice I was hearing and not my own pride." Bosenac picked up the partially completed radio. "I took the parts when Rytov wasn't looking. Please don't punish him."

Vereshchagin paused, as if considering his response. "For the last few hours, I have been taking counsel of my fears. Although it is dangerous for us to strike the Blues too softly, I believe that destroying three dams will be sufficient for our purposes. It does no harm for me to tell you first. Please pray that I have not miscalculated."

Bosenac bowed his head. "Thank you, Colonel."

Vereshchagin took the radio from Bosenac and tossed it to Gu, who caught it neatly in his right hand. "None of this happened," he told Gu. "Please take these pieces to the armsroom."

L-Day plus 476 [2-river Rain 14]

"THERE IT IS. WHERE DO YOU WANT TO PUT DOWN?" CORPORAL Erasmus van Rooyen asked Section Sergeant Thys Meiring. A second Sparrow carrying Meiring's partner followed at a respectful distance.

Impossibly tall and gleaming white in the starlight, dam B was a graceful arc curving between massive granite cliffs. White water shot from sluices far below. Meiring's eyes could not accept the disparity between the immense monsoon-swollen lake on one side of the dam and the seemingly trivial river on the other.

"Where do you want to put down?" van Rooyen persisted.

Meiring, whose sobriquet was "Bad Hand" because of a permanently stiffened finger, finally nodded. "How much fuel you got?"

"Enough to get back if another storm front doesn't move in. Not much reserve."

"Right shoreline then. Look for a solid spot. If you don't see one, slow down and I'll get out if you promise not to drop me in the lake."

"Promise." Van Rooyen laughed as the ungainly little plane caught the updraft from the dam. "They say muck stinks if you stir it up. You watch out for yourself, Section Sergeant."

The Sparrows set down recon teams at the other two dams the following night. To the Blues, prophetically, it was the third day of river, in the fourteenth year of Rain.

HIMS *Zuiho* [4-river Rain 14]

"*STUNDE NULL*," COLDEWE SAID, REVERTING TO THE LANGUAGE of his youth. "Zero hour." He was uncharacteristically subdued as *Aoba* departed to place the two shuttles brought from Suid-Afrika into position, perhaps brooding over being asked to remain behind.

For a departure meal, Jan Snyman's men had voted for *Rassetegai s Ryboi*, a flaked pastry fish dish, and fruit tarts. Aichi's platoons had asked for *shiruko*, red-bean soup, and sweet *ohagi* served with the last of the apples.

Meri Reinikka shook the cobwebs from his head. "Do you know what strikes me as funny, Anton? A blue man spent his entire life preparing to build those dams, and I spent my entire life preparing to bring them down. What took years to build we will destroy in minutes. Men are better at destroying things."

Kolomeitsev snorted. "I know this, Meri—the Blues who built the dams trimmed canyon walls and cut away riverbed to put them in place. To build, you must destroy what is there in order to raise a foundation. War is only a leveling. It is what is raised after that is meaningful."

Vereshchagin watched until *Aoba*'s outline dwindled on the screen. His appetite gone, he set aside his plate, square in shape as a sign of mourning. "To raise, and to raze. The two words mean different things, and yet they have much in common."

"Remember Hanna Bruwer's old kylix, the one with all the mended cracks?" Coldewe said suddenly. "Rikki brought it with her."

Vereshchagin did not trust himself to speak.

Nicola Bosenac had retired to his cabin after giving absolution and communion to those who desired it. The Iceman jested, "Father Nicola has been solemn of late. Perhaps we could drum up a few christenings to cheer him."

"If losing a few dams doesn't convert the Blues," Coldewe said, knowing how The Iceman's mind worked, "we'll have to really show them we're serious."

"The Blues are singularly unlucky," Kolomeitsev said.

L-Day plus 479 [5-river Rain 14]
Dam C: 2150 hours

AS UBOREVICH'S SCATTERED FIRST SECTION OF NO. 9 PLATOON finally assembled, Platoon Sergeant Kaarlo Kivela rubbed the ankle he had banged coming down. "Any final thoughts before we go in?"

Superior Private Eloff, entrusted with a special mission, glared at him. "I still say it's not right!"

Uborevich glanced up at the heavens.

Dam C, farthest upriver of the three, was a low structure three kilometers wide, built of four great arches. Water was pouring down the massive spillway, and more was flowing through the penstocks that turned the turbines. Kivela touched his radio. "Nine point one-one. Break. Kivela here. Donkey, are you where you can see?"

Donges was, and Kivela whispered, "Let's go."

With Donges's gp machine gun in position to provide fire support from the rock face, Kivela led six men and a dog named Greta down a goat's path to secure what looked to be the powerhouse and substation. Uborevich blew the "telephone" cable and took three more men on bicycles across the top of the dam to clear the smaller complex on the far side.

Inside the powerhouse, a handful of surprised Blue engineers, technicians—circus clowns, for all Kivela knew—ignored Kivela's clumsy instructions to lie down on the floor.

They died.

Kivela absently fed a fresh magazine into the silenced submachine gun he held in his hands. "You know how this works?" he asked his grizzled little engineer, Moushegian.

Moushegian stared down at the unfamiliar control panel and threw up his hands. "Short of pushing every lever, I haven't the slightest clue."

"Wire the turbines, and we'll start pushing every lever."

Moushegian began selecting appropriate charges from his bergen, muttering to himself, as Kivela's men finished clearing the near-side pumping station.

Kivela turned to Eloff. "It looks like we're all clear here. You want help to do the honors?"

"No, I can do it," Eloff replied, clearly disconsolate. "But it's purely unnatural! Unnatural is what it is!"

Kivela patted him on the shoulder. "There's a time for all things, like it says in the Bible someplace. Go to it."

While Eloff trotted off to plant a sign marked with a white gallows insignia and the word BANG! on top of the dam beside the spillway, Kivela watched Moushegian wiring the turbines in their ceramic shafts. "Sometimes we blow up dams," he murmured to himself, looking downstream, "and sometimes we don't."

Kivela wasn't sure whether the Blues would know what "bang" meant, but he was fairly sure they'd figure it out.

Not otherwise occupied, Snack Bar Meier found some sheeting in one of the overhead storage cabinets and used it to cover the bodies.

Eleven minutes later, with help from Donges up top, Moushegian finally found the lever that controlled the scouring galleries. After pushing open the gates to release a torrent of water—the merest fraction of the reservoir's capacity—rushing downstream, Moushegian wired the controls.

Still wondering to himself why absolutely nothing had gone wrong, Kivela took his men to the far side to rendezvous with the transport that was supposed to pick them up. At 2238 hours, expedition time, dam C's turbines began exploding.

Cuextla: 2242 hours

KEKKONEN LOOKED AT DE KANTZOW AND KEYED HIS RADIO. "Recon point one. Break. Lieutenant Wessels, everything is still quiet here. Where are you?"

Like most of the other buildings in the veritable warren of structures in Kekkonen's immediate vicinity, the building where Wanjau's signal had come from was immense, perhaps thirty stories high and with a roof as large as four football fields. However, Kekkonen could see all of the roof from where he sat, and Lieutenant Wessels, the recon platoon leader, and the rest of his people were clearly neither present nor accounted for.

"I always love these frosting finely timed operations. You know, the ones where you got to synchronize your frosting time display and that sort of thing," de Kantzow reminisced.

"Shut up, DeKe!" Kekkonen listened. "Yes, sir. We're on top of the building. . . . Uh, Lieutenant, what do you mean you're on top of the building. We're here. Where are you?"

"Problems?" de Kantzow inquired.

"Give me a fix on our position," Kekkonen said astringently.

De Kantzow did so, and Kekkonen compared positions with Wessels. "They're about twenty blocks away. I guess we might be a little rustier at this than we thought. Wessels is so mad he could spit. Are we on the right building or is he?"

"We are," de Kantzow said confidently. "You know, this frosting kind of thing wouldn't have happened in the old days."

"In the old days, we had Prigal," Kekkonen pointed out. "I'm talking to Miinalainen now. Wessels must really be mad. He has a team inside already, and these buildings are like mazes. It's going to take him a while to get them out, and even longer to get here. We need to be on our way before the dams go up. Miinalainen wants to know if we want to try to rescue the contact team ourselves or abort?"

De Kantzow looked down at Dolly, who was still sitting inside the small Sparrow aircraft that had brought them. "Dolly, what do you think?"

Dolly wagged her tail.

"She's for it," de Kantzow announced, scratching the dog under the chin.

"Okay. Miinalainen and Wessels say do it. You lead."

Dam B: 2252 hours

FROM THE ROAD RUNNING ALONG THE TOP OF DAM B, LIEUTENant Mika Hiltunen stared far down the air face of the dam at white water and a vast array of workshops and maintenance plants the Blues had built along the canyon walls to either side. The view made him slightly dizzy; the reservoir at his back was considerably larger than the parish in which he had been born.

He looked away from the chasm in time to see Kokovtsov's shuttle pass between two water-intake towers and slow almost to stalling speed ten meters above the wavelets, its noise swallowed up by the rushing water.

"We keep telling Coconut you are not really supposed to fly

a shuttle that low," he told the private standing next to him, a cowboy named Lin.

As they watched, the clamshell doors in back of the shuttle opened and a drag chute popped out, jerking the loaded assault boat free. As soon as the boat cleared, four men in scuba gear jumped into the water after it.

"Captain Sanmartin used to love the reef animals, used to talk people into going to help collect them." Hiltunen shook his head. "Never thought it would ever come in handy."

The boat threw up a massive waterspout as it hit and disappeared beneath the surface. A few seconds later, as the ripple it created spread, it popped up. Hiltunen watched until the first of the frogmen bobbing in the water managed to swim to the boat and climb aboard.

"A river runs through this land," Hiltunen whispered, "and we will set it free."

Lin looked at him. "Are you feeling okay, sir?"

Cuextla: 2309 hours

"IT'S SPOOKY HOW EMPTY THIS PLACE IS," KALLE KEKKONEN murmured. He pointed to a door. "How about this one?"

De Kantzow shrugged, and Kekkonen tried the lever. "It's locked."

De Kantzow growled something that probably did not qualify as a tribute to Kekkonen's perspicacity.

As the two of them had rapidly discovered, the Blues only ran stairwells from one floor to the next, and scattered them around. There was even less consistency in the cryptic characters inscribed on the doors. The metallic whine of the building's air-conditioning was unsettling.

Kekkonen handed de Kantzow his submachine gun. "I have a picklock." He produced it from his side pocket and carefully inserted it into the oval hole in the barrel of the door handle. His patient fiddling failed to produce results. De Kantzow busied himself scanning the ceiling for stray cracks.

After a moment, he nudged Kekkonen aside. "I have a picklock, too." Thumbing the safety on Kekkonen's submachine gun, he fired one round into the door, pausing to observe penetration and ricochet. Satisfied, he nodded and fired the rest of the magazine into the door in short, carefully aimed bursts. He pivoted on his left foot and executed a savage kick that snapped the door free of its lock.

Kekkonen accepted his submachine gun back. "You know, DeKe, you take all the fun out of this."

"You and your frosting mathematical probabilities," The Deacon growled as they stopped inside. "I told you we should have turned right."

The room had high, vaulted ceilings and elaborately woven tapestries on the walls. A very long table and dozens of carefully carved chairs filled most of it. The floor was covered with ornate scrollwork. "DeKe, this looks like a throne room or something," Kekkonen whispered.

"It's almost as fancy as the whorehouse we trashed on Odawara," The Deacon solemnly agreed.

Dolly wandered over to investigate the brilliantly decorated high seat. She walked around and sniffed at it a few times. A few seconds later, Kekkonen said softly, "DeKe, did you just see what I just saw?"

De Kantzow shook his head. "No. And you didn't either."

Dolly walked back to Kekkonen wagging her tail. He reached down to pat her. "Do you think she knows?"

"No." The Deacon shook his head. "Not a chance."

Kekkonen considered. "If we tell anybody, do you think they'll believe us?"

"No." The Deacon shook his head. "Not a chance. Come on, we're frosting short on time here."

Landing Zone One: 2314

MAJOR AICHI GLANCED AT KOKOVTSOV AND TOUCHED THE RADIO in the shuttle's darkened cockpit. "Recon point one-three. Break. Aichi here. Sergeant Salchow, how is the road?"

Assistant Section Sergeant "Abdullah" Salchow, head of the three-man recon team "occupying" the six kilometers of road arbitrarily designated Landing Zone One, replied, "You're clear to land, Major."

Kokovtsov let down his landing gear and began to measure his approach. Seconds later, an 88mm round from a recoilless gun lit up the night.

The radio clicked. "Salchow here. *Now* you're clear to land, sir."

Kokovtsov chuckled as the massive shuttle glided to a halt.

Mikhail Remmar's Cadillac and a slick rolled down the ramp and sped off carrying a half section of Aichi's second platoon to establish a blocking position farther up the road. Another section pushed a transport plane out the back and locked its wings into place, while the rest of Aichi's men filtered into position along the dikes. Moments later, the transport flew off to retrieve the first and second sections of No. 9 platoon. Kokovtsov flew the shuttle off to circle.

Supply Dump: 2320 hours

FROM *AOBA*'S FAVORITE HIDING PLACE BEHIND THE LESSER moon, Jankowskie and Kobayashi monitored events on the planet's surface with what remained of their satellite array.

"So far we appear to be on schedule," Kobayashi said.

Jankowskie nodded to the signals rating. "Jan, this is Detlef. Unless you say otherwise, we are going to make with our part of the program."

Maintaining radio silence, Snyman made no reply. Jankowskie turned to Kobayashi. "Let's go."

Moments later, *Aoba* and *Chokei* emerged over the water side of the planet, flamed two Blue satellites, and deposited precision-guided, five-hundred-kilogram projectiles on a half-completed offshore missile complex and three observation stations the Blues had established on oceanic islands.

Accelerating to the highest speed they could manage in atmosphere, the two warships waited until just before the supercontinent appeared on the horizon and then discharged most of the projectiles remaining in their magazines, carefully calculating on inertia, prevailing winds, and the rotation of the planet to carry them to their targets. The two ships broke for open space.

As they did so, *Chokei* positioned herself above *Aoba*, and *Aoba* launched her lifeboat—crudely doctored to imitate *Chokei*'s radar signature—on a preset course that carried her in the wake of the projectiles launched.

A dozen Blue missiles rose to greet the lifeboat, and three of them turned it into atomized dust. Fourteen minutes later, the first five-hundred-kilogram bomb directed itself at an airfield on the continent's bleak western coast, and the rest drifted down at intervals. Although some projectiles had their flight disrupted by the explosions that vaporized the lifeboat, and others lost track of their targets in the overcast, bombs are very accurate; they almost always hit the ground. The result was pandemonium.

The goal, of course, was to keep the Blues unenlightened about the nature of the attack as long as possible. Conditioned to expect assault from space, the Blues would find it difficult to distinguish the demolition of dam B from the other reports flooding in.

Jankowskie gestured to the signals rating. "Jan, Detlef again. Hope you're well. It looks like somebody kicked over an anthill down there. A blizzard of radio traffic, spent missiles in many directions, and aircraft sorties everywhere." He chuckled. "I haven't seen this much excitement since my mother took me to the World Cup."

Cuextla: 2342 hours

"FREEZING HELL, THEY HAVE TO BE AROUND HERE SOMEwhere," de Kantzow quietly complained. He halted and held up one hand when he saw Dolly stop. Silently exchanging weapons with Kekkonen, de Kantzow turned a corner and emptied the magazine of Kekkonen's silenced submachine gun into a crowd of armed Blues.

"You get them?" Kekkonen wheezed.

A fusillade of shots answered his question. "Frosting hell," The Deacon replied. He armed a grenade and flipped it around the corner. When it went off, he knelt down and poked his head around to observe results. He promptly loosed a fléchette round from his s-mortar. "One of them twitched," he explained, handing back Kekkonen's submachine gun.

"That rips it," Kekkonen said, slamming a fresh magazine into his weapon. "We're almost out of time, and the Blues know we're here."

"You got any ideas?"

Kekkonen bent down and patted the dog. "Dolly, you remember Isaac? Go find Isaac!" Dolly bounded off. "Do you think—" he started to say.

"Just shut up and follow her," The Deacon said.

Seconds later, they found her pawing a door. "You teach her to shoot, and we're out of a job," de Kantzow commented as Kekkonen blew the lock off.

The room was empty. Dolly whimpered. "You want to try again?" Kekkonen asked her.

Two Blues later, they found the right room.

"You people sure make a lot of noise," Corporal Kobus Nicodemus observed. "What kept you?"

"Leave everything. We've got to move fast," Kekkonen panted. "I'll take point, DeKe, you bring up the end."

"You have an extra weapon?" Isaac Wanjau inquired softly. De Kantzow handed him his sniper's rifle and two spare magazines, while Kekkonen sheepishly produced a second submachine gun for Kobus Nicodemus. Motofugi and Marais assisted Dr. Seki.

Landing Zone One: 2347 hours

THE TILT-ROTOR LOWERED ITSELF, ALLOWING ITS WHEELS TO touch. The huge propellers kept spinning as Platoon Sergeant Kivela rushed Uborevich's section off the plane, shoving laggards out bodily.

As the transport lifted to pick up Hiltunen, Aichi sent Uborevich to reinforce Remmar and the infantry half section up the road. He watched as they pedaled their little bicycles into the darkness.

Twenty minutes later, Kokovtsov's shuttle reappeared out of the night and roared to a halt on the highway. Emerging from the sodden fields, Aichi's men began laying strings of mines across the road. At a nod from Mikhail Remmar, Prigal drove Cadillac 14/3 out of a ditch and delicately knocked down the back wall of a stone toolshed. A few minutes work around the doorway with a cutting bar gave Remmar a clear field of fire.

Dam A: 2349 hours

MAJOR JAN SNYMAN HAD GIVEN EACH OF THE DAMS NAMES: dam C with its multiple arches was the opera house; dam B was the tower. Both depended upon horizontal arch action rather than sheer size and weight to hold back water. In contrast, dam A was the wall, the great wall—low, squat, and massive.

Built of layered earth and rock around a huge ceramic spillway, it was 160 meters high and nearly four kilometers long. At a guess, 250 million cubic meters of earthen fill had gone into its construction, and it held back a sea 420 kilometers long, intended to supply water to the fields along a thousand kilometers of riverbank for thirty-five rainless nine-days.

Dam A was the point d'appui, the fulcrum, which is why Reinikka had recommended a nuke, and why Jan Snyman had assigned himself to the assault. And along the entire lonely stretch of dam that Snyman had selected, for the entire twenty-seven minutes it took to maneuver the assault boat into position and tie it down at the sixty-meter mark, Snyman, carrying a shot-up black umbrella Karaev had lent him, and the third section of No. 9 platoon saw not a single Blue.

It was all very anticlimactic.

They set all three detonators—Reinikka believed in backing up his backups—for a time seven hours hence, and basically got the hell out of there.

The tilt-rotor that came to pick them up was even on time.

Dam B: 2356 hours

"IT FIGURES," HILTUNEN SAID, UTTERLY DISGUSTED.

The explosives-laden assault boat had hung up halfway down the dam. Engineer Sergeant Nikoskelainen suspected one of the hydroplanes had caught on a trash rack.

"How much longer?" Hiltunen demanded.

Nikoskelainen scratched his head. "They're working at it with cutting bars. Maybe another ten minutes." He shrugged. "Mika, you ever try to cut through four centimeters of steel underwater?"

The wave of bombs from *Aoba* had already hit, which meant that the delicate timing that was intended to cover their activities was already wrecked.

"What happens if we blow it in place?" Hiltunen asked.

Nikoskelainen thought about it for a moment. "Probably nothing much. The way they got the boat hung up down there, the axial cavity of the charge isn't parallel to the dam, which means the detonation shock wave and the expanding gases aren't going in the right direction." He considered explaining the mechanics of an underwater bubble pulse and decided against it. "You lose a lot of effort that way. I could show you the math."

"Frost it, that's six-point-whatever tons of explosive down there!"

Nikoskelainen thought for a moment more. "Mika, this stuff this dam is built from isn't brittle like concrete. What the charge has to do is to shape the shock wave of the blast so that it spreads laterally from two plane surfaces, splitting the material and creating enough sideways motion in the structure so that the water can just blow the whole thing open." He elbowed Hiltunen in the ribs. "Of course, *I* wanted to use a nuke, but *somebody* said that the Blues would notice a nuke, which would cause problems for Jan downstream. Of course, that was when we thought we'd be on schedule."

Hiltunen felt his radio. "What is it?"

"Meiring here." Thys Meiring was one of the two reconnaissance-platoon scouts who were now manning listening posts. "More company, Mika. Looks to be a couple of dozen of them, this time. They're standing around the roadblock arguing."

Hiltunen had ignored the roadblock the Blues had positioned on the winding road that led to the top of the dam, until several of the Blues manning it interested themselves in the activity on the lake, whereupon Section Sergeant "Mother Elena" Yelenov and the four-man team providing far-side security eliminated the problem and stacked the bodies out of sight. Unfortunately, the problem was back.

Hiltunen, who ordinarily didn't swear, swore succinctly and to the point.

"The roadblock again, huh?" Nikoskelainen eyed Hiltunen sympathetically. "Don't you just hate interruptions?"

Hiltunen stared at Nikoskelainen. "Just get the bomb in place."

He rode his bicycle toward the far side. Realizing what a target he made against the partially moonlit water, he ended up crawling the last quarter kilometer.

By the time he arrived, the Blue patrol had decided to investigate, and Mother Elena and several friends had resolved the matter. Unfortunately, in the process, Private Lin took two rounds through the upper body, and several of the Blues escaped.

Hiltunen hoped it would take them a while to find a radio and call in help.

Cuextla: 2358 hours

"THE FROSTING PEOPLE FOLLOWING US," DE KANTZOW WHISpered, "are getting close."

Wanjau caressed his rifle. "All right."

"One is all it takes, and the Variag wants you back." De Kantzow shook his head. "Isaac—if some frosting thing goes wrong, tell Lara I tried. Just tell her that."

Wanjau nodded and left.

De Kantzow listened to the footsteps of the Blues. Waiting until he judged that the stairwell was full, he tilted his body forward and fired three fléchette rounds into the mass of bodies. He followed up with an incendiary grenade and reloaded as he ran down a narrow corridor that snaked in and out, his ears full of the sound of small-arms ammunition exploding from the heat of the thermite.

He stopped opposite two doors. "Frosting hell, was it a left or a right?" He noticed one door had LEFT, IDIOT! emblazoned on it in flaming red brush strokes.

When he reached the top of the last set of stairs, the roof was crowned in black smoke from smoke grenades. "I sent your Sparrow on ahead," Lieutenant Wessels explained. Still thoroughly annoyed, he turned the detonator key at his belt and blew the last two sets of stairs into scrap.

De Kantzow followed Wessels on board the transport. Slamming himself into a seat, he watched as Miinalainen and Kekkonen poured five hundred rounds from a 7.7mm gp machine gun into the smoking hole in the roof, just in case, as the tilt-rotor bounced itself into the air and leveled out.

"Why are you frosting grinning like that?" de Kantzow asked Kekkonen sourly. His body ached.

" 'Tell Lara I tried.' See what happens when you marry a girl half your age? You get silly."

Seeing Rikki Sanmartin, her hair cut impossibly short, sitting between Dr. Ando and Gerrit Myburgh, de Kantzow swallowed what he intended to say.

"Life's a circle, Deacon," Kekkonen observed philosophically. "I started out behind a machine gun, and now I'm back."

It wasn't until the transport was about to land that de Kantzow noticed he had been shot cleanly through the left shoulder.

Landing Zone One: 2359 hours

LIEUTENANT TSUKAHARA SAW MAJOR AICHI APPROACHING IN the darkness and snapped to attention.

Aichi returned the salute. "A quiet evening, isn't it, Tsukahara. How are the men?"

Aichi had placed his first platoon behind the shuttle and his second platoon and a mortar team in reserve. Six kilometers up the road, he stationed Uborevich's first section of No. 9 platoon, who had more mobility because of their bicycles, and Mikhail Remmar's half of the light attack detachment.

"Straining to prove themselves worthy, honored Major," Tsukahara replied. Anxious to keep any kind of criticism from his voice, he searched for words. "To be so far from Earth for so long and not to even see an enemy!"

"Perhaps you could show me your positions. I would like to reinforce my orders to withhold fire to the last instant to keep our presence unsuspected as long as possible," Aichi said, watching carefully to see if Tsukahara took this as a reflection upon his own abilities. He was relieved to see that Tsukahara, a conscientious officer, did not.

As Tsukahara proudly walked him through, Aichi was pleased to see that the positions interlocked and covered the ground.

As they looked out over the blank expanse of roadway, he explained quietly, "Ours is a dry, unostentatious mission, Tsukahara, yet one completely necessary to success. To be successful, our expedition's attack must be carried out as swiftly as a flashing demon and withdrawn as fast as a passing wind. We must cover that withdrawal."

"All the same, Japanese racial quality is especially not well suited for such missions," Tsukahara argued. "It hardly seems like war."

"Please tell me, Tsukahara, what is this phenomenon of war?" Aichi smiled. "Some people believe that war is like sumo wrestling: a display of one brilliant feat is all that is desired. In war, the quick stroke is what the conjurer uses to deceive. At this moment, two men in a small Sparrow are doing more to bring victory by infecting plants than the rest of us combined."

He continued, "I have learned very much from Colonel Vereshchagin. In his view, an ideal war would not even be fought. I agree."

Tsukahara flinched ever so slightly.

"I do not believe that we can depend on fighting prowess or even divine favor to bring victory, Tsukahara. God does not aid those who do not carry through an effort. Victory must be wrung by effort from the hands of hard fate. I feel strongly that it only comes through unselfish devotion."

"*Hai*, honored Major." A thought struck Tsukahara. "Honored Major? What will happen after the ships from Earth arrive?"

"That is not our concern," Aichi said, filled with doubt.

9/2 In Transit: 0000 hours

"I WAS GETTING WORRIED ABOUT YOU," THE TRANSPORT PILOT said. "There are Blues all over on the far side."

Lieutenant Hiltunen strapped himself in the copilot seat, and Engineer Sergeant Nikoskelainen squeezed forward to join him. "We've broken contact. Let's get out of here," Hiltunen ordered.

Three small explosions lit up the trail they had climbed.

"Now, we've broken contact," Nikoskelainen corrected.

"When is the dam set to blow?" the pilot asked, lifting his clumsy plane into the air and hurling it down the cliff toward the river so that he could build up some quick airspeed.

"Now," Nikoskelainen said, staring out the window.

A huge geyser of white water erupted fifty meters into the air. The Blues on top of the dam who were looking around for the source of the engine noise were suddenly knocked down. For a moment, Hiltunen thought he saw the semicircular arc of the dam actually ripple in a wavelike movement that dampened out after a second or two. "Nothing happened!" he said, utterly shocked.

Nikoskelainen silently pointed to a jet of water springing from the face of the dam. He began counting, "Ten, nine, eight, seven . . ." When he got to "one," the jet turned into a stream and the cracks spread. Suddenly, the face of the dam gave way and the entire left side crumbled.

"It helps if you know some math," Nikoskelainen said, nodding sagely.

For the first time since he parachuted away from the shuttle, Mika Hiltunen began to relax. He never felt the metal slivers that ripped through his body several moments later.

9/3 In Transit: 0016 hours

IN THE TRANSPORT'S COPILOT SEAT, MAJOR JAN SNYMAN touched the radio. "Ten point one. Break. Snyman here, Stefan, we're on our way in. What is your situation?"

"No contact here thus far." Lieutenant Stefan van Deventer,

the No. 10 platoon commander, was one of The Iceman's protégés and had formerly commanded No. 2 platoon, which was something very few officers were capable of. Van Deventer said crisply, "The recon platoon's tilt-rotor just landed. The contact team is aboard, and we are initiating refueling procedures."

"What?" Snyman said, almost to himself.

"Major Aichi says the transport sent to pick up the dam B force went down on the return flight about fifteen kay from the dam. Five dead." Van Deventer's voice sounded unnaturally calm. "Unless you say otherwise, I'm sending the recon platoon tilt-rotor to pick up survivors and fly them on to Major Aichi. Major Aichi has agreed to wait. I estimate that this will keep Major Aichi's shuttle on the ground an additional two hours, twenty minutes."

While Snyman's shuttle had two tilt-rotors at its disposal—its own plus the one from the recon platoon—Major Aichi's only had the one that was now a burned-out wreck. The hair-fine timing in execution that Snyman had prayed for was coming unstrung.

It was on the tip of Snyman's tongue to release Aichi and have the transport return to Landing Zone Two, but he knew that this would add an extra 120 kilometers to the distance the plane had to cover. It would also place the contact-team scientists and Rikki Sanmartin in considerable risk. He closed his eyes. "Pilot willing, Stefan? All right. Hold the plane there until I get in."

"No, *sir*," van Deventer said sharply. "The pilot goes alone. I am not holding up the plane a minute longer than it takes to refuel it, and Colonel Hans and Isaac and your *wife* would have my *head* if I let you go on the flight to grandstand. Let Aichi handle it."

"All right, Stefan," Snyman said, cursing his own impotence. "Snyman out."

When his transport landed, the recon transport was already gone. Van Deventer had begun pulling in his men, who had yet to see a single Blue. As Daniel Savichev's Cadillac came in, No. 10 platoon pushed Snyman's transport aboard the shuttle with a practiced ease. The shuttle took off seven minutes later.

Snyman made his way back into the cargo bay to make sure people were strapped in and all equipment was bolted down. He noticed Dr. Seki sitting hunched up with an airsick bag in his hand and an amused, animated look in his eyes.

"Major Snyman, why are your men whistling?" Seki asked, as

the shuttle turned sharply to the right on its way to the desolate northern coast.

"It is somewhat difficult to explain," Snyman said diplomatically, as the whistling—half in earnest—intensified.

Isaac Wanjau, looking thinner but happy, grinned. "Russians whistle when other people would boo. Our No. 2 platoon used to call itself 'The Devil's Own,' and we put a lot of people from No. 2 platoon here in No. 10. They suspect that this may be the last operation for them, and they didn't even get to shoot anybody. You can imagine how disappointing this is."

Landing Zone One: 0124 hours

"HOW MUCH LONGER?" AICHI ASKED KIVELA. A FEW BLUE VEHIcles were stashed at both ends of his oblong perimeter along the highway, their surviving occupants gagged and guarded.

"Another hour, maybe." Kivela looked up into the sky as another Blue military plane, sleek and needle shaped, flew overhead in the distance, hoping against hope that his flak team could knock it down if it began a firing pass. "I feel naked with the silly shuttle just sitting there."

"There is insufficient fuel for it to take off and fly around," Aichi observed as the Blue plane disappeared. "How long have you been preparing the shuttle's camouflage net?"

Kivela chuckled. "I think Kalle Kekkonen sent back a chunk of road to study the day we landed. We always thought we might have to do this, you know. Oh, my!" He peered out into the darkness. "We're in for it, now," he whispered. "Those aren't civilians. It looks like an entire motorized company."

He touched his radio. "Nine slash one. Break. Kivela here. Wait for the lead vehicle to run a mine." He looked at Aichi. "We'll be able to shoot at about half of them. I make the intervals between vehicles about ninety meters. See if you can get the mortar to drop some rounds on the rest of them."

Aichi listened to the engines of the approaching vehicles. "We have a Hummingbird reconnaissance drone we can launch."

"Do that," Kivela said.

Two hundred meters to his right, Mikhail Remmar watched the Blue column from his toolshed. His gunner, Valeska, was already measuring the distance, waiting for Kivela to assign targets.

"Superior Private Remmar," Mikhail said in a quiet, commanding tone of voice, "please remove the gum from your mouth. It lacks respect for the people we are about to kill."

She did so without ever taking her eyes from the view screen.

The Blue column stopped when the first vehicle touched off a mine. It was a serious error.

An 88mm recoilless gun got the second and third vehicles in view, the 12mm machine gun on the slick claimed two more, and Valeska Remmar put high-explosive rounds into the remaining eleven. Riflemen and machine gunners, assigned sectors, cut down survivors. From two kilometers away, the 105mm mortar dropped shells on the vehicles farther back.

In a matter of seconds, half of the Blue force disappeared. The firing ceased almost as suddenly as it began. Several minutes passed before the shocked Blues saw fit to return it.

Mikhail Remmar watched Kivela crawl up to the lead vehicle to examine the shattered body of a Blue whose name was Kikhinipallin. "Superior Private Remmar, that was very fine shooting," he said with a father's pride, and that of a vehicle commander. Then he looked over at Prigal. "Why are you glum? And why are you squirming like that?"

"I, uh—"

"Spit it out."

"I, uh, forgot to hook up my tube."

"Your what?"

"My urine tube!" Prigal shouted.

With the rest of the armored car's crew—father and daughter—momentarily disabled, Prigal cautiously backed the Cadillac to a hull-down position in a ditch.

Reinforcements arrived for the Blues twenty minutes later.

Landing Zone One: 0211 hours

LOOKING DOWN THE LINE OF BURNED-OUT VEHICLES, KIVELA absently noted that roasted Blues smelled even worse than roasted humans.

War is hell for average people. The Variag's special refinement was to make it hell for their leaders, too.

A round slammed into the dike a few meters from Kivela's head. More holed the Blue truck parked behind him. Although Aichi had released the Blue drivers they had detained once the shooting started, the trucks were a magnet for incoming fire.

Kivela touched his radio. "Nine point one-one-four. Break. Kivela here. Moushegian, the Blues are back in toolshed B."

"They don't learn, do they?" Moushegian replied. A few seconds later, Kivela saw a flash from the stone structure as Moushegian touched off another directional mine hidden in the thatch. A handful of Blue soldiers were trying to work their way around the flank that faced the mountains, but it would be at least another half hour before they made their presence felt, if at all. In accord with The Iceman's plan, Aichi had blown four canal locks to flood the fields on the river side, activated mines strewn along the dikes, and used the mortar to scatter more mines on the main road to the south. The Blues did not like the mines.

Aichi broke into Kivela's transmission. "Aichi here. Platoon Sergeant Kivela, what is your situation?"

"No change. We can hold our own for now." Although Uborevich's section had suffered two dead and three wounded, the Blue company fronting them was largely spent.

"Please inform me immediately if this changes. Tsukahara's platoon has been pushed off the mound, and I will need to use second platoon to regain it."

"Major," Kivela said earnestly, "the Blues aren't very good, but they're awfully quick to react. The only thing keeping us alive is the fact that the ones with rifles don't seem to talk to the ones flying planes. We ought to think about getting out of here."

With Blues at either end of the highway, the situation was getting very uncomfortable. The fact that the Blues hammering Tsukahara's platoon were within five hundred meters of Kokovtsov's shuttle was especially disturbing.

"One moment, Platoon Sergeant." There was a pause as Aichi issued orders to his second platoon. "Please continue."

"Sir, sooner or later, the Blues are going to figure out what they're doing. If I disengage right now, it will still take my people fifteen minutes to reach the shuttle." Kivela tried to add urgency to his appeal. "Once the Blues see the shuttle, none of us are going home. The Variag can send another shuttle to pick up Mika's section tomorrow night—after dam A blows, the Blues will be too busy evacuating folks to notice."

Although Kivela had friends aboard the tilt-rotor, he tried not to allow friendship to affect his professional judgment, and the odds against their holding out until the tilt-rotor arrived were getting worse.

"The transport is low on fuel," Aichi responded, "and it will be difficult to conceal." He added diffidently, "After dam A explodes, the Blues are likely to view a shuttle landing as a prelude to another attack and respond vigorously. We must either wait for the transport or resign ourselves to abandoning these men."

Kivela conceded the point, and he was not pleased by the thought. "Major, can I ask you a personal question?"

"Please?"

"You're risking both your platoons for a dozen of our people. I know why I'm staying. Why are you?"

It wasn't the sort of question Kivela usually asked an officer, but the circumstances were unusual.

"Excuse me one moment," Aichi said, and Kivela waited, listening to the mortar crew pump out 105mm rounds in support of second platoon's attack. Mortar rounds were beginning to run scarce.

"In listening to Major Kolomeitsev I have come to understand what the Imperial defense forces were like when he and Colonel Vereshchagin first became Imperial officers," Aichi said. "Although the present defense forces are no longer subject to the baleful influence once exercised by the security ministry, in some ways they are like an egg, unformed. Having not fought a war for a number of years—indeed, no one really contemplates fighting a war anymore—they no longer have a clear tradition. This highway is perhaps a good place to begin a new one. I do not like leaving men behind. Is this sufficient?"

"Yes, sir. And thank you, sir. Kivela out." Kivela touched his radio. "Nine point one. Break. Kivela here. Bory, I just talked with Major Aichi. We're going to hold here until Mika's tiltrotor arrives. If I happen to buy it, you do what Major Aichi tells you." He paused. "Aichi's a good man."

Landing Zone One: 0243 hours

"REMMAR-*SAN*, THE NATIVES NEXT TO THE CANAL LOCK ARE BEcoming annoying." Lieutenant Tsukahara had consolidated what was left of Aichi's first and second platoons, positioned them along what was in effect a final line of defense. "Please give me three rounds."

With the mortar gone—the Blues had finally managed to coordinate an air strike—Mikhail Remmar's Cadillac found itself acting as self-propelled artillery. Using the eyes of the pilotless

Hummingbird reconnaissance drone hovering over the battlefield, Valeska Remmar obediently turned the Cadillac turret 180
degrees and pumped three 90mm armor-piercing rounds through
the earthen embankment by the lock.

At a nod from Mikhail, Prigal moved the armored car to its
fourth fallback position before the Blues could return the favor.
Prigal blinked owlishly. "Valeska, you know why Hummingbirds hum?"

"Because they don't know the words." She grinned and
reached over to slap him backhand across the arm. "My mother
told me that one."

"Hush," Mikhail told them. "We are receiving a transmission."

"Uborevich here." With Kivela down, Uborevich had taken
command of what was left of the force holding the far end of
the runway. Fortunately, they'd managed to get the wounded and
even some of the dead out after the last Blue assault.

"Mikhail, the transport's about to come in. We're going to
pull back and let the machine guns cover our withdrawal." On
either side of the road, gp machine guns mounted with a camera
eye and controlled by joysticks from the shuttle would maintain
the illusion that Uborevich's men were still in position. "You
give us six minutes, then you follow."

"*If* practicable," Remmar stressed. "I'm sending one of my
crewmen with you. It will only take two of us here."

"I thought you would. Okay, send her."

Mikhail reached down beside his seat and pulled out one of
the little bicycles. "Superior Private Remmar, you are detached."
His voice softened. "Give your mother my love. Now, get out of
here! Now! That is an order!"

She hesitated just long enough to kiss him, then obeyed.

"You could have told her you loved her," Prigal complained.

"She knows that." Remmar reached up to close the hatch.

Uborevich said, "Okay, I see her. Good luck, you two. And
Mikhail, if Gerrit changes his mind, can I marry her?"

"I'll see you in hell, first!" Remmar grinned. "I'll save you a
cool spot. Remmar senior out." He looked at Prigal. "You have
any complaints?"

Prigal shook his head. "No."

Remmar grinned. "Colonel Hans told me I could make you a
superior private if I wanted to."

Prigal shrugged. "Why spoil perfection?"

Sensing something was up when they heard the tilt-rotor's engine droning, the Blues came forward. The two remote-controlled machine guns lasted only a minute or two. Then fourteen 90mm high-explosive projectiles in a span of eighty-six seconds discouraged them.

"You *are* slow," Prigal observed. He looked at Remmar. "You know, there's a rumor these people are cannibals."

"Prigal, what do you care?" Remmar said irritably. "You've been eating goose all your life."

IN THE SHUTTLE'S COCKPIT, KOKOVTSOV BEGAN FEEDING POWER to his engines even before the clamshell doors closed. "What about Remmar and Prigal?" he asked Aichi.

"They will not be joining us," Aichi said.

Van Rooyen, who had taken over as Kokovtsov's copilot, reached over and flicked several switches. "Let us know when you want us to fire, sir." Aichi was startled by a small explosion on the nose of the shuttle as Kokovtsov began taxiing down the runway.

"Shuttles are not armed," Aichi exclaimed.

"This one is." Kokovtsov said apologetically. "We've got a 30mm gun and some rocket pods mounted behind the heat shield Ras just detached. We'll have to replace it before we come down through an atmosphere again."

Van Rooyen looked at Kokovtsov strangely. "You're awfully talkative tonight, Coconut."

Kokovtsov shrugged. "We're still on the ground."

The shuttle picked up speed. "All kinds of shooting up ahead." Van Rooyen appeared nervous.

Aichi tried to master his own emotions. "Rocket pods are unguided. We would be firing on Remmar as well."

"I know." Kokovtsov added uncharacteristically, "That dumb grunt is my friend."

Aichi caught his breath and nodded. "Corporal van Rooyen, please fire at Flight Sergeant Kokovtsov's direction."

Kokovtsov reached over and adjusted the angle on van Rooyen's weapons package. Then he lifted the shuttle's nose and shouted, "Now!"

As Kokovtsov fought to keep the shuttle on course, van Rooyen's training took over. In the space of eleven seconds, he fired 192 four-kilogram rockets and one thousand rounds of 30mm.

"Leib' God," he muttered, as awed by the display he had unleashed as the Blues who were its recipients.

Heaving itself from the improvised runway, the shuttle began skipping a complicated course toward the sea. The abandoned tilt-rotor began burning with an incandescent light from a case of incendiary grenades Meiring had dumped on board. "Lightening the nose makes it tough to fly," Kokovtsov said, as if to disguise his own feelings.

He looked at Aichi with a degree of compassion. "Major, go on back with your people. If we get hit, there isn't anything you can do up here."

Aichi made his way to the shuttle's cargo bay. Seeing that his men were watching him, he peeled away his face shield and stopped beside Valeska Remmar, who was sitting with her face in her hands. He bowed.

"On behalf of His Imperial Majesty's government, permit me to express my condolences, Juffrou Remmar." Then he found a vacant seat and sat, absolutely drained.

"Shame about poor, old Prigal," Private Eloff said to break the silence.

Slowly and deliberately, Thys Meiring began relating all the Prigal stories he could remember: Prigal's Moonshine, Prigal's Island, Prigal's One-Legged Truck, and all the others.

Moments passed. Aichi heard Kokovtsov's voice in his ears. "Kokovtsov here. *Aoba* says Blues are swarming all over dam A. They've opened the sluice gates, and they're using divers."

With hours before the bomb was set to detonate, Aichi was anguished by the thought that the Blues might find the bomb and disarm it, that everything they had done was for nothing.

"It—" He felt himself becoming dizzy. "It would be very unfortunate if the Blues were able to save the dam."

He heard Kokovtsov say, "I wouldn't worry much. Meri Reinikka built the thing, and Meri doesn't like people messing with his stuff." There was a break in the conversation. Then Kokovtsov added, "*Aoba* says the bomb just went off."

Aichi saw Uborevich looking at him. He rose to his feet. "I have just been informed that dam A has been destroyed."

A few people started to cheer.

At a nudge from Uborevich, Snack Bar Meier lurched to his feet. "Hey! Don't do that." Meier looked slightly abashed. "A lot of people are dying down there."

The cheering quieted as abruptly as it had begun.

"Consistency has never exactly been one of our strong points," Thys Meiring explained to a slightly shocked Mitsuru Aichi.

Three hours later they reached *Aoba*.

L-Day plus 480 [6-river Rain 14]

A HUNDRED-METER WALL OF WATER AND MUD CAME SWEEPING down the valley, scooping up mountains of trash and debris and turning fragments of demolished orchards and bridges into battering rams. Although the cresting wave flattened out and tumbled as it rolled forward, the inexorable pressure of water behind it built it back again.

When the slope of the land decreased, the rolling wave spread and slowed to become a gentle flood, hour by hour, that floated houses away and filled the buildings in the cities and the irrigation ditches with mud. It broke the aqueducts and scoured the village ponds, leaving no source of clean water. The faster shipping in the river escaped out to sea. The water carried slower ships and barges inland and dropped them unceremoniously.

When it ebbed, the flood left undermined levees, washed-out roads, hundreds of thousands of piles of debris, and a gaping hole in the power net. Where the seawalls in the delta broke, the inland sea flowed in to taint the soil. Growing crops were washed away or covered in silt.

Having warned a hydraulic society of its vulnerability, Vereshchagin communicated a more ominous warning, advising the Pochteca to check the plants growing on a hillside terrace and warning them not to allow these plants to come into contact with others.

HIMS *Zuiho* [9-river Rain 14]

"WE COULD TALK ABOUT THE WEATHER, ALTHOUGH PEOPLE down below might think it impolite under the circumstances," Coldewe commented. "Any idea what we should do for an encore?"

"The next move belongs to the other side," Vereshchagin said distantly. "Pia Szuba, who incidentally is fascinated by all she has seen, says that our attack is a ritual fight of the kind men once waged with arrows and spears, in that it is merely a medium for impressing upon the Blues how seriously we view their breaches of good manners and how unpleasant the consequences."

Coldewe held up a worn Imperial coin. "You call it. Chrysanthemum says she's completely right. Crowns says she's completely wrong." He looked at Vereshchagin with a measure of sympathy. "Which one is it, Mika or Mikhail?"

"Both of them. And Prigal. Somehow, losing Prigal is the cruelest blow."

Coldewe shrugged. "You know, he probably liked going out this way. In a week or so, somebody will make up a new verse to 'The Whistling Pig' about him, which will counterbalance the four verses about him that are less than flattering."

"Do you need assistance writing it?"

Coldewe grinned and shook his head. "If I wait a few days, someone else will beat me to it." He looked at Vereshchagin coldly. "How's your heart?"

"Natasha told you?"

"Piotr. He doesn't expect you to make it back, and he wants me to start taking the long view of things—the fate of planets and galaxies and that sort of thing." Although Coldewe's tone was flippant, his eyes were troubled.

"I sometimes wonder whether James Wolfe arranged it best."

"Quebec?"

Vereshchagin nodded. "To die in the moment of victory, in a victory that sealed a war. 'Now God be praised, I will die in peace.' "

"Good man. I read somewhere that he said he would rather be the author of Gray's *Elegy* than have beaten the French."

"Do not worry, Hans." Vereshchagin smiled. "I promise not to die until I am no longer needed."

Esko Poikolainnen thrust his head through the doorway. "Sir, *Aoba* reports that the Blues are blowing up missile silos."

"We've won," Coldewe said.

"Strange that it never feels like winning. Stay with me a moment." Vereshchagin switched on his terminal to page Dr. Seki in the half of the ship set aside as a quarantine zone. "Dr. Seki, I am told you are well."

"Quite well, honored Vice-Commissioner." In truth, Seki looked like hell, but his spirit was defiant.

"I am told that the Blues have begun blowing up their missile silos."

Seki stared for a moment, then nodded. "During our period of captivity, the naturales believed themselves to be in a position of complete control. This had an interesting effect on the nature of my discussions with Spoagusa. It is even possible that I was able to persuade him of our expedition's continued peaceful intentions." Seki paused. "Although subsequent events may have damaged this impression."

Vereshchagin was well aware that Seki deplored the devastation that the expedition had wrought on the planet, believing it unnecessary, and he silently blessed Seki for this. "Our intentions have not changed. Are you prepared to reopen discussions with the Blues?"

"Of course, honored Vice-Commissioner. Who do you wish to accompany me?"

"Dr. Marais, I think, and perhaps Father Bosenac." Vereshchagin smiled impishly. "I would like him to relate to them the story of Noah and the Flood."

"I would anticipate success. I would expect that they understand you better now. I am certain that I do."

"Please make them understand that I want hostilities to end. There is a grief every commander feels at seeing people he has sent out come back cold and stiff. For me, it has happened so often that I have learned to live with it, to tolerate it, but I have never gotten used to it, and I want it to stop."

"I will faithfully convey your sentiments."

Vereshchagin paused. "Tell the Blues they must destroy all their remaining missiles and terminate their fusion program until we have a better basis for trusting one another."

Seki smiled. "And they must return Brit Smits."

"And the bodies of the others we had to leave behind. One must always keep faith."

The best rumor of all was that Simon Beetje finally got back his wife, or possibly vice versa.

EPILOGUE

In Orbit, HIMS *Zuiho* [6-tetrahedron Rain 16]

DRESSED IN BATTLEDRESS, WITH A READER PROPPED UP UNDER his nose, Hans Coldewe found himself plowing through Dickens's *Our Mutual Friend*, which was an accurate measure of his boredom. He found himself hoping the ending had changed. Unfortunately, it hadn't.

Esko Poikolainnen thrust his head inside. "A shuttle from the frigate *Kinugasa* just docked. Admiral Hoshino is on board."

"Thanks, Esko. We mustn't keep the admiral waiting." He made his way to the shuttle bay, and saluted smartly as Hoshino was piped on board. "Lieutenant-Colonel Hans Coldewe, acting commander, Neighbor task group."

Hoshino, dressed in Navy blue, returned Coldewe's salute, seemingly oblivious to the honor guard from Major Aichi's first platoon. He examined Coldewe. "I understood that Lieutenant-Colonel Anton Vereshchagin was in command."

Coldewe gestured. "Perhaps we should go to my cabin."

"Perhaps," Hoshino agreed, motioning for his staff officers to remain.

Coldewe entered the compartment and waved Hoshino to a seat. "Tea, Admiral?"

Hoshino accepted a cup. "I find myself in a most unusual position."

"I imagine so. Why Colonel Vereshchagin, not Commissioner Vereshchagin?"

"Commissioner Mutaro has died, so, of course, his temporary appointments have ceased to be valid." Hoshino stared into his tea. "What is the situation here in your estimation?"

"Relations with this planet's inhabitants are tolerably good, although we had to iron out a few difficulties along the way. In a few decades or so we might actually begin to understand this place. It's all in our report." Coldewe patted a thick stack of material. "Some of the germs down below have demonstrated a propensity for people, which is a serious nuisance, and I have half the ship in quarantine. Now that your squadron is here, I imagine most of our people would like to go home."

The word "quarantine" attracted Hoshino's interest, but he allowed little of it to show. He sipped at the tea and then set his cup aside. "I think their desires can be accommodated. My orders are to return *Aoba* and *Zuiho* to Earth as soon as possible."

The tea Hoshino was drinking was warm water with a slight tea flavoring. Coldewe wondered whether the admiral would say anything about it and decided he wouldn't. "It would be prudent to have the ships stop at Suid-Afrika to resupply."

"Logistical considerations make it necessary to stop at Suid-Afrika," Hoshino agreed without batting an eye. He shifted ground. "I have spoken to Major Aichi and Captain Kobayashi at some length."

Coldewe smiled. "I know. You were burning up the ship-to-ship lines. I hope you're authorized to promote Major Aichi. He's earned it. I could write him a recommendation."

"That will not be necessary." Hoshino fidgeted, obviously uncomfortable. "We noticed the absence of corvette *Jintsu* as well as ongoing repair work on the planet's surface. Major Aichi and Captain Kobayashi mentioned hostilities."

"Those were some of the difficulties. Is there a problem with this?"

"Commissioner Mutaro's original dispatch caused the government a great deal of difficulty. As you may perhaps imagine, many persons viewed this expedition as highly irregular. Under these circumstances, I have been directed to return Lieutenant-Colonel Vereshchagin to Earth." Hoshino did not say "dead or alive," but his voice implied it.

"Aren't you taking a chance coming here unescorted?" Coldewe said softly.

"I have no great liking for the orders I have been given." Hoshino tilted his head. "And I rather doubt that an armed escort would afford me any greater security."

Coldewe nodded. "Good point."

"Major Aichi and Captain Kobayashi declined to discuss Colonel Vereshchagin. They suggested I speak with you."

Coldewe hesitated for a second or two. Then he picked up a stoppered porcelain kylix, shook it a little, and handed it to Hoshino. "Anton was suffering from degenerative heart disease when he took this job, you know. As Virgil said, 'All the best days of life slip away from us poor mortals first; illnesses and dreary old age and pain sneak up.' We have a battalion cemetery on Suid-Afrika. We'll be adding a few urns this trip. Hendricka Sanmartin provided this one. It's an heirloom and it would grieve her to lose it." He looked Hoshino squarely in the eye. "I think there would be an unfavorable reaction if it went to Earth."

Hoshino studied the kylix for a moment, then handed it back. He changed the subject. "Major Aichi strongly recommended that I retain certain personnel to facilitate the changeover. He also said something about blue underwear that I am not certain I quite understood."

"I think people in question will be amenable. I rather suspect they'll keep you from making a few mistakes."

"He suggested retaining Major Piotr Kolomeitsev. I regret the inexpedience."

"Things down below are considerably confused. The governing authority we have been dealing with has been displaced, and there's a rebellion or two going on. Major Aichi says that it's more confusing than the Meiji restoration." Coldewe paused. "I've been relying on Piotr quite heavily."

"The situation here does present numerous complexities," Hoshino reflected. "Allowing him military rank is completely out of the question. Perhaps it might be possible to retain him in a civilian capacity."

"I don't think he'll mind," Coldewe said, aware that The Iceman could draw salutes dressed in a loincloth. As long as people chose to fight wars, there would be a place for a Piotr Kolomeitsev. "When do you plan on releasing *Aoba* and *Zuiho*?"

"I anticipate retaining them only long enough to transfer records and key personnel. As you might imagine, my government is exceedingly anxious to have firsthand news. You have been here quite a long time."

"Yes," Coldewe said distantly, "that's certainly true."

When Hoshino returned to *Kinugasa*, Coldewe made his way to A deck. Stopping in front of a cabin, he knocked on the door. "Anton? The Imperials are here."

"Please come in." Vereshchagin, dressed in civilian clothes, was seated with a terminal in his lap. He opened his eyes. "The Imperials are here? You could have said something."

"And spoil the surprise?" Coldewe grinned. "A very nice admiral named Hoshino asked about you. I mentioned that you were retired, blissfully cultivating your mind and writing your memoirs."

"This is work. We should have brought a historian along." Vereshchagin raised an eyebrow. "Is that what you told him?"

"Well, not exactly, no. Should I call him back?"

Vereshchagin cleared his throat. "What did you say exactly?"

"When he mentioned sending you back to Earth, I handed him Hanna's old kylix and implied your ashes were inside."

"Eventually, but not quite yet. And he believed you?"

"Of course not. It was empty. But the admiral probably suspects that if he did send you back, we'd burn down Tokyo again." Coldewe winked. "Besides, if he's read any of our other reports, he must realize how inelegant it would be for us to close out our Imperial careers on a truthful note."

Terminus a quo, Suid-Afrika

YEARS LATER, NEAR THE END OF HER SECOND TERM AS PRESI-
dent of the Republic of Suid-Afrika, Hendricka Sanmartin-Cillie
named her first daughter Hanna Antonia, in memoriam.

For her first birthday, the child was given a music box that
played "The Whistling Pig."

ABOUT THE AUTHOR

ROBERT FREZZA was born in 1956 at Bolling Air Force Base and grew up around Baltimore, Maryland. He graduated from Loyola College in Baltimore with a B.A. in history and was commissioned as a second lieutenant through the ROTC program. He then went on to University of Maryland Law School to learn a trade and avoid ending up as a second lieutenant of infantry in Alabama.

After serving on active duty for three years in Germany as a captain in the Judge Advocate General's Corps, he went to work for the army as a civilian attorney. He served as Deputy Chief of the Personnel Claims and Recovery Division of the U.S. Army Claims Service and is a graduate of the Army Management Staff College.

A third-generation Baltimore Orioles fan, he enjoys reading, theater, and arguing military history. He lives reasonably quietly in Glen Burnie, Maryland.

DEL REY ONLINE!

The Del Rey Internet Newsletter...

A monthly electronic publication, posted on the Internet, GEnie, CompuServe, BIX, various BBSs, and the Panix gopher (gopher.panix.com). It features hype-free descriptions of books that are new in the stores, a list of our upcoming books, special announcements, a signing/reading/convention-attendance schedule for Del Rey authors, "In Depth" essays in which professionals in the field (authors, artists, designers, sales people, etc.) talk about their jobs in science fiction, a question-and-answer section, behind-the-scenes looks at sf publishing, and more!

Online editorial presence: Many of the Del Rey editors are online, on the Internet, GEnie, CompuServe, America Online, and Delphi. There is a Del Rey topic on GEnie and a Del Rey folder on America Online.

Our official e-mail address for Del Rey Books is delrey@randomhouse.com

Internet information source!

A lot of Del Rey material is available to the Internet on a gopher server: all back issues and the current issue of the Del Rey Internet Newsletter, a description of the DRIN and summaries of all the issues' contents, sample chapters of upcoming or current books (readable or downloadable for free), submission requirements, mail-order information, and much more. We will be adding more items of all sorts (mostly new DRINs and sample chapters) regularly. The address of the gopher is gopher.panix.com

Why? We at Del Rey realize that the networks are the medium of the future. That's where you'll find us promoting our books, socializing with others in the sf field, and—most importantly—making contact and sharing information with sf readers.

For more information, e-mail delrey@randomhouse.com